THE CLOCKWORK HOUSE

WENDY SAUNDERS

For my dear friend Elisha
Who loves a good ghost story.

ALSO BY WENDY SAUNDERS

The Guardians Series 1

Book 1 Mercy

Book 2 The Ferryman

Book 3 Crossroads

Book 4 Witchfinder

Book 5 Infernum

Book 6 A Little Town Called Mercy

The Guardians Series 2

Book 1 Scarlett

Book 2 The Veritas

The Carter Trilogy

Book 1 Tangled Web

Book 2 Twisted lies

Book 3 Blood Ties

*I*t was strange, Ava thought to herself as she watched the plain pine box containing her mother lowered into the dusty ground, she was technically an orphan now.

Her t-shirt stuck uncomfortably to her back as ponderous beads of sweat rolled lazily down her spine, collecting at the waistband of her threadbare jeans. The dark tendrils of hair which had escaped her messy bun, were plastered to her neck as the raging inferno of the midday sun beat down on her unprotected head.

Who the hell thought getting buried at midday was a good idea?

She squinted and tried to focus on the monotonous monotone of the preacher. Even with her sunglasses protecting her eyes from the harsh glare of the sun, she was still seeing spots and weird reflections of light.

The coffin hit the hard, compacted ground with a thud and Ava shifted uneasily. This time it had nothing to do with the heat. Her mother was really dead, this was it, her eternal resting place. She reached down inside herself for something, anything, that felt different.

Nothing.

Well no, not exactly nothing. She felt sad, of course she did, but the bald-faced truth of it was that although her mom was dead, nothing had really changed. She didn't feel any different which only served to confirm one uncomfortable fact. That even when her mom had been alive, Ava had always been alone.

Caroline Annabeth Wallace, or rather 'Serenity' as she'd always been known to her friends, had lived life very unapologetically on her own terms. She'd blown from town to town, commune to commune, with all the turbulent grace and unrelenting ferocity of a summer storm, on a whim, and with no regard for the daughter she dragged along in her wake.

Her mother had loved her, Ava had never doubted it, she'd simultaneously both baffled and annoyed her and she may not have always understood her, but she'd loved her none the less.

Ava rolled her shoulders uncomfortably; her skin felt like it was melting off her body in the relentless Arizona heat. She glanced down at the small plaintive whine of her dog Bailey, who sat at her side, pressing her heavy body against her legs.

'Alright girl,' she murmured under her breath as she stroked her head, 'not long now.'

The droning sermon ran on and on. Like the opening credits of Star Wars, it felt like it was never going to end, and no one was really paying attention. Bailey gave a dissatisfied sniff and trotted off, stretching out under the scant shade of the nearest tree, her long pink tongue lolling out of her mouth as she panted heavily.

Knowing she wouldn't go far Ava once again turned her attention back to the mismatched assembly of characters pretending to listen to the eulogy, as if it were the most riveting thing in the world and they weren't all stoned out of their minds. A riot of tie dye assaulted the eye, along with beads, bare feet and Birkenstocks. Everywhere Ava looked was long hair and sweating bodies, overlaid with the unmistakable scent of weed, which hung over the proceedings like a miasma.

Well, Ava thought absently, at least her mom had gone out the same way she lived; high, at one with nature and the very center of attention.

She let out a slow breath and blinked the sweat from her eyes. It was typical that her mother had managed to die during one of the hottest months on record, thank you climate change, but then again, her mom had always loved the bright blazing sunshine. The hotter the better as far as she'd been concerned, unlike her daughter who'd always preferred cooler, overcast, moodier weather.

Ava supposed it reflected their personalities perfectly. Her mother had always been a glass half full kind of girl, whereas Ava didn't have a glass, or if she did, hers would not only have been very definitely empty but also possibly smashed on the ground with someone stealing the pieces.

The reading finally concluded, and the mourners shuffled forward to toss brightly colored, wilted flowers onto the coffin. Ava waited until they slowly began to drift away one by one, in pairs and small groups. Stepping forward she stared down into the open grave, scuffing the toe of her frayed sneakers in the dusty ground as she frowned, at a loss as to what to say.

'Bye mom,' she murmured finally, 'say hi to dad for me.'

Her fist tightened around a limp bunch of wildflowers she'd stopped at the side of the road and picked on her way to the funeral. Half of them were probably weeds she thought to herself in amusement, but they looked pretty, so she figured what the hell. Her mom probably would have liked them anyway; she'd never really liked hot house flowers cut at the peak of perfection.

Perfection, she'd told her, was overrated. Freedom was everything.

It was just as well, Ava mused ruefully. She couldn't have

afforded to buy flowers anyway, not even from the local gas station. With one final lament she tossed the flowers down onto the coffin and watched as they landed with a faint thud and parted in the middle, sliding slowly off either side of the curved lid to be crushed along the edges of the grave.

Figures.

She shook her head and turned around to find a familiar face standing right behind her.

'I'm gonna miss her,' he murmured, his eyes flickering over Ava's shoulder and lingering on the gaping hole in the ground.

'Baz,' she nodded in greeting, she'd known him since she was a kid. He'd been one of her mom's oldest friends and also, unbelievably, her lawyer.

His hair was steel gray shoulder length and his eyes a vivid cornflower blue. His weather-beaten face was tanned and etched with deep lines. He wore loose fitting harem pants decorated garishly, patterned in primary colors and on his feet were battered leather sandals. His only concession to the formality of the occasion was a rather boring gray pin-striped tie, which knotted tightly around his neck and lay against his rainbow tie dyed t-shirt.

'I like your tie,' her mouth twitched in amusement.

'Thanks,' he nodded seriously. 'Ava...I'm sorry about your mom, she was one of a kind.'

'That's one way of describing her I suppose,' Ava murmured.

'If you're feeling up to it,' he continued, 'I need to read you her will.'

'Mom didn't have a will.'

'Yes, she did,' Baz corrected her.

'But mom didn't have anything worth putting in a will,' Ava shook her head. 'What'd she do? Leave me her stash of weed and the last couple of kegs of her homemade daisy wine?'

4

'Ah her daisy wine,' Baz smiled in remembrance, 'the first time I had your mom's wine I lost six days.'

'You're lucky you didn't lose your internal organs,' Ava muttered.

'Good times,' he chuckled.

'If you say so,' Ava shrugged.

'Anyway,' Baz shook his head, 'the will. Can you stop by the cottage?'

'Is that really necessary?' she replied in annoyance.

She was down to her last thirty bucks and had been sleeping in her truck for the past week. She was almost out of gas too, the trip to Arizona had pretty much cleaned her out. There was a diner just down the street advertising for a temporary waitress. She really should try sweet talking the owner into giving her a job for a couple of days until she had enough money to blow town again, not spending the day reminiscing with Baz about her mom.

'It really is important Ava,' he told her bluntly, sensing her reluctance. 'There was a lot about your mom you didn't know.'

'What do you mean?'

'Just stop by the cottage and we'll talk,' he patted her arm comfortingly.

'Fine,' she blew out a breath.

She watched him walk back across the cemetery as she reached into her bag and pulled out a bottle. Taking a deep gulp of the lukewarm water she headed toward her dog who watched her approach with a thumping tail. Kneeling down next to her Ava slowly poured the water into her hand and watched as Bailey lapped it up enthusiastically.

'Is that better girl?' She stroked her head gently, 'wanna go for a ride? Huh?' She rubbed her fur soothingly, 'looks like we've got somewhere to be.'

Bailey jumped to her feet as Ava stood and slipped the half empty bottle back into her bag, dusting off her jeans. She turned and took one last look at her mother's grave as it was being filled in. Her heart suddenly thudded dully in her chest and her mouth turned down. Everything suddenly felt so final.

Bailey nudged her legs with her blunt nose as if sensing her hesitation.

'Come on then,' Ava sighed and headed back toward her truck.

Opening the door Bailey jumped up into the cab and curled up on the bench next to her. Pulling away she flicked the radio on and idly flipped through the stations for a few minutes before finally switching it back off.

She drove through town slowly, barely registering the bustling farmers' market. Turning onto one of the main streets her eyes were once again assaulted with a cacophony of bright colors. It was Bisbee pride and everywhere she looked were rainbow flags, brightly dressed people in elaborate costumes and rainbow beads.

She smiled; she couldn't help it. She could feel it in the air, the sense of community. It was a celebration, filled with music and laughter, but despite the flamboyantly dressed patrons her heart still ached, and one thought pounded in her aching head like a relentless bass drum. Mom is dead... mom is dead...

She wound her way through the streets leaving the sounds of celebration behind her. Bisbee, Arizona wasn't such a bad place to live considering some of the shit holes her mom had dragged her through over the years. Although Bisbee had been one of her mother's favorites, probably because Baz was there, it hadn't called to Ava, she didn't feel it in her soul.

She'd always thought she'd know it, the place she would call home. She'd traveled far and wide, both with her mom and on her own as soon as she was old enough, but she'd never found it, her place in the world, the sense of belonging she craved. Lately she'd begun to wonder if her soul was just as restless as her mom's had been.

6

Before long she pulled up outside Baz's place. What he'd affectionately referred to as 'the cottage' was in reality a rather squat, single storey building with chipped clapboards and peeling yellow paint.

Ava glanced over at Bailey, who'd lifted her head and pricked her ears.

'What do you think?' Ava asked her.

Bailey cocked her head, blinking her large dark eyes as her tail thumped rhythmically against the torn seat.

'That's what I thought,' Ava sighed. 'Come on, let's get this over with.'

Opening the door and stepping down onto the sidewalk she felt Bailey jump down behind her. They crossed the dry, sparse patches of brown grass and headed for the house which had a beaded curtain instead of a screen door.

Shaking her head, Ava reached out, parting the strands of shell colored beads to reveal an open door.

'Baz?' she called out.

'Come in,' his disembodied voice echoed back, 'something to drink?'

Stepping through the curtain with her dog she followed the voice through to the back and found Baz in the kitchen.

'No thanks,' she shook her head, 'I'm good but can I have a bowl of water for Bailey?'

'Of course, of course,' he nodded bustling around the kitchen as he filled a brightly colored clay bowl and set it down on the tiled floor before reaching into the refrigerator and pulling out a beer for himself. He popped the top and took a deep swig, swallowing with an audible gulp as his eyes locked on hers.

'Come,' he nodded toward the doorway and pushed away from the counter with Ava following behind him, leaving Bailey contentedly lying on the cool tiles lapping at her water.

The room he led her into was a warm inviting living room.

The walls were covered with bright hand painted murals of forests and sunsets. Sun catchers hung from the ceiling, rotating slowly with the displacement of air as they passed beneath them. Along one wall was a sagging couch and beside it stood a roughhewn bookcase covered in photos, some framed, others simply propped against each other, their edges curling with age.

Ava froze as her gaze fell on one in particular. She reached out with trembling fingers and lifted the dusty frame from the back of the shelf. Her dark eyes studied the image even as her fingertips traced the lines and curves of the picture.

A young man stared back at her through the lens of the camera. His long dark curly hair reached the base of his neck and hung forward into his laughing eyes. Bare chested and barefoot, and wearing nothing but cutoff jeans he sat astride a gorgeous black 1944 Indian Scout. Incidentally, the same motorcycle which she knew would claim his life only months after this photo was taken. She glanced down to see the smiling five-year-old girl in front of him wearing pigtails and aviator sunglasses, her grin almost identical to his.

She looked across to Baz who'd settled himself comfortably on the worn out old blue couch with a huge glass bong planted between his legs.

'You still have this picture of me and my dad?'

Baz wrapped his lips around the end of the pipe and inhaled deeply, the water in the bulb of the glass bubbling slightly as he pulled away and leaned back against the cushions, his head falling back as he released a long slow stream of smoke.

After a moment he blinked and spoke.

'Yeah.'

Ava moved over to the seat opposite him and sank down slowly onto the tasseled afghan cover and waited. She'd spent enough time with her mother over the years to know how to deal with a stoner.

She waited patiently.

'He was a good man,' Baz spoke again after a few more moments, his voice low and raspy, his gaze pensive. 'He loved you and your mama.'

'Yes, he did,' Ava replied quietly as her gaze was once again drawn to the photograph in her hands.

'He was my best friend,' Baz murmured, 'nearly broke your mama when he died... guess they're together again at last.'

He leaned forward over the bong and sparked up his lighter, taking another deep pull.

Ava placed the photo frame down on the untidy coffee table in front of her and glanced up at the wall above Baz's head. It was almost impossible to believe that the guy sitting in front of her lugging a bong was a bona fide lawyer, but it was true according to the framed certificates and credentials on the wall.

'Baz,' she sighed in frustration, 'what did you want to talk to me about? I don't mean to be rude but everything's still a little raw. I'm not really ready to sit here and reminisce about my dead parents.'

'No,' he agreed as he exhaled another thick cloud of smoke, 'you're here for the reading of her will.'

He reached into his pocket and pulled out a rumpled piece of paper. Smoothing out the creases he laid it on the couch next to him and began patting down his torso as if he couldn't quite recall what he was looking for.

Spying a pair of tortoise shell glasses on the table, peeking out from under a TV guide, Ava retrieved them and handed them to him wordlessly.

'Ah,' he nodded in approval, unfolding them and sliding them onto his face before picking up the paper.

'As it's just the two of us,' he began, 'we'll skip some of the formalities. They put me to sleep anyway...' He scanned down the document and cleared his throat.

'I, Serenity Cortez, formerly known as Caroline Annabeth Wallace, being of sound mind and body... yadda yadda yadda... and hereto do leave all my worldly possessions to my daughter and only child...'

'But mom didn't have any possessions,' Ava replied mildly, 'so isn't this all a bit unnecessary?'

'Ah wrong!' He waggled a finger at her.

Placing his bong on the coffee table he stood and crossed the room to retrieve a dog-eared manila folder. Moving back to the couch he sat down and opened it.

'Her estate is as follows... whoa...' he blinked and sank back against the cushions, 'head rush...'

'Here, let me,' she held out her hand as he passed her the folder.

Opening it, Ava scanned down the page, some jewelry, an old pocket watch and... her gaze stopped on the monetary figure below. She blinked, blinked again, then re-read the same line three times. When the figure didn't change, she looked up at Baz with her mouth open.

'Just because your mom didn't live for money, didn't mean she didn't have any. She chose to live life the way she wanted. That...' he pointed to the folder, 'didn't mean anything to her, she always said she wouldn't be defined by dollar signs.'

Ava felt her stomach swoop and her head begin to pound at her temples. The shock was quickly replaced by a sharp painful jolt of anger.

'It might not have meant anything to her,' her eyes burned furiously, 'but it would have meant something to me. With just a fraction of this I could have gone back to school, gone to college, instead of clawing my way from one day to the next, living in my truck, trying to scrape together enough money for food and gas. My life could have been so different, I could've been different.'

'Your mom wanted the best for you,' Baz shook his head, 'she loved you more than anything. She wanted you to experience life, not get caught up in the chains of materialism.'

'The chains of materialism?' she whispered angrily, 'is this some kind of joke? Is it materialism to want to have a home? A bed of my own? Not a sleeping roll on the floor of whatever shack we happened to be living in with twenty other people?'

'Your mom did what she believed was best,' he shook his head in regret, 'no matter what I said to her. She made her choice for right or wrong.'

'No matter what you said?' Ava frowned suspiciously. 'What do you mean?'

'I agree with you,' Baz sighed. 'I always thought you should've had a home, some stability. It's what your dad wanted.'

'My dad?' she replied in confusion, 'but mom always said he was a free spirit and refused to be tied down.'

'That's the way she liked to remember him because it fit with what she wanted,' Baz corrected her. 'The truth is, your dad was from a huge family, at least he was, until they were all killed back in El Salvador right before he fled to the US. He wanted to build a family and a home here. I still remember the look on his face the first time he held you in his arms. He promised you a home, promised to keep you safe and happy, but he died before he could. Serenity took you and moved on. Don't get me wrong I loved your mama, but that woman was always running.'

'From what?'

'She wouldn't say,' Baz shook his head. 'What I do know was that she was an incredibly intelligent woman, she invested her money wisely over the years. When she found out she was dying she cashed it all in and had it placed into a bank account in your name.'

'I don't know what to say,' Ava glanced down at the paper miserably, watching as the ridiculous number of zeros taunted her. 'She didn't even tell me she was sick. I never even got the chance to say goodbye.'

'She didn't want you to see her like that,' Baz replied quietly. 'In the end it happened so quickly... and well... cancer's never a pretty way to go. She wanted to spare you that.'

Ava blew out a slow breath as she flipped through the paperwork. 'I suppose at least I don't have to worry about eating tomorrow,' her eyes fixed on the bank statement in her name as a terrible weight settled on her chest.

'Keep reading Ava,' Baz settled back comfortably, lighting a joint, 'the money's not all your mom left you.'

Ava turned back to the folder and forced herself to keep reading.

'The Lynch House, Midnight Island?' She frowned, 'a house? Mom owned a house?'

'Kind of,' he replied slowly.

'What do you mean kind of?'

'She inherited the house,' he puffed out a ring of smoke, 'it's been in her family for generations. Your mom was born on the island, but she never lived in that house. Her family, the Wallaces, had another place which was sold after your grandmother passed.'

'I've never heard of Midnight Island, mom never mentioned it.'

'It's a small island off the coast of Maine.'

'So, let me get this straight. This house, the Lynch House, has been in my family for generations but they didn't live in it?'

'That's right,' Baz nodded, 'been in the family as far as I know since the late 1800's. I don't know what happened, but it hasn't been inhabited since then.'

'That's a bit weird isn't it?' Ava frowned.

'Look the truth is, your mom didn't want to leave you that house. She tried everything to get rid of it over the years. It's been an albatross around her neck since your grandmother passed away.'

'She didn't want me to have the house?'

'Nope,' he shook his head.

'But why?' Ava replied in confusion.

'I don't know,' he shrugged, 'but I always got the feeling she was afraid of something. That's why she would never go back to the island.'

'If she hated that house so much, why not just sell it?'

'She would have,' he drew on his joint slowly, 'but the fact is, the house has been on the market since the fifties. No one wants to buy it.'

'No one?' her brows rose in surprise. 'I expect it's probably a ruin by now.'

'You'd be wrong about that too; I spoke with the realtor on the island when I was getting Serenity's affairs in order. The house is not habitable but as far as I'm aware it's still structurally sound... more or less...'

Ava rubbed her face tiredly, somewhere behind her eyes a vicious throbbing had begun.

'I don't know Baz, it's a lot to take in.'

'I know,' he nodded sympathetically, 'but there is one thing you should know.'

'What's that?'

'Your mom loved you, more than anything in this world. Her parenting skills may have been unconventional at best but never doubt you were everything to her.'

Ava nodded; her throat tight with a burning sensation she couldn't swallow past. Blinking back the tears she stood slowly.

'Thanks Baz.'

'Don't be a stranger okay?' He relit his joint which had gone out.

'Don't worry Baz,' she gave a small smile, 'I know where to find you.'

'Here,' he picked up the photo of her and her dad and handed it to her. 'You should keep this.'

'Are you sure?' her eyes widened.

'I got dozens of memories of him up here,' he tapped the side of his head, 'you should have that.'

'Thanks,' she whispered as her eyes filled with tears.

He nodded once and she turned for the doorway. She didn't even need to whistle for Bailey. Sensing her movement, the dog scrambled to her feet, her claws skittering against the tiles as they headed back out through the beaded curtain and into the front yard.

Opening the door to her truck she waited for Bailey to scramble up before climbing in behind her. Placing the folder and framed picture down on the seat next to her, she stared out the dusty windscreen aimlessly.

She felt Bailey crawl into her lap as if she could sense her distress. She reached up and licked Ava's chin, nudging her with her nose.

'Alright girl,' Ava murmured absently as she ran her hands over her thick fur as much to comfort herself as her dog.

There was so much she didn't know about her mother. Serenity had never spoken about her family or where she came from. Occasionally she'd talk about Ava's father as if to keep the fading memory of him alive, but even then, all Ava really knew was that he'd been born in San Miguel, El Salvador and fled aged 18 during the civil war. He'd met her mother in San Francisco. It was love at first sight and Ava had been born nine months later, almost to the day.

But if what Baz had said was true and her mother had been born on Midnight island, there was a slim possibility she still had family there, maybe some aunts or uncles, possibly even some cousins. She could at least discover some of her family history, maybe even figure out why her mother had run.

She couldn't deny that the mysterious house was nagging at her like a persistent toothache. The curiosity was almost overwhelming. Why would her family not want the house and refuse to live in it? And why, in all the time it had been up for sale had no one wanted to buy it?

'What do you think?' she murmured as she looked down at her dog.

Bailey's ears twitched, her tail thumping against the exposed foam of the seat that was being held together with peeling duct tape.

'Okay then,' she blew out a breath as she nudged Bailey out of her lap.

She clambered over to her side, turned in a circle a few times before settling down and tucking her head onto her paws, watching Ava with dark liquid eyes.

'Are you ready for an adventure then?' Ava asked.

Bailey's tail thumped against the seat once more.

'Alright then,' Ava picked up her sunglasses and slipped them back onto her face. Turning the key in the ignition the engine struggled and spluttered to life. Ava's mouth curved at the corner.

'I guess we're heading to Midnight then.'

2

'*D*on't look at me like that,' Ava blinked.

Bailey sat at her feet staring up at her with dark eyes.

'Seriously, it's not my fault.'

The dog snorted.

'It's the rules,' Ava protested.

Bailey lifted a paw and nudged her.

'I can't,' she sighed, 'you'll get me in trouble.'

Bailey butted her legs with her head and looked up at her with sad eyes.

'Urgh, you're killing me here,' Ava looked back along the deck to make sure no one was watching. 'Fine but you'd better behave.'

Ava reached down and unclipped the bright red leash from Bailey's collar. The second she was free she nipped the leash from Ava's hand and stuck her head through the railing, opening her mouth and letting go.

Ava leaned over the railing and watched the bright red trail of leather swirling down beneath the water. She watched in silence for a few moments before turning back to her dog.

Bailey sat back down on her haunches, her thick bushy tail swishing against the deck happily as her mouth lolled open in a wolfish grin.

'You'd better hope the guy in charge doesn't catch you off your leash, it's a long swim back to the mainland.'

Bailey jumped up, rubbing her body along Ava's legs and nuzzling her hand.

'Okay girl,' she smiled softly as she stroked her.

Her gaze was drawn back to the water which rippled and danced, glittering as the sunlight caught the waves. She drew in a deep relaxed breath, almost tasting the salty air on her tongue as the hot summer breeze tugged at her long dark hair. There was a tremble of excitement in her belly, a quiet whisper somewhere in the back of her mind as she got her first good look at Midnight Island.

'So, this was where my mom was born,' she murmured as she rested her hand on Bailey's head, her sharp gaze taking in every detail as the island grew larger across the small expanse of water.

The smooth rocking of the waves was soon replaced with the thunderous boom and crash of the waves against the base of the cliffs. Her eyes were drawn up and she caught her first glimpse of a huge gray stone building staring out forlornly across the water.

Her stomach clenched against the sudden and renewed fluttering, a strange mix of nerves and curiosity. She'd never owned anything in her life other than her truck and now she technically owned what looked like a rambling Victorian mansion on a cliff top.

Her hand released her dog and gripped the rusted white railing as she unconsciously leaned closer. She couldn't see much from her vantage point now that they were heading in closer to the dock, but for a second... she shook her head, she wasn't a whimsical person at all, but if the house had been a person, she would say that it had almost felt like it had locked its gaze on her and was watching.

Shaking off the strange feeling she pushed away from the railing and turned. Heading down the battered metal steps to the lower deck, she stopped abruptly.

A pair of amused blue eyes watched her, dropped to her dog who stood pressed against her legs, then lifted back to lock onto Ava's wary gaze.

His lips twitched.

Jack, she'd heard him called when she'd first boarded the ferry. The captain of the rusted, but seaworthy, 'Sea Witch' had barked orders down at the younger man standing in front of her now.

Despite the fact the captain was much older, with a heavily lined, weather beaten face, and the guy in front of her was gorgeous in a kind of rugged fisherman kind of way, there was enough of a resemblance for her to assume some kind of familial relationship between the two.

'You should head back to your vehicle miss,' the corner of his mouth curved. 'We'll be heading in to dock soon and my uncle is real strict about animals on leashes.'

She nodded, her cheeks flushing as he threw her a disarming smile. Jesus, the guy was really good looking. She moved past him with Bailey following in her wake as he stepped aside. Even Bailey looked back and wagged her tail.

'Flirt,' Ava whispered, a small smile playing on her lips as she looked down at her dog and they walked companionably back to her truck. Ava ran her hand over the smooth shiny paintwork, then opening the door, she stepped back and allowed Bailey to jump up as she climbed in after her. Breathing deeply, she inhaled the scent of brand-new leather.

It was extravagant, she knew it, but she'd also never had anything brand new in her life. When she'd learned just how many zeros were in her bank account, thanks to her inheritance, she could admit, she'd gone a little crazy. She'd bought herself a brand-new truck, driven it straight off the forecourt of the nearest dealership. She'd thrown away all her worn tatty clothes and bought herself new ones. Nothing fancy, just jeans, t-shirts and sweaters. She'd even thrown away her battered old sneakers and now wore bright red converse.

In retrospect she really hadn't spent that much, in fact she'd barely made a dent, a scratch even, but to someone who was used to counting every nickel and dime it still felt a little frivolous.

There was a slight bump as the ferry slid into the dock, which shook her from her thoughts and before she knew it, she was driving down the ramp and onto Midnight Island.

The dock bustled with unfamiliar sights and sounds. There were stacks and stacks of lobster traps, fishing boats returning and unloading huge crates of fish, and a flourishing market with people everywhere calling out loudly.

Usually Ava would have been fascinated, drinking in every new sound and smell ravenously but today she couldn't focus, couldn't think of anything but the house on the cliff. It was almost as if it was calling to her, singing to her blood.

She pulled out the directions she'd been given over the phone. Unfolding the paper against the wheel, without taking her eyes off the narrow winding road, she navigated her way through charming cozy little streets and past busy restaurants and quaint tourist shops.

Following the road up and away from the main part of town she passed into the quieter, more residential areas, past cute cottages and summer rentals. Feeling the tranquility of the island wash over her she relaxed, unaware of the small unconscious smile tugging at her lips.

Glancing every now and then at the little hand drawn map she followed the road. The houses and buildings slowly began to disappear until there was nothing left but empty road ahead of her, flanked by tall trees, which speared up into the sky with their twisted, gangly trunks and lush canopies. All her anxiety began to drain away and the feeling of peace once again washed tantalizingly over her. Finally, she reached the top of the cliff and the tree line opened up to reveal a huge gray building.

COURTNEY KELLER CLIMBED out of her mom's Chrysler and smoothed down the skirt of her new suit. It was mortifying having to drive a minivan, she thought as she flipped her blonde waves over one shoulder with a careless toss of her head. It wasn't like it was her fault what had happened to her own car. She just hadn't seen the low wall while she was reversing, nor the trash cans as she'd tried to compensate and pulled forward sharply. It was also really unfair her parents wouldn't help her out with the repairs, after all she'd only just gotten her realtor's license and it was going to take some time for her to start earning decent money.

She glanced up at the grim looking house and shuddered. The place gave her the creeps and for good reason; having grown up on the island she was well acquainted with the history of the Lynch House.

She deliberately turned her back on the house, but the feeling persisted, sly spindly little fingers which skittered down her spine, causing a light perspiration to break out at her temples.

She glanced down at her watch, an expensive looking knock off one of her aunts had brought her back from a trip to Thailand, but she had to admit it was a pretty good fake. It had fooled most of her friends and that was all that really mattered.

She shifted as her heels began to sink slightly into the gravel, which was partially overgrown with moss, and tightened her fingers around the file she held in front of her like a shield.

Wishing she hadn't come out to the remote spot on her own she refused to turn and look at the house again, just in case...

Feeling an uneasy churning in her belly she once again glared at her watch as if it hadn't only been fifteen seconds since she last checked. Where was the woman? The ferry was on time, she'd checked herself. It should have docked nearly half an hour ago.

She could only hope the stupid woman bought the rat-infested flea hole of a house. Not only would it get it off their books but would also earn her a nice commission and the respect of her colleagues. As the newest member of the team she was pretty darn low in the pecking order which is why she'd been sent out to deal with this house in particular. The simple fact was no one else wanted to deal with it and she couldn't blame them. Still she was sick of getting all the jobs no one else wanted. How was she supposed to prove herself and earn any kind of decent money if they wouldn't give her a chance?

She glanced up at the unmistakable rumble of an engine and the crunch of gravel beneath tires. Smoothing out her forehead, her smile widened showing off the pretty white veneers which had been her eighteenth birthday present. She once again smoothed down her red power suit and tucking the file under one arm, waited for the huge black truck to park beside her.

AVA CLIMBED out of the truck, with Bailey jumping down behind her as she approached the young woman smiling at her like a toothpaste commercial.

'Miz Cortez,' the girl offered her hand politely, her smile dimming slightly as her eyes dipped to the big dog at Ava's side.

'Hi,' Ava took her hand and shook brusquely. 'Don't worry about Bailey, she doesn't bite.'

'I'm Courtney Keller of Gillespie Realtors, may I be the first to welcome you to Midnight Island,' she forced her smile up another watt. She really wanted this sale, even if it meant she got mauled by what looked suspiciously like a wolf.

'Thanks,' Ava murmured absently, her gaze already drawn to the towering building behind them. 'It's bigger than I thought.'

'Twelve bedrooms,' Courtney beamed enthusiastically, 'and an absolute steal for a property of this size and location.'

Ava stared up at the house, it was pretty much the size of a mansion. It was at least three storeys. A flight of stone steps led up to a huge double entranceway above which was a balcony. Above that was a gorgeous old rectangular statement window and directly above that a smaller metal balcony and another massive rectangular window, this time topped with a steeply gabled roof.

To the right was a large circular section which looked like a tower. The second storey metal balcony continued to wrap around the tower to the back of the house. The third-floor windows of the tower were each framed with stunning brick-work arches and the whole tower was topped off with a tall cone-shaped roof.

To the left of the building was a slightly shorter squatter tower, which instead of being smoothly rounded seemed more angular, almost hexagonal. The windows were slightly less ornate, just plain sash windows, some of which she could see were either cracked or missing glass panes altogether. The roof was less conical than the other tower, with another more angular gabled roof.

The back of the building or at least what Ava could see of it, seemed to be a rectangular shape. The third floor once again had a small metal balcony like the front of the house and the third-floor window was framed by a brick arch which ended in a sloping pitched roof. Next to it, right at the edge of the main roof, sat a huge tall chimney stack.

Ava glanced along the roofline and from what she could see there seemed to be several smaller chimneys, perhaps half a dozen in all, leading her to surmise that there were real fireplaces in most of the rooms, typical of the time period.

She was desperate to get a closer look, but the ground level was all boarded up and the entire perimeter was surrounded by a metal fence, punctuated at intervals by signs warning, KEEP OUT and DANGER!

'So,' Courtney opened her file, although she needn't have bothered. She'd already learned every detail about the house, determined to be the one to sell the ancient turkey and win the approval of her peers.

'The house,' she began, 'was built in the mid-19th century by a noted architect from Boston; he liked to vacation here with his family. They owned the house for twenty years until he passed away and his son sold it to the Lynch family. It has remained in their family since then. Now the house hasn't actually been inhabited since 1919 so it still retains all of its original features.'

'I don't suppose there's electric or running water then?' Ava mused quietly.

'There are actually several bathrooms with toilets, however they do date back to the late 1800's and would need some updating. I believe the property when it was last inhabited was lit by gas lamps so the electric would also need installing, but it's a charming period property. There is a working water pump at the back of the building and it also comes with several acres of land and a private beach at the foot of the cliff.'

Courtney threw that in with a wide enticing smile.

'Uh huh,' Ava murmured, only half listening to Courtney as she studied the house. It was massive, what the hell was she going to do with such a huge property? It wouldn't sell, judging by the length of time it had been on the market, especially not in its current condition. If she had any hope of selling it on it would need to be rehabbed before she could flip, it and that would take some serious dollars. She had no doubt, that even with the ridiculous amount of money it would take to make it livable she could afford it, maybe even make a profit on it. A sizeable one given the location and the private beach, but did she even want to sell it?'

Courtney's heart started beating faster, she could see that the woman was actually considering it. She might actually pull this sale off. Her stomach clenched in excitement as she tried to school her features into the cool, aloof professional she was.

'So, what do you think?' Courtney asked after a moment of silence.

'I think,' Ava replied quietly, 'that it looks sad.'

'Sad?' Courtney frowned.

'Sad and neglected, like it's been waiting for someone to bring it back to life, to make it happy again.'

'Well,' Courtney beamed, 'well then, if you're interested in making an offer, we can...'

Ava turned back; her dark eyes fixed on the girl.

'An offer?'

'An offer to buy the property,' she confirmed. 'As I said it's an absolute steal at this price.'

'I think there's been some misunderstanding,' Ava replied, 'I'm not buying the house.'

'Pardon?'

'I'm not buying it because I already own it,' Ava told her. 'I just wanted to have a look at it, so it seemed best to call the realtors and have them show me around.'

'Oh,' Courtney frowned, 'oh...' she repeated flatly, any trace of warmth gone from her demeanor.

'I understand it's been on the market since the fifties?'

'That's right,' Courtney replied sourly as she watched her commission disappear before her eyes like a fine mist.

'And no one was interested?'

'They came close, a couple of times in the seventies and eighties but no one actually made an offer.'

Ava turned back to the house her lips pursed thoughtfully.

'Take it off the market,' she decided.

'Excuse me?' Courtney replied.

'Take it off the market,' Ava repeated.

'You're going to live here?' Courtney asked incredulously.

'I don't know yet,' she shook her head, 'but I do know that it won't sell in this condition. Either way it needs a lot of work.'

'Understatement,' Courtney muttered under her breath.

'I'd like to take a look inside,' Ava turned back to her. 'Do you have the keys, or something we can pry the boarding loose with?'

'No, I don't,' Courtney shook her head. 'The realtors don't keep the keys to the property, not since...'

'Since what?' Ava asked curiously.

'Nothing,' Courtney swallowed uncomfortably, 'um... Mr Pearson, the lawyer in charge of the estate keeps the keys at his office. You'll need to see him.'

Ava's eyes narrowed curiously. All of a sudden Courtney didn't seem to want to look her in the eye and her lips were tightly pinched together as if she were holding something back.

'Okay then,' Ava answered slowly after a moment, realizing the girl wasn't going to be any more forthcoming. 'Well thanks for your help.'

'You're welcome,' she muttered sulkily. 'If you want to follow me back down into town, I'll show you where his offices are.'

'Thanks that would be great.'

'No problem,' Courtney responded trying to remember her manners.

Ava watched the girl stomp as gracefully back to her car as she could in those ridiculous heels which were already covered in dust from the gravel. She couldn't have been more than her early twenties and seemed more like a kid playing dress up in her mommy's dramatic red power suit. Driving a minivan wouldn't help her get taken seriously either but each to their own.

Whistling for Bailey they climbed back into her truck and headed back down into town. As they drove down the Main Street, Courtney honked her horn and pointed to a glass fronted office with 'Pearson Attorney at Law' stenciled onto the window in a perfect arch of gold lettering.

Ava honked in thanks and pulled into a parking space directly opposite the building, watching as Courtney sped off in her minivan not paying much mind to the speed limit.

Ava headed into the office with Bailey in tow. A loud distressed squeal demanded her attention as the glass door swung shut behind her.

'No dogs!' The short rotund woman with a tightly curled perm practically climbed onto her chair. 'No dogs in here!'

'Oh um,' Ava frowned, 'I'm really sorry but it's too hot out there to leave her in the truck. Honestly, she's very well behaved. I know she looks a little intimidating but she's a big softie, she won't harm you I promise. I just need a few moments with Mr Pearson.'

'Do you have an appointment?' she demanded, her face turning red as she watched Bailey with beady eyes, as if she expected her to pounce and sink her teeth into her at any moment.

'No, I'm afraid I don't, I've only just arrived on the island, but we have spoken on the phone. My name is Ava Cortez.'

'You can't see him without an appointment, so you'll just have to go back wherever you came from and take that beast with you.'

'It's alright Philippa,' a deep calm voice intruded, 'I have a few minutes.'

Ava looked across and got her first look at Dennis Pearson and unlike Baz, he actually looked like a lawyer with his carefully parted salt and pepper hair, his neatly groomed beard and well-tailored dark blue suit.

'Ava,' he crossed the room and held out a hand, 'it's nice to finally meet you.'

'Thanks,' she shook his hand. 'Sorry about Bailey, it really is too hot to leave her in the car.'

'It's no problem,' he waved his hand. 'Why don't you both come on back to my office, Philippa is a little uneasy around large dogs.'

'Sorry,' Ava muttered contritely as she passed by his flustered assistant. As he closed the door to his office, she caught a glimpse of the small woman as she flopped back into her chair, her hand pressed to her rather ample, heaving bosom.

'What can I do for you Ava?'

She watched as he retrieved a bottle of water from his desk drawer. He set an empty coffee mug down on the floor beside Bailey and filled the cup so she could drink. Bailey, being the unladylike slob that she was, simply stuck her nose in the cup, following it as it moved slowly across the floor, causing the water to lap up and over the sides like a miniature tsunami and making a complete mess of his pristine floor.

'Sorry,' Ava winced.

'It's alright,' he chuckled good naturally, 'I have dogs of my own.'

'Oh?'

'Labradors,' he grinned, 'big, bouncy and boisterous, so compared to my heathens she's actually very well behaved. German Shepherd?'

'Yeah,' Ava replied looking down at her dog who sat back on her haunches watching them, her long, wet pink tongue dripping slobber and water, 'although given the size of her I sometimes wonder if she's half werewolf.'

He laughed loudly.

'You've just arrived on the island I assume?'

'A few hours ago,' she nodded, 'I've been up to the house and had a quick look at the place. I met one of the realtors.'

'Which one?'

'Courtney Keller.'

'Ah yes,' he smiled in amusement, 'she went to school with my daughter. She's only just recently got her realtor's license; it's so new it still squeaks if she turns around too quickly.'

'I think she was a little disappointed when she found out I already owned the house.'

'I'm not surprised. Marv who owns the realtors has been trying to off load it since he took over the business from his daddy back in the late seventies. I believe he was offering a hefty bonus to anyone who could sell it. I expect Courtney was seeing dollar signs the minute you drove up.'

'Something like that,' Ava agreed, 'she didn't seem to happy when I told her to take it off the market.'

'You're not selling?' he replied in surprise. 'You're going to keep it?'

'I honestly don't know yet,' she shook her head, 'but as we've already seen, it won't sell in the condition it's in now. So, I either have it rehabbed and flip it, I fix it up and live in it or I bulldoze it to the ground and sell the land.'

'Is the last a serious contender?'

'What the bulldozing part?'

He nodded.

'No,' she replied after a moment, 'it's such an old house and although it's in a bit of a state you can see how beautiful it must have looked in its glory days. Although it would be easier and infinitely cheaper, I can't bring myself to knock it down, not unless it's too far gone to save it.'

'I see,' he leaned back in his chair and studied her. 'You look a little like her you know.'

'Who?'

'Caroline,' he answered simply.

It was a jolt to hear her mother called by her birth name, she had only ever known her as Serenity.

'You knew my mom?'

'I did, although I was a few years older, we went to school together,' he told her softly. He wasn't going to tell her that everyone knew who the Wallaces were because of their wealth and connection to the Lynch House. 'I suspect you favor your father more, but I can see a little of her in your features,' he continued. 'She always was a free spirit, the island never sat well on her. I wasn't surprised when she left as soon as she turned eighteen.'

'Yeah, sounds like mom alright,' Ava replied, 'she was never big on responsibility.'

He heard a tiny trace of bitterness coloring her tone, but he politely chose not to mention it.

'Anyway,' Ava changed the subject, 'Courtney mentioned you have the keys to the house?'

He leaned back studying her for a moment longer before opening one of his desk drawers and retrieving an old, heavy bunch of ancient looking keys.

'Why do you have them?' she asked curiously, 'I just would've thought the realtors....'

'We thought it best that I hang on to them,' he laid the keys on the desk in front of her. 'There have been several break-ins over the years, kids mostly scaring themselves with ghost stories and dares.'

'Ghost stories?'

'Like any house of that kind of age,' he shrugged, 'it's primed for attracting gossip and rumors. I wouldn't pay any attention, but I will warn you the keys won't do you much good.

Other than the padlocks for the safety fences we had to board up the entire ground floor after...'

'After what?' her eyes narrowed.

'It isn't safe,' he hedged around her question as he reached for a yellow legal pad and picked up a pen. 'I can't guarantee what state the interior is in, you shouldn't go in until it's been thoroughly checked and declared structurally sound. Here's the number of a local construction business, its family run, has an excellent reputation. They take care of pretty much the whole island and although they're based here, they do take on work over on the mainland too, so if you do decide to fix up the house, they're the ones you need to speak with.'

'Thanks,' she reached out and took the paper as he folded it and handed it over.

'Sorry to cut this short,' he looked down at his watch, 'but I do have another appointment.'

'Not at all,' she scooped up the keys and tucked the paper in the pocket of her jeans. 'Thanks for your time.'

'My pleasure,' Dennis smiled, 'make sure you stop by and let me know how things are going.'

'I will.'

Giving him one last look, she opened the door and hurried through the office as quickly as possible before Philippa freaked out again.

Once back in her truck she pulled out the paper Dennis had handed her and read his neat scrawl. Not only had he given her the name and number of the construction business but also instructions on how to get there.

She could've blamed the fact that she spent the next hour driving around in circles on the fact she'd been reading his map upside down, or the fact that none of the roads were marked clearly, but what the hell, it was a pleasant enough drive and she certainly got to see more of the island and the more she saw, the more she liked.

Her mother had always avoided places like this, instead preferring big bustling cities or dry, dusty, arid towns in the middle of nowhere. Perhaps small costal islands and towns reminded her too much of home, but then again, she never did understand what was going on in her mother's head half the time.

But now, surrounded by the scent of briny waters and watching the glittering waves sparkle around the edges of the island she felt a strange sense of contentment. As the air cooled and the sun began to dip toward the horizon, setting the skies ablaze with powerful slashes of pink and purple, she abandoned any thought of finding the construction company and drove back toward town as her belly began to rumble loudly.

She parked out front of a local bar and grill. Now that the sun had gone down the air was cooler, so leaving Bailey in the truck she headed inside.

KELLEY TORE his gaze away from the game on TV as a collective denial rose up from some of the regulars. Although they still watched avidly, despite their rather vocal disapproval Kelley had already lost interest, he wasn't really a sporty kind of guy anyway.

He picked up a cloth and resumed wiping down the smooth glossy wood of the bar. Absently glancing across to the doorway he saw her immediately. It took him a moment to process that he'd stopped cleaning and was just standing staring.

She stood out; even in jeans, a plain white tank, red sneakers and without a scrap of make-up she was stunning. All gold skin, dark eyes and hair as black as Indian ink. He watched as she crossed the room, heading toward the other end of the bar. She didn't take a seat, instead she picked up a menu and began to read.

'Hey, what can I get you?'

Ava looked up at the tall guy standing smiling at her from the other side of the bar. Her gaze dipped from his face to his torso and back up again.

'Umm,' she glanced back down at the menu.

'You eating?' he asked.

She nodded.

'Well,' he smiled easily, 'the lobster rolls are really good.'

'Huh,' she looked up, her gaze locking on his eyes. Under the dim lights she couldn't really tell what color they were, but they were light. 'I've never had lobster before.'

'You've...' his eyes widened slightly, 'what never?'

She shook her head, her mouth curving slightly.

'That's practically sacrilegious around here.'

'That right?' she replied in amusement.

'You know, we're going to have to remedy that, stat.'

'Maybe next time,' she smiled suddenly, and he stopped and blinked. 'I'll take the cheeseburger and fries thanks, if you could wrap it up to go.'

'Uh,' he shook his head as if to clear his thoughts, 'to go, right.'

She continued to scan down the menu.

'Can you add the steak with that.'

'Steak?' His eyes drifted over her slim hourglass figure, pausing briefly on her small waist, 'you want a steak too?'

'Uh huh,' she nodded.

'Any other sides with that?'

'Nope,' she replied simply, 'just the steak, rare... so it faintly whispers moo.'

'Okay...' he set his order pad down, 'you do know how big the burger is right? You seriously telling me you're going to down a twelve-ounce steak too?'

No,' her mouth curved, 'it's for my dog.'

'Your dog?' he repeated slowly, 'you're going to buy your dog an eighteen-dollar steak?'

'Why wouldn't I?' Ava shrugged, 'she likes steak and besides if I don't give her something good to distract her, she won't let me eat my burger.'

His head tilted a fraction as he studied her curiously.

'Okay,' he smiled a moment later, 'one burger, one steak coming right up. It may take a little while, why don't you take a seat and I'll get you something to drink?'

'Coke please,' she slid onto the bar stool and watched as he placed her food order.

He filled a tall glass and slid it in front of her.

'You're new on the island then?' he leaned on the bar in front of her.

'Yeah,' she took a sip of her ice-cold drink.

'Vacation?'

'Family business,' she replied vaguely.

'You have family on the island then?' he asked curiously.

'You ask a lot of questions,' her eyes narrowed slightly.

'But that's how you get to know someone,' he smiled.

'You never heard of stranger danger?'

He chuckled lightly shaking his head, 'more often than I'd like.'

She frowned at the weird response.

'Kelley Ryan,' he held out his hand.

She stared at his hand suspiciously before glancing back up at his expectant face.

'Ava,' she grudgingly offered, as she took his hand and shook as briefly as she could without being rude.

'Ava?' he left it hanging. 'Or is it one name like Cher or Madonna, or maybe Sting.'

'Cortez,' she replied, trying not to be charmed.

'Ava Cortez,' he rumbled, his mouth curving as he studied her, 'I'm pleased to meet you.'

She refused to let her name on his tongue heat her belly, or any other part of her for that matter, despite the warm gravelly tone of his voice. She was there to deal with the house and find out if she had any living family, not scratch an itch with any of the locals, no matter how appealing they were.

'So where are you from?'

'Lots of different places.'

'Are you always this prickly?' he asked in amusement.

'Yes,' she replied flatly.

His name was called loudly from the other end of the bar, so he excused himself reluctantly and moved further down and began filling drinks orders.

She sat quietly sipping her coke and watching him. His frame was tall and just the right side of lanky to not be skinny. His skin, paler in the winter months she guessed was tanned, his hair, a medium brown with licks of sun kissed blonde, hung to his collar, long enough to run his fingers through but not so long as to look untidy. She still wasn't entirely sure what color his eyes were, his smile was easy and genuine, but the face damn it, he was entirely too gorgeous for his own good.

The women flocked to him like a half-price sale at Nordstrom, she noticed. Each of them starry eyed, pouted lipped and with cleavage he could trip over if he wasn't careful. But she noticed he ignored every single one of them, other than a polite smile, in favor of glancing in her direction every few moments as if to satisfy himself she was still there and not some figment of his imagination.

It would be flattering if she wasn't so suspicious. A man that good looking had to know the effect he had on women. He couldn't be that oblivious to the disappointed pouts and sulky frowns he left in his wake.

He would be trouble; she could just tell. Probably best to steer well clear of him.

'ORDER UP.'

There was a hearty boom of a voice punctuated by the dainty tinkle of a small bell.

Kelley headed back her way, stopping to pick up her order which was in a brown paper bag.

'Can you throw a couple of beers in there?' Ava asked.

'Sure,' he folded a couple of napkins and tucked them into the bag before retrieving a couple of cold bottles from the small refrigerator behind him.

'So,' he smiled easily, 'where are you staying while you're on the island?'

'Why?' she asked suspiciously.

'How else am I going to call you up and ask you to dinner, you still need to try the lobster remember?' he winked, 'the locals won't accept you until you do.'

'I don't think....'

There was a loud and sudden crash from the kitchen followed by profuse stream of profanities.

'Hold that thought,' Kelley turned toward the kitchen, 'seriously, don't move I'll be right back.'

He disappeared through the doors into the back and Ava sighed. He was too appealing for his own good, or maybe her own good. She shook her head, she wasn't looking to start anything up, even anything casual, she had too much on her mind. Shoving her hand into her pocket she pulled out a handful of bills and dropped them on the bar as she picked up the bag of food and her two beers.

Shame, she glanced once more in the direction Kelley had disappeared before she deliberately turned and walked out the door.

Climbing back into her truck, Bailey immediately stuck her nose into the bag.

'NO!' Ava snapped firmly, 'you have to wait. If not, you can sit in the back.'

Bailey obediently sat down, her tail thumping against the seat, a small plaintive whine at the back of her throat.

'That's what I thought,' Ava nodded as she tucked the food down in front of the seat and backed out onto the road.

They headed back through the town, up the narrow winding road, following the route they'd taken earlier in the day. It was almost full dark now, with only her headlamps to guide the way through the tree lined road.

Finally, it opened up and Ava pulled up, parking a short distance from the house on the patchy grass.

'Come on then girl,' she climbed out with Bailey hopping down enthusiastically next to her. 'Would you look at that?' she breathed.

The full moon reflected off the ocean making it glitter and shimmer restlessly, and in that one instant, with the cool night air tugging at her hair and the salty scent of the ocean in her nostrils combined with the soothing sound of the waves crashing against the base of the cliff, she fell hopelessly in love. Whereas her mom had needed the heat and the desert, Ava realized, she needed the ocean.

Smiling to herself she climbed up into the flatbed of her truck and settled back down beside Bailey as she unwrapped their food.

After they'd eaten, Ava had enjoyed a cool beer as she lay back staring at the pinpricks of light in the vast indigo sky above her, and for the first time in her life, she felt peaceful. She watched for the longest time, snuggled back against her bags, with a full belly, the comforting weight of her dog pressing across her legs and the lullaby of the ocean crooning softly to her. Her eyes began to get heavy, drifting closed, and as the moon watched over her, high in the sky, Ava didn't notice the tiny flickering of a solitary candle in the topmost room of the darkened house.

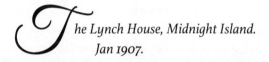

he Lynch House, Midnight Island.
Jan 1907.

SHE REACHED out with gentle hands and as she peeled the dressing back, he whimpered in pain as the stained cotton took a layer of oozing skin with it.

'Shush,' she whispered.

'It hurts.'

'I know it does,' her eyes widened nervously as she glanced at the closed door, 'but if you make a noise, she'll hear you.'

The small boy clamped his lips closed so tightly they turned white, his eyes filled with pain and fear. She resumed her task, working quickly to avoid causing him any more pain. The skin of his stomach was angry and red, peeling in patches, his groin and his upper thighs weren't much better. There was still no improvement. All she could see were blisters and dead skin. He would bear scars for the rest of his life, but he would recover as long as the wounds did not become infected.

'Why does she hate us?' he asked as she pulled his nightshirt down over the fresh dressings and drew the blanket back over him.

'Hush,' she soothed him, 'don't think about that now.'

She stood quietly, wincing slightly as the floor creaked beneath her stockinged feet. She tried to move as quietly as possible. She removed her dark blue woolen dress and laid it over the back of the plain wooden chair, leaving her in only her pantalettes and chemise as she perched on the edge of the bed and removed her black wool stockings.

She stood slowly and as she turned, the dim flickering candlelight highlighted the angry red slashes across the backs of her arms, her shoulders, and her back, disappearing underneath the white lace of her chemise.

'Does it still hurt?' he asked in a small voice as he stared at the thin vicious marks of the switch. His tummy hurt when he looked at them; she'd been punished because she'd tried to stop HER, from hurting him. It hadn't mattered anyway; she'd still scalded him and beaten his sister. 'I can put some salve on it.'

'No love,' she whispered, 'it doesn't hurt.'

She turned away from him, so he couldn't see the lie in her eyes. It was painful, every time she moved it burned and ached, but there was only a little salve left and his need was greater.

She grabbed her long nightshirt and pulled it on over her undergarments and shivered, her breath puffing out in little white misty clouds. It was so cold in the topmost room, but the servants weren't allowed to light the fire.

She climbed into bed beside him, clambering under the blankets and pulling him in close.

'Sleep now,' she murmured, rocking him gently in her arms.

'Will you tell me a story?' he whispered sleepily.

'Only if you close your eyes,' she murmured, her brow furrowing slightly as she felt the intense heat from his small, thin body.

Blowing out the candle, they lay together in the darkness as she *whispered to him. Tales of faraway lands, of towers and palaces, of wild animals and elephants, the wonders of the world.*

'Will we go one day?' he murmured, his voice slurred, 'you and I?'

'Of course, love,' she stroked his damp hair, 'as soon as I'm old enough I'm going to take you away from this place, far far away from this house, from her. We'll be free and she'll never ever hurt us ever again.'

'Promise?' he mumbled.

'I promise,' she kissed his clammy forehead, 'now sleep.'

She held him in the darkness as he slipped into dreams, not knowing that he would be dead before the dawn.

4

_A_va's head broke the water and she dragged in a lungful of air. The early morning sun was bright and the air warm, although her skin pebbled under the cool water as it rippled and shimmered around her, catching the rays of light and reflecting them back.

Wading over to the rocky ledge she retrieved her bar of soap and began to wash, as Bailey barked happily and jumped in and out of the waves, playing like an excitable puppy. Then again, Ava couldn't really blame her. Up until this point neither of them had spent any real time along the coast, now they found themselves on a beautiful little island and it felt good.

Ava dunked under the water to rinse the lather. She'd bathed in some pretty questionable places over the years thanks to her transient lifestyle, courtesy of her mother but there was something liberating about bathing in the ocean. Clean and fresh, with her skin smelling like a curious mixture of coconut and saltwater, she waded back to the shore and grabbed her towel. Completely at ease with her nakedness she toweled off and pulled her clean clothes on.

There was no way anyone could see her from this vantage

point. The top of the cliff jutted out so that the beach was barely visible from above and the cliffs either side curved outwards so that her little beach was nestled in a U shape, almost like a small lagoon. The route of the ferry from the mainland passed the other side of the cliff and so there was no way anyone could intrude on her little slice of heaven.

Climbing up onto a huge boulder, with a bottle of water in one hand and her toothbrush in the other, she began to clean her teeth as she stared out at the water.

Something tugged at the edges of her mind. A strange dream from the night before, but even now, she found she couldn't quite recall the details. She wasn't sure why it was bothering her so much, especially as she couldn't remember it, but she'd woken with a heaviness in her chest and an inexplicable feeling of unbearable loss and sorrow.

Ava rinsed her mouth out and sighed. Trying to put the uneasiness from her mind, she stared out across the deep blue water.

It certainly was a gorgeous spot and from what she'd seen of the island so far, it was a charming little community. Why would her mom want to leave?

She found herself wishing she'd known about Midnight Island before her mom had gotten sick, then she could have asked her about it. Not that Serenity would have answered, she was a champion evader when she wanted to be. That was how she managed to die of cancer without Ava even knowing she'd been sick.

No, she shook her head, even if her mom had still been alive, Ava doubted she'd have told her anything about her childhood home. Which meant, she would have to figure it out for herself. Maybe talk to some of the locals, and while she was at it see if she could dig up some information on the house itself, but first on the agenda was tracking down the owner of the construction company and getting someone to check the internal stability of the house. She had to admit she was beyond curious to see inside.

With that thought firmly in mind she pulled her sneakers on and gathering up her towel and belongings she whistled for her dog, who gazed longingly at the sea one more time before letting out a series of barks and following her up the roughly hewn steps carved into the cliff face.

Hope Ryan leaned back in her chair, rubbing her hugely swollen belly with a sigh of frustration. She picked up the report she'd been trying to read and yawned widely. She was at the 'not getting any sleep' phase of her pregnancy due to the fact that A) she couldn't get comfortable and B) her unborn babies wouldn't let her. Then when she added in C and D, her four-year-old twins and her seven-year-old daughter, she was beginning to wonder if she'd ever sleep again.

Was it even possible to die of lack of sleep? Or did she just have a crappy temperament and hallucinations to look forward to? If it was hallucinations, she was hoping for one which involved no kids, her pre-pregnant sized body (minus the stretch marks), a deserted tropical island and a manservant named Raoul, in tiny trunks who served her cocktails all day long. Her husband wasn't allowed; he was banned from her tropical hallucinations on account of the fact it was his fault they'd ended up with so many children. Well, she didn't know if it was genetically his fault, but she was the one with the swollen ankles, so damn it he was taking the blame.

Turning her attention back to the mind-numbing report about lumber discount, she blinked again, watching as the letters just blurred together. Dropping the report back down on the desk she glanced out the window and saw a black truck pull in. It wasn't one of theirs; it was too new and definitely too clean.

Being of a curious nature, Hope would've gotten out of her chair and waddled over to the window to get a better look, but she wasn't sure she could. She was willing to bet her hips were firmly wedged in the stupid chair. In fact, it was entirely possible that when it was time to go home her husband would have to simply wheel her out in the chair and strap her to the back of his rusty red pick-up.

The door to the office opened and the first thing Hope saw was a huge ball of gold and black fur bound over to her, sniffing her excitedly and rubbing its whole body against Hope, making the office chair roll back against the wall.

'God, I'm really sorry,' a female voice winced.

Hope laughed as the enormous dog licked her face and shuddered with delight as she ran her hands over its fur.

'It's alright,' Hope laughed again as she gave the dog a good-natured shove when it tried to crawl up into her lap where there was clearly no space thanks to her massive belly. 'I was just sitting here feeling sorry for myself. He? She?'

'She,' Ava confirmed.

'She,' Hope nodded as she looked up properly for the first time and caught sight of the stunning dark-haired woman, 'has cheered me up.'

'Yeah,' Ava smiled affectionately at her dog, 'she's good at that. She's really maternal though, she loves pregnant women and babies. She's very protective and extremely intelligent.'

'I always wanted a dog,' Hope sighed, 'but my house is enough of a zoo these days.'

'If she's too much I can always leave her in the truck.'

'She's no trouble,' Hope smiled. 'Anyway, what can I do for you?'

'Oh right,' Ava wiped her palms on her jeans and held out her hand. 'I'm Ava.'

'Hope,' she reached out and shook Ava's hand.

'I've recently found myself in possession of an old house

and its not been inhabited for a very long time. I need someone to come and check it's structurally sound so I can decide what to do with it. I was referred to you by my lawyer, um Mr Pearson.'

'Oh Denny,' she nodded, 'he plays golf over on the mainland with my father in law. They think we don't know what they're really up to when they head over on 'business',' she punctuated the air sarcastically with quoty fingers. 'Anyway... sure, we can get someone out to look at your property for you.' She started searching the cluttered desk for a notepad and pen.

Suddenly the door opened, and Ava froze in surprise. The guy from the bar the night before casually strolled in. He barely nodded in her direction, giving her a polite distant smile as if he hadn't been flirting with her barely twenty-four hours earlier.

She watched with wide eyes as he leaned over Hope, rubbing her huge belly and dropping a kiss on her lips.

'I thought you were heading home?' he asked softly.

'Yeah well,' she replied a little sourly, 'I'm pretty sure I'm wedged in this dumb chair.'

Ava's expression hardened as her gaze dipped to Hope's left hand and sure enough there was a thin gold band on her finger. What an asshole, she thought to herself; how often had he cheated on his obviously pregnant wife?

'Oh, I'm sorry,' Hope apologized. 'Ava, this is my husband Killian. Killian this is Ava.'

'We've met,' Ava replied flatly.

'Have we?' Killian frowned as he held out his hand.

'Yes,' she replied, 'only you told me your name was Kelley.'

'Oh,' Killian chuckled, 'what's he done this time?'

'Excuse me?' she replied in confusion.

'Kelley's my idiot brother,' Killian shook his head.

'Oh,' Ava's eyes narrowed thoughtfully, 'twins?'

'Don't even mention that word around here,' Hope shook

her head, 'or you'll be cursed. Killian and Kelley are twins, their dad and uncle are twins, these...' she rubbed her belly are our second lot of twins. You want my advice stay well away from the Ryan gene pool or you'll be up to your neck in your own miniature football team before you know what's happened. Seriously, run now, save yourself.'

Ava laughed genuinely.

'Sorry,' she apologized to Killian. 'I met Kelley last night at Dusty's Bar and Grill and he spent the whole time hitting on me. Then I walk in here this morning and saw you with your obviously very pregnant wife...'

'Hold the phone,' Hope interrupted, 'back up there. Kelley was hitting on you?'

'Yeah,' Ava nodded, 'although given the number of women hanging all over him practically fighting for his attention, I'm sure it's second nature to him.'

'Oh my God,' Hope clapped her hands together in delight and giggled.

'What?'

'Kelley never flirts with anyone; in fact, I can't even remember the last time I saw him actually interested in a woman.'

'Oh please,' Ava scoffed, 'have you seen him? What am I saying; of course, you have. You're married to the mirror image of him. Kelley has trouble written all over him.'

'No,' Hope shook her head in amusement. 'You'd think that but if you actually get to know him, you'll realize he's genuinely oblivious to the attention.'

'Uh-huh,' Ava replied dryly, the disbelief written clearly on her face.

'Anyway,' Killian interrupted, 'I'm sure you didn't come here to discuss my brother, so what is it we can help you with Ava?'

'Cortez,' she added.

'Cortez,' he mused thoughtfully for a moment. 'Hang on... Cortez... aren't you the one who's inherited the Lynch place?'

'That's right,' Ava nodded, 'how did you know?'

'Phil,' Killian replied in amusement.

'Who's Phil?'

'Phillipa, Dennis Pearson's assistant,' he answered. 'News travels pretty fast around here, but if Phil knows about it, it practically hits light speed.'

'Oh.'

'Oh my god,' Hope whispered in horror, 'you actually own the Lynch house? THE Lynch House?'

'Uh, yeah,' Ava frowned, 'why?'

Killian shot his wife a warning look which she completely ignored.

'It's only the most haunted house in the whole of New England.'

'Haunted?' one of Ava's brows rose slowly.

'That's an exaggeration,' Killian stared pointedly at his wife. 'The fact is, the house comes with a history just like anywhere else, but you add into that the fact that it's been uninhabited since the twenties and you got nearly ten decades of teenagers gossiping and making up stories to scare each other. Then those stories get told and embellished. It's a load of bull.'

'Tell that to Todd Hinton and Declan Tilman,' Hope muttered.

'An accident and a tragedy,' Killian replied sharply as he stared at his wife.

She stared back.

'What's going on?' Ava frowned. 'I feel like everyone's talking in code. Is there something important I'm missing here?'

'Look Ava,' Killian turned his attention back to her, 'like I said, the house has a history as much as any property its age. It's a beautiful building, a gorgeous example of Victorian architecture that frankly it was a crime to allow it to deteriorate into the state it's in now.'

'Well I'm looking to change that,' Ava replied. 'As I was telling Hope just before you walked in, I'm looking for someone to come out and take a look at the house. I need to see if it's structurally sound and if it's worth saving.'

'Buildings like that are always worth saving,' Killian scratched the stubble at his chin thoughtfully, 'but it won't come cheap.'

'You let me worry about that,' Ava answered. 'Can you take a look at it and tell me if it's safe?'

Hope let out a snort.

'I mean safe enough to go inside without worrying if the ceiling is going to fall on my head,' Ava clarified.

'I have to admit,' Killian's lips curved into a slow grin, 'ever since I was a kid I've wanted to see inside the place.'

'Well now's your chance Mr Ryan.'

'Killian,' he corrected. 'Well alright then, why don't we head out now and take a look?'

'You're not serious?' Hope's mouth fell open in shock. 'You're not actually going inside?'

'It's the only way to tell if its sound,' Killian replied easily. 'Don't worry baby,' he leaned over and kissed her reassuringly, 'nothing's going to happen.'

'But...'

'Trust me,' he smiled.

'Fine,' she muttered sourly, 'go right ahead, but if there is an angry ghost and you die, leaving me to raise five children by myself, I swear to God I'll kill you.'

Killian chuckled. 'I'll be back in a few hours.'

'If you're not, I'll be sending your dad to look for your dead body,' Hope called out as Killian and Ava stepped outside with Bailey in tow.

'Is she serious?'

'About what?' Killian replied in amusement, 'the ghost, or my dead body?'

'Both.'

He huffed out a laugh.

'She probably is serious.'

'Do you actually believe in ghosts?' Ava asked curiously.

'No,' Killian replied as he stopped next to Ava's shiny truck, 'I don't believe in ghosts, but then again I was always the more pragmatic kid. It was Kelley who was always staying up half the night under his bedclothes with a flashlight, scaring himself to death with comic books.' He shook his head at the memory, a smile curving the corners of his mouth. 'He loved Hellblazer... Nice truck by the way.'

'Thanks,' Ava beamed as she stroked the top of the doorframe.

'You know, you look at that truck the way most women look at shoes.'

'I'm not most women,' she replied.

'I'm beginning to see that,' he mused quietly, after all it would take an exceptional woman to turn the head of his notoriously picky brother, if indeed that was what happened. Making a mental note to call his brother first chance he got he nodded toward the door. 'Why don't you head on up to the house? I'll be right behind you.'

Nodding Ava climbed back into her truck with her dog and pulled out of the small parking lot, heading back up toward the house.

True to his word, by the time Ava pulled up in front of the rambling old Victorian property Killian's rusty red pick-up pulled in right behind her and parked.

'Hey.'

Ava turned just in time to catch a bright yellow hard hat.

'You're going to need that,' he nodded to the hat in her hands and watched as she put it on. 'Probably best if you leave your dog out here just in case. I don't want her to get hurt; if there's loose debris on the ground it could injure her paws.'

Ava nodded in agreement as Killian tilted his head back and took a long hard look at the huge building.

'You're lucky it was constructed with brick and stone. 'If she'd been a timber structure, I doubt she'd have lasted this long... you've got some broken windowpanes on the second and third floors, it will have exposed the rooms to damage from the wind and rain coming in off the coast. It's possible the upper floors have deteriorated but we won't know for sure until we get inside. You got keys?'

'Yes,' Ava replied fishing in her pocket for the large bundle of keys the lawyer had given her, 'but the entire lower floor is boarded up.'

'Not a problem,' he reached into the flatbed of his pick-up and rummaged through the tools until he came up with a crowbar.

'Stay,' Ava told Bailey, who didn't look happy but found a patch of sun warmed grass and hunkered down, yawning with a stretch of her tongue and a slight whine before dropping her head on her paws and settling in for a nap.

It took several attempts to find the right key for the padlock but finally the gate scraped open with a groan of protest. Killian was the first to head up the stone steps which still seemed to be perfectly stable and past two small stone lion heads mounted on the wall either side of the bottom step.

By the time she reached Killian he'd already pried off one panel of rotting wood, propping it up against the curve of the rounded tower to the right and was working on the second panel. It finally gave with a loud splintering and cracked in two, showering the ground with chunks of wood.

'Would you like to do the honors?' he stepped back.

Ava stared at the old double doors. They were rotten; even she could see they couldn't be saved and that was fine. A doorway like this needed something brighter. Panels of stained glass which would catch the dying rays of the light reflecting off the ocean and throwing a myriad of colors across the foyer she imagined she would find on the other side.

She fumbled through the keys for the right one and she slid it into the lock, imagining it turning smoothly as she opened the doors and let them romantically glide open, but it didn't. It was wedged. No matter how hard she tried the lock refused to budge, as if the house was somehow trying to keep them out.

'Hmm,' Killian examined the lock, 'it's rusted through. It can't be helped, we'll have to break in. The doors are past saving anyway.'

Ava nodded and stood back.

There was sharp crack, and the lock gave, splintering off a huge strip of rotted wood.

'Ready?' he turned to her and grinned.

'Yes,' she replied placing her palm on one of the doors, her belly tensing with a mixture of excitement and nerves.

Killian reached out and placed his palm on the other door and together they pushed them open. There was an almost audible rush of air, as if the house was taking its first breath in over a century.

She lifted one foot and slowly crossed the threshold. As she stepped inside the house it was as if she'd crossed some secret gateway from one world to another. She swayed momentarily; the air pressure was different, heavier somehow, like the oppressive weight of an oncoming storm. Her ears buzzed slightly and for a second, she could've sworn she heard a whisper, barely more than a sibilant hiss.

She shifted her weight to step further into the house when she felt Killian grab her upper arm gently and hold her in place.

'Wait.' She watched as he leaned down and lifted two heavy flashlights he'd placed beside the doorway. Switching one on, he handed it to her before lifting his own. 'Better stay close to me just in case; I don't want any of the flooring giving way under you.'

She nodded and allowed him to step in first. Standing on the threshold while he checked, she studied the strange time capsule. If they were correct this place hadn't changed in over a hundred years. Although it was a mess, it was a curious glimpse into the past that few were privileged to experience.

They found themselves standing in the darkness of what appeared to be a large foyer, the beams of their flashlights high-lighting a large staircase winding upward.

There was a sudden, loud bang in the stillness. Somewhere in the house a door slammed causing Ava to flinch involun-tarily and turn to Killian.

'Don't let anything Hope said spook you,' he shook his head in amusement. 'Some of the windows upstairs are either broken or missing panes, so as soon as we opened the front entrance it created a draft.'

Ava nodded, it made sense. She lifted the beam of her flash-light a little higher and the light caught on the dust motes spin-ning in the air, displaced by their sudden intrusion. Directly above the staircase seemed to be a second-floor balcony draped with huge curtains of delicate spider webs which fluttered slightly, but it was still too dark to see beyond that.

'We'll be able to get a better sense of the place once all the boarded windows on the ground level are uncovered,' Killian told her as she followed him to the left through a doorway and into what looked like a library. It was hard to tell; it was so dark she could only catch glimpses of her surroundings under the beams from their flashlights.

She lost sight of Killian after a moment, though she could hear him moving around close to her. She let her beam of light sweep across the far wall revealing rows of bookcases. The glass doors hung open or simply hung off their hinges as if a small tornado had blown through the place, and the floor was littered with the carcasses of splayed books, pages torn, spines broken. It would all have to go of course, Ava mused to herself. Even the books still on the shelves were probably infested with silverfish.

The drapes at the window had all but rotted away, nothing more than moth eaten shrouds hanging limply from either side of the boarded window. Ava moved further into the room, the ground uneven from the debris, some of which seemed to crunch under her feet. She lifted her flashlight to the ceiling and saw large chunks of plaster had crumbled away revealing thin strips of lath.

Something brushed against her leg and she dipped her beam of light down, but she couldn't see anything. She took another small tentative step forward and heard the unmistakable grind of cracking glass under her sneaker. She glanced down again, and this time found a small framed photograph lying on the floor.

Reaching down she grasped the edge of the frame and lifted it, tilting it slightly to allow the shards of loose broken glass to fall to the dusty floor. Once she was sure she wouldn't cut her fingers on the glass she lifted the flashlight and shone it on the picture.

In it was a rather austere looking woman perched on a chair, her back so straight it looked as if it were bolted in place. Her waist was tiny thanks to a tightly laced corset beneath her dress which had large puffy sleeves. Beside her with his hand chastely resting on her shoulder, stood a tall, smartly dressed man, with neatly parted hair, a curved moustache and a pocket watch on a chain, tucked into his waistcoat. The other side of the woman was a small boy of maybe six years. He too had neatly parted hair, a stiff white collar and short pants which stopped just above his knees.

She felt Killian move closer, felt the solid presence of his body standing just behind her. The tiny hairs on the back of her neck and her arms rose, as if she were suddenly surrounded by static electricity, which prickled long her skin and buzzed in her ears. Somewhere in the room she heard a weird sound, not quite the tick of a clock, more like a clicking, whirring mechanism.

'Do you hear that?' she asked Killian as he stood silently behind her... Killian? She repeated when he didn't answer.

'Ava?' Killian called out, the beam of his own flashlight hovering somewhere outside the entrance to the room.

She spun around, her flashlight flickering across the darkened room, her heart beating a little faster. That was strange, she could've sworn he'd been standing behind her.

'I'm coming,' she replied quickly as she turned and headed out. She didn't notice as one of the glass fronted doors creaked and swung inward twenty degrees, revealing a tall shadow hovering behind her.

'Killian?' Ava stepped back into the foyer still holding the picture.

'Over here,' his muffled voice replied. 'Careful there's a small step down into the room.'

She crossed over toward the other side of the wide staircase. Following his voice, she watched her feet as she stepped down and found herself entering another huge, almost cavernous room. The ground didn't seem to crunch under the soles of her sneakers this time, instead it felt like sturdy wood.

Once again lifting her flashlight she cast the beam around the space, but it was impossible in the near darkness to gauge the dimensions of the room. Stepping forward, she let out a small cry of pain as she rapped her knee smartly on something hard, causing the harsh screech of wood against wood to echo through the room.

'Are you okay?' Killian's disembodied voice floated across the stale air.

Ava sucked in a sharp breath as the vicious pain in her kneecap dulled to a muted throb.

'I'm fine,' she replied gazing down at the piece of furniture she'd collided with.

It was a wooden table of some kind, with a hinged lid and an attached chair. Recognizing it as an old school desk she looked up, flashing the light across the room and sure enough there were several more desks all lined up neatly.

Ava tucked the photo frame carefully under one arm. Holding the flashlight in one hand she reached out and touched the worn wood, feeling the rough grain against the pads of her fingers as she traced the grooves and indentations.

Peter, she mouthed quietly. Someone, at some point had carved his name into the desk, only the 'r' was back to front and the rest of the letters were a mismatched assemblage of different sizes and capitals. The owner of the name had obviously been quite young.

'Well everything looks pretty sound down here,' Killian suddenly appeared next to her. 'Do you want to come upstairs and check out the second level? The light will be better up there as the windows haven't been boarded up.'

'Sure,' Ava nodded despite the fact he could barely see her.

They climbed the main stairs which forked halfway up. She quietly followed behind Killian as he went from room to room, checking floors, ceilings, window frames and walls. She didn't pay him much mind; her gaze was taking in all the details of the house she hadn't been able to see downstairs. The space had been flooded with light from the many windows, despite decades of dirt and grime on the panes which were still in place.

Plaster had chipped away from the ceiling in many of the rooms. The exposed floorboards, likewise, were in a pretty rough condition and in almost every room the wallpaper peeled and drooped down the walls in great swathes. Drapes hung tattered at broken windows, but the furniture remained in place.

One of the first things she noticed was the sheer amount of small child sized beds. Due to the large size of most of the rooms, they had easily fitted three to four beds per room. Each was still made up with graying sheets and heavy blankets in not much better condition than the drapes.

Still it was eerie. Children's tin toys lay splayed across the floor, china dolls were propped on beds or tucked into chairs in the corners of the room. It was as if the occupants had simply walked out and left everything as it was.

A rocking horse suddenly creaked and shifted in the breeze from the broken windowpane. Ava stepped closer, noticing a small tin carousel with brightly painted, chipped horses. Reaching out with inquisitive fingers, it slowly began to turn, the ancient mechanism nudged into motion by her touch. The haunting lullaby filled the room in its stilted and uneven way, the music barrel obviously having been damaged over time.

'That's creepy,' Killian shook his head as he turned to leave the room and Ava followed.

They moved up another smaller flight of stairs to the third and topmost floor, as they moved carefully down the corridor Ava stopped dead in front of a plain wooden door. She couldn't say why she'd stopped, all she knew was her heart was pounding loudly in her chest, her mouth was dry, and her hands had involuntarily curled into fists.

Reaching out slowly, she pushed the door open with a loud creak of protesting hinges and stepped into the room.

It wasn't anything special. There was a small fireplace along one wall, and a single, solitary window opposite. In the corner of the room was an old bed, the mattress long since rotted away and beside it a plain wooden chair.

Her dark eyes locked on the bed and her chest ached like a

huge weigh was crushing her breastbone. A hot, hard ball of pain burned in the back of her throat and she couldn't swallow.

'Are you okay?'

Ava blinked and turned to find Killian staring at her oddly.

'Yes,' she replied, 'why?'

'You're crying,' he frowned.

Ava lifted her hand and felt the wetness on cheek.

'It must be the dust,' she muttered turning away in embarrassment. Had she been crying? Worse still, why hadn't she realized it?

Killian stared at her silently, his expression unreadable as he studied her.

'Come on,' he said finally and nodded toward the door, 'I've seen enough for the moment. Why don't we get some fresh air and talk outside?'

She nodded mutely, not trusting her voice as she followed him from the room and headed toward the stairs. A static prickling sensation began to tickle between her shoulder blades causing her to momentarily pause and glance behind her but there was nothing there.

Shaking off the strange feeling she hurried to catch up with Killian as he stepped out of the main doors and into the bright sunlight.

As the warmth began to seep back into her body, she found herself closing her eyes, tilting her face toward the sun and drawing in a deep breath, the sad, lonely feeling she'd experienced earlier slowly dissipating.

'Are you sure you're okay?'

Ava opened her eyes to find Killian holding out a bottle of water and watching her curiously.

'I'm fine,' she took the bottle gratefully and unscrewed the cap. 'Such a lot has happened in such a small space of time, I guess I'm still trying to process it all.'

He nodded in understanding.

'Well, I don't know that my initial assessment is going to lessen the load or add to it.'

'Lay it on me,' she leaned back against the stone wall and took a sip of her water.

'Well, she's solid,' he tipped his head back and took a massive gulp of his own water. 'They sure don't build 'em like they used to. Don't get me wrong there's a shit ton of work involved, but the bare bones of her are sturdy and she's a beauty. Early to mid-19th Century, there's a lot of original features that can be saved, but just as much will have to be stripped out and replaced. It's a hell of a job.'

'How much hell are we talking?'

'On the exterior alone,' he rubbed the back of his neck thoughtfully, 'it's tough to tell until we've got some scaffolding up and can take a closer look, but from what I can see, some of the mortar between the brickwork is crumbling, that will need attention asap. All of the windows will have to be stripped out, you'd want to keep the originals, so they will need to be refurbished and all of the glass panes repaired or replaced. That alone will take a specialist craftsman.'

She watched as he leaned down and scooped a chipped roof tile from the long grass.

'Can't tell just how much damage the roof has sustained from here, but most likely that will need to be repaired and re-tiled. We can use newer ones, but in order for them to match we'll need to see if we can get our hands on originals saved from other old buildings. All the doors will need replacing, all the chimneys cleaned and repaired. The balcony railings will need to be checked, but they'll probably need to be replaced too. The whole place will need wiring as its never had electricity, plumbing, or heating. The drainage will need to be looked at and that's just the basics. The interior is a whole other story. We'll be able to get a better look at the ground floor once the boarding is down and we have some light to work with, but walls, ceilings and floors will all need replacing. The list is endless.'

'Uh-huh,' Ava replied absently as she stared up at the house.

'Ava,' he drew her attention back to him. 'The house has been neglected for so long, we could quote you, get halfway through the build and find a whole host more problems. It's a money pit. Given the age of the property it's going to be a lot of conservation work. You'll need specialist craftsmen and women, and that won't come cheap.'

'How much, ballpark?'

'You're easily looking at seven figures with a re-furb on this scale.'

She turned and looked up at the house again; this time she felt a very distinct tug deep in her belly.

'Okay,' she decided.

'Okay?' he frowned, 'okay? Ava did you hear what I just said?'

'Every word.'

'You've seriously got that kind of money?' he replied in surprise eyeing her target jeans and plain sneakers.

'I've got more than enough; my inheritance will cover it.'

'You could easily blow through it and then some,' he shook his head. 'Don't get me wrong I'm dying to get my hands on this house. A re-build like this rarely comes along but I don't want you to commit to this and end up blowing through all your savings.'

'I've lived without money before,' she shrugged, 'I can do it again.'

His eyes narrowed thoughtfully as he stared at her.

'You're serious about this aren't you?'

'Yes, I am,' she replied quietly. 'I don't know what it is,' she glanced back up at the house. 'I feel... I feel like the house has been waiting for me. I guess that sounds pretty dumb huh?'

'Not at all,' he shook his head.

'Okay,' she blew out a breath and pushed herself away from the wall, holding out her hand, 'let's do this then.'

'You sure?' Killian's eyes twinkled with boyish excitement and he reached for her outstretched palm.

'I'm sure,' Ava nodded.

Their hands clapped together, and they shook firmly. The front door of the house slammed shut so loudly and abruptly part of the wood frame splintered away making them both turn their heads to stare.

'Man,' Killian grinned, 'Hope is gonna freak out.'

Ava rolled her eyes and shook her head.

'So, what's first?'

'There's so much to do,' Killian trotted down the steps heading for his pick-up where he retrieved a tatty notepad with curling edges and a stubby pencil. 'I'm not letting anyone else get their hands on this project, I'll personally oversee every step myself. Fortunately, all the other work we've got on at the moment is fairly straight forward so I've got good guys I can put in charge. That'll free me up. I'll hire in extra crews from the mainland. We need to get the exterior done and the whole place weatherproof before the weather turns. It seems like we've got plenty of time now but when you factor in that I still need to hire crews, draw up plans, order in materials and equipment, we're going to need to hit the ground running.'

'Wow.'

'Yeah,' he nodded as he leaned against the hood of the truck and began to scribble notes. 'A lot of the interior work can be carried out during the colder months, so we really want to nail down the basics first. I know a great architect over on the mainland. I'll see if he can track down the original blueprints to the house and come out and meet with you. You'll want to keep the exterior as true to the original as possible but inside you'll be able to modernize, kitchen, bathrooms etc.'

'I feel like my head's spinning,' Ava frowned.

'That's what I'm here for,' he told her reassuringly. 'I'll get straight on this and come back to you with a plan and some numbers. Once you're satisfied, we'll get the contracts drawn up. You've already got a lawyer; you going to continue to use Dennis?'

'I guess so.'

'I'll give him a heads up,' Killian noticed the broken photo frame in her hand. 'What's that?'

'Oh,' Ava lifted it and stared at it thoughtfully now that she could see it in the bright daylight. 'I found it in the library. I couldn't help but notice that in the other room there was a load of old-fashioned desks and upstairs there seemed to be a lot of children's beds.'

'Well,' Killian scratched his chin slowly, 'the house used to be used as a school back at the turn of the century.'

'Did it?' Ava replied curiously.

Killian eyed the old black and white photo in her hand.

'If you want to know about the history of the house you'll want to talk to Bunty.'

'Bunty?' Ava's brows rose.

'Bunty McCarthy,' Killian answered. 'She runs a little tourist shop almost directly opposite the ferry, Bunty's Boutique. She also happens to be the chairwoman of the island's historical society. If you want to know anything about the history of the island Bunty's your woman.'

'Thanks,' Ava murmured thoughtfully, 'I might just do that.'

'Okay well, I'm going to get going,' Killian smiled. 'I'll have to break the news to Hope and then I have a lot of groundwork to do before we can get started. Where are you staying?'

'Here,' she glanced around as if it should be obvious, 'it's my land after all.'

'Here?' his eyes widened in surprise, 'you can't stay here? The house is in no way livable.'

'Not in the house,' she shook her head. 'I slept in my truck last night, but I have a tent I'll pitch tonight.'

'You can't stay here Ava; before long it's going to be a very noisy, dirty building site.'

'I've lived in worse places believe me,' she shrugged.

'You know,' Killian shook his head in amusement, 'you'll have to come over to the house. You can have a beer and a burger and tell us your life story. I have a feeling it's fascinating.'

'Maybe,' Ava replied.

'Well okay, look if you're dead set on staying here at least upgrade from a tent to an RV or something. You need something sturdier than a tent. Once we get the equipment and supplies in, there'll be temporary rest rooms on site, but trust me, you don't want to be sharing them with a dozen guys. They have habits that would make a monkey blush. You're going to want some sort of temporary home with a bathroom and kitchen space. I'll make some calls and see what I can come up with.'

'Thanks,' Ava smiled genuinely.

'Cell number?' he pulled his own phone from his pocket to save her number.

'Don't have one.'

'You don't...' he broke off and sighed. 'You'll need one of them too, unless you have a deep-seated moral reason for not having one.'

'No reason,' she shook her head, a small smile playing at her lips, 'just didn't need one before.'

'Well you'll need one now,' he told her as he climbed into his pick-up, 'if for no other reason than Hope can call you twenty times a day to make sure I'm not being murdered by the ghosts.'

Ava laughed and held up her hand as he backed up and

swung round, disappearing down the road. Alone once again she whistled for Bailey who came trotting over obediently.

'Well,' she hunkered down beside her best friend and stroked her fur as she stared up at the old house, 'looks like we might have a home after all.'

5

Ava strolled leisurely down the winding street as the cool breeze rippling off the water tugged at her hair. It had taken some convincing, but Bailey stayed in the truck. After all, Ava couldn't imagine anyone named Bunty who ran a boutique would want a huge German Shepherd lumbering around her shop.

It wasn't even as if she could leave her at home, considering they didn't currently have a home and she certainly couldn't leave her in the small tent she'd set up for the night. Maybe Killian was right, Ava mused, perhaps she should consider a temporary trailer or an RV of some kind.

Ava stopped as the small store came into view. It was a sweet little building, painted pale blue with brilliant white trims. The sign above the shop read _'Bunty's Boutique,'_ in an elegant curling script and inside the windows hung lacy white curtains.

Crossing the street to the front entrance Ava found herself grateful she'd left Bailey behind although she missed her furry shadow. Pushing open the door in a merry tinkle of bells, she stepped inside and glanced around. She'd barely had time to take in the neatly stocked shelves filled with all manner of pretty little items when an older woman suddenly appeared behind the counter, summoned by the dainty bell mounted above the door.

Her hair was almost pure white and styled in a smooth bob which curled under her chin. Her skin was softly lined and dusted with a fine sheen of powder; her lips were a pearly pink to match her nails. She wore a double strand of pearls at her neck and a pair of thin wire framed glasses hung from a gold chain over her blouse of ivory silk.

'May I help?' she asked politely as her violet blue eyes studied Ava.

'Uh,' Ava shifted slightly under the intense scrutiny of the immaculately dressed woman. 'I'm looking for Bunty McCarthy?'

'Well you've found her.' She stepped out from behind the counter, smoothing her dove gray slacks as she offered her hand. 'And you are?'

'Ava,' she stepped forward and took the woman's hand, 'Ava Cortez.'

'Ava?' Bunty's eyes widened and her grip on Ava's hand tightened so unexpectedly that she almost yelped. 'Well, as I live and breathe,' she smiled widely, 'Hari's granddaughter, all grown up.'

'Who?'

'Hari?' Bunty repeated, her elegant brow folding slightly, 'your grandmother, Harriet Wallace? God rest her soul.'

'Sorry,' Ava apologized in embarrassment, 'I don't really know anything about my grandmother.'

'Oh, that Caroline,' Bunty rolled her eyes in exasperation. 'She couldn't run away from home quick enough. I assume if she hasn't told you about your grandmother, she's probably explained precious little else.'

It was still strange hearing people refer to her mother as Caroline.

'Serenity... I mean mom,' Ava corrected herself, 'was a very private person.'

'Nonsense,' Bunty pursed her lips until they wrinkled, 'your mother was a little madam who always wanted everything her way. Still, you're here now,' she patted Ava's hand fondly. 'Come on, let's have a cup of tea. I have a bridge game in an hour with the rest of the ladies, but for now I think I can close up a little early.'

Before Ava could open her mouth to protest Bunty marched across the room, flipped the closed sign on the door and turned the lock with a tiny little click.

'Come along, don't stand there staring dear, follow me.'

Unable to do much else Ava skirted around behind the counter, following the older woman through into a small parlor and kitchenette.

'Take a seat dear,' Bunty nodded toward the round table covered with a lace tablecloth as she picked up the kettle and set it to boil. 'Do you prefer tea or coffee?'

'Either,' Ava slid awkwardly onto a dainty white chair with a pink padded seat and glanced around the room. It was neat as a pin, just like the stranger in front of her, who was currently laying out cookies in a ruthlessly decorative formation on a china plate.

'How long have you been on the island?' Bunty asked as she continued to bustle around the small kitchenette, her back to Ava.

'Since yesterday,' Ava replied absently as she studied a delicate porcelain figurine of a cat standing on its hind legs playing a fiddle. 'I met Killian Ryan this morning, and he suggested I speak with you about the house I inherited, um... the Lynch House?'

There was a sudden clatter as Bunty fumbled with the

teacup. Her spine stiffened as she took a moment to place the cup and saucer carefully down on the tray in front of her, before twisting her head to look at Ava, her gray eyes unreadable.

'Of course, you'd be curious about the house,' she replied with a polite, if not slightly distant smile. 'It's only natural.'

'It's not just the house,' Ava continued as Bunty turned back and lifted the now full tray. 'I'd like to know about my family, about the people I come from. Serenity...' she shook her head, and corrected herself again, 'mom...'

'Don't keep correcting yourself on my behalf dear,' Bunty shifted aside a small copper jug filled with cheerful flowers and set the tray down on the table. 'Call your mother whatever you'd like. I don't like to speak ill of the departed, but Lord knows I've had a few choice names for that girl over the years.'

'You don't seem to like my mom very much,' Ava's head tilted unconsciously as she watched Bunty.

'It's not like that, I loved that darn stubborn child. She was my God-daughter after all.'

'She was?' Ava's brows rose in surprise.

'Not that she would have ever acknowledged it,' Bunty's mouth set in a firm disapproving line. 'Hari, your grandmother, was my dearest friend for more years than I can count, and I miss her every single day, but it was hard to watch your mother break her heart over and over again.'

'Why did she?' Ava replied curiously, 'mom I mean. Why did she leave? She never spoke about her family at all; I didn't even know about Midnight Island until after she'd died.'

'There were so many reasons,' Bunty waved her hand dismissively and brushed the question aside. 'So, tell me where you are staying? The Pryce's guesthouse over on Violet Avenue? It's funny, I don't recall Susanne mentioning a young lady staying with them.'

'No,' Ava watched as Bunty set a teacup in front of her and

began to pour from a pretty lavender colored teapot, 'I'm staying up at the house.'

'What house would that be dear?'

'The Lynch House,' Ava muttered absently as she watched the stream of dark steaming liquid fill her cup.

Bunty set the teapot down so abruptly the table rattled.

'Excuse me?' She blinked owlishly as if she hadn't quite heard correctly.

'I'm staying up at the Lynch House. Seeing as I own the land it seemed silly not to make use of it,' Ava shrugged.

'But the house is... uninhabitable,' Bunty finished after a moment's deliberation.

'For the moment,' Ava agreed, 'that's why I have a tent. Although I have to admit Killian does have a point. A tent isn't going to be very practical once the work on the house gets underway. I'm thinking about upgrading to a small trailer or RV temporarily.'

'You...' she began but broke off as if trying to make sense of what Ava was saying, 'what do you mean for the moment? What work?'

'I've decided to restore the house.'

'You've,' Bunty's voice was almost lost on a breathy exhale and for one ridiculous moment Ava wouldn't have been surprised to see her make the sign of the cross against her chest.

'It won't last much longer,' Ava replied, 'it's really now or never. It won't sell in the current condition it's in but even if I wanted to keep it, I can't allow it to deteriorate further.'

'You can't allow it?'

'I know that sounds silly,' Ava shook her head. 'I don't know, I guess as its been in my family for such a long time and they've allowed it to fall into such a state I feel responsible for it.'

'You sound like your grandmother,' Bunty muttered.

'Do I?' Ava replied in surprise, somewhat taken aback. 'What was she like?'

'Hari?' Bunty smiled as she once again picked up the teapot, this time filling her own cup. 'She was very kind; she had a soft spot for everyone. She loved animals and children; she'd have loved to have had a huge family, but it wasn't to be. The birth of your mother was hard, and after Caroline was born, she was told it was too dangerous for her to bear any more children. I think she would've adopted but then your grandfather passed away unexpectedly. A car accident, it was late and dark... and it was raining...' her voice trailed off.

'She never married again?' Ava picked up her tea and took a thoughtless sip, wincing as she burned her tongue in the process.

'No,' Bunty shook her head. 'For some there's only one and your grandfather was the sun, the moon and the stars to her. He was my cousin you know, fourth, once removed on my mother's side.'

'I didn't know,' Ava murmured, 'I don't know anything about my family.'

'Well we shall have to remedy that won't we?' Bunty patted Ava's hand as it lay against the tablecloth.

'I'd like that,' Ava replied, quiet and genuine as she stared down at the contrast of her golden skin against the stark white table linen.

Bunty studied the stunningly beautiful young woman as she toyed with a loose thread. The girl was an enigma. She had the kind of gorgeous, exotic looks of a movie star yet there wasn't a stitch of make up on her flawless skin.

If she looked really hard, she could see a trace of her old friend Hari and her wayward daughter Caroline, around the mouth, the full bottom lip, the line of her nose but it wasn't obvious. The girl's looks had to have come from her father.

'Are you alright?' Bunty asked as the silence began to stretch out between them, 'you seem... pensive?'

'Sorry,' Ava shook her head, 'I'm being rude.'

'Not at all,' the older woman assured her.

'It's something about this island,' she frowned, 'about being here. I have this feeling in my chest, in the pit of my belly and I can't figure it out. I don't recognize it so I can't even put a name to it. Everything happened so fast. Serenity dying... I didn't even know she was sick, until she was already gone. She didn't bother to tell me she was dying of cancer. Didn't even give me the chance to say goodbye. She made the choice for me, like always.'

Bunty's mouth thinned.

'That sounds like Caroline,' Bunty sipped her own tea in a valiant effort to keep from saying what she really wanted to, but it was plain to see the girl needed some careful handling. She may have come across as independent and capable, but there was a vulnerability there, just a shadow, the merest hint in those dark eyes.

'I want to know where I came from, who I came from,' Ava looked up, her gaze locking with Bunty's. 'Can you help me with that?'

Bunty stared at Ava for several long silent seconds almost as if she were weighing a decision of some sort. She slowly set her teacup back in its saucer, tapping her pearly pink fingernail against the delicate china.

'I can,' she finally answered her violet gaze unwavering, 'but it does not come without warning or consequences Ava. Once you go down that road, there is no turning back and you may not like what you find.'

'I don't understand.'

Bunty sighed deeply. 'Your family's roots run deep here on the island. There is not a single brick or blade of grass that has not been touched by their legacy. Your mother didn't want any part of it, she ran as far and as fast as she could and she never looked back, but your grandmother felt that same connection, that same responsibility as you do. We both spent decades searching for the truth and what we found came with a terrible price. Your grandmother was never quite the same... after...'

'What do you mean?' Ava frowned.

'She'd always been so happy, so kind, but the weight of the secrets of your family pressed down upon her, a heavy burden that in the end smothered her. I don't want you to suffer as she did. If you want my advice, bulldoze that house to the ground and forget it ever existed.'

'What could possibly be so bad?'

'Ava,' she began slowly.

'No,' she shook her head firmly, 'I'm tired of everyone else making decisions for me or keeping me in the dark. This is about me, about what I need. I need to know where I come from. It's important to me. Do you have any idea what it feels like to be adrift in the world with nothing and no one to anchor you? No one to turn to; no home to run to?'

'No,' Bunty admitted, 'I don't.'

'This is my choice,' Ava replied firmly, 'and I want to know.'

'Maybe,' Bunty sighed again glancing at the slim gold watch at her wrist, 'but not this evening. I have to go soon, or I will be late.'

'Will you help me though?' Ava asked softly.

'Yes,' she replied after a long moment, her tone carrying a hint of reluctance, 'but I suggest you go away and think long and hard Ava, because truth always comes at a terrible cost.'

KELLEY'S CAR made it almost to the top of the long winding road before it shuddered and rolled to a stop, the headlights flickering in the dying twilight before cutting out completely.

'Okaaay,' Kelley reassured himself as he glanced through

the tree line to the huge ominous outline of the Lynch House. 'I'm sure it's a total coincidence,' he muttered under his breath. 'Nothing at all to do with the big scary house on the other side of the trees.'

Shaking his head in denial he grabbed the heavily laden brown paper bag from the passenger seat, and the two bottles of beer nestled beside it, and climbed out of the car.

'Nothing at all creepy going on,' he mumbled to himself as he hiked through the trees further up the road toward the cliff top. 'Just taking an evening stroll, absolutely nothing to worry about.'

The crack of a branch breaking, and the sudden sharp hiss of the wind had him freezing in his tracks, his body tensing as he stopped and listened, his eyes darting about warily. There was a distant hooting high up in the trees but otherwise nothing out of the ordinary.

'You're such an idiot Kelley,' he shook his head as he started walking again. 'She's going to think you're some kind of crazy stalker.'

He was right, he knew he was. The calmer more rational part of his brain had told him to wait at least until daylight, but when his brother had stopped by to grill him about the dark-haired stunner who'd pulled a Cinderella on him the night before he'd been surprised. Even more surprised to find that she was part of the Wallace family. But if he'd been surprised to find she'd inherited the most infamous house on the island, he'd been downright shocked to find she'd set up camp on the doorstep and not only that, but that she planned to renovate the old death trap.

He couldn't help it, the place freaked him out and had done since he was a kid. In the tenth grade he, along with a couple of his friends, Johnnie Baxter and Benny Malone, had hijacked a six pack from Johnnie's dad and headed up to the bluff on a dare. They'd chugged the beer and raced their bikes to the top of the cliff, although weaved their bikes may have been more accurate, considering they were all novices to alcohol and, rather embarrassingly, well on their way to being drunk after only two beers apiece, determined to confront the ghost of Luella Lynch herself.

They hadn't confronted the ghost; his friend Benny crashed his bike into a tree and broke his leg. Johnnie hadn't been much help either. He'd burst into tears at the first sign of trouble, more concerned with his dad finding out about the beers they'd lifted. Kelley had taken one look at the bone poking through Benny's flesh and vomited back up the beer, before passing out and hitting his own head on a rock.

As a ghost hunting mission, it had been a complete failure. Getting Benny back down the hill with a concussion and trying to explain his friend's broken leg hadn't been a picnic either. His own father had seen right through their rather elaborate cover story and had delivered a blistering lecture followed by a grounding that had lasted the rest of the semester. A little harsh Kelley had felt, but the one little pearl of wisdom he had gained from their little adventure was don't drink and ride.

The tree line began to thin out and beyond it he could see the clearing which led up to the huge imposing gray building. His hands began to sweat a little and his stomach began to roll. For a second, he'd felt like his sixteen-year-old self about to hurl up his contraband beer, but this time it had nothing to do with broken bones or torn flesh, it didn't even have anything to do with the enormous creepy-ass house.

He hadn't felt like this since he'd asked Nancy Kitteridge to Homecoming, well over a decade ago. He was moments from being face to face with a girl he really liked, and he was pretty certain he was about to make a complete idiot of himself, incidentally just like he had with Nancy. He hadn't at the time realized his sneaker was untied and instead of being smooth and suave, he'd managed to trip over his own laces and crash into the water fountain, once again knocking himself out.

Come to think of it... he'd managed to knock himself unconscious with alarming frequency as a kid. Perhaps he had some sort of permanent brain damage. That was surely the only explanation for him driving out to the scariest spot on the island at nightfall, to see a girl he barely knew, and who may or may not end up thinking he was some sort of psychopath.

Still, he'd always had the luck of the devil, or so his uncle continuously told him. Sure, he'd knocked himself out rather ungraciously in front of the prettiest girl in school, but he'd come to, on the ground, with her peering over him in concern. She'd helped him to the nurse's office, said yes to the dance and they'd dated for nearly four months until her parents decided they were moving to Wichita, of all places.

Randomly he found himself wondering what had happened to Nancy Kitteridge.

She was probably married with three kids by now. Most people his age were, with the exception of his brother who was almost up to five, but then again, he was cheating by having them in pairs. Not that Kelley had given any thought to marriage and kids. He'd been perfectly happy with his life just the way it was... until she'd walked through the door and ordered an eighteen-dollar steak for her dog.

It was like being hit with a lightning bolt.

He was like one of those dumb sheep who kept electrocuting themselves on the same stretch of fence and couldn't wait to be zapped again. So, instead of waiting until a civilized hour and introducing himself properly, he was creeping through the rapidly darkening woods, well not creeping, stalking, no that sounded even worse... walking purposefully to her makeshift camp to... what exactly? Get to know her? Ask her out on a date? Propose marriage? Jesus, he really hadn't thought this one through. This was probably why he was still single.

The trees parted and he stepped into the clearing. The light was all but gone, casting long shadows. A short distance away he could see a large dark truck parked on the grass; beside it was a tent and an open campfire. Sitting at the edge of the fire holding onto some kind of large cooking pan was the dark haired, golden skinned woman who'd ruthlessly consumed his thoughts for the past twenty-four hours.

He took a hesitant step forward and as he did a spicy, mouth-watering scent wafted toward him on the night breeze. Drawn toward her and the delicious smell his stomach growled, although whether that was due to the woman or the food, he wasn't sure.

His gaze focused on her as he crossed the distance more confidently. She seemed utterly engrossed in whatever it was she was cooking, and he found himself unconsciously trying to walk louder. A pointless task; his shoes sunk into the soft grass muffling the sound of his approach. He really didn't want to sneak up on her and scare her but in the near darkness and silence of the clifftop, with nothing but the sound of the sizzling pan and the boom of the waves at the foot of the cliff, he feared it might be inevitable.

He was about to clear his throat loudly to announce his presence when a huge shadow loomed out of the darkness, snapping and snarling as it barked loudly forcing him to stop dead and back up a pace.

Ava looked up and blinked in surprise. For a moment she wondered why Killian had returned to the house so late but as she was about to open her mouth her eyes narrowed, and she realized it wasn't the contractor she'd met earlier in the day.

'Kelley?' she guessed.

He smiled at her, pleased she'd remembered his name.

'Hello Ava,' he replied easily.

'Bailey!' Ava called loudly when her dog continued to bark, 'enough! You'll wake the dead with all that noise.'

'Please don't say that,' Kelley's eyes flicked uneasily to the house to the left of them.

'Bailey, back up girl.'

Kelley watched as Ava's dog backed up, stepping into the circle of light cast by the fire as he moved forward, and he got a proper look at her.

'Whoa! Holy shit that's an enormous dog! Was she created in a lab?'

'No,' Ava's mouth twitched, 'she's part German Shepherd part bear.'

'When you said dog,' Kelley's eyebrows rose as he continued to stare at Bailey, who was in turn watching him mistrustfully, 'I don't know, I just pictured something small and cute that would fit in your purse.'

'Would have to be a pretty big purse,' Ava continued to stir whatever it was simmering over the fire in an enormous shiny, silver, flying saucer shaped pan.

Kelley grinned, 'Big? I think you'd have trouble fitting her in a packing crate.'

'Why do you think I drive a huge truck?' Ava glanced up, a small smiled tugging at the corner of her lips. 'Why are you here Kelley?'

'Came to welcome you to the neighborhood,' he gave her a cute, slightly lopsided smile, held up the bag and shook it. 'I brought dinner, although whatever the hell you're cooking smells a hundred times better.'

'What's in there?' she asked curiously.

'Burgers cooked just the way you like it and steak for your dog.'

'You bought Bailey a steak?' she stopped stirring and stared at him.

'Seemed like the thing to do at the time,' he shrugged.

'Bailey,' Ava called out after a moment, 'let him sit down.'

Bailey turned her head toward Ava, letting out a little sniff of discontent but she moved out of his way none the less, trotting over and sitting next to her mistress obediently as she continued to watch Kelley warily with large unblinking black eyes.

'I thought you were your brother just now,' she watched him take a seat on a small log she'd placed beside the fire.

'I heard that's not the first time today that's happened,' Kelley glanced at the fire, noting that she'd taken the time to dig the firepit down into the ground, encircling it with huge rocks from the beach. Either side of the pit she'd laid logs just large enough to sit on. She was obviously a woman who was no stranger to the outdoors.

'No,' Ava snorted quietly. 'I walked into his office this morning and met his heavily pregnant wife. Then he walked through the door and I thought it was you. Embarrassing.'

'You're not the first one to make that mistake and you won't be the last,' Kelley grinned. 'I have to ask Ava, what the hell are you making? It smells entirely too good for something cooked on a campfire.'

'It's Thai street food,' she twisted the pan over the flames, swirling the red colored contents around the inside with a sizzle as she reached into a paper bag and retrieved some leaves which she dumped in. 'Bay leaves,' she informed him at his curious look.

'You know how to cook Thai street food?'

'Among other things,' she nodded. 'This is Massaman Gai; it's one of the milder Thai curries with Persian influences. Are you allergic to nuts?'

'No,' Kelley shook his head.

'Would you like to try some?' she offered.

'I thought you'd never ask,' he grinned.

'It's almost ready,' she nodded.

'You like to cook then?'

'I love to cook,' Ava replied absently as she concentrated on the sizzling pan, 'even if it's just for me.' She glanced down and gave Bailey a sharp look.

Fascinating, Kelley thought, the dog actually looked away guiltily. If she'd been a person she'd have been whistling in mock innocence.

'Bailey's not allowed any. Last time I made curry she snuck some from my plate. You cannot even begin to imagine the mess she made in my truck. I had to air it out for a week.'

Kelley laughed loudly as Bailey barked once at Ava, almost in protest.

'What?' she replied to her dog, 'you and I both know it's true. Need I mention the chocolate incident?'

Bailey whined and looked away again.

'That's what I thought.' Ava replied.

'Amazing,' he murmured.

'What is?'

'It's almost like she understands everything you say,' Kelley replied in fascination.

'Oh, she understands plenty,' Ava shook her head. 'Her breed's very intelligent anyway, but we've been together since she was born. She more or less ignored her mother unless she wanted feeding and attached herself to me. As it's just me and her on the road, on our own, pretty much most of the time, I think we've just come to understand each other.'

'On the road?' he leaned forward and propped his elbow on one knee and his chin in his palm, 'you travel a lot? For pleasure or work?'

'You ask a lot of questions,' her dark eyes flicked back to him.

'It's how you get to know someone,' he smiled. 'Ask me anything, I'm an open book.'

'Sorry I don't read much,' she shook her head.

'A challenge huh?'

'If you've got a steak in that bag you might want to give it to her. It might sweeten her up or she's going to growl at you the whole time you're here,' Ava changed the subject.

'She always like this with strangers?' he asked as he reached into the bag.

'No,' Ava shook her head, 'she actually has a very sweet disposition.'

'So, it's just me then?' he asked perplexed as he unwrapped the steak.

'Yeah,' she nodded.

'Oh,' he frowned, 'dogs usually love me. I've never had one dislike me before.'

'She doesn't dislike you,' Ava reached down beside her for a bowl. 'She's wary of you and protective of me. She's unsettled, we're in a new place and its dark, and you're a stranger.'

'But she met my twin earlier?'

'Dogs have over three hundred million smell receptors in their noses,' she began to spoon the curry into the bowl. 'You and your brother may look almost identical but trust me, to her you'd smell very different.'

'Oh,' he held up the steak and Bailey's ears pricked, she lifted her furry face and sniffed before turning to look at Ava.

'It's okay,' she nodded.

Bailey moved forward carefully taking the steak from Kelley's hand before dragging it back over to devour it at Ava's side.

'She asks your permission first?'

'In some of the places we've lived in over the years, people will feed the dogs any old crap. It's not good for her, so I taught her not to accept food from strangers.'

'What sort of places?' he handed her one of the beers he'd brought, noticing that she discreetly checked to make sure the bottle was sealed and not tampered with in any way. It made him wonder exactly what sort of life she'd lived that she'd be so cautious, not just for herself but with her dog too.

'Just places,' she shrugged as she handed him a bowl of curry and a slightly bent metal spoon.

'What about your family?' Kelley spooned a mouthful of curry, making a hum of pleasure as it hit his tongue. 'So good, where the hell did you learn to cook like this?'

'Here and there,' Ava smiled.

Kelley swallowed his mouthful and studied her carefully, his light-colored eyes appearing even paler in the dancing firelight.

'Ava,' he spoke softly, 'I know you don't know me yet, but you can trust me. I may come across as a bit of a stalker, but I am genuinely interested in getting to know you, no strings attached. I'm harmless I promise.'

Harmless, Ava almost snorted. There was nothing harmless about just how appealing the guy was, or how her belly jumped and tied itself into nervous knots when he was near, but... she was forced to admit, she would be working closely with his brother for the foreseeable future and she couldn't avoid everyone on the island. She'd spent her whole life wondering what it would be like to have a permanent home, a place to belong and when she was finally presented with the possibility of one, she didn't want to inadvertently alienate her potential friends and neighbors.

The problem was, she was rusty and out of practice. It had been her and Bailey for such a long time now it was hard to remember how to interact with people on a social level.

'I can go if you want me to?' Kelley interrupted her thoughts, 'I don't want to make you uncomfortable.'

'Finish your curry before it gets cold.' Ava shook her head and set the cooking pan on a nearby pile of rocks to cool as she picked up the large wooden spoon she'd used to cook with and ate directly from the pan.

'Don't you have another bowl?' Kelley frowned.

'Nope,' she spooned some more into her mouth. 'Like I said, it's usually just me and Bailey. I wasn't expecting company.'

'I feel bad now,' he frowned, 'I didn't mean to impose.'

'You're not,' Ava sighed, 'I'm just a little prickly with people of the two-legged variety. I'm out of practice.'

'Are you planning to stay on the island permanently?' he asked curiously. 'You're one of the Wallaces aren't you?'

'So I'm told,' she nodded as she continued to eat. 'Apparently Harriet Wallace was my grandmother, but I never knew her. Serenity wasn't real big on sharing personal details.'

'Serenity?'

'My mother,' Ava replied matter of factly.

'You call your mother Serenity?'

'Called, she's gone now, died just before I came here.'

'I'm sorry,' Kelley murmured as he studied her.

Ava shrugged.

'Her name was Caroline Wallace, but she was always known to everyone as Serenity. I don't know why,' Ava mused dryly. 'The only time there was anything serene about her was after she'd smoked her way through an entire bag of purple haze.'

'Where did you grow up?' Kelley cracked his beer open and took a swig. 'I don't remember Hari ever having her grand-daughter to stay.'

'Hari?' Ava repeated curiously, 'you knew my grandmother?'

'It's a pretty small island, everyone knows everyone, but in this case, Hari was friends with my grandmother Alma. They played bridge together every Tuesday.'

'What was she like, my grandmother?'

'Hari?' Kelley smiled, 'she was a kind woman, tiny, with the sweetest smile. She baked the best cookies around, even better than my grams, although if you tell my grandmother that I'll call you a dirty rotten liar.'

Ava smiled, damn it she didn't want to be charmed but she was charmed. She didn't want to like him either, but she did.

'Communes,' she offered randomly with a sigh.

'Sorry?'

'I grew up in communes,' she explained self-deprecatingly, 'sexy huh? Surrounded by a bunch of grubby half naked hippies who were stoned 99.999 percent of the time.'

'Do they still even have communes?' Kelley wondered, 'I know they were big in the seventies, but I thought they'd pretty much died out by the eighties.'

'Oh, they're still around if you know where to look,' Ava opened her own beer and took a slow thoughtful sip. 'That's where I learned to cook. By the time I was twelve I was cooking more often than not, for anything between twenty and sixty people at any given time.'

'Wow.'

'Yeah, I learned pretty early on that if I stayed in the kitchen no one really bothered me. Once I hit puberty, I started getting a lot of attention I didn't want.'

'I'll bet,' Kelley frowned. 'What about your mom?'

'Oh, she was around,' Ava rose from her seat and moved across to a large tub of cold soapy water and began to scrub the pan. 'Serenity wasn't big on laying down rules and boundaries for me. She wanted to give me the freedom to explore my sexuality, but I had no intention of exploring it with those guys. I mean each commune is different, don't get me wrong I'm not stereotyping anyone, but more often than not these communities are polyamorous or polygamous, which is basically a justification for a free for all.'

It was no wonder she was so guarded Kelley thought to himself as he handed her his empty bowl and spoon.

'I can do that if you want?'

'It's okay,' she took the bowl and dunked it in the water.

'I can't imagine what it must have been like growing up like that.'

'It wasn't all bad,' Ava shook her head as she set the clean bowl and the pan against the rocks at the edge of the fire to dry. 'Just different.'

'It doesn't sound like a very safe way to grow up.'

'I was always safe,' Ava sat back down in her original seat and picked up her beer as Bailey curled into the side of her legs. 'Don't get me wrong, there were a couple of occasions when certain guys didn't want to take no for an answer and got quite aggressive, but Serenity got me out of there pretty quickly. Say whatever you like about her, the one thing she always did was protect me.'

'She sounds like a complicated woman,' Kelley rolled the half empty beer bottle between his palms.

'Complicated?' Ava smiled, 'no, not that complicated. She loved freedom, she loved rolling from one day to the next never knowing where she was going to land or what adventure the world would bring. She loved endless possibilities and not being tied down, and most importantly she loved weed.'

'Sounds like you've lived an interesting life,' Kelley replied. 'I've never left Midnight, well except on vacation but my roots are here, it's my home.'

'You're lucky then,' Ava murmured as she studied his face, 'I've never had a home. We settled for a while in San Francisco, when Serenity met my dad.' Her voice trailed off as she began to pick absently at the label on her bottle. 'We were a family for a while.'

'What happened?'

She looked up and blinked; she'd been lost in her thoughts and for a moment had forgotten about him.

'He died,' she replied, 'motorbike accident, it was a blind corner, the sun was low. The truck driver never saw him.'

'I'm sorry,' Kelley replied genuinely, 'are you close to your dad's family?'

'They're dead too,' she chuckled, 'are you sensing a theme here? My dad came over from El Salvador when he was a teenager, his whole family were killed in the civil war.'

'Wow,' Kelley's brows rose, 'I don't' know what to say. I can't imagine what that's like. I come from a huge family. We are legion, I've lost count of how many cousins I've got.'

'So, I hear from your sister in law.'

'She's a sweetheart,' Kelley grinned.

'She warned me to stay away from you.'

'She's a crazy woman who doesn't know what she's saying due to a massive hormonal imbalance.'

Ava laughed out loud; it was the first time he'd seen her really laugh. Not a polite, slightly amused chuckle but an honest to god belly laugh. She lit up like a roman candle and he found himself staring at her like a stunned gazelle.

'I liked her,' Ava smiled.

'She liked you too,' he shook his head in amusement, 'judging by the twenty messages she left on my phone, grilling me about the woman I met in the bar the night before.'

Ava looked up as the sky rumbled suddenly, very loud and very close.

'Looks like it's going to storm,' Ava murmured as she began to pack away all of her herbs and spices and utensils before the rain hit.

'Yeah,' Kelley gazed at the turbulent sky.

The stars had disappeared and the black vastness above them was now a boiling swirling mass of dark gray streaks.

'You should probably go,' she packed everything into the back of her truck and covered it over.

There was another loud bang, setting Bailey barking madly and the sky lit up like the fourth of July, highlighting the choppy ocean in the distance, the blackness of the water punctuated by the white frothy edges of the turbulent waves.

'You're seriously going to make me walk back in the storm by myself?'

'You're not scared, are you?' she tilted her head as she watched him.

'Yes,' he grinned, 'I'm terrified. You should probably stay close and hold my hand.'

'Nice try,' she chuckled as the first fat drops of rain began to fall.

They stood staring at each other as the rain began to pound down, soaking them almost instantly.

'Welcome to Maine,' he told her with an amused smile. 'The weather's temperamental.'

'Oh, for heaven's sake,' she rolled her eyes and peeled back the opening to the tent, 'get in.'

'I don't know if I should,' he blinked demurely, 'I'm not that kind of boy. What if you're using the storm as an excuse to take advantage of me?'

She found herself laughing out loud again.

'Just get in the tent before I change my mind, I'm getting soaked here.'

Kelley threw her a grin and ducked into the tent, stumbling and falling to the ground which was covered with sleeping bags, blankets and pillows. He twisted as he hit the ground, jarring his shoulder as he rolled onto his back.

Still as suave as ever, he thought in amusement but at least this time he'd not knocked himself unconscious. Suddenly a big wet dog bounded into the tent, trampling all over him, the sheer weight of her knocking the breath from him in an audible whoosh, her long tail slapping him in the face and her huge paws crushing his balls.

He rolled to his side groaning in pain, feeling slightly nauseous.

'You alright?' Ava climbed into the tent and zipped it closed, laying down beside him.

'Yes,' he wheezed.

'Sorry about Bailey, you're in her spot.'

'I noticed,' he sucked in a breath as he tried to adjust his jeans.

'Just so you know,' Ava glanced at him, 'you're only staying until the rain lets up and if you try anything Bailey will maul you, starting with your dick.'

'Understood,' he breathed through the throbbing ache in his balls.

Bailey crawled between them forming a huge barrier which smelled of wet fur. She glanced down at Kelley, growling low in her throat in warning before her long pink tongue lolled out of her mouth and for a second, he could've sworn she was laughing at him.

They lay there all three of them, staring up at the roof of the tent, watching as it lit up with each bolt of lightning streaking across the tempestuous sky. They talked in hushed tones, of little things, silly things, they laughed and little by little Ava found herself beginning to relax.

The man lying on the other side of her dog was entirely too tempting for her own good. He appealed to her on every level, from his gorgeous face and crooked smile to his self-deprecating sense of humor.

They waited for the storm to blow itself out or move on, but as they lay there together, warmed by the heat of Bailey's huge furry body and lulled by the rhythmic patter of the rain against the canvas, they both drifted into a deep comfortable sleep.

6

*K*elley was suffocating, trapped in a dream wasteland somewhere between waking and a total lack of anything resembling consciousness. In this strange dream world, he was being pursued by a huge flying rug of gold and black fur. There were steaks attached to his clothes and as he tried to run, the ground kept turning into a strange gooey red curry. He turned as the rug swooped down and suddenly, he was falling. The rug blanketed him, covering his nose and mouth as he gasped for air.

He woke with a jolt, struggling to breathe under the huge hairy mountain of fur laying on top of him. He pushed and shoved, until finally he managed to move the dead weight a fraction and suck in a loud breath.

'Bailey,' he wheezed as he shoved the heavy lump again.

She whined and rolled over onto her back, crushing his stomach and burying the side of his head with her face.

'Would you two like some privacy?' an amused female voice spoke.

Kelley shuffled and struggled underneath the weight of the

huge dog, managing to get her off his face as he looked up and saw Ava peering into the tent.

'Help please,' Kelley grimaced as Bailey shifted.

'I think she's changed her mind about you,' Ava's mouth twitched.

'Please get her off me; she weighs a ton.'

Deciding to take pity on the poor guy, Ava straightened up, holding the tent flap open as she let out a loud whistle.

'Bailey, breakfast.'

He'd never seen a dog move so fast. He doubled over and groaned as her claws dug in and she scrambled ecstatically in an attempt to get out of the tent, trampling him like a wet rag in the process.

After a few moments Kelley crawled out of the tent and climbed to his feet, gingerly stretching out the kinks in his spine and rubbing his sore belly.

'Here,' Ava handed him a coffee in a tin cup.

'God bless you,' Kelley inhaled the fumes of the dark bitter brew, almost reverently.

'I don't have any milk.'

'Black's fine,' he took a long, satisfying gulp, not caring that it was still slightly too hot, burning his palate. He let out a deep breath and yawned, his fingers tangling in his hair as he pushed it back from his face. 'Sorry,' he yawned, 'I didn't mean to fall asleep last night, I swear.'

She studied him slowly. It was the first time she'd actually seen him in daylight and, while he did look almost identical to his twin, she could see the subtle differences. Kelley's hair was leaning toward the shaggy, needing a haircut. His warm chestnut hair, naturally lightened on the ends by the sun, hung in his eyes and grazed his collar. His skin was lightly and unevenly tanned, highlighting intensely green eyes, which at the moment were filled with sleep but were no less potent as he watched her over the rim of his cup.

For a moment they stared at each other until Bailey wandered over, having cleaned her bowl, and butted Ava in the legs. Ava looked down as her dog brushed past her, rubbing her full body against her affectionately.

'I honestly don't know how you haven't suffocated sharing a tent with her,' Kelley shook his head.

'She doesn't sleep on me like that,' Ava laughed lightly. 'Sometimes she'll lie across my legs, but she's never actually rolled all over me.'

Kelley looked down at Bailey who was watching him with dark liquid eyes.

'Decided I'm alright, have you?' he asked her.

She responded by jamming her nose in his crotch.

'Jesus Christ Bailey,' he swore as he doubled over and moved back sharply, trying not to spill the rest of his coffee. 'Boundaries... you didn't even take me out to dinner first.'

'I'm sorry,' Ava tried to cover her laugh with her hand. 'I guess somewhere between last night and this morning she's decided she likes you.'

'What about you?'

'What about me?' her eyes glittered in amusement.

'Have you decided you like me too?'

Ava laughed again. In fact, she hadn't laughed this much in a while and it felt good.

'I guess you're okay,' she replied.

'Ava really, all these compliments will just go to my head.'

'I'm sure you get enough compliments,' Ava leaned back against her truck.

'Huh?'

'Nothing,' she shook her head as she gazed up at the house.

Kelley followed her gaze and took another sip of coffee.

'I guess it's not so scary in the daylight,' he mused.

'What? The house?' Ava asked.

'Yeah, half the island's population have come out here as

teenagers and kids, scaring themselves stupid and trying to catch a glimpse of the ghost.'

'What ghost?'

'You seriously telling me you've been on the island what, two days, and you haven't heard about the ghost of Luella Lynch?'

'No,' she climbed up onto the hood of her truck and once again glanced up at the house. 'Everyone gets all cagey and tight-lipped about the house, like it's some big secret. It's just a house, a big sad old house that's been neglected for far too long.'

'Ava...Ava, Ava,' he tutted as he propped himself casually against the side of the truck. 'I can see I'm going to have to educate you.'

'Go on then,' her mouth curved, 'educate me.'

'The story begins back at the turn of the century. The Lynch family had already owned the house for nearly fifty years, though most of the family had passed away. All that was left was Eleanor Lynch, her daughter Luella and her young son Edward. Luella, it seemed, was a very disturbed child, and even worse as a teenager. Legend says she murdered her younger brother when he was only eight years old, by drowning him in the bath. The mother, Eleanor, had Luella locked away in an asylum in Maine where she stayed for several years, until the doctors decided she was not considered a danger. She'd managed to convince them her brother's death had been a tragic accident although Eleanor never fully believed it. Lonely in her old age, she relented and allowed Luella to return home.'

'Still not really scared yet,' Ava shook her head.

'That's because I haven't got to the good stuff yet,' he replied. 'Now, where was I?'

'Luella returns home after a stint in rehab.'

'Very funny,' he glanced up at the house. 'Anyway, Luella returns home, furious with her mother for having her locked away for so long. She locked her mother, who was now old and frail, in the attic room, keeping her prisoner as she once had been. Trying to put her past behind her and present a respectable face to the world, Luella married a young teacher, from Boston I think, and together they opened the house as a school.'

'Yeah,' Ava murmured absently as she stared back at the house. 'I saw all the children's desks when I was in the house yesterday. Your brother said it had once been used as a school.'

'You were inside the house?' Kelley blinked slowly, 'actually inside it yesterday?'

Ava nodded.

'Good God Ava, you've got a set of brass balls.'

'Like I said, it's just a sad, old, neglected house,' she told him pointedly, 'and I'll thank you to leave my balls out of it,' she added impishly. 'So, go on, tell me how this tale of terror ends, cause I gotta tell you, right now? I'm just not feeling it.'

Kelley shook his head in disbelief as the corner of his mouth curved.

'One night in 1919, Oct 31st to be exact...'

'Halloween?' Ava's brows rose mockingly, 'not very original.'

'The 31st Oct 1919,' Kelley continued, 'was the worst storm on record. Houses were destroyed, part of the island was flooded, and lightning struck this very cliff causing part of the cliff edge to break away and crash into the sea below. The storm raged all night and when it finally calmed with the dawn, all the parents of the children at the Lynch school, knowing that the cliff had been struck by lightning, rushed to the house to find their children.'

'And?' Ava asked expectantly.

'And nothing, they were all gone,' Kelley replied.

'Define all gone?'

'Disappeared without a trace, meals were left untouched, beds unslept in. Toys left scattered on the floor. Luella, her husband and all the children had vanished. There were no bodies, no blood, nothing.'

'Is that it?' Ava frowned, a bit disappointed, 'they all just vanished? Where does the supposed ghost come into it then?'

'There was talk of hidden passageways and rooms beneath the house. They say Luella snapped during the storm and dragged the children down into the hidden rooms, murdering them all as she had her brother. Unable to face what she'd done, she locked the concealed doorways and died down there amongst the corpses of the children she'd killed.'

'Okay,' Ava shook her head, raising her hand. 'First, there is not a shred of evidence that anyone was murdered,' she began to tick off her fingers. 'Second there were no bodies; third I'm guessing the distraught parents searched the house from top to bottom?'

Kelley nodded as he conceded the point.

'Did they ever find these so-called hidden rooms?'

'No.'

'Exactly,' she replied. 'I'll admit it's a bit weird, but you said yourself the island flooded, and part of the cliff collapsed. It's just as plausible that they were trying to reach somewhere safer and were swept out to sea and drowned.'

'There are other things,' he continued, 'over the years.'

'Such as?' her brows lifted in challenge.

'Strange things in the house; flickering lights in the high windows.'

'The reflection of the moon on the windowpanes,' Ava countered.

'Weird noises.'

'All old houses have weird noises,' Ava laughed. 'Seriously Kelley, the house is not haunted, I guarantee it.'

'Okay then, back in the eighties, three kids broke into the house on a dare. Todd Hinton, Declan Tilman and Julia Mays, but only Julia walked back out again. Todd was found at the bottom of the staircase, just below the second-floor balcony and Declan threw himself from the Clifftop.'

'That's sad,' Ava shook her head. 'How old were they?'

'Eighteen.'

'An accident and a suicide, so young,' she shook her head. 'Such a waste of life.'

'That isn't what really happened. Julia was nearly incomprehensible by the time they found her the next morning. She'd spent all night in the house alone and whatever it was she saw drove her mad. She was never the same again; she's been in and out of mental institutions ever since.'

'I still think it's all urban myths and rumors,' Ava shook her head. 'You grew up on the island so it's different for you, but I don't believe in ghosts.'

'Think what you like,' Kelley shook his head, 'but everyone on the island knows. Luella Lynch still walks those rooms, as the ghosts of the children she murdered hide from her.'

'Seriously?' Ava stared at him, 'that's not even a good story. There are so many holes in it I could use it to strain soup.'

'Why would you strain soup?'

'Never mind,' she sighed.

'All I'm saying is there's no way you'd get me in that house,' he held up his hands. 'Now,' he pushed away from the truck, 'that coffee has gone straight through me. Where's the restroom?'

'In the house.'

Kelley stared at her blankly.

'There won't be any temporary restrooms on the site until the building crews arrive, so I'm afraid you'll have to rough it and pee behind a tree.'

'Are you serious?' he blinked.

'Welcome to the joys of outdoor living,' she grinned.

He walked away muttering something Ava didn't quite catch. Smiling to herself she rinsed out the cup she'd handed

Kelley and made herself a coffee. She turned to gaze out across the sparkling ocean, breathing a sign of contentment. She had just raised the little tin cup to her lips and taken a slow contemplative sip when she heard Bailey barking loudly.

Turning around sharply, her gaze swept over the little makeshift campsite and then over to the house. Unable to see her dog, she placed the cup down by the firepit and followed the barking. She jogged to the edge of the large house and rounded the corner. Toward the back of the property, some distance away, she could see Bailey as she pranced excitedly on the spot, tail wagging as she leapt in the air and caught a ball which had been tossed to her.

Ava shook her head in amusement; for all his protests Kelley had obviously fallen for her soppy dog. She headed toward them. Every time Bailey caught the ball she would trot forward, disappear out of sight for a few seconds, presumably to drop it at his feet, then back up again, tail wagging, as she waited for it to be thrown again.

'I knew you couldn't resist her,' Ava laughed as she approached. 'I thought you were going to pee not play catch with my dog.'

She stopped by Bailey who was sitting on her haunches, ball in her mouth as she grinned, tail thumping against the dry, browning grass. Turning her head, she frowned in confusion. There was no one there, just an empty brick alcove in the wall.

'Kelley?' Ava looked around but there was no one and no way he could've disappeared without her seeing him. 'Kelley?'

Kneeling down beside Bailey she reached out and took the ball from her dog's mouth, turning it over in her hands as she studied it.

'Where did you get this girl, huh?' she rubbed Bailey's coat.

The ball was small and hard, like a baseball, and made from a dark tanned leather which was partially cracked in places from age. The stitching was worn almost smooth and across the middle, branded untidily like it had been done with a heated penknife were the initials *P. L. M.*

Ava turned and glanced thoughtfully at the concealed alcove. She could've sworn someone was throwing the ball to her; she'd watched Bailey jump up and catch it in her mouth. Perhaps she'd managed to bounce it against the wall somehow and caught the rebound.

A sudden, terrifying scream pierced the air and had Ava standing abruptly. Dropping the ball thoughtlessly from her suddenly lax fingers, she left it lying in the tall brown patch of grass and ran back toward the front of the house.

The screaming seemed to be coming from just inside the tree line. Heading straight for it, with Bailey loping alongside her, she came to a skidding halt just in time to see Kelley zipping up his jeans and looking absolutely mortified. In front of him stood a group of well-dressed elderly ladies, one of which she recognized.

'Mrs McCarthy?' Ava frowned as she stared at a slightly shorter woman, she didn't recognize, swooning in Bunty's arms.

'Bunty dear, call me Bunty,' she corrected fanning her friend casually as if she caught her fainting every other day. 'Sorry about Betty, she has a nervous disposition. We were on our way to visit with you, but it seems one of the trees came down in the road last night, so we left the car and walked the rest of the way. Although it's a pleasant morning for a stroll through the woods, we weren't expecting to see quite so much of Mr Ryan here.'

'Nonsense,' another lady, wearing candy floss pink, ruffled chiffon, smiled slowly as she winked a heavily mascara clad eye at Kelley who seemed to flush an even deeper shade of red. 'It's always a pleasure to run into one of the Ryan boys.'

Kelley took an involuntary step behind Ava as if he could somehow use her as a human shield.

'Uh,' Ava replied awkwardly, 'um okay, well welcome... I guess.'

'Hey,' a deeper male voice intruded and as they all turned to look, Killian appeared through the trees. 'Have I interrupted something?' he glanced around, noting all the older ladies before landing on his brother. 'Kelley?' he greeted curiously, 'I thought that was your car further down the hill.'

'Crapped out on me last night,' he replied. 'Sorry, beg your pardon, broke down last night,' he amended when one of the other ladies, this one with a carefully sculped perm, wearing a peach twin set and a small golden cross, glared at him.

'Last night?' his eyes glittered in amusement as they dipped to Ava for the barest fraction of a second. 'I kept telling you the sparkplugs needed cleaning.'

'Yeah yeah,' Kelley scratched the back of his neck uncomfortably, 'I've been meaning to get it serviced.'

Killian shook his head as he turned to Ava.

'What are you doing here? Ava asked. 'I thought we'd agreed to meet at your office later today?'

'Welcome to island living,' Kelley muttered in her ear, 'where your business is everyone's business, and everyone drops by unannounced.'

'We did,' Killian ignored his brother, 'but I managed to get an RV for you to use temporarily.'

'You did?' her eyes widened a fraction. 'Wow, that's really good of you.'

'I was just bringing it up when I ran into a snag. Did you know one of the trees came down last night?'

'I didn't hear it but yes, Bunty here just told me,' Ava nodded.

'I saw your car behind it,' Killian nodded. 'If you want to give me your keys Mrs McCarthy, I'll bring it on up for you after I've arranged to clear the road.'

'Thank you, Killian, so kind of you, and how is Hope?'

Bunty smiled, heaving up her swooning friend and dumping her on the cougar who was still eying up Kelley like he was her next meal. 'Here Ivy, take Betty.'

She reached inside her purse and withdrew a small set of keys which she handed to Killian.

'She's doing fine, thank you Mrs McCarthy.'

'What brought the tree down?' Ava wondered out loud. 'I didn't see any lightning and I didn't think the wind was strong enough.'

'It wouldn't have taken much,' Killian shook his head. 'I checked the tree and it was rotten the whole way through, it would have come down sooner or later. Anyway, I'll call in a couple of the guys and have them help me clear the road.'

'I'll come and help you,' Kelley answered quickly, as Ivy began to edge closer to him, still holding onto the semi-conscious Betty.

'Coward,' Ava whispered as he turned and shot her a disarming grin.

The strange little oddball group of women stood and watched for a moment as the two ridiculously good-looking men disappeared back through the trees.

'Well then,' Bunty turned to Ava, 'let me introduce you to everyone. This is Ivy and Betty.'

Ivy had a light fine wave of hair artfully secured behind one ear with a small sparkly clip, the rest of it sat coiled over her bony shoulder in thin waves, so heavily sprayed with lacquer it moved in a giant clump whenever she shifted her head. Her lashes, which may not have been her own, were thick and black, over a layer of pale pink eyeshadow which propped up her penciled-on eyebrows like scaffolding. Her dress was the same sweet candy shade of pink and a riot of ruffles, which hurt to look at too long.

Betty had ceased swooning the minute the boys had disappeared and now stood unaided, clear eyed and assessing, as if she'd never been indisposed. She wore a no-nonsense maroon pant suit and sensible heels.

'That over there is Barbara,' she pointed to the woman in the peach twin set with the small gold cross, 'then we have Esther.'

She pointed to a little woman with a sweet little cloud of pure white hair, and wrinkled skin.

'Esther,' Bunty said loudly, 'SAY HELLO TO AVA.'

Esther glanced over at Bunty who was waving to get her attention.

'No thank you dear,' she replied in a soft voice, 'it's too early for dinner.'

'She's always forgetting to change the batteries in her hearing aids,' Bunty rolled her eyes as she turned to the last woman in the group, 'and this is Norma.'

Norma stood with knitting needles in her gnarled hands as she clicked away quietly. Her yarn bag had big hooped handles which were looped over her bony wrist. A winding trail of deep green yarn trailed from the bag to her needles where it was knotted and looped ruthlessly to become part of the long green shapeless ooze, which every so often she would tuck into her bag.

'What's she knitting?' Ava asked curiously as she eyed the sickly green monstrosity.

'A scarf,' Bunty replied, 'it's all she can knit. She attempted a sweater once; it was so large you could fit two people in it.'

'And that was just in the sleeves,' Ivy laughed, though not unkindly. Instead she stared at her friend with honest amusement and affection, as opposed to the predatory smile she'd sent Kelley.

'Well that's everyone then,' Bunty clapped her hands together. 'Now you've officially met the Midnight Island Historical Society and ladies weekly luncheon club, you should join us. We're always looking for new members, in fact you can take your grandmother's place, God rest her soul. We do miss Hari something dreadful.'

'I knew a Harry once,' Ivy mused thoughtfully, 'a sculptor he was,' she winked at Ava. 'Good with his hands.'

'We meet Tuesdays and Thursdays,' Betty informed her, 'you should come to our luncheon this week. We're having bouillabaisse, a bit fancy for my taste but it was Ivy's turn to choose.'

'Ah, maybe,' Ava replied carefully.

'We're also the members of the Knitting and Crochet Guild, and the Apple Pie Society, but it gets slightly cumbersome to rattle off all of our titles,' Barbara brushed an invisible speck of lint from her sleeve.

'Barbara is our club secretary,' Bunty told her helpfully.

'Apple Pie Society?' Ava replied.

'We're in charge of the yearly Apple Pie fair,' Barbara nodded her head. 'People come from all over to taste our pies. Lorna Pritchard has an orchard over on the west side of the island; it's over a hundred years old, comes from her daddy's side of the family. Of course, the name is a bit uncouth. I've always thought Pritchard's Orchards doesn't have very much panache for such an old esteemed orchard. I have suggested to her and her husband Richard on several occasions that they might want to change it. Of course, he's lucky he didn't have to take her name when they wed, I mean, can you imagine being married to someone named Richard Pritchard? Ridiculous.'

'Be kind Barbara,' Bunty admonished her.

'She's just sour because she never married,' Ivy whispered. 'When she dies it's going to be a case of 'return unopened' if you know what I mean.' She lifted a thinly penciled brow.

'God has another plan for me,' Barbara lifted her chin, 'besides you never married either.'

'That's because I'm too much woman to limit myself to just one man,' Ivy attempted to flick her hair, but merely succeeded in lifting it up in one great flap and plopping it back down in exactly the same position, right to the millimeter. Seriously, the woman needed to lay off the hairspray. Ava sincerely hoped Ivy didn't smoke because she was most likely, extremely flammable.

Ava couldn't help the smile threatening to tug at the corner of her lips as she listened to the chattering women.

'Anyway dear, why don't you show us where you're staying. Seeing as our darling Hari is no longer with us, we feel a certain responsibility to make sure her only grandchild is well taken care of, so just think of us as your surrogate family.'

'Uh huh,' Ava's eyes widened, not really sure what to say to the eccentric but well-meaning guild of old ladies.

Ava glanced around and noticed Bailey had stealthily slunk away. It seems she didn't know how to take their sudden visitors any more than Ava did.

'Come along then,' Bunty took Ava's arm and wrapped it companionably through her own as she began to steer her in the direction of the house. 'Do you know, I haven't been up here in years? The last time was with Hari.'

'Was it really?' Given no other choice Ava fell into step beside Bunty. 'Did she come up here often?'

'Not often,' Bunty shook her head, 'but occasionally. Sometimes she'd bring me for company, at other times she wanted to be left alone with her thoughts. She always felt a pull toward the house, something others couldn't understand. To them it was just an old wreck used to frighten unruly children and over imaginative teens.'

'Is there any truth to it?' Ava asked as they ambled along, with Ivy and Barbara bickering behind them, followed by Esther who wandered along happy to just be with her friends, and Norma, who was so engrossed in her knitting that she was being herded by Betty so she didn't accidentally collide with a tree.

'Ah so you've heard some of the gossip then, have you?' Bunty smiled.

'I guess.'

'It was only a matter of time I suppose. Let me guess? The rather handsome young Kelley Ryan?'

'He thinks its haunted,' Ava snorted.

'Yes well, Kelley always fell into the over imaginative teen category.'

'What do you think?' Ava asked curiously.

'I think everyone who looks at the house sees what they want to see,' Bunty replied. 'Killian sees a sad old building in need of repair; Kelley sees a mysterious old house filled with restless spirits and secrets, and Hari...'

'Yes?' Ava asked, 'what did she see?'

'Hari,' Bunty shook her head and sighed, 'saw her family's greatest shame. I think she loathed the house as much as she loved it. She was bound to the house, and it was a bondage that held her in its thrall until her last breath. She could never escape it.'

'Why did no one ever live there?' Ava glanced at Bunty. 'Why did it sit empty for so long?'

'It's been empty ever since the great storm of 1919,' Bunty answered. 'After the disappearance of all those children, the house gained a reputation. Some believed it was haunted, some thought it was cursed, some figured it was just flat out plain bad luck. I'm afraid once the stigma stuck no one would touch it. It would be like trying to sell the hotel from the Shining.'

'The Shining?' Ava's mouth quirked.

'I've been known to indulge in the odd Stephen King, it's my guilty pleasure,' she whispered conspiratorially. 'But don't tell the ladies, it's not on the approved reading list for the Midnight Book Club.'

'You're members of the book club too?' Ava asked in amusement.

'We are the book club,' Bunty replied with a shrug, 'we like to keep busy.'

'So,' Ava backtracked to Bunty's earlier comment about the house, 'some of the legend is true then? Those children did go missing?'

'Great heavens, a wolf!' Barbara exclaimed loudly as they stepped out from the trees in view of her little campsite, where Bailey was laid out in the sun on a sparse patch of grass.

'That's Bailey,' Ava introduced her to the assembly of startled women. 'She's my dog but don't worry she won't hurt you.'

'It's huge!' Betty blinked, still holding onto Norma and her bottomless knitting bag.

'She's part Sasquatch,' Ava replied dryly.

'Is this where you're staying?' Bunty glanced around in disapproval, noting the small scruffy tent next to the brand-new truck, both of which were behind a crude firepit. 'Oh no, no, no, no, this simply won't do at all. Pack your things young lady, you'll stay with me for a while until you get on your feet.'

'I am on my feet,' Ava replied as she disentangled herself from Bunty's arm and headed over to the firepit which was currently devoid of anything but ash from the night before.

Ava took a seat on the log as Bailey loped over to her and pressed her face into her lap waiting to be stroked.

'You can't honestly think that living like a... a hobo is preferable to staying with a friend or even at the local guest house,' Bunty frowned. 'If it's a question of money...'

'It's not,' Ava shook her head. 'It's kind of you to offer Bunty but I have money, I just don't want to stay anywhere else. This is where I want to be.'

The moment the words left her mouth she realized they were true.

'Well it certainly is a heck of a view,' Ivy turned to look out across the brilliant, glittering sea.

'I can't imagine why on earth you'd want to stay here,' Betty settled herself on one of the log seats. She glanced up at the house looming over them and shuddered, 'especially on your own, with everything that's happened there. It's not just haunted you know,' she whispered, 'it's cursed.'

'Now, now, Betty,' Bunty admonished with a cluck of her tongue, 'it's nothing of the sort. Kindly remember we are the historical society not the literary society. We deal in documented historical fact not flights of fantasy.'

Betty harrumphed slightly, her lips pursed, as she tucked her hands neatly in her lap.

Ava watched as one by one the ladies seated themselves around the cold firepit.

'Why would you think its cursed?' Ava asked curiously. 'I mean, I've heard the stories about it being haunted...'

'Don't encourage her Ava,' Bunty frowned.

'Oh, hush up Bunty,' Betty waggled her finger at the other woman, 'you can be such a stick in the mud sometimes. The girl asked a question and if she's brave enough to camp out here on her own she's brave enough to hear the answer.'

Bunty sighed loudly and rolled her eyes heavenward.

'It was the curse of the Lynch family,' she began, her voice more suited to the firelight at midnight, rather than a cold dead firepit in the middle of a bright sunny morning. 'It all began with Ephraim Lynch, the patriarch of the Lynch family back in the mid-19th century. He bought the house from a well-known Boston architect.'

'No, no, no,' Barbara interrupted, 'you're telling it all wrong. He didn't buy it from the architect, he bought it from his son.'

'Oh, for heaven's sake,' Betty huffed, 'tomato tomahto, the fact is the previous owner sold it to Ephraim Lynch. At first the SON,' she looked over at Barbara pointedly, 'of the architect who built the place didn't want to sell, but Ephraim had his mind set and would not be swayed. By all accounts he was a very hard man. If he set his mind to something none dared stand in his way.'

'I heard the son had gambling debts,' Ivy added.

'Get on with it,' Barbara made a speeding up motion with her hand.

'I'm getting to it,' Betty replied indignantly, 'if you would all just stop interrupting.'

'Married the maid he did,' Norma suddenly piped up as she pulled her long green anaconda of a scarf from her bag and held it up against Ava's body, as if she were measuring it. 'Such a scandal.'

'It wasn't the maid,' Bunty finally intervened. 'She was a local girl from a well to do family, but she was only sixteen when she married Ephraim, who was by that time forty-three.'

'Ew,' Ava murmured.

'It wasn't unheard of to marry that young back then. I mean, this would have been,' Bunty shook her head, gazing skyward as she cast her mind back, '1867? Or thereabouts.'

'It is kinda gross though,' Ava frowned. 'I mean, I know some young women like their sugar daddies, but sixteen seems really young. Why would her parents allow it?'

'I imagine they would have insisted.'

'Why would they...' Ava's voice trailed off as her nose wrinkled. 'Oh, double ew.'

'Poor child,' Bunty shook her head, 'shotgun wedding at sixteen and she was dead within half a year.'

'Dead?' Ava's brows rose.

'A seven-month baby and died in childbirth. He was too big for her small body; she bled to death.'

'God rest her soul,' Norma murmured as the click clack of her knitting needles resumed.

'Do you mind,' Betty replied primly, 'I'm telling this story.'

'Go ahead then,' Bunty flipped her hand.

'Thank you,' Betty replied. 'Now, where was I? Ah yes, the

babe, well poor girl died in childbirth, but the boy survived, Ephraim's son whom he named Edison. Now, he also has an unfortunate story. He grew up alone in the house with only his father and a constant stream of wet nurses and maids, for curiously none of them ever stayed long. When he was in his twenties Edison married. He and his bride left Midnight the very night of the wedding. She did not even spend one night under the roof of her new father in law, instead they left the island and headed to New York. They had not been there long when Edison was involved in a terrible automobile accident, this would have been in eighteen ninety...... three?'

'Two,' Bunty corrected.

'1892,' Betty nodded shooting Bunty a look. 'He survived, barely, but he was paralyzed. With no income and no means of supporting themselves they had no choice but to return to Midnight Island and to his father's house. The following year Edison's wife Eleanor gave birth to a daughter, Luella.'

'But how?' Ava frowned. 'If he was paralyzed, surely he wouldn't be able to...'

Ava broke off as Betty's brows rose and she gave her a very pointed look.

'You're not actually suggesting that...'

'The child was not Edison's daughter but half-sister? That his wife was impregnated by her father in law?' Betty replied. 'There's no proof of course, there was some local gossip, talk of an affair, but the records show that Eleanor became pregnant several times in the following years as her husband's health deteriorated. There were four stillbirths, before she gave birth to a son, Edmund, in 1899, six years younger than his sister Luella. Her husband Edison died in Dec 1898 a full seven months before the boy was born. It was reported that Edison had taken a turn for the worse in October of that year, as the weather worsened so did his condition. He simply would have been too frail, too ill to impregnate his wife.'

Ava shook her head slowly as she tried to process what she was being told. Glancing up, she met Bunty's eyes. The older woman quickly looked away, her cheeks pinching, and her lips pressed together in a tight line. She was holding something back, of that Ava was certain. Bunty McCarthy knew far more than she was letting on to the other women of the historical society and Ava was determined to find out what it was.

'I heard that the little boy, Edmund is it? died. I was told he drowned in his bath and that it was Luella who killed him.'

'Stuff of nonsense,' Bunty sniffed. 'The boy did drown, but it was nothing more than an accident. Luella was never accused of killing her brother. That's just juvenile islander gossip.'

'She was never committed to an asylum then?' Ava asked.

'No,' Bunty shook her head. 'She did run away from home though, was gone for a good few years.'

'Why did she come back then?' Ava leaned further forward. 'I thought she turned the house into a school.'

'She did,' Bunty replied. 'Her mother, all alone in the house, suffered a stroke. Unable to care for herself, Luella returned to the island only to find all the family's money was gone, depleted over the years since Ephraim Lynch's death in 1902. They were flat broke. Luella opened the house as a school. At first it was only attended by the children on the island, then gradually she expanded it and many children came from the mainland and boarded at the house as it generated more income. After a while Luella employed a young teacher from Boston by the name of Jonathan Sedgewick. He boarded at the Morgan guest house for a time as it would not have been proper for him to live under the same roof as Luella, who was unmarried.'

'So, what happened next?' Ava had propped her elbows on her knees and was resting her chin on her fists as she watched Bunty in rapt fascination.

'Luella and Jonathan must have fallen in love, or decided it was mutually beneficial for them to wed. They married in January of 1919 and that fall came the storm and with it, the disappearance of not only Luella and her husband, but every child in that house.'

'What about her mother?' Ava asked.

'No one knows,' Betty shook her head, picking up the story once again from Bunty. 'There's no record of her at all after the stroke. We don't know if she died; there's no burial plot for her in the cemetery where Ephraim and Edison are both buried.'

'Wait a minute,' Ava frowned. 'If they all died or disappeared without a trace, that means I'm not descended from them? So how did I end up inheriting the house?'

'You're not a direct descendant,' Bunty told her, but her mouth once again thinned slightly, and her eyes were guarded. 'Ephraim had a younger sister; she left the island after their parents died of Typhoid. From what we understand she had nothing to do with her brother. She married and had children, who in turn had their own children. Several decades after the disappearance of Luella, the town council declared her legally dead. They tracked down Ephraim's sister's descendants, the Wallaces, and the house passed to them. They moved back to the island, but they never lived in the house.'

'So, Luella would have been my great, great aunt or something.' Ava mused.

'Something like that,' Bunty muttered quietly as she watched Ava, her blue eyes unreadable.

Ava opened her mouth to speak once again but before she could utter a word, a loud car horn blared. She looked across to the entrance to the woods and saw a huge RV driving up, followed by a small neat silver Honda.'

'Ah, my car at last,' Bunty stood and smoothed down her slacks. 'Well Ava dear, I'm afraid we shall have to leave you now.'

Ava stood and watched as the RV parked alongside her

truck. The compact Honda parked opposite and behind them both came Killian's red pickup. Killian climbed out of the RV and tapped the side as he headed toward Ava.

'She's solid,' he grinned, 'much better than a tent. You've got a small kitchen, seated area with table, a toilet and shower, and most importantly, a double bed, big enough for you and that half dog, half bear that's permanently attached to you.'

'It's mine?' Ava's eyed widened as she glanced lovingly at the RV, the way some women might eye diamonds.

'Don't get too excited, its only on loan,' Killian told her. 'Mr Wilson loaned it to you.'

'Who's Mr Wilson?' Ava frowned, 'and why is he loaning me his RV?'

'Mr Wilson is the retired principle of the local high school; he's friends with my dad. Usually he takes off for the summer with his wife, who's a retired nurse. They like to take to the open road for a few months, but their daughter has just given birth to their first grandchild after years of IVF and they don't want to miss a moment of it.'

'You gossip like an old woman Killian,' Kelley laughed as he opened the door of the Honda and unfolded his tall frame from the small car.

Killian shook his head and rolled his eyes.

'Anyway,' he continued, 'it's yours for the time being.'

'Thank you,' she replied sincerely, itching to get inside and take a look around. Instead she followed his gaze and watched as two huge guys climbed out of his pick-up. One was older with a leathery, weather beaten face and a wild grey beard. The other was younger but with a day's worth of scruff on his face and colorful tattoos covering both forearms. Both of them wore plaid shirts and beaten up old jeans.

'That's Judd and Hank,' Killian nodded. 'They helped us to clear the road; you shouldn't have any trouble passing now.'

'Thanks,' Ava offered them a smile.

'Ma'am,' they both nodded in turn.

'Well we're just gonna head back now,' Killian climbed into his pickup as Judd and Hank hauled themselves into the back.

'Well now just you hold on there a hot second,' Ivy smiled with siren red lips as she fluffed her platinum hair. 'If you would be so kind, could I trouble you for a ride?'

'Ivy May Harding,' Barbara chided, 'her hand involuntarily toying with the gold cross at her throat.

'Oh, hush up, you always sit up front with Bunty. I am not squeezing into the back seat of that pint-sized car with Betty, Ester and Norma again. Why she near on punctured one of my lungs with those knitting needles. I keep telling Bunty she needs a bigger car before one of us gets skewered by Norma. Well, it's not going to be me, no siree. Boys?'

'Miz Harding,' Killian replied, 'of course you're welcome to ride with us. I can drop you home on my way back to my office.'

'Thank you kindly. You boys must be so thirsty after all that manual work. You must come in for some of my home-made lemonade,' she beamed widely as she swept past Kelley, pinching his butt with a saucy wink. 'I insist.'

He shot Ava a look of sheer panic as he stepped closer to her.

'What's the matter Kelley?' she chuckled, 'allergic to lemons?'

'More like allergic to Miz Harding,' he growled under his breath. 'If you have a moment Ava,' he took her arm and drew her gently away, missing the narrowed glare Ivy shot his way.

'What is it Kelley?'

'I'd have preferred not to do this with an audience,' he glanced over his shoulder at the three men and six older ladies watching him raptly. For a second, he almost expected them to break out the popcorn.

'Do what?'

'Ask you out,' his mouth curved into the most adorable smile and once again her belly clenched.

'Ask me...?' her mouth fell open, at a loss as to what to say. 'Kelley I've barely been on the island forty-eight hours; I'm not looking to date anyone. I don't even know if I'll stay once the house is completed. I may sell up and move on.'

'It's just dinner Ava,' he smiled, 'not a proposal. I'd really like the chance to get to know you, no expectations, but what can I say? We've already spent the night together.'

There was a sharp hiss of air and Ava glanced across to see Betty's eyes widen.

'Nothing happened,' Ava replied loudly. 'We fell asleep with my dog planted between us like the Great Wall of China.'

'So? What do you say?' Kelley asked hopefully as she turned her attention back to him. 'I mean, you cooked last night, so I owe you a meal. This is the perfect opportunity for you to try our local lobster.'

'I don't know,' she frowned.

'Just think about it, okay?' he grinned as he walked backward toward his brother's truck.

'Fine,' she took in a deep breath, 'I'll think about it.'

Resisting the urge to fist pump the air in triumph, Kelley turned and practically skipped to his brother's pick up, deliberately skirting past the cab where Ivy sat expectantly beside his twin, looking like she'd swallowed something sour. Kelley vaulted easily over the side and planted himself in the bed of the truck alongside Hank and Judd.

'What?' Kelley asked.

Hank took a long drag on his cigarette and stared at him.

'You got it bad boy,' he shook his head.

Ava watched as the truck pulled away, ruthlessly ignoring the little flutter in her belly when Kelley smiled her way.

A few moments later the ladies departed, with hugs and air

kisses, as a firm, 'no refusal' invitation was issued to their next luncheon.

Finally, Ava was once again alone with her thoughts. Although her mind was filled with all the things, she'd learned about the Lynchs, a seriously dysfunctional family to say the least, she found her thoughts kept returning to the question of who had been playing fetch with her dog earlier.

Something tugged insistently at the corners of her mind, but every time she reached for it, it tattered and tore, scattering like ashes blown from a bonfire.

Before she could reason why, she found herself once again retracing her steps around the side of the house to where she'd dropped the ball in the dry dusty grass.

She searched and searched, but as the sun began to beat down mercilessly, high in the midday sky, the strange little leather ball was nowhere to be found.

7

*T*he Lynch House, Midnight Island.
Jan 1893.

HER BACK ARCHED *off the bed, as another ear-splitting scream tore from her lips. Her abdomen clamped painfully with another breath-stealing, vice-like grip. She felt a rush of hot thick fluid gush from between her spread legs, her soiled nightgown hiked up to her waist, exposing her tight, swollen belly.*

A grim-faced woman kneeled between her thighs, her sleeves rolled up to her flabby elbows, her enormous bosom heaving with every breath. Her face was pock marked, her lips slack and wide, her cheeks ruddy and well rounded.

She prodded and poked between her legs, her thick fingers intrusive and unwelcome as she shoved them inside her intimately.

'I can feel the babe's head,' her voice was raspy with age and too much love of the tobacco leaf. 'Not much longer now.'

She wanted to slap at those hands, to instinctively cringe away from the humiliating examination, but the pain ripped through her belly once again and she couldn't think, couldn't breathe. All she could feel was an enormous amount of pressure between her legs, and suddenly there was stretching and burning as she felt her skin begin to tear.

She looked down in horror to see a small head sticking out of her, covered in a thick white fluid and smears of blood. She would've screamed then, if one final excruciating wave of pain hadn't gripped her stomach so hard it robbed her of breath. Given no other choice, her body simply took over and clamped down hard, expelling the tiny bawling infant into the waiting hands of the old woman, in a gush of blood and other fluids.

She turned her face away from the ugly blob of bloodied flesh, with its wet patch of dark hair and flailing limbs.

She fell back against the pillows breathing heavily, her pale cheeks stained with tears and sweat.

'Oh my,' the old woman cooed as she wiped the babe clean and wrapped her in a fine white linen. 'It's a girl madam, and she's a beauty.'

'Take it away,' she whispered harshly, not bothering to turn her head. 'I don't want it.'

'But madam,' the old midwife frowned, 'she's your daughter.'

'I said...' she replied coldly, 'take it away.'

Not to be deterred the woman edged around the huge, heavy, canopied bed and held the babe in front of her, peeling back the linen to reveal a tiny delicate face.

She stared at it numbly, until it opened its eyes and stared back at her. The horror washed over her in waves, almost choking her with the rage and disgust she felt.

It had his eyes and they bored into her soul, mocking and cruel.

'Get rid of it,' she hissed.

The babe began to cry then in earnest, as if it could somehow feel its mother's rejection. It squirmed and mewled in the old woman's arms, red faced and shrill.

'But madam, she's hungry, she needs to nurse.'

She lay there, staring at the rich fabric of the damask drapes, trying desperately to block out its cries. Her breasts, tender and swollen, began to harden painfully as they flooded with milk, her nipples wet as the child continued to scream. She felt warm milky liquid dripping onto her rib cage, saturating the front of her ruined nightgown but she couldn't bear the thought of it against her skin, or the feel of its tiny mouth clamped to her nipple suckling.

The very thought repulsed her.

'Madam,' the old woman tried again as she rocked the babe.

'I SAID TAKE IT AWAY!' she turned and screamed.

The woman stumbled back a few paces, holding the tiny babe to her ample bosom protectively. She turned quickly, in a swirl of heavy skirts and headed toward the door, stopping abruptly when a huge imposing frame blocked her way.

'Sir,' she swallowed nervously.

He was tall, and powerfully built. His dark eyes dipped down to the mewling bundle in her arms, his jet-black hair glowed in the candlelight, so it almost looked wet, swept back from his face. Two wings of pure white flared out from his temples making him look even more dangerous.

'It's a girl sir,' she held out the squalling bundle for him to see, but he didn't look. He'd already lost interest.

'Take it to the wet nurse on the third floor,' his voice was low and gravely. Devoid of any warmth it sent shivers skittering down her spine as she dipped her creaky knees in a half curtsey and shuffled hurriedly past him.

He gave no more attention to the old woman or the child, his black eyes were fixed on the woman laying on soiled sheets, her exposed thighs stained with blood as she buried her face in her pillow.

His mouth curved slowly as he reached out and slowly closed the door to the sound of her bitter weeping.

8

*A*va pulled her knees up and wrapped her arms around her legs as she smiled softly. Bailey was dozing, spread out across the small double bed in front of her. She wiggled her toes and buried them comfortably in Bailey's fur as she didn't seem to mind. Glancing around the place she was currently calling home another strange rush of warmth stole through her chest.

This was the first time she'd ever lived in an RV and she had to say, she was pleasantly surprised. It didn't look that big from the outside, but it had way more room on the inside. It was ridiculous how much living space she now had. Behind the driver and passenger seats there was a small booth with a square Formica table and padded benches. Opposite was a stove and sink. Then there was the door beside that, with steps down to exit the vehicle. A long sofa ran along the opposite wall and at the end was a small bedroom containing a double bed, and a bathroom with a toilet and shower.

Some might have turned their noses up at the modest accommodation but to Ava it was a small slice of heaven, her own heaven. No more sleeping in her truck, which was well on its way to giving her a crick in her neck that no chiropractor would be able to fix. No more questionable motel rooms, with busted locks, things growing in the shower and disturbing stains on the sheets which looked as if they hadn't been laundered in a decade, because it was all she could afford, and definitely.... definitely, no more communes. No more sharing bathroom space with twenty other people, no sleeping on pallets listening to the other people in the same space snoring, or worse grunting and groaning in the darkness, noises she'd discovered far too early in life.

Ava closed her eyes for a minute and drew in a slow breath. Silence. Well, other than her dog's soft snore, and the gentle sounds of the ocean, which crept through the open window at her back even as the sweet, salty breeze tickled her neck and danced down her spine.

There was no one else; it was just her and her dog, on her very own cliff top. She sighed loudly in pleasure, causing Bailey's ears to twitch as she lazily opened one eye.

'What do you think?' Ava muttered quietly as she looked down at her best friend. 'Is this home?'

Bailey thumped her tail a couple of times before closing her eyes again.

Ava wasn't certain, but it sure came close. She'd never felt such a pull toward a place before. She wasn't sure whether to breathe a sigh of relief or not. For a while there, she'd wondered if the apple had fallen a little too close to the tree and that she had been doomed to wander restlessly like her mother had. Except, for Serenity, it was a choice rather than a punishment, but for the first time ever she'd felt the tug deep in the pit of her belly.

Maybe it was just wishful thinking; maybe it was the tenuous tie of long dead relatives she knew nothing about. All she knew was the desperate desire for roots, for something sturdy to hold on to. A place to belong.

The problem was, her roots were slowly disappearing. Her family tree had withered away until there was nothing, but dry fossilized roots hidden by decades, centuries even, of gossip, rumor and supposition, shrouded in legend. If she had any hope of uncovering the truth and discovering who and what she came from, like an archaeologist, she'd have to peel it back layer by layer.

Her dark eyes fell on the brand-new large leather notebook she'd purchased the day before, that was laying open on the bed beside her. Page after page was now filled with her neat handwriting as she'd meticulously documented everything she'd been told about the Lynches and about the house itself. Every single scrap of information, from Killian and his wife Hope, to Kelley and the eccentric ladies of the historical society.

Half of it was crap of course, in fact probably more than half if she was being totally honest. It was going to take a while to weed through decades of teenage over-imagination and small island gossip.

It was intriguing though, she had to admit, plus it gave her something to occupy her time. After all there wasn't much she could do while the house was being ripped apart and put back together. She could help carry debris as the house was cleared and she could wield a paintbrush fairly efficiently, but that was the sum total of her manual labor skills.

It was the thrill of uncovering a century old mystery that had her skin tingling and her blood pumping. She glanced across at the photo frame she'd recovered from the house. At that moment it was nestled on a plastic bag to stop any broken glass from falling onto the bed. Sliding it over so it was directly in front of her she picked up the frame, careful to hold it over the plastic. She'd dusted out most of the broken glass and was now able to study it more carefully in the daylight, than she had been within the dim confines of the boarded-up house.

The woman in the picture really did have the tiniest waist, making her chest look oddly puffed out like a hen. Nestled against the dark gown she wore was a small round locket on a long chain, a detail Ava hadn't noticed the first time. The little boy standing beside the well-dressed woman, wore short pants but his legs were covered with long socks, stockings almost, ending in tightly laced boots. The picture was black and white so it was hard to tell what colors they might have been wearing. The boy had very light hair and pale eyes. Although the woman had darker hair, her eyes looked eerily similar to the child. The man looked like neither of them.

They had to be a family unit Ava guessed. Photography was very expensive back then and certainly not done on a whim. Turning the picture over she studied the back of the frame. It was now nothing more than withered leather and tiny flaps of rusted metal holding the picture in place. Digging her fingernails in Ava managed to scrape the metal leaves aside so the back loosened, and as she removed the brittle leather something fluttered into her lap.

It was a small lock of hair, barely more than one tiny blonde curl, tied with a faded, musty blue ribbon. She pulled the photograph from the frame, staring at the back of it. Printed in a neat typeset were the words LHJ Linden Photographic Studio. Her gaze wandered further down the yellowed paper to a looping scrawl in faded black ink which read, *My darling Peter...*

Ava picked up the lock of hair, holding it gently in her fingertips as she turned the photo back over and stared at the three faces.

'So, which one's Peter?' she mused out loud.

It had to be the kid, she concluded. If the lock of hair belonged to someone in the picture, the young boy was the only one with fair hair.

'Who are you?' Ava whispered curiously.

She looked up sharply as Bailey suddenly sprang up from

the bed and darted toward the door, barking loudly. Tucking both the picture and the lock of hair in her notebook, she shut it carefully and secured it with an elastic band before shoving the remnants of the damaged frame into the plastic bag to dispose of later.

Swinging her legs over the edge of the bed she padded to the door on bare feet and swung it open. Before she could stop her Bailey leapt out, barking playfully as she dashed off.

Unable to see what had her dog so worked up Ava climbed absently down the steps from the RV while she stared across to where Bailey had disappeared around the corner of the house.

'BAILEY!' she called out, but as her foot hit the dry grassy ground she cried out at a sudden sharp stab of pain in her foot.

She sat down heavily on the steps and lifted her injured foot, propping it on her other knee so she could inspect the sole which had begun to ooze blood. She could see the corner of something protruding from her flesh. Reaching out with shaky fingers she grasped it as firmly as she could as it was already wet with her blood and pulled hard. A sharp hiss passed her lips as she turned the object over on her palm.

It looked like part of a seashell. Her brow furrowed in confusion, and as her gaze dropped to the ground beneath the last step, her eyes widened in surprise. Hopping carefully down the last few steps, she kneeled down close to the ground.

In front of her was a neatly arranged circle of pretty seashells, all of them perfectly shaped and intact, with the exception of the one she'd had the misfortune to step on. Tiny little fan shapes and miniature conches, all in delicate shades of pale pink, peach, cream and beige. There was not a hint of dirt or seaweed. It was as if someone had gone to great lengths not only to pick the most pleasing shells but had also taken the trouble to clean them too.

Inside the small circle of shells was a posy of wildflowers. She recognized them, as most of them grew abundantly along her cliff. Long green stems and tiny bud like flowers and bells in white, purple and pink, all hand-picked, were arranged neatly and tied with several long blades of grass. It was sweet, the whole thing was simple and almost childlike, but what a strange thing to do.

Her brow folded into a frown as she tried to figure out who would leave them and why? If it was a welcome to the neighborhood kind of gift, why hadn't they knocked on the RV and spoken to her in person?

Pulling her phone, which she'd been finally forced to get on account of all the building works about to commence on her property, out of her pocket she snapped a couple of pictures before leaning down and carefully collecting all the shells, so Bailey didn't cut her paws. It was fortunate she'd missed the whole thing when she'd bounded energetically down the stairs and leapt off the last step.

Lastly, she picked up the small bunch of flowers and headed back up into the RV, almost forgetting her injured foot as she contemplated the strange gift. She placed the flowers in a world's greatest mom mug she'd found in the cupboard and filled it with water. Leaving the shells on the table beside the mug, she turned and saw the bloodied footprints she'd left along the floor.

Wincing slightly at the mess, after all, as cozy as it was, the RV didn't technically belong to her, she grabbed a cloth and wrapped it around her foot to stop the bleeding as she cleaned up the mess. Once that was done, she found a small first aid kit under the sink. It didn't take long to clean and cover the small wound as it wasn't deep. Slipping her sneakers on, she grabbed her keys and went in search of her dog.

It was easy to find her, she wasn't too far from the same spot she'd been playing in a few days earlier, only this time she didn't have a ball, she was just rolling around in the grass, like she would if Ava was rubbing her belly.

'Bailey?' Ava called out and watched as she scrambled to her feet, dashing over as she panted happily. 'Crazy dog,' she shook her head in amusement as she bent down and rubbed her fur. 'Wanna go for a ride?'

Bailey's ears pricked up and she barked loudly.

'Need some supplies,' Ava stood and headed toward the truck with Bailey dancing along at her heels. 'You're going to have to wear the leash though.'

It was almost comical the way Bailey skidded to a halt and glanced up at Ava reproachfully.

'Don't look at me like that,' Ava shook her head, 'it's only until the locals get used to you. You're like the size of a small pony.'

Climbing up into the cab of her truck she left the door open and leaned out.

'You coming or not?'

Not needing to be told twice Bailey leapt up into the truck and settled next to Ava as she slammed the door closed and gunned the engine.

She took a slow leisurely drive down the winding cliff road toward the town, with the windows down as she breathed in the sea air. She parked by the docks and took her time buying supplies. Work was due to begin the next day on the house; by mid-morning the crews Killian had managed to hire from the mainland would have arrived on the early ferry. Some of them, she knew, according to Hope who had continued to call her daily with updates, would stay on the island, lodging at the various guesthouses and with friends. Some would make the daily commute.

There wouldn't be much for her to do on site other than make decisions about what she wanted doing to the house and what she was prepared to pay for, but there was one thing she could do and that was feed everyone. She loved to cook and thanks to her upbringing was not only used to cooking for large amounts of people but often cooking outdoors.

She bought stacks of disposable plates and cups, a coffee urn, a huge barbecue, okay that had been a little extravagant but, in her defense, she'd never owned one before and it had been on sale down at Samsons' Hardware. She'd spent the last few days building up the fire pit and stocking up on fuel, which had largely involved long walks in the woods with her dog while she collected fallen branches and twigs.

She bought large pans and fresh produce, all locally grown, and loaded it all up in the back of her truck while she watched as the boats came in, unloading huge traps and crates filled with fresh lobster and fish. The fish she could handle, she had a real way with pan fried fish, but she was determined to learn to cook lobster, something she still had yet to try.

The thought of lobster rolls had her mind involuntarily turning back to Kelley, the sexy bartender who was not only determined to take her out on a seafood date but who'd been conspicuously absent for the last few days. She hadn't seen or heard from him since the night of the storm when they'd fallen asleep in her shabby little one-man tent, and the next morning when he'd gone to relive himself and accidentally flashed a bunch of little old ladies.

The thought made her lips twist momentarily into an amused smile, but it soon vanished when she contemplated how quickly he'd abandoned his pursuit of her. She should've been relieved that he'd left her alone. After all, she wasn't on the island looking for love she was there to discover her family roots and rebuild an old house, but damn it if she wasn't a little disappointed that he'd apparently lost interest so quickly.

Still, she shouldn't have been surprised. As a bartender he had women falling over themselves to get to him. She knew, she'd seen it with her own eyes the night she'd rolled into town. He could have any woman he wanted, even Hope had alluded as much. Why on earth would he want a prickly loner who lived out of her truck, with an oversized dog who'd tried to smother him in his sleep.

Her mouth twisted down and her brow furrowed. The more she thought about it, the more annoyed she became, until it was an unpleasant slippery eel twisting and lurching in her belly. She was glad he hadn't called or bothered to pursue her; she wasn't interested in the slightest. If he wanted to go and sleep with some cheap bar slut, then he was welcome to.

She hadn't realized that, as her inner voice ran away on a mental rant, she'd been walking aimlessly, following roads and paths away from the main docks and shops, until she wasn't quite sure where she was. Looking up she saw a big friendly sandstone colored building with Midnight Middle and High School written across it in neat silver letters. Despite the fact that it was summer, and school should've been out, there were various cars scattered about and a bunch of kids heading out the main entrance.

Gripping Bailey's brand-new blue leash in her hand Ava crossed the street and headed toward the building. She figured she could flag down someone and ask for directions back to the docks.

She saw a cluster of kids and moms not far from the entrance. She was already heading toward them when they parted and she stopped dead in her tracks, her mouth falling open in confusion. She blinked hard but the sight in front of her remained the same.

It was Kelley, standing in amongst the kids and parents, laughing and smiling. He wore his trademark blue jeans, but he'd paired them with a button-down shirt and jacket, and he was wearing thick rimmed glasses that were just the right combination of studious and nerdy.

Oh boy, her stomach swooped as she stood there staring at him. She'd just about convinced herself she'd inadvertently wandered into some kind of alternative reality, one where Killian and Kelley had neglected to tell her they were triplets instead of twins and that there was in fact another Ryan brother, when he looked up, his eyes locked with hers, and his face broke into a wide and genuine smile.

He excused himself from the students and the parents. Funnily enough the moms looked more disappointed at his departure than the students as he jogged over to her.

'Ava!' he greeted as he stopped in front of her, 'I've been thinking about you for days.'

He drank in the sight of her like he was dying of thirst and she was an ice-cold beer. Like before, she didn't have a stitch of make up on and her thick inky black hair was piled up on top of her head in a messy knot, leaving a few errant strands curling against the damp skin of her neck in the heat. Unable to help himself his eyes peeled scandalously down her body. She was wearing the tiniest denim shorts revealing long toned legs, with skin the color of honey, which ended in her trademark red sneakers.

'Hey,' Ava's brow rose, 'I'm up here.'

'Well, there's not an inch of you that's not perfect is there?' he muttered almost to himself.

'There's no such thing as perfect,' she scowled.

'Stunning then,' his green eyes met hers as he smiled.

'What are you doing here Kelley?' she asked in confusion. 'I thought you worked in a bar?'

'That?' What? No,' he shook his head, 'I just help out at the bar sometimes. This is where I work.'

He indicated the school behind him.

'You're a teacher?' she tilted her head slightly as she studied him.

'I am,' he grinned. 'Got the scars to prove it... I teach 7th grade English. Nothing like trying to wrangle a bunch of cocky twelve to thirteen years olds into enjoying the literary classics.'

'Literary classics huh?'

'That's right,' he replied with a slow nod. 'I do feel Captain Underpants was sadly underrated for its literary genius, but my kids are beyond that now. Our most recent read was Watership Down. At first, they didn't want to read a book about a bunch of... and this is a direct quote... 'dumb rabbits', but I had them all crying into their textbooks by the end of the semester.'

'So, you traumatized a bunch of twelve-year olds?'

'Oh, totally scarred them for life,' he nodded, 'but their lives will be so much richer for it.'

'Uh-huh,' she couldn't help but smile. He had the whole nerdy professor thing going on, hot nerdy professor, and god damn if he wasn't pushing buttons, she wasn't even aware she had.

'I thought school was out for summer?'

'It is, but we teach summer school and a whole bunch of extra credit classes.'

'Oh,' she scuffled the toe of her shoe absently against the ground.

'Anyway,' he smiled again, 'I'm glad I ran into you. I've been wanting to see you for the last couple of days, but it's been crazy. I've been covering some of the other summer classes as well as my own for the faculty staff on vacation, and I was trying to cover shifts at the bar.'

'Bye Mr Ryan!' a chorus of kids called out.

Kelley lifted his hand and waved.

'Well I...uh...oomph,' whatever she was going to say was lost as she was jerked sharply to the side. Bailey had collapsed to the sidewalk with a mournful whine, rolling over and tangling her heavy body in the offending leash, almost yanking Ava's shoulder from her socket, as she chewed at the blue woven cord.

'She doesn't like her leash,' Ava rolled her eyes as Bailey gave another plaintive whine. 'Quit being such a drama queen;

you know why you have to wear it... jeez...' Ava sighed. 'What?' she shrugged her shoulders when she caught Kelley watching her with a smile.

'Nothing,' he shook his head, 'I love that you talk to her like she's a human.'

'Yeah well,' Ava frowned as Bailey continued to gnaw at the leash, 'she likes to pretend she's stupid, but she understands plenty.'

'So...' Kelley grinned, 'classes are done for the day, you're here, I'm here. Some might call that fortuitous.'

'And some might call it a coincidence.'

'Come on Ava,' he reached out and tugged a loose strand of her hair gently, 'let me buy you dinner?'

'Isn't it a bit early for dinner?'

'I skipped lunch,' he replied, 'so any food is good. We could walk down to the beach; I'll buy you a lobster roll and an ice cream.'

'What kind of ice cream?' her eyes narrowed thoughtfully.

'Best on the east coast,' he grinned.

A small smile tugged at her lips as she watched him.

'Okay,' she replied after a moment.

'Yeah?' his smile widened.

'Sure,' she shrugged.

'Okay,' he backed up slowly, 'I've just got a few things to tie up. Give me ten minutes, I'll be right back.'

'Okay,' she nodded as she watched him walking slowly backward.

'Okay,' he repeated, 'and you'll be right here?'

'I'll be right here,' she smiled slowly.

She watched as he threw her another gorgeous grin before turning around and darting back into the school.

'Oh boy I'm in trouble,' Ava muttered.

She had to admit she was having a hard time resisting all the nerdiness and boyish charm wrapped up in a sinfully good-looking man. It was a dangerous combination. She'd thought she had him pegged the first night she met him, but she was just starting to get what Hope meant about him being oblivious to the female attention he received. He just wasn't that shallow.

She was also starting to feel slightly guilty for all the nasty thoughts she'd had earlier when she thought he was just ignoring her. The guy was just busy. He had a life; he had a job... well two jobs apparently. She kept trying to squeeze him into a box that didn't fit him, and he'd simply just laugh and climb straight back out. It was confusing the hell out of her. She felt like she was trying to navigate shark infested waters, with no paddle, in a capsized canoe.

She had no experience to draw on. It wasn't like she was a virgin by any means. She'd scratched plenty of itches over the years when she'd felt like it, but both parties had been looking for no strings, mutual satisfaction topped off with an amicable 'see ya later' in the morning.

Kelley wasn't like that and just what the hell was she supposed to do about him? He made her want, although if you'd asked her what, she wouldn't have been able to tell you, only that he tugged at her, just like the island did.

'Hey, you look like you were a million miles away.'

Ava looked up in surprise as Kelley reappeared in front of her holding a battered brown leather satchel. She glanced down at her watch; true to his word he'd only been just over ten minutes.

'Come on Bailey,' Ava tucked at the leash, dragging her protesting dog to her feet. 'So how come you work at the bar too?' Ava asked. 'Are teachers' salaries really that bad?'

'No,' he laughed as they walked side by side, not quite touching. 'My uncle owns the bar and grill, but he has a bad knee. Played some football in college, was good enough to have gone pro, but an injury shot his knee. It's been getting steadily worse for the past couple of years, but he was too stubborn to do anything about it. The last few months he's barely been able to walk, so I've been helping out as much as I can. He's going in for surgery on the mainland next week, so I'll run the bar for him while he recovers.'

'That's good of you,' she murmured.

Kelley shrugged, 'it's what you do for family. His kids, my cousins, are all married with families of their own and demanding jobs. They don't have the time to help out. They would if they could, but I'm the only one who doesn't have a life outside his job.'

He laughed, but it wasn't filled with self-derision or mockery but a genuine amusement and affection for his family.

'You're a very easy-going guy,' she remarked.

'I doubt my students would agree with you,' he chuckled.

'Did you always want to be a teacher?'

'Yeah,' he nodded, 'I did, even when I was a kid. I'd grade my brother's papers for him, it drove him nuts. Killian hated school, he just loved to build things.'

'But not you?'

'I hate to ruin your manly image of me but I'm pretty much a spaz if you put any kind of tool in my hand. Now if you want someone to quote you Hemmingway, I'm your man.'

'Hemmingway?'

'Or Shakespeare, Poe, Yeats?'

She stared at him.

'The mighty pyramids of stone, that wedge-like cleave the desert airs, when nearer seen and better known, are but gigantic flights of stairs... of course, that was Henry Wadsworth Longfellow, an American poet from the late 19th century, but it's one of my favorites.'

He glanced at Ava as she watched him quietly and he smiled.

'Of course, I also love Harry Potter,' he shrugged, 'I mean, who doesn't. What about you?'

'What about me?'

'Favorite book?'

'I don't read much,' Ava murmured.

'Okaay,' he replied slowly, 'well how about work then? What do you do when you're not renovating old haunted houses?'

'This and that,' she shrugged, 'waitressing mostly.'

'Wasn't there anything in particular you wanted to do?' he asked curiously. 'I mean when you were a kid, astronaut? Rockstar?'

'No,' she smiled.

'What did you want then?'

A home was what she'd always wanted more than anything, but that seemed way too personal to share with him, so she merely shrugged instead.

'I like to cook,' she answered finally.

'Never thought about being a chef?' he asked.

'Never stayed in one place long enough,' she answered honestly.

'You looking to change that?' he asked seriously as they stopped along the railings, looking down at the beach.

'I don't know,' Ava replied quietly as she stared out at the glittering ocean. 'There's something about this place, it calls to me.'

She turned to look at him and flushed, she hadn't meant to say that out loud.

'I'm glad,' he smiled, 'because selfishly I want you to stick around.'

'Trust me,' Ava scoffed, 'I'm nothing special.'

'Why would you think that?' he asked seriously.

'Because it's true,' she shrugged.

She really believed that, he realized as he studied her dark eyes. She was carrying so much baggage and he was willing to bet every dime he owned that most of it wasn't hers. She was like a fascinating puzzle that he was dying to take apart and figure out.

'Well you're wrong,' he replied confidently, 'and sooner or later I'm going to prove it to you, but for now I believe I promised you lobster rolls.'

'Where are we going?' she asked as he grabbed her hand, trying to ignore the warm fluttery feeling in her stomach as he towed her along, 'because you know, most restaurants won't allow dogs...'

'Just there,' Kelley pointed to a small... well it was little more than a wooden shack, with plastic furniture set out in front of it, covered with bright red and white checked paper tablecloths. 'Most places on the island serve lobster, but if you want the best, then you want Ma James. That's her place just ahead, and she doesn't mind dogs.'

Her heart did a little flip and then a long slow roll when she realized he'd chosen a place that would include her dog.

'Take a seat,' he steered her toward a nearby table where she'd still have a perfect view of the ocean, 'I'll be right back. What do you want to drink?'

'Anything is fine,' she shook her head. 'I don't mind.'

Bailey hunkered down beside her as she slid onto one of the seats beneath a huge yellow umbrella and anxiously toyed with the salt and pepper shakers on the table, beside a metal napkin dispenser with the Coca Cola logo splashed across the side.

She'd never really done the whole dating thing. Usually if she wanted to get laid, she'd pick some guy up in a bar, not that that happened very often. She wasn't one to sleep around after all, but this whole getting to know each other, sitting having a meal overlooking the ocean? The whole thing just smacked of romantic intentions and she had no idea what the hell she was doing.

Kelley, who she'd originally dismissed as a player, had not only turned out to be highly educated but really intelligent and interesting. She hadn't even finished high school for god's sake. In fact, who was she kidding, she'd never even gone to high school. He was so far out of her league it wasn't even funny.

She watched him as he approached the open front of the hut and greeted a short plump woman with curly iron gray hair, ruthlessly pulled back from her tanned, heavily lined face, while her huge golden hooped earrings swung, every time she moved her head.

Ava couldn't hear what they were saying but every now and then Kelley would glance back at her and smile, almost as if he was reassuring himself that she hadn't disappeared. When he finally returned to their table with a heavily laden plastic tray, the first thing he did was place two disposable bowls down on the ground in front of Bailey, one filled with water and one filled with meat.

'What's that?' Ava asked.

'Chicken, sorry no steak for you today Bailey,' he petted her head as he stood and took a seat opposite Ava, 'and no lobster either. Ma James says shellfish isn't good for dogs.'

Ava blinked as she sat staring at him.

'Damn it, Kelley, stop it,' she frowned.

'Stop what?' he replied absently as he placed a soda in front of her, alongside a small oval, red plastic basket lined with paper and containing a sub roll stuffed with a delicious smelling meat and dressing.

'Stop making me like you,' she frowned.

'Can't,' he grinned, 'it's all part of my devious plan.'

She watched as he picked up his own sub and took a huge bite, his eyes rolling in pleasure.

'Sorry if I'm being rude,' he apologized after he'd chewed and swallowed, 'I'm literally starving.'

'I have no idea what to do with you Kelley,' she murmured.

'I have a few ideas,' he grinned, 'but for now, it doesn't have to be any more complicated than two people sharing a meal and talking.'

'About what?'

'Anything you like,' he took another bite, 'anything you like.'

And they did. They talked for hours, about everything, about nothing and all the little things in-between. The weird thing was, it wasn't hard. Just like the night they'd fallen asleep side by side in a pokey little tent with the rain drumming down on the canvas and the thunder crashing high above them. Being in his company was effortless.

By the time the long afternoon passed toward evening they were walking along the docks, side by side, eating ice creams just as he'd promised.

'You were right you know,' Ava finally said.

'About?'

'The lobster rolls were amazing. Now I'm going to have to learn how to cook them,' she mused. 'Do they really boil lobsters alive?'

'I try not to think about that part,' Kelley winced. 'I'd rather it just ended up on my plate; I don't need to know how it got there.'

Ava laughed as she looked out across the marina. The last of the boats were coming in and the docks were still laden with huge crates of fish and lobsters.

'What's that big building over there?' she pointed to a large warehouse sitting slightly back from the dock.

'That's where they pack and process the catch,' Kelley licked his ice cream. 'Just around the corner is the fish market.'

'Fish market,' Ava stopped suddenly. 'Uh, we should probably go back.'

'Why?' Kelley asked curiously.

'Because Bailey...' whatever she was about to say was drowned by a joyful bark, and as Ava blinked, all she saw was a blur of black and gold fur disappearing toward the warehouse. She raised her left hand to find a bright blue leash dangling from her wrist, gnawed off at the end. 'Shit,' Ava swore, 'hold this.' She thrust her own ice cream at Kelley and sprinted after her dog.

She ran flat out, rounding the corner of the building.

'BAILEY!' her voice cracked like a whip causing her dog to skid to a halt.

Ava approached her slowly. Bailey was standing quivering, her body trembling at all the scents surrounding her. Her ears pricked up and her nostrils flared.

'Stay,' Ava commanded as she edged closer, the smell of fish so strong, she gagged a little.

Bailey's eyes flicked to the right and Ava's followed. Her stomach clenched as she realized why the smell was particularly strong here. There were barrels and barrels of fish guts. Her eyes flicked back to Bailey who wagged her tail.

'DON'T...YOU...DARE...' Ava whispered; her eyes wide in warning.

Bailey wagged her tail again and lunged at the nearest barrel. Ava dived for her, but it was too late. As she grabbed her collar, they both tumbled into a barrel, overturning it and sending it careening into the next one, showering them both with slimy fish parts.

Ava wrestled her dog, but it was no use, the floor was too slippery. She had no purchase to climb to her feet and haul her dog away. Bailey was having the time of her life rolling over and over, rubbing her fur into the smelly fish goo.

Ava finally managed to grab her and haul her against her body, holding her in place. She looked up as the sound of laughter rang in her ears. Kelley stood almost doubled over with laughter, an ice cream in each hand.

'You think this is funny?' she asked angrily.

'I'm sorry,' he drew in a deep breath and started laughing again, 'it's just...' he continued to laugh.

Ava's eyes narrowed dangerously.

'Bailey,' her voice was ominously low, Bailey thumped her tail against the ground making wet slapping noises.

'Ava, wait!' Kelley sobered, reading the intent in her eyes. He held up his hands, but it lost the desired effect as he was still holding two melting ice cream cones.

Ava's eyes flashed as she lifted her hand from Bailey's collar and released her.

'Sic him girl,' she whispered, and Bailey leapt forward.

Kelley took an involuntary step back as she pounced and tackled him to the ground, rolling over and over him, rubbing her face against his, licking him ecstatically. He gagged at the stench of her rotten fishy breath.

'Bailey stop!' he tried to breathe through his mouth as she began to lick the ice creams he was miraculously still clutching, although he'd now crushed the cones in his fists as he fought off the giant playful, rancid smelling dog.

Ava climbed to her feet marching over to Kelley as he lay on the floor. She leaned over him, saluted him with her middle finger, before turning and stalking away, whistling for her dog, who once again in a mad scramble after her mistress managed to crush his balls, leaving him groaning on the ground amongst the fish guts.

IT HAD TAKEN him more than a few minutes to catch his breath and several more for the ache in his groin to ease, after which he'd tenderly hauled himself to his feet and gone after Ava. He hadn't found her anywhere. He'd stalked back to the school to retrieve his own car and driven straight up to the house on the cliff with the windows cranked down and his head hanging out to try and avoid the smell which was emanating from every inch of him.

He should have driven home, showered for an hour straight after burning his clothes, but he hadn't. He hadn't even given it a second thought; he was climbing out of his car in front of her parked truck before he could even question his motives.

He was pissed off, really pissed off. Okay maybe he shouldn't have laughed but dammit, did she really have to set her tame bear on him? He doubted he'd ever be able to get the stench off him and the nasty oily goo was now beginning to dry on his exposed skin, making it feel stiff and itchy.

He climbed out of his car, not even bothering to slam the door. After all it would need a good airing, for probably the next thousand years or so.

He marched over and pounded on the door of her RV but got no response. Glancing around, he couldn't see her or her damn dog anywhere. His gaze tracked over to the dark boarded up house looming over him and he involuntarily shuddered. If the house had eyes, he'd have sworn it was watching him.

Deliberately turning his back on it, he reached for the door handle on the RV. He froze at the distant sound of barking and once again glanced around. He couldn't see them, so he followed the sound of Bailey's playful barks.

It led him to the edge of the cliff and upon closer inspection he realized there were stone steps carved into the cliff face leading down. Curious, he followed them, winding slowly down until he found himself stepping out onto a small hidden beach.

It was a tiny little paradise, flanked on either side by the curve of the cliffs. Huge boulders and craggy rocks piled up on one side of the small cove where the cliff at some point had crumbled and crashed into the beach below. Kelley had no idea this place even existed. Then again, he'd never been brave enough to explore anywhere near the infamous Lynch House.

His anger had simmered down to irritation on the long climb down from the top and even now the irritation was giving way to a peaceful sense of wonder. It was like being inside a painting; the sky was streaking with deep stains of pink and purple as the sun began its descent and the dying light caught on the rippling waves making them sparkle. He moved further out from the base of the steps onto the beach, his ruined sneakers sinking into the sand as he once again followed the sound of barking. He rounded a huge rock and stopped dead.

Every thought drained from his head, and his jaw went slack.

Ava rose out of the water like a mythical Siren, her back to him and the beads of sea water glistening off her golden skin in the dying light. Her hair spilled down her back, slick and glossy like a streak of black paint, to the top curve of her buttocks which were just visible above the water.

Alerted to his presence, Bailey, who'd been frolicking happily in the waves, began to bark in earnest causing Ava to turn her head, her midnight eyes locking on his.

He spun around quickly putting his back to her to give her some privacy as every inch of his body grew warm despite the rapidly cooling evening air.

'Uh sorry,' he stuttered. 'I was looking for you, I didn't mean to intrude. I mean, I didn't know you were... you know... naked.'

Ava waded across to one of the larger rocks jutting out of the water, where she'd rested her soap and shampoo, and crossing her arms on top of it she leaned against it, effectively shielding her body from prying eyes.

'It's okay Kelley,' she replied, 'you can turn around. I'm decent... more or less.'

'I uh...' he turned his head and found her leaning against a rock like a mermaid, watching him curiously.

He was so cute, she thought to herself, all embarrassed and trying not to look at her.

'I'm sorry I laughed at you,' he stuck his hands in his pockets and kicked the sand like a surly teenager.

Definitely cute.

'I'm sorry I set my dog on you,' as the corner of her mouth curved into a smile.

'Well okay then,' he nodded, trying desperately to resist the temptation to look at her and all her glorious, wet, naked skin, 'I should probably go.'

'Why?'

'What do you mean why?'

'Does my body bother you?' she tilted her head as she studied him.

'Is that a trick question?' he replied. 'I don't think there's any way for me to answer that without sounding like an idiot or a creep.'

Ava laughed.

'Kelley,' she shook her head in amusement, 'get your clothes off and get in here, the water's lovely.'

'I'm sorry what?' he blinked, pretty sure he misheard.

'I said, get naked and get in here,' she laughed again.

'That's what I thought you said,' his eyes narrowed as he stared at her, not sure if she was serious or not.

'I'm not inviting you in for sex, let's get that straight now, but seriously, I can smell you from here.'

'And who's fault is that?' he crossed his arms.

'Yours, for laughing at me,' she smiled. 'Come on, I've got soap... and shampoo,' she picked up the bottle and waved it at him.

He had to admit, he wanted the soap and shampoo more than anything at that particular moment. Every time he got a whiff of himself it turned his stomach.

'And it doesn't bother you?' he asked curiously, 'skinny dipping on a secluded beach with a guy you've only just met?'

'Kelley, I was raised by a bunch of hippies. We spent entire summers naked when we were kids.'

'We're not kids,' he pointed out.

'I'll behave myself if you will,' she grinned, 'besides we have a giant lumbering wet dog as a chaperone.'

'A valid point,' he nodded.

'Come on then?' she challenged him, 'unless you're chicken?'

His green eyes narrowed once again as he kicked off his shoes and peeled off his socks. Next went the jacket and shirt, followed by his jeans until he stood in front of her interested gaze in nothing but tight black boxers.

She lifted an eyebrow in challenge.

'Yeah, yeah,' he shook his head. 'Turn around, the water's probably freezing, and I won't be looking my best.'

She threw her head back with a silvery peal of laughter before turning and diving into the water.

Yanking his boxers down and kicking them off he ran for the water.

'Shit... cold... cold...cold,' he chanted until he was far enough out to dive cleanly in and swim out to the rock.

She watched, treading water comfortably while he lathered up and soaped his body, pleasantly surprised to find his tall slim frame, which tended toward lanky, was actually hard and wiry with flat washboard abs and a delicious v which disappeared down below the water line.

'You know you're pretty fit for a teacher,' she mused.

'Don't objectify me,' his mouth curved in amusement, 'anyway, I may teach English, but I also coach the swim team.'

'Looks good on you.'

'So, you do this often?' he asked as he washed and scrubbed his hair.

'What? Roll in dead fish guts and get naked with the local teaching faculty.'

'No,' he snorted, 'bathe in the ocean. I have to say, it's a completely new experience for me.'

'I've done it a few times since I've been here,' she admitted, 'before I didn't have an alternative. This time, I didn't want to stink up the shower in the RV. It's a pretty confined space and I needed to wash Bailey too. This seemed like the best option.'

'Sensible.'

'So why the swim team?' she asked.

'It was the only sport in high school I didn't suck at,' he replied with a laugh. 'Killian ran track and field, played football and basketball. My idea of working out was turning the pages of a comic book but put me in the water and I was unstoppable.'

Ducking under the water he rinsed off the last of the shampoo and as his head broke the surface and he took a deep breath he swam over to her. He ached to reach for her, to pull her body in until they were pressed tightly to each other as they sank beneath the waves, but he didn't. He respected her boundaries even if she was the most tempting thing, he'd ever seen in his life.

They splashed and played like kids, laughing like idiots until the sun went down, the temperature dipped, and they were losing the light. Wrapped in nothing but towels, they gathered up their ruined clothes and chased each other up the stone steps to the cliff top, before finally collapsing in the back of Ava's truck, still wrapped in their towels, with Bailey spread out across their legs as they shared a bottle of Don Julio and watched the stars winking to life in the vast indigo sky.

Neither of them noticed as the front door of the house swung slightly open, nor did they see the small child like footprints and a trail of broken seashells leading into the house.

elley groaned at the loud thumping sound; his head was splitting as he threw his hand up to protect his eyes against the harsh glare of the blazing sunlight, but merely succeeded in slapping himself in the face.

He murmured a soft Ow and began to half doze once again.

He was aware of the warmth of the sun against his bare skin and the cold hard metal of the truck bed at his back. He swallowed tightly, his mouth dry and still tasting of tequila.

His arm was dead from being pinned beneath another body. He didn't need to open his eyes to know who it was. She was curled into his side, naked skin pressed to his where their towels had slipped and gone askew during the night while they'd slept or passed out drunk. He wasn't sure which had come first. At some point one of them had pulled a rough old blanket from the truck bed over them but again he couldn't quite recall who.

He could feel the heavy weight of Bailey over his legs, her body rocking slightly as her tail wagged, banging lightly against the side of the truck in a steady rhythm.

Aware he should probably move or something, he shifted

slightly but Ava mumbled something unintelligible and snuggled closer. Her hair wrapped around him in long fragrant
ropes, smelling of the sea, which once again made him think of
mermaids, which inevitably led back to him picturing her
naked in the dark water of the cove.

He'd move in a minute...

He was just drifting back off when the loud thumping
began again. It took him a second for his hungover brain to
realize it wasn't pounding inside his skull but at the side of the
truck they were currently sleeping in. Cracking open one
bloodshot eye he winced against the bright glare stabbing his
eyeball like a thousand tiny sadistic pins.

Damn Don Julio.

He felt Bailey leap up, this time her whole body wagging in
excitement as she leaned over the side of the truck. Pulling
himself up onto his elbows, Kelley blinked a couple of times as
his eyes slowly began to focus and found himself staring at a
beige clad chest and an official looking badge. His gaze slowly
traveled up the length of a freshly pressed uniform before
stopping on a familiar face shaded by a wide brimmed sheriff's
hat.

'Uh...'

'Morning Kelley,' the deep voice rumbled.

'Hi Dad...' Kelley swallowed thickly.

'DAD?' Ava shot up next to him clutching the blanket to her
chest, her eyes wide with embarrassment.

She blinked her gritty eyes a couple of times, but the hallu-
cination wouldn't clear. There was an extremely good-looking
older guy standing at the side of her truck, with the same trademark smile and green eyes as Kelley. His skin was tanned a
pleasing caramel color and his gray shot hair was combed
neatly beneath his hat.

He watched her with an unreadable expression as he petted
her dog. Bailey woofed in greeting and relished the attention.

'You must be the Miss Cortez I've been hearing so much about,' he offered his hand.

'Um humm,' she nodded slowly, her voice disappearing as she shook his hand, clutching onto the blanket for dear life in case she accidentally flashed the local Sheriff, who also appeared to be Kelley's father, apparently.

'August Ryan,' he introduced himself, 'but most folks around here call me Gus. I see you're already well acquainted with my boy.' He nodded toward Kelley who was yawning silently.

'Dad, what are you doing up here?' he squinted, wishing he had his glasses.

'Got a call from Francis down at the Pack and Plate yesterday afternoon, says there was an incident involving you, a woman and a dog.'

'Yeah sorry about that,' Kelley sat up, 'we'll go down and apologize later.'

'Oh God, I really am sorry about that,' Ava flushed. 'You can blame that giant idiot there; she can't resist fish gut aroma. If it stinks you bet your ass, she's gonna roll in it. I may never get the smell out of my truck.'

Gus laughed, a slow warm rumble in his chest as his eyes twinkled in amusement. He reached out and ruffled Bailey's fur.

'She sure is a big girl.'

'Yeah well,' Ava muttered sourly, 'she is half moose.'

He chuckled again.

'Are you two going to get dressed? Or am I going to have to haul you in for public indecency?'

'Last I checked this was private property,' Kelley replied easily.

'Tell that to your brother, who was heading up behind me with a full crew and several large trucks of equipment.'

'SHIT.' Ava's eyes widened as she leapt up and shuffled to

the end of the truck, grabbing the blanket and wrapping it around herself as she slid off the tailgate and dashed for the RV, leaving Kelley scrambling to cover himself with the small towel.

'I like her,' Gus watched as the door to the RV slammed shut. 'Make sure you bring your girl home to meet your mama.'

'She's not my girl,' he flashed a cheeky grin, 'but I'm working on it.'

'So I see,' he sighed. 'Just keep the public nudity to a minimum.'

'You got it,' he climbed down from the truck carefully, wearing nothing but the towel knotted around his waist.

'Where are your clothes?' Gus frowned.

'In the trunk of my car covered in fish guts and goop.'

Gus shook his head slowly.

'Honestly Kelley, I don't know how you get yourself into these messes sometimes. It's like the spring formal all over again.'

'Hey, that wasn't my fault,' Kelley protested.

Suddenly he felt a tug and the towel loosened around his hips. It slid from his skin and he just about managed to snag it in time, holding it up in front of himself as Bailey growled and pulled on the other end.

'Bailey, ah shit.... cut it out, will you?' he swore as he yanked hard on the towel.

She growled again playfully, her tail wagging as she enjoyed their impromptu game of tug of war.

'I'm serious,' he hissed to the dog as his father stood back with his arms crossed, his eyes filled with amusement. 'Um a little help here?'

'Sorry son,' he shook his head. 'You got yourself into this mess, you get yourself out.'

'That's just cruel,' Kelley scowled.

'It's character building,' Gus informed him.

Suddenly Kelley heard the loud blare of a horn and several

trucks rumbling into the clearing. Bailey gave a final yank and the towel slid from his grasp as he tried to cover himself.

'BAILEY!' he growled as she pranced out of reach with the spoils of war dangling from her mouth like a 1st place ribbon.

Spinning around, he searched frantically for something to cover himself with. He ended up grabbing the nearest item, which happened to be one of Ava's brand-new frying pans which were stacked next to the fire pit. He held it in front of him like a shield.

The trucks parked up one by one and doors began to open as the crew piled out, laughing openly and wondering what the hell they'd just walked into.

Killian climbed out and headed over with a wide grin, as he nodded first to his dad then to his naked twin.

'What the hell did you do this time?'

'Nothing,' Kelley replied, tilting his chin and trying for as much dignity as he could manage while wearing nothing but a kitchen utensil.

Killian lifted his phone and Kelley heard the unmistakable click.

'Oh, come on,' he whined.

'You wait till Hope sees this,' Killian snorted.

'Very responsible,' Kelley scowled. 'You know there's a very real possibility she could end up laughing her way into premature labor.'

'Thanks for the concern,' Killian smirked, 'but trust me Bean and Button aren't in any hurry, a fact Hope reminds me of at least every half hour.'

Kelley glowered at his brother as he lifted his phone and snapped another picture.

'That one's for Grandma.'

'Oh great,' Kelley rolled his eyes, 'just give the old lady a heart attack, why don't you?'

'Oh please, it's not like she hasn't seen you naked.'

'Yeah when I was like five,' Kelley snapped.

'All right that's enough you two,' Gus intervened.

The sound of a door rattling had him looking across to the RV. Killian watched the look on his brother's face with great interest as Ava climbed down the steps. She was wearing denim shorts and a tank, but her red sneakers, which were now ruined, had been replaced with army boots. She scraped her long thick wild hair back, wrapping it into a messy knot.

'Dude you're drooling,' Killian whispered in amusement.

'Huh?' Kelley replied, not listening to a word he was saying.

'What's going on?' Ava stopped in front of him and glanced down at her new frying pan.

'Bailey stole my towel,' he admitted sheepishly, 'she has a freakishly strong grip with her jaw. You sure she's not part python?'

Ava's lips twitched as she turned and tucking her fingers into her mouth, she let out the loudest, shrillest whistle he'd ever heard. After a few seconds Bailey bounded back into view still carrying the towel which now looked as if it had been chewed to death in a shark attack.

'Hand it over,' she stared Bailey down, who let out a token woof of resistance. 'Bailey,' she warned.

Trotting over reluctantly she spat the soggy mess at Kelley's feet.

He leaned down ignoring the loud wolf whistle behind his bare ass and picked up the towel, dangling it between his fingertips.

'Thanks,' he replied dryly as he stared down at the dog who looked completely unrepentant. 'I don't suppose you have another one?'

'Sorry,' Ava replied trying not to smile, 'hang on a minute though.'

She disappeared back into the RV, reappearing moments later with the small tartan blanket they'd been sharing.

'All right boys, show's over,' she dismissed them.

'She's right,' Killian decided to take pity on his brother. 'Let's get set up and get to work.'

They all moved away murmuring amongst themselves as Ava approached Kelley and stopped directly in front of him, with barely a few inches between them as she glanced down.

'That a frying pan in your pocket or are you just pleased to see me?'

'Both,' he smiled slowly.

She leaned in and wrapped the blanket around the back of him, covering his rather fine ass as he lifted the frying pan and she continued to wrap the blanket around him like a kilt.

'There,' she smiled as he handed her the frying pan, 'very William Wallace.'

'So, you do read.'

'No,' she laughed lightly, 'Mel Gibson fan.'

'Mel really?' he asked in disbelief.

''Fraid so,' she nodded.

'Thank you for coming to my rescue,' he swayed closer to her.

'You're welcome,' the barest hint of a dimple appeared in her left cheek as she looked up at him. 'Sorry I abandoned you, I panicked.'

He tucked a stray strand of hair behind her ear.

Impulsively she rose up on her toes and planted a kiss on his cheek, feeling the rough scratch of a day-old stubble against her lips.

'I think we can do better than that,' he murmured, enchanted by her.

Every thought drained from her mind as his lips pressed against her mouth, soft and warm. The whole world seemed to tilt as he wrapped his arms around her and dipped her backward sinking deeper into the kiss. It was only when she heard the familiar click of a camera, they both looked up, blinking like deer caught in a set of headlights as she still clutched the frying pan.

'That's one for the family album,' Gus grinned.

'Dad,' Kelley hissed.

'Go on,' Ava laughed and righted herself, giving him a little shove with the pan. 'You'd better go find some clothes.'

'I'll call you later,' he dropped a light kiss on her lips as he headed toward his car and climbed in.

'Well this is going to be interesting to watch,' Killian grinned to his father.

Ava turned around to find the two Ryan men watching her.

'Don't you both have something to do?' she asked pointedly, her cheeks flaming slightly with embarrassment.

'As a matter of fact, I do,' Gus adjusted his gun belt, 'dinner at our house on Sunday Miss Cortez. Kelley will pick you up.'

'Oh I...' her brow folded into a frown.

'And welcome to the island,' he patted her shoulder as he walked past.

'But I...'

'Don't bother Ava,' Killian shook his head, 'it's easier just to go along with it. Mom makes the best pot roast, and Grandma's peach cobbler is awesome, but don't tell Hope I said that. She's been trying to perfect her cobbler for the last five years and it always manages to look like it's been run over by a truck.'

'I feel like I've just been run over by a truck,' Ava frowned.

'It gets easier,' he laughed. 'Welcome to island life, where your business is everyone's business.'

'Kelley said the exact same thing,' she grumbled.

'Well in this case he's right,' Killian grabbed the frying pan she was still holding on to and began to tow her back toward the house. 'Speaking of business, I've got a friend of mine coming in on the afternoon ferry. He's an architect and trust me when I say you're going to need one. Once we get inside and shore up the structure, it's going to need some serious remodeling, but for now we'll get the fencing down and the scaffolding up. We need to get a good look at the roof. Once we're sure the house is more or less safe, we'll start ripping out the guts. We'll save anything that can be saved but from our preliminary look the other day I can't say I'm hopeful.'

'It's okay,' she shook her head, 'I'm not sentimental, and I'm also not sure I'm even keeping the house, so do what you need to do.'

He stopped and turned to stare at her.

'You not planning on staying on island then?' he asked thoughtfully.

'I don't know,' she shrugged glancing round at her cliff top. The portable restrooms were being backed into the clearing strapped to the flat bed of a beeping truck, while several big burly guys were making short work of disassembling the protective metal fences surrounding the property, stacking them up at the edge of the woods.

Her gaze trailed up the huge, gray, sooty looking building in front of her and her heart gave another dull thud. Once again, she felt that weird little tug, like someone was squeezing her solar plexus.

'It's a lot of house for just one person,' she murmured, 'what would I do with it?'

'I don't know,' Killian answered as if she'd been speaking to him, instead of musing out loud. 'Share it?'

She turned to look at him dryly, her brows rising slowly.

'Just saying,' he held up his hands, 'although, you wouldn't get Kelley through the door. He's terrified of the ghost of Luella Lynch.'

Ava rolled her eyes and shook her head.

'Is there anything I can do to help?' she asked staring back at the guys unloading planks and metal poles for the scaffolding.

'Not at the moment,' Killian raised his hand in acknowledgement, nodding as one of the men signaled for him.

'I'll come and find you later,' he told her, 'until then...'

'Stay out of the way?' she replied.

'More or less,' he grinned. 'I don't think my brother would forgive me if I let you get hurt.'

She rolled her eyes again.

'Go,' she shooed him away.

'Okay,' he backed up a few paces, 'but the same goes for your dog. Keep her out of the way for the moment; I don't want her getting injured either.'

'Got it,' she nodded as he turned and jogged toward the others.

She wandered back toward the fire pit and whistled for Bailey. She passed her time building up the fire, keeping it fairly small. The sun was high in the sky and it was roasting already. The last thing she needed was a blazing inferno, however she did want some breakfast. She set the tin kettle to warm on the edge of the fire for coffee and grabbed her oldest most battered pan.

Ten minutes later she was settled on a log seat with Bailey dozing at her feet, eating scrambled eggs and toast, watching the bustling activity around her. The old fencing quickly disappeared from the site and she watched as the metal structure was erected level by level around her building.

After the first hour of just sitting there watching, she was well and truly bored. The initial excitement had worn off and she was itching for something to do.

She set the huge metal urn she'd bought on the edge of the fire, resting it on several grapefruit sized rocks she'd collected from along the beach. Slowly it began to churn and bubble contentedly, filling the clearing with the tantalizing scent of coffee. Slowly one by one, it drew the crew and she happily plied them with coffee and bottles of water from the stack she'd bought days before.

By mid-morning an old blue Chevy Tahoe drove into the clearing pulling up alongside her truck. She watched as an old guy with a yellowing beard climbed out, removing his hat and wiping the sweat from his forehead with a bright red bandana which he shoved back into the back pocket of his jeans.

'My it's a hot one,' he smiled as he held out his hand. 'Name's Jed, from Island Market, you spoke to Martha yesterday?'

'That's right,' Ava returned his friendly smile as she shook his hand.

'Got your order in the back,' he nodded toward the car. 'Gotta say that's an awful lotta meat for such a skinny girl.'

Ava laughed, hiking a thumb over her shoulder toward the bustling crew behind her.

'Got a lot of mouths to feed.'

'So I see,' he nodded. 'So, it's true then, you fixing the place up?'

'Looks like,' she replied.

'I'm glad,' he decided after a moment. 'It was awful sad to see such a fine-looking building rotting away.'

'You not a ghost enthusiast then?' she asked.

'No Ma'am,' he turned his wide brimmed hat over in his hands before placing it back on his head to shield him from the sun beating down on his thinning hair. 'I couldn't say if there's such a thing or not, but I do hate wasted potential. That house there is part of our island history and it don't deserve such cruel neglect.'

'Well I'm glad to do my part for the island then,' Ava decided, charmed by the old man.

'Is it true you're Hari's grandkid?'

'That's right,' she replied.

'She was a fine woman,' he nodded, 'a real looker. Knew

your granddaddy some too. He was a good man, shame what happened to him.'

'I heard he died in an accident,' she replied.

'That's right,' he nodded. 'Taken too soon, God rest his soul. Still,' he changed the subject, 'where should I put this then?' He opened the back of the Tahoe to reveal several large coolers and crates.

'Just there is fine,' she indicated the shaded side of the RV.

She tried to help but Jed was having none of it. He waved her off and, in the end, she just stood and waited for him to finish.

'Thanks,' she handed him a wad of bills and shook his hand.

'You gonna be feeding them on a regular basis?' he nodded toward the crew.

'Probably,' she replied. 'I like to cook, and it gives me something to do.'

'Well you mind those boys pay you. You can't be feeding them all for free,' he warned her in a kind of sweet overprotective way, 'and you're obviously gonna be needing supplies on a regular basis, so come down to the market and we'll open you an account. Make sure you get a good discount too.'

'Thanks Jed,' she smiled genuinely as her heart softened, 'that's really kind.'

'Well you're part of the island now, Miss Cortez and we take care of our own.'

'Ava,' she corrected, 'please.'

'Ava it is then,' he nodded as he climbed back into his car and leaned out of the open window. 'Now make sure you stop by; I'll tell Martha to expect you.'

'I will,' she promised, standing back as he drove away.

Wasting no time, Ava broke open the new barbecue she'd purchased the day before, eager to play with her new toy.

Before long she'd set up a folding table, fired up the grill and was cooking up a storm.

KILLIAN ROUNDED the corner of the building. He'd spent the last half hour inspecting the glass summer house at the back of the property, but as he approached all he could see was a cluster of his men gathered around, near Ava's truck and RV. He headed over to see what was going on when he caught the smell of something delicious wafting on the breeze.

The crowd parted and he found Ava in the middle of them, beside a folding table which was piled high with salad, drinks, condiments, plates and napkins. Ava herself was standing beside a grill upon which were dozens of fat, sizzling sausages and burgers.

'Hey Killian,' she greeted him as she handed a plate to another of his men, 'you hungry?'

'I am now,' he stopped in front of her. 'What's all this?'

'Lunch,' she replied easily, 'I figured y'all would be hungry.'

'Ava you don't have to do this.'

'I know,' she shrugged as she flipped the burgers, 'but I wanted to. It gets tedious just cooking for myself. Besides its going to get pretty boring around here, if all I'm doing is watching you guys play with power tools.'

He laughed and shook his head, 'well at least tell me these bums are paying you.'

'What? No way,' she replied, 'it's on me. It's the least I can do.'

'Are you crazy Ava?' Killian answered incredulously. 'It's not like we're doing you a favor, you're paying us a lot of money to fix the place up.'

'I know,' she smiled.

'Don't worry boss we got it covered,' a gruff voice cut through the crowd.

Killian turned to look and saw his foreman Bo holding a large can stuffed with bills and loose change.

'Here you go Ma'am,' he set the can down on the edge of the table.

'You didn't have to do that.'

'Fair's fair, Miss Cortez. You feed us, you get paid, although you may come to regret it. They're like a pack of stray dogs. Feed 'em once and they'll keep coming back for more.'

Ava laughed delightedly.

'I think I can handle that, and its Ava,' she handed him a plate loaded with food.'

'Thank you, Ma'am,' he smiled, 'Ava,' he corrected at her raised brow.

'Looks like you're gonna be a hit around here,' Killian looked over at the grill with interest. Shoving his hand in his pocket he came up with a handful of bills and dumped them in the pot.

'What do you want to drink?' she asked.

'I'll take a soda,' he replied as she loaded up a plate for him.

'You want potato salad with that?'

'Sure,' he watched as she scooped it out of a large mixing bowl and dolloped a generous amount on the side of his paper plate.

'You make that from scratch?' he wondered out loud.

'Only way to make potato salad,' she handed him the plate and a napkin.

He took a mouthful and sighed in pleasure. The meat was perfectly cooked with just a slight smoky taste, the rolls were fresh, the salad crisp and the potato salad was just pure creamy deliciousness. He chewed slowly as he glanced around thoughtfully, taking in the whole set up she had going on. It was industrious; there wasn't any power anywhere. She'd made use of the fire pit and the grill, cooking confidently on an open flame like she'd done it a thousand times before. She easily chatted with his men as she kept up a steady pace, never burning anything. She had a talent for feeding people, he could almost see the little love hearts in his guys' eyes as they thanked her and ate her food.

'You fixing to do this on a regular occasion?' Killian asked.

'That's the plan,' she nodded as she handed out the last plate and began to clean up the mess.

'We've got some portable generators coming up this afternoon. We can't get the house wired into the main grid until the whole property's weatherproof, so we're having to bring the power with us. We'll rig you up some over this side of the clearing.'

'That would be great,' Ava replied enthusiastically.

'You need some kind of cover too,' he mused. 'You can't prepare food out in the full sun, so maybe a canopy of some sort. I'll have something fixed up for you by tomorrow.'

'You don't have to do that,' she replied as she began to stuff used plates into a large trash bag, 'you've got enough to do.'

'It's the least we can do,' Killian shook his head. 'You look after us, we look after you. That's how it goes.'

Her heart gave another helpless tug and she blew out a breath. She was in very real danger of falling in love with the whole damn island at this rate.

Saved from having to form a response, Ava looked over at the sound of another vehicle driving onto the site. This time it was a sleek silver sports car.

'Flashy bastard,' Killian grinned as the car pulled in and parked. A tall guy of medium build with sandy blonde hair climbed out, wearing a button-down shirt with the sleeves rolled to his elbows and tailored slacks. He peered at them from behind a pair of Ray Bans and waved.

'Drew!' Killian placed his empty plate down and wiped his hands.

'Did I just miss lunch?' he grinned as he confidently sauntered over.

'I can fix you a plate if you're hungry?' Ava offered. 'There's still some left.'

'No thank you sweetheart,' he removed his glasses and tucked them into the collar of his shirt, 'I've had lunch. You must be Ava?'

'That's right,' she wiped her hand on her denim shorts before offering it to the pristinely dressed man in front of her.

'Andrew Duffy,' he smiled warmly as he shook her hand, 'but please, call me Drew.' He glanced up at the house and whistled. 'She sure is a beauty.'

'Yeah the house isn't bad either,' Killian laughed and elbowed Ava good naturedly, causing her to roll her eyes.

'Are you the architect then?' she continued to clean up.

'Sure am,' he leaned back against his car, 'and I can't wait to get my hands on your house. It's a dream to work on an original Talbot.'

'Talbot?' she questioned.

'George Isaiah Talbot. He was practically the Michelangelo of 19th century architecture. He was born in England but moved to Boston as a young man. Some of his Victorian follies are just gorgeous, but buildings this size? He only built a few of them and this one is extra special because it was his private residence. He built it specifically for himself but after he died, his son, who didn't have half his talent but had a lot of gambling debts, was forced to sell it, to your ancestor I believe, Ephraim Lynch.'

'So I'm told,' she replied.

'He must have been very shrewd,' Drew nodded. 'I've seen the bill of sale and he bought the house for well under its actual value. Talbot's son must have been desperate.'

'That's a sad legacy.'

'Isn't it?' Drew agreed. 'Anyway, I'm itching to see how much of the original features have survived. I've tried to track down the original blueprints to the building but so far, no luck, which is really strange. All of Talbot's blueprints were preserved and archived, every single last one of everything he ever built, except this particular house.'

'Is that strange?' Ava shrugged, 'I mean it was over a hundred and what...fifty years ago?'

'We'll see, won't we,' Drew replied. 'I've got my people trying to track them down.'

'Will it matter if we don't have the original blueprints?'

'It would make my job easier if I had access to the originals, not to mention more interesting, but I can do without them. It just complicates thing a little as I'll have to measure everything by hand.'

'So, what now?'

'Now,' Drew pushed away from the car and leaned in, retrieving a hard hat, a folder, and several other items, 'now we take a little stroll through your house and make some notes.' He turned to look at Killian. 'Can we go in?'

'Sure,' he nodded, 'just be careful. Stick to the ground level for now. We've got most of the supports in; fortunately, the main structure's still pretty solid. The boarding is just coming off the windows now so you should have some natural light to work with. We'll tell you when you'll be able to get a look at the upper levels, but it probably won't be today.'

'I can work with that,' Drew nodded. 'Ava? You ready?'

'Wait,' Killian asked, 'where's Bailey?'

'Asleep in the RV,' she replied. 'She'd have gone nuts while I was cooking sausages.'

'Okay,' he nodded in satisfaction.

'Who's Bailey?' Drew asked.

'My dog,' she answered easily. 'Just give me a moment will you. I need to finish cleaning up before we go in.'

'No problem,' he leaned back against the car and watched

her as she bustled around, storing food and picking up empty paper plates.

'You may as well pop your eyes back in there, pal,' Killian leaned against the car beside him. 'Kelley's already staked a claim.'

'Damn,' Drew's eyes trailed down her long, tanned legs. 'You Ryans have all the luck.'

Killian grinned. 'Hope says hi by the way.'

'Does she?' he glanced across at his friend. 'You know I should hate you for marrying my prom date and knocking her up.'

'Hey,' he smiled, 'it was your choice to leave the island for the bright lights and big city.'

'Yeah and I'm beginning to think I might've made a mistake,' his eyes landed on Ava.

'Really?'

'No,' Drew smiled. 'As tempting as that tall drink of water is, I'm happy where I am.'

'Okay I'm all done,' Ava headed back over to them, taking the hard hat Killian offered her and putting it on.

Drew chuckled and shook his head.

'What?' Ava asked.

'You even look good in that ugly yellow plastic.'

'Hey, yellow worked for Snow White,' she relied.

'So it did,' he pushed away from the car. 'Come on then princess, let's go fix your castle.'

She smiled widely at him and for a second, he had to stop and blink. It was like being blinded by the sun and the hell of it was, that she wasn't even aware she was doing it.

'It's lethal, isn't it?' Killian murmured, 'that smile of hers.'

'Your brother doesn't stand a chance,' Drew laughed in delight.

Ava headed toward the house. She could see the boards being prized from the lower windows and was eager to get another look inside, this time in bright daylight. Killian disappeared leaving her solely in the company of Drew whose entire attention was fixed on the house in front of him with an almost reverent focus.

They climbed the stone steps, bypassing the lion statues and rusted metal lamps, and headed toward the front entrance, which was wide open, with work crews wandering in and out, still carrying large planks of wood and metal scaffolding poles.

Once again, just as it did the first time, as she entered the house Ava felt that tiny shift, so faint she wondered if she were imagining it. But the air felt somehow heavier, like it was heavy with static electricity.

'Can you feel that?' she asked Drew.

'Feel what?' he murmured staring up at the huge staircase which split and curved up either side of the foyer to a second-floor balcony.

The was a loud, splintering sound behind them and the foyer was suddenly flooded with light.

'Wow,' Ava murmured looking up at the huge columns supporting the staircase.

Her gaze drifted slowly down to the floor and her eyes widened. There was a huge canvas rug with a delicate floral design at its center and around the edges. Beneath it was an incredibly complex tiled floor, decorated with geometric shapes.

'This is perfect,' Drew kneeled down to study the tile, 'and mostly undamaged. You're going to want to save this. Help me move this rug, will you?'

'What do you think that is?' Ava asked as she eyed a huge, circular, black tar like stain in the center of the rug.

'I'm not sure,' he glanced up toward the ceiling looking for any signs of a leak, 'could be anything. Let's move it out, I want a better look at the flooring.'

They each grabbed a corner of the rug and began to fold it

over, dragging it to the edge of the foyer to be taken outside, but as Ava glanced back, she realized the stain was still in the same place. Whatever it was, had obviously gone through the rug and onto the floor where, instead of appearing black, it had an almost reddish, rust colored hue to it.

'I wonder what it is?' Drew frowned as he pulled out his phone and took several pictures, not only of the stain itself but the entire floor, including close ups of the patterned tiles. 'It looks like dried blood.'

'Very cheerful,' Ava shook her head.

'Maybe an injured animal got in,' he mused, 'or maybe something leaked from above. Anyway, whatever it is there's a good chance once we identify it, we'll be able to clean it and restore the original tiles. If you just wait here a moment, I'll grab Killian and get him to pack some protective layers down, so they don't get damaged with all the foot traffic moving through here.'

She nodded as he disappeared out the front door, dragging the old stained rug with him. She stood waiting patiently for him, staring absently at the peeling wallpaper, when a movement up on the second-floor balcony caught the corner of her eye.

She turned to look but couldn't see anything. Losing interest, she was about to head back out to find Drew when she heard a quiet patter, almost like a bounce. She shifted over, moving closer to the stairs and through the banisters saw a small round object rolling slowly down the steps. She watched mesmerized as it hit the ground, bounced a couple of times and rolled across the tiles, stopping when it hit her boot.

Reaching down she picked it up and turned it over in her palm. It was the same brown leather baseball she'd left lying in the tall grass outside, she was sure of it. She lifted her fingers and traced the rough scarred letters burned into the skin of the ball. It had to be the same one. What were the chances of there being two identical balls? And what was it doing inside the house?

She heard another noise, like a shuffle from the balcony above and looked up. For a split second she could have sworn she saw... suddenly she felt a hand grasp her shoulder and she nearly jumped out of her skin.

'Sorry... sorry!' Drew held his hands up as she spun around, grasping the ball in her fist. 'I didn't mean to scare you, I called but you were a million miles away.'

'It's okay,' a half laugh rushed out on a heavy breath. 'Do you know if there are any work crews upstairs on the second floor?'

'Not that I know of,' he shook his head. 'As far as I know they're all busy checking and re-enforcing all the rooms down here first. Why?'

'Nothing,' she shook her head glancing at the strange ball, 'no reason,' she frowned. 'What do you want to look at first?'

'Let's start with the right wing,' he nodded toward a door, before walking purposefully toward it and leaving her to trail along in his wake. 'This would have originally been the front parlor, mostly used for receiving guests, although I can see that it was adapted as a school room.' He wandered through the scattered rows of single wooden desks with hinged lids and attached seats.

The flooring in this room was partially obscured by tides of dry decayed leaves which had obviously blown in through the broken windows sometime before the place was boarded up.

Ava leaned down and picked up a small rectangular slate board. Eerily, it still had the first few letters of the alphabet scrawled across it in a child's untidy looping lines.

'There's quite a few damaged windowpanes,' Drew studied the frames, 'but I think they can be salvaged. I know a guy who specializes in these old sash windows.'

'That sounds like a lot of work,' she carefully set the slate board on one of the desks.

'It is,' he agreed, 'but trust me, things like the windows and roof tiles you want to save if you can, so it's in keeping with the period of the property. New ones just wouldn't suit the aesthetic of the building.'

'I guess,' Ava hummed. 'I suppose I haven't really thought about it.'

'Well now's as good a time as any,' he pulled out a small handheld object and pressed a small button, emitting a thin red light across the room to the opposite wall. He stared at it for a second then scribbled something in his notebook.

'What's that?' she asked curiously.

'A laser measuring tape,' he replied as he continued to take different measurements of the room and scribble them down in his book along with a roughly sketched floorplan. 'I'm still hoping to get my hands on the original blueprints, but if I can't I'm going to have to try and make temporary ones. Anyway, you were about to tell me your plans for the building.'

'I was?'

'You must have some idea of what you want to achieve here,' he stopped scribbling and looked up at her.

'Not even in the slightest,' she admitted. 'This is all still pretty new to me. I didn't even know this house existed until a month ago.'

'Do you plan on living here?'

'I don't know,' she frowned. 'Sorry, I know I'm not being much help.'

'That's okay,' he shook his head. 'Don't worry, we'll figure it out. A lot of the time these kinds of projects are a work in progress anyway. How about we start with the basics? Do you want to completely modernize or stay true to the original building?'

'A little of both I guess,' she chewed her lip thoughtfully. 'I want to save as much of the original features as I can, I think it would be a shame not to, but also it needs some modernizing. I doubt whoever ends up living here will want to pump water from a rather questionable well.'

'Well you're right about that,' he laughed, 'so we'll restore the exterior, the windows and the roof and keep it as close to the original design as we can. Inside is a different matter. Once the building is weathertight, we'll install electricity and plumbing. You'll want modern bathrooms and half baths on each floor, depending on how many bedrooms there are. Likewise, you'll want a new modern kitchen and heating. Once we've got a layout of the interior, we can have a look at each room. There is some leeway for moving interior walls and changing the layout but that will be up to you.'

'Okay,' she nodded.

'Shall we continue then?' he indicated toward a doorway at the far end of the room.

'Sure,' she replied following along behind him.

For the most part she watched him work. They uncovered a scullery, a butler's pantry, another parlor and a gorgeous metal framed sunroom with huge paneled windows reaching high above in a dome shape, not only letting in the light but giving an incredible view of the headland for miles in each direction and out across the ocean.

Ava wandered from room to room, the curious little baseball clutched in her hand as Drew measured and muttered and drew rough sketches and illustrations in his book. Content to just wander through the rooms she was amazed at just how much of the original features had survived. It was like walking through a time capsule.

'Ava!' Killian's voice called from one of the other rooms, 'there's another delivery for you!'

Excusing herself from Drew who was still lost in his work she navigated her way through the confusing maze of rooms, and sub rooms, and adjoining rooms, and finally found herself back in the front foyer. Dodging all the workmen she hurried out of the main entrance and down the steps, to find herself standing in front of a small van with 'Elodie's Flowers for Every Occasion' splashed across the side in delicate swirling baby pink lettering.

'Miss Cortez?' a gangly teenager asked, his voice a little squeaky as if it wasn't quite done breaking yet. Likewise, his arms and legs seemed too long for his body and his face was scattered with fine red pimples.

'That's me,' she nodded.

'Sign here please,' he thrust a clipboard and pen at her, dark crimson slashing across his cheekbones as he tried not to look at her long, tanned legs.

Signing it quickly she handed it back and watched curiously as he leaned into the van and pulled out a huge bouquet of brightly colored flowers in shades of blue and green.

She barely noticed as the embarrassed teen climbed back into the van and peeled out of the clearing. Her eyes were fixed on the flowers, a huge smile creasing her cheeks. Nestled between all the pretty flowers, mounted on thin sticks, were little cardboard cut outs of frying pans, fish heads and tails, and mermaids.

She pulled out the card, although she didn't need to read it to know who it was from.

Thinking of you X

She climbed up into the RV closing the door behind her, not wanting anyone to see as she pressed her face into the flowers and inhaled the sweet scent. She wasn't sure what most of the flowers were, only that they were pretty and that no one had ever given her flowers before. Well other than the strange little posy of hand-picked flowers and seashells someone had left the day before.

She set Kelley's flowers down on the seat and reached for

the wildflowers, frowning in confusion. The mug was still filled with water but the tiny little purple bell-shaped flowers which had been fresh and vibrant only the day before, were now brittle and dead. She reached out to touch one, watching as it crumbled against her fingers.

Her eyes widened as she looked down at the table to find that the beautiful tiny seashells, she'd piled neatly next to the flowers, had crumbled away and were now nothing more than a pile of dust.

10

*I*t had been two days and he hadn't stopped thinking about her. He found himself slightly jealous that his twin got to spend every day with her while he worked on that huge creepy ass house of hers. The jealousy was only made worse when he found out Drew was back in town and that he was working on the Lynch house too.

They'd gone to school together, the three of them, Drew, Killian and Kelley. Only Drew had been captain of the football team and had a notorious reputation with the ladies. He'd been like love heroin to the girls of Midnight High back then; he'd gone through the entire cheerleading squad, the gymnastics team and half the swim team too. It seemed Drew had a type, and it was stunningly beautiful with a tight, toned, athletic body. Everything Ava was, dammit.

He'd wanted to go see her since the moment he'd driven away wrapped in nothing but an old thin tartan blanket. That had sure given his neighbors something to gossip about as he'd strolled into his apartment, but every time he'd tried to get away his uncle had demanded his attention.

He loved the man but jeez, he was obsessive about his beloved bar. He was only a week away from his surgery now, which meant he was in a lot of pain, he was frustrated and just straight up bad tempered. Everything Kelley did was wrong; despite the fact he was giving up all his free time to run the damn bar. Free time he could have spent with Ava; free time, that Drew was spending with her.

His fingers gripped the wheel as he drove slowly up the winding road, pulling over as a truck ambled down in his direction. Once it had passed, he started back up toward the cliff top. Pulling into the clearing he eased his car toward Ava's truck only to find there wasn't much space.

Now, instead of just the RV, the truck and the fire pit, there was a large square canvas canopy set up with tables covered with condiments, plate, cups and coffee urns. Dozens of mismatched plastic tables and folding chairs were set up like a little alfresco dining area, and over the fire pit was a metal stand with two huge flying saucer shaped pans sizzling side by side.

His mouth was watering by the time he found a place to park and climbed out. The sweet and spicy scent of something wickedly delicious filled the warm summer air as he strolled over.

Ava was standing in front of the fire her skin flushed from the heat, her midnight hair tied back with a lavender colored bandana and a chef's apron tied over her trademark denim shorts.

'Hey,' he greeted as she looked up and smiled at him.

'Hey,' she continued to stir each of the pans simultaneously.

'That smells incredible,' he inhaled deeply as he peered over the edge of the nearest pan.

'Today it's burritos,' she replied easily, 'served with braised bean rice. You have a choice of chili or Cajun chicken as a filling, and there's also fresh sour cream, fresh guacamole and homemade salsa. You hungry?'

'Yeah,' he murmured watching her as he unconsciously rubbed his belly, although whether he was hungry for the mouth-watering food or the temping woman serving it, he wasn't entirely sure.

'Take a seat,' she nodded to a nearby table.

He watched her as he slid onto the faded plastic chair. Gone was the guarded wariness she'd displayed since arriving on the island. He'd never seen her so relaxed and happy as she pulled tortillas wrapped in foil from where they were warming by the fire and began to load them with crisp salad, rice, meat and sour cream.

'You want a bit of everything?' she glanced up.

'Please,' he nodded.

'Thanks Ava,' a huge thickly muscled guy with a dark beard dropped a handful of bills into a huge can on a nearby table. 'Best burritos I've ever had.'

She beamed her cheeks flushed with pleasure.

'You're welcome Luke, tell Aiden he's going to miss out if he doesn't hurry.'

'Will do,' he nodded.

'You've got quite a little industry going on here,' Kelley nodded to the overflowing pot of cash.

'What? oh that,' she laughed. 'They wouldn't take no for an answer. I kept telling them they didn't have to pay me, but they insisted on contributing toward supplies.'

'Here,' she slid the plate onto the table in front of him along with a soda. 'I haven't seen you around for a few days, you been busy?' she asked casually as she threw a couple of empty plates into a huge trash can and began to wipe down one of the tables.

'My uncle's getting a bit antsy waiting for his surgery,' Kelley cracked open the can of soda and took a swig. 'He's been micromanaging every single decision I've made regarding the bar. I think he's just nervous about the surgery and riding me takes his mind off it.'

'Yeah your dad said.'

'My dad?'

Ava nodded across to another table and as Kelley glanced over her shoulder, he saw his father sat comfortably, his hat resting beside his plate, his hands filled with a burrito and his cheeks puffed out like a squirrel as he chewed. He managed a half grin and a thumbs up in Kelley's direction before he turned his attention back to his lunch.

'He hasn't missed a meal,' Ava laughed, 'I'm beginning to think he likes my cooking. Yesterday it was Tuscan chicken with Italian herb rice and warmed ciabatta. He had two helpings.'

Kelley shook his head, a smile curving the corner of his mouth as he lifted the tightly packed burrito and took a huge bite, moaning in appreciation as a myriad of flavors instantly burst across his tongue.

'Marry me,' he mumbled around his mouthful of food.

Ava laughed in amusement.

'I hate to burst your bubble there, pal,' Killian slid onto the seat next to him, 'but our Ava here gets twenty proposals a day around here.'

'Our Ava?' Kelley's brow rose.

'We've staked our claim, she's ours. She has to stay here and cook for us forever.'

'How's it coming along?' Ava asked in amusement as she slid a loaded plate in front of Killian.

He leaned in and breathed deeply, before lifting the huge cigar shaped roll and biting out a massive chunk.

'Ummm,' he chewed slowly, 'I think you've outdone your-self this time.'

'Wait till you try my chicken Po'boy with Asian style vegetables.'

'Now you're just teasing,' he took another bite as she

laughed. 'It's coming along well. All the supports are in place on the second and third floors, and the scaffolding's complete. She's sturdy as a rock now. We'll be back up on the roof taking a closer look at the damage this afternoon, though we were up there this morning and found something strange.'

'What?' Ava asked in interest.

'They look like air shafts,' he replied with a slight wrinkle of his forehead. 'I've never seen anything like it on this type of building. We can't figure out where they run to or why you would need them.'

'That is a bit weird I guess,' Ava mused.

'Anyway, I want to go back up and get a closer look, see if I can figure it out. We're going to start removing the roof tiles to get a better look at what's underneath, but it looks as if the whole roof will need to be replaced. Most of the beams are rotten. While we're doing that, we'll also begin to cement back in any of the loose bricks in the exterior façade. Some of the mortar has crumbled away on the topmost window arches of the tower.

We'll start removing the windows and packing them up for transport. It seems Drew's window guy has just taken on a partner which has freed up some of his time, so he's agreed to restore all your windows. But given the sheer number of them, it'll take a while and we really need them back in before the weather turns.'

'Can I get back in the building this afternoon then?' she asked as she continued to tidy away plates and wipe down tables.

'You actually spend time in there?' Kelley asked.

'Most afternoons,' she nodded, 'if I'm not in the way. Drew's in the middle of drawing up the plans for the build and I'm looking for inspiration. At the moment the interior is divided up into lots of smaller rooms and we're toying with the idea of opening a few of them up into larger living spaces.'

'Uh huh,' Kelley replied slowly.

'You should come with me,' she told him. 'You need to get over this fear of yours and realize there's no ghosts.'

'That's what they want you to think, then they wait until you're alone...'

'You should have been writing novels rather than teaching English with that imagination of yours,' she shook her head. 'I mean if you're too scared...'

'You calling me chicken?' his eyes narrowed.

'If the feathers fit.'

'Fine,' he replied flatly.

'Fine,' she repeated in amusement, 'you can come trash picking with me.'

'Trash picking?' his brow rose questioningly.

'There's loads of stuff left in the house,' she explained, 'a lot of it damaged to varying degrees. So, I've been collecting it all up and sorting what can be saved or not.'

'What sort of things?'

'Framed photographs, paintings, candlesticks, ornaments, and I found a carriage clock yesterday. China, silverware, just general stuff you'd find in a house of this size, only most of it dates back to the late 19th century and I kinda feel like I have a responsibility to save as much of it as I can. Even if it doesn't end up back in the house, I could always donate it to a museum or something.'

'Sounds fascinating,' Kelley leaned in closer his eyes afire with curiosity. 'So it's like treasure hunting?'

'Something like that.'

'Cool,' he grinned, 'okay I'm in.'

'Your storage shed should be arriving tomorrow so I'll pull a couple of the guys to assemble it for you,' Killian told her as he finished the last of his burrito and wiped his mouth on a paper napkin, tossing it on the plate. 'Then you can start storing stuff from the house in there.'

'Thanks,' she grinned before turning to Kelley. 'Everyone's pretty much done. Give me a little time to clean up and I'll show you the house.'

'Sure,' he nodded.

'I can't believe you actually let her talk you into going into the house,' Killian shook his head. 'That place terrified you as a kid, you had nightmares about it for years.'

A fact Kelley was well aware of, but if she kept smiling at him like that, with that little whisper of a dimple in her left cheek, he was pretty sure he'd probably follow her into Freddie Kruger's boiler room and not bat an eyelid.

'I hope you boys are behaving yourselves,' Gus wandered over.

'Well Kelley's wearing clothes, so I consider that progress,' Killian smirked.

Kelley threw him a withering look.

'If that girl keeps cooking like this, I'm going to have to take the old belt down a notch,' he patted his full stomach comfortably.

'Hey Dad,' Kelley glanced up at him as he rested against the back of his chair, 'can you stop in on Uncle Dusty later. He's approaching a major freak out. He was talking about cancelling his surgery.'

'Oh, that Dustin,' Gus shook his head, 'he never did like the doctor's office, even when we were kids. He's even worse with hospitals, that's why it's taken him so long to get his knee looked at.'

'Yeah well, he's a nightmare. I get that he's worried but he's driving me insane. It's not like I don't have anything better to do than run his bar for him. Don't get me wrong I'm happy to help, but the constant criticism is getting a bit much.'

'I'll talk to him,' Gus nodded. 'Anyway, I'd better head back; I'll see you later.'

'Bye Dad,' Killian mumbled, watching as their father set his hat back on his head and strolled back to his squad car, whistling casually. 'I'd better get back to work too.'

Kelley watched as his brother stood up and rummaged around in the pocket of his jeans before stuffing some bills into the can.

Unfolding himself from the chair he did the same, noticing just how much money she had in the can. He let out a low whistle.

'It's a nice little business you've got going for yourself here,' Kelley remarked.

'Oh, it's not a business,' Ava shook her head as she continued to scrub the large pans clean, 'I just like to cook. The boys are just paying for the groceries.'

'Ava do you have any idea how much you've made?' he asked curiously.

She shrugged her shoulders.

'I don't know,' she rinsed off the pans and utensils and set them to dry in the sun. 'I just shoved the can in the RV with the other ones. I haven't counted any of them yet.'

He'd never met anyone before who was so supremely unconcerned about money.

'Have you thought about doing this as a business?'

'What? Cooking?' she frowned. 'It's not really worth it. Once the building work's finished, I won't have anyone left to feed.'

'I wouldn't be so sure about that,' Kelley smiled, 'but I meant have you thought about setting up your own little place in town?'

'Like a restaurant?'

'Why not?' he shrugged.

Ava laughed as she untied her apron and hung it over the table.

'Honestly I wouldn't know where to start. I like to cook, that's the beginning, middle and end of my skill set.'

He watched as she snagged a couple of hard hats and placed one on his head.

'Come on, I wanna show you the haunted house,' she grinned.

'That's not funny.'

'It kinda is,' she grabbed his hand and towed him toward the house.

'Where's Bailey anyway,' he glanced around. 'I would've expected to be mauled to death by now.'

'She's in the RV,' Ava shook her head and sighed. 'She's not very happy about it but a construction site is not really a good place to let her roam free.'

'Uh huh,' Kelley murmured as he stopped at the top of the stone steps and stared up at the building.

'It's okay,' she whispered, 'I won't let anything happen to you.'

'Hey, I'm working with decades of childhood fears here,' he cast a dry look in her direction before sucking in a deep breath. 'Okay I can do this.'

'Sure you can,' she replied softly without a hint of teasing as her hand tightened reassuringly in his.

'Okay,' he exhaled loudly, and lifting his foot he stepped over the threshold into the foyer. 'Whoa, did you feel that?' he murmured.

'What?' she looked up at him curiously.

'Nothing, I guess,' he frowned. 'It just seemed... never mind, it's probably that overactive imagination of mine.'

'It feels like low pressure, like the air before a storm, somehow heavier,' she told him softly.

'Yeah,' he replied as he stared at her thoughtfully, 'that's it exactly.'

'Strange,' she muttered, 'no one else seems to be able to feel it.'

'Guess that means we've both got overactive imaginations,' he smiled down at her.

'Come on, I'll show you around.'

She kept his hand in hers as she steered him through the lower rooms, past the parlor which had been converted into a school room, an old billiards room, the music room with a damaged piano, through the scullery and servants' quarters, until they reached another door.

'What's in there?' he asked curiously.

'I don't know if I should show you,' she winced, 'being an English teacher and a lover of books and all that.'

Even more curious now, he stepped through the doorway down into what looked like a library, except all the glass fronted cabinets stood empty with their doors flung open, and the floor was littered with the corpses of damaged books.

'Damn,' he whispered.

'Yeah,' Ava stepped further into the room, wandering past the half empty bookcases to where an old, heavy desk stood not quite in the center of the room.

She stood and stared out into the room, an unreadable expression marring her features.

'What?' Kelley asked as he followed her into the room.

'Nothing,' she shook her head.

'Tell me,' he stopped in front of her.

'It's just,' she sighed, 'I keep trying to see it.'

'See what?'

'The house,' she frowned, trying to find the words to explain. 'Drew keeps asking me what I want to do with it, what my vision is of how it should look and no matter how hard I try I just can't see it.'

'That's not a bad thing Ava,' he replied. 'You don't have to have all the answers.'

'You wanna know something stupid?'

'Sure,' he smiled, 'I love stupid.'

That earned a small smile, followed by a wistful sigh.

'My whole life, all I've ever wanted was a home.'

He wasn't sure what he was expecting her to say but that quiet, heartfelt admission tore at his heart. He'd had a home, filled with love and surrounded by a big, noisy, interfering family, which apparently, he'd taken for granted.

'A home?'

'Serenity loved to move around a lot,' she shook her head. 'The wanderlust she called it. It was always a new place, a new town, a new city, a new commune, new faces. Nothing ever stayed the same. I'd make friends and then she'd just uproot me again. Sometimes I almost hated her for it. In the end I just stopped making friends, it hurt too much when I had to leave.'

'I'm sorry,' he frowned, 'that sounds like a lonely way to grow up.'

'It wasn't all bad,' Ava shrugged. 'Serenity loved me, in her own way, but I would lie on the ground on whatever sleeping pallet I could find, sometimes if I was lucky I got an actual bed, and I would dream of a home of my own, one that I never had to leave.'

'That's understandable,' he murmured.

'But do you know what I've just realized?'

'What?'

'That in all the time I had this dream of having a home, I never once pictured what it would look like,' she replied in confusion. 'Now I'm faced with the very real possibility of actually having a home and I still can't picture it. I'm beginning to think there's something wrong with me. That maybe I am just a nomad like my mom.'

'There's nothing wrong with you Ava,' he took her arms gently, so she was facing him and tilted her chin up until their eyes met. 'Have you ever thought that maybe it wasn't the house you were dreaming of, but the sense of belonging.'

'I don't understand,' she frowned.

'Ava, a home is more than just bricks and mortar, its more than picking out window treatments and fancy furniture. It's the people around you, who love you. People you know you can count on to be there for you, a place in the community. I watched you out there, and it was more than you just cooking for a few people, it was you making a connection, making a place for yourself.

It's all right there in front of you if you really want it, if you're brave enough to step up and take it. So, you don't know what color you want to paint the walls, okay. So, you don't even know where you want to put said walls, big deal. What matters is deciding whether or not you belong here on the island with us.'

'Kelley,' she murmured.

'Of course,' he grinned, 'selfishly I want you to stay just so I can have another chance at getting you naked, this time hopefully without a wet dog and an ocean between us.'

She laughed and a little of the heaviness on her shoulders lifted. She opened her mouth to speak when she suddenly heard a loud cracking sound.

'What was that?' she asked worriedly.

The sound came again, alarmingly close.

They both looked down at the floor between their feet, where a large jagged crack suddenly appeared in the parquet flooring. She barely had time to look up, her eyes widening in shock as they locked on to Kelley's, when the floor suddenly splintered and gave way, and the next thing they knew they were both falling.

In that one terrifying moment of freefall, surrounded by darkness, she felt Kelley's arms wrap around her protectively and then they hit the ground.

Somehow, he'd managed to cushion her fall, although it had still knocked the wind out of her. She rolled off him, coughing through the dust and debris which had been thrown up into the air with their combined impact.

'Kelley?' she croaked as she groped for him in the darkness, 'Kelley, are you okay?' She coughed again.

For one terrifying moment in the blackness and silence, her heart almost stopped, fearing the worst, until he groaned and rolled over.

'Kelley,' she breathed in relief as he moved.

'What the hell?' he looked up at the gaping hole above them. 'WATCH OUT!' he suddenly yelled, grabbing her in the darkness and rolling her underneath him as he shielded her from more splintered wood, old books and debris that showered down on them.

There was a loud, ominous, grinding sound and the heavy old desk toppled into the hole, wedging its massive bulk in the opening, suspended precariously above them. They both looked up in horror as it slid another inch closer to them, dislodging a fresh shower of splinters and dirt.

'AVA MOVE!' Kelley grabbed her roughly and dragged her across the floor as he scrambled back, cocooning her with his body. The desk crashed through the floor and smashed to the ground, narrowly missing them by inches and throwing up a fresh cloud of sharp splinters and choking dust.

'AVA! KELLEY!' Killian's voice shouted desperately through the wide gap. 'GET SOME ROPE AND FLASHLIGHTS, I CAN'T SEE A THING!' he yelled loudly to his crew. 'AVA! KELLEY! CAN YOU HEAR ME?'

Kelley shifted as the dust subsided, reaching for Ava in the darkness.

'Ava?' he whispered urgently, 'are you okay? Are you hurt?'

'I'm okay,' she wheezed, 'a little banged up but I'm alright.'

He blew out a deep breath. Unable to see her, he reached out for her and cupped her face to assure himself she really was okay, pressing his forehead to hers in relief.

Killian's frantic voice came again through the ragged hole above them.

'We're okay,' Kelley called up, as he helped Ava stand on shaky legs.

'Jesus Christ Kelley,' Killian's voice was filled with relief. 'I'm gonna kill you for shaving the next ten years off my life.'

'Yeah?'

Ava could hear the grin in Kelley's voice.

'Come down here and say that.'

'Don't tempt me,' he replied irritably.

'Ava?' Killian called, 'are you okay?'

'Yeah,' she replied, 'Kelley broke my fall.'

'Good to know that hard head of his is good for something,' he grumbled. 'Hold on we'll get you out of there.'

'Kelley,' Ava called to him softly, as she ran her hand along the wall and felt smooth wood and ridges. 'This is wood paneling; I think we're in another room.'

'Killian!' Kelley shouted up, 'drop down a couple of flashlights so we can see where we are.'

'Okay,' came the reply, 'heads up.'

Ava watched as Killian switched on each of the flashlights and dropped them down the hole, one by one. Kelley caught them easily and handed one to her as he scanned their surroundings.

They weren't in a room but a corridor, with a faded red runner along the wooden floor, dark wood paneling along the walls and candle sconces mounted at intervals to the end, where there was a closed door.

'I knew it,' Kelley shook his head. 'I told you there were hidden rooms and passages beneath the house.'

'Yeah, yeah,' Ava frowned, 'let's just hope you're not right about anything else. I'd hate to open that door and come face to face with the ghost of Luella Lynch.'

'Don't even joke about it,' Kelley's eyes widened a fraction.

They both stared at the door highlighted by the twin beams of their flashlights.

'Are you thinking what I'm thinking?' Kelley muttered.

'Pretty sure I am,' she replied reluctantly.

His heart was pounding in his chest like a bass drum and he could feel the powerful wave of adrenalin surging through his veins. He was scared but it was rapidly being elbowed roughly aside by a sense of curiosity, so strong it almost tugged him off his feet. He'd never been able to resist a mystery and here he was being presented with the mother of them all.

'WHAT'S GOING ON DOWN THERE?' Killian yelled.

'Hold on Killian,' Kelley replied, glancing at Ava who gave the barest nod of her head. 'We're just going to take a look.'

'I don't think that's a good idea,' Killian shouted back. 'We've got ropes; we're going to pull you back up.'

'In just a minute,' Kelley argued. 'We're down here now and it looks stable enough. We're just going to take a quick look.'

'Great,' Killian muttered irritably. 'First you can't get him in the house, now you can't get him out.'

Kelley climbed over the ruins of the desk which was blocking the corridor and reached out to help Ava over the debris. They walked slowly down the corridor until they were standing in front of the heavy mahogany door.

'You sure about this?' Ava asked.

'We're just going to take a look,' Kelley muttered. 'No harm ever came from just taking a look.'

'Great, maybe they can inscribe that on our gravestones… *'Kelley said we were just going to take a look…'*

She heard him chuckle lightly.

'Ready?' he asked.

'As I'll ever be,' she breathed, 'but just so you know, you're paying for my therapy when this is all over.'

He laughed again as he reached for the brass doorknob.

The stillness of the corridor seemed to amplify the clicking as the lock turned and slowly, like something out of a Bela Lugosi movie, the door creaked open with a disturbingly loud high-pitched whine.

There was nothing but darkness beyond. Kelley felt Ava's hand sneak into his and at that point he wasn't entirely sure if she was comforting him or he was comforting her. They shuffled tentatively forward and caught a glimpse of metal in the beam of the flashlights. It took a few moments to realize that it was an elaborate, metal framed staircase spiraling down into the darkness below.

Kelley glanced across to Ava.

'Should we?' he asked, not sure whether he wanted to hear a yes or no.

'I wonder what's down there,' she muttered as she stared into the black well of twisting metal.

'There's only one way to find out.'

She lifted her flashlight so she could see his face.

'I will if you will,' he challenged.

'Guess we're going down then,' she sucked in a fortifying breath. 'After you.'

'Somehow I knew you were going to say that,' he muttered as he let go of her hand and stepped onto the stairs, testing to see if they were still strong enough to bear weight. 'They're sturdy,' he told her quietly. 'Locked away down here they weren't exposed to any corrosive elements, so we should be okay.'

'Okay then,' she replied grasping onto the handrail, 'I'm right behind you.'

They circled down into the blackness below with only the pinprick of light from the flashlights to guide them. In the stillness, with only their labored breath to break the silence, the temperature dropped as they slowly descended, and their exposed skin pebbled in the cool air. Finally, after what seemed like an eternity, they reached the bottom and found themselves facing another heavy wood paneled door with brass hinges.

Ava watched as Kelley reached out and grasped the small round handle and twisted. There was a small audible click and the door swung open easily on well-oiled hinges, which seemed somehow more ominous than the creaking hinges in the corridor high above them.

The first thing Ava noticed was the ground beneath her feet. It didn't have the soft give and warm creak of aged wood, nor did it have the rough metallic clang of the spiral staircase. This time they found themselves standing on cold hard tile.

The room didn't seem to fit the rest of the house, Ava thought to herself. It was cold and sterile. The walls, as she turned a slow circle, were plain white utilitarian tile, edged in a deep green colored tile which bordered the strange room, at the top, middle and floor level, breaking up the stark whiteness.

Her beam of light fell on a long rectangular table sitting in the center of the room. It was mounted on a circular base and footplate. She slowly edged closer and reached out with trembling fingers to touch it. It was smooth and ice cold to the touch, and made, it seemed, of porcelain.

It wasn't entirely even, she realized. It sloped ever so slightly down to a deep rectangular sink with a metal hand pump mounted on the side. Unable to help herself she lifted the handle, which was heavy and stiff, but after a few grinding, experimental pumps it spewed out a stream of dark urine-like, rusty water.

Beside the porcelain table was a small metal tray on wheels and sitting atop it was a large urn like bottle. The label was worn, and she was unable to read the confusing writing, but it contained some kind of fluid. Placed neatly beside it was a long length of rubber hose, wound up like looping entrails.

She looked up to see where Kelley was and found him

standing beside a heavy desk upon which was a gas lamp, a pot of quills and several stacks of dry parchment-like papers. Next to the desk were huge apothecary shelves revealing rows and rows of glass jars and bottles in varying sizes and containing all sorts of things, from dry leaves and powders to liquids and several gooey looking items they couldn't even identify.

Kelley's beam of light highlighted a long row of books as he shuffled along slowly reading the titles. '*The Anatomie Generale,*' By Marie Francois Bichat in three volumes. There were another eight heavy volumes by someone called Sommerring. '*Anatomy of Bones and ligaments, Anatomy of the muscles and vascular system, Microscopic anatomy of the nervous system, including the brain, the spinal cord and the ganglia...*' There even appeared to be an original copy of Grey's Anatomy dated 1858.

'What the hell is this place?' Ava breathed heavily.

Kelley turned slowly, his light falling on the pale table in the center of the room.

'I hate to say it,' he swallowed thickly, 'but I'm pretty sure that this is some sort of mortuary.'

'A mortuary?' she replied in confusion. 'What would a mortuary be doing down here? The house itself is out in the middle of nowhere, and right now we're pretty deep underground, in fact we're probably inside the cliff itself.'

'I don't know,' he shook his head. 'I have no clue why there would be a room like this hidden beneath the house. I've never even heard a sniff of a rumor about anything like this.'

'Kelley look,' her light fell on another doorway, 'that's not the door we came in.'

Kelley turned and looked behind them. Sure enough, and easily confused in the darkness, there was a second door.

'Ava,' Kelley muttered, 'I'm not so sure. I mean, hidden corridors and empty rooms are one thing but this... this is a whole hell of a lot of creepy. I've got a weird feeling in my gut. I'm not sure we're gonna like what we find behind that door.'

'We have to see,' her stomach turned over and over in nervous somersaults. She didn't want to open that door any more than Kelley did, but something told her she had to. If she didn't it would keep playing on her mind. She had to know the truth, whatever it was.

This time it was Ava who reached for the door. Like the door to the mortuary it turned with a small click and swung open easily with a strange hiss of air, as if the room were somehow taking its first breath in over a century.

Unable to help herself she stepped into the room and the temperature plummeted even further. Her breath was expelled from her blue tinged lips as a fine lacy mist and she shuddered, her fingers and toes suddenly numb.

She stepped further into the room and felt her feet sink into a lush carpet. The walls were decorated with silk wallpaper with filigree motifs and delicate floral patterns. Mounted on the wall was a brass plate. No, a grate she mentally corrected herself, with a small lever below it which would allow the plate to slide horizontally back and forth to open what she could only assume this far underground was an air vent of some sort.

The vent was in the closed position and deep in the heart of the cliff surrounded by rock. The naturally cool temperature had almost perfectly preserved the room, like a time capsule.

She turned to the right and found a huge four poster bed, with a canopy and heavy drapes. The sheets and blankets were still neatly made up as if it were merely awaiting its owner's return.

There was a strange buzzing in her ears as she stared at the bed. She tilted her head, unconsciously straining to listen. It was weird, it almost sounded like whispering, only it was too low to make out the words. She turned slowly, her flashlight trailing along the wall to the opposite side of the room. Her heart and stomach jolted violently as her mouth fell open in a silent scream, unable to force any sound from her frozen vocal cords.

She could hear the whoosh of her adrenalin fueled blood gushing through her veins and pounding in her ears as she stared, unable to process what her eyes were seeing. Built into custom alcoves in the walls were ornate glass coffins, seven of them in all and they weren't empty...

Seven women lay, as if asleep, naked, on pillows of pale silk and lace, surrounded by dried flowers, with blood red petals, the edges curling and blackened with the stench of death.

The women were, for the most part, almost perfectly preserved. Three of them, each with dark hair and full breasts lay languidly, a cruel parody of a slumbering lover, their skin dried and slightly withered.

The next two, one a redhead and one a blonde, were laid out, still naked but in a more demure fashion, with barely any hair at the juncture between their thin desiccated thighs and breasts that were small and underdeveloped. It betrayed how young they had been at the moment of death, barely on the cusp of womanhood.

The sixth one seemed somewhere in the middle, age wise. A young lady in the burst of youth, but unlike her companions in death, she had not fared so well. There was a great jagged crack in the glass wall of her coffin. Her skin had crumbled away leaving parts of her torso collapsing inwards. Her face had begun to decay, revealing patches of bleached white skull and grinning teeth beneath her paper-like flesh and her eyes were nothing more than sunken hollows.

Ava shuddered. It was like she'd walked into a horror show, only these weren't wax models and she couldn't just head for the nearest emergency exit. She was trapped deep below ground in a room of death and her muscles were tensed so tightly it physically hurt.

Her eyes slowly fell on the last corpse. Part of the wall above the casket had cracked away, not enough to breach the wall of the room but the plaster had come away and crashed down in a sheet, smashing the glass of the coffin and breaking the seal. Like her companion, her skin had disintegrated leaving only patches of her humanity left, bones protruding from dried leather-like flesh and scattered with dried petals and stick like stems.

Somewhere in the dim recesses of her mind Ava seemed to recall someone had told her the cliff had been struck by lightning. She couldn't have said how or why she knew, but the moment the thought occurred to her she understood beyond a shadow of a doubt that, that was what had happened. The moment the lightning had struck the cliff the plaster had cracked away and crashed through the coffin, revealing the rough stone wall behind.

Ava was afraid. She could feel the fear, dry and tasteless in her mouth, making it hard to swallow, but there was something else. Her mind seemed kind of distant, like she was standing outside her body looking at the grisly scene.

The whispering in her ear began again and without stopping to wonder why, she stepped forward, reaching for the girl in the broken coffin. Her vision narrowed, blurring at the edges like a tunnel. She just had to touch her papery skin, just once, she had to know...

'AVA!' Kelley's voice cracked like a whip, his tone so sharp and unfamiliar it snapped her out of the strange trance as he rushed toward her.

Grabbing her arm, he yanked her back.

'Don't touch her!' he told her urgently, yanking off the lavender colored bandana holding her hair back, and pressing it over her nose and mouth. 'She's been embalmed with arsenic. When the glass was broken it released the fumes from her body and they've been building up inside this sealed room... the whole room is toxic.'

With his t-shirt pulled up over his mouth and nose he dragged her from the room. She dropped her flashlight as she stumbled along behind him, holding the bandana to her mouth. Her head was swimming and she was dizzy. She held onto his hand, the only warm safe thing in the darkness, and trusted him to lead her out.

Holding onto Ava's hand tightly with one hand and leading the way with his flashlight with the other, he dragged her through the mortuary and back up the winding staircase, along the corridor, lifting her over the broken desk as he approached the light spilling down from the wide-open hole in the ceiling.

There were two ropes dangling down ready for them, as several concerned faces peered through the gap.

'Killian!' Kelley called urgently as he secured the rope around her waist, 'pull her up.'

He watched as she was hoisted up through the hole before scrambling up the second rope, agile as a monkey. He climbed over the jagged edge, losing some skin on his palms and shins to the splintered wood. As soon as he was free, he lifted Ava into his arms.

'Kelley, what is it?' Killian asked in concern.

'Get everyone out of the house,' Kelley told him as he carried Ava from the room toward the main entrance, with Killian barking orders to his men to clear the site.

Kelley stumbled out into the daylight, the sudden brightness stabbing his eyes like pins after the darkness of the hidden rooms. He stumbled down the steps, collapsing to his knees with Ava still in his arms.

'Ava?' he pulled the bandana from her mouth, 'are you okay?'

'Feel sick,' she croaked as she turned and dry heaved.

'Get her some water,' Kelley barked to Bo, the foreman who was standing hovering anxiously nearby and who took off for Ava's supply of refreshments without having to be asked twice.

'What the hell Kelley?' Killian dropped to his knees next to them, 'what happened down there?'

'You need to call Dad,' his serious green eyes locked on his brother. 'We've got a room full of dead bodies down there and they're all poisonous.'

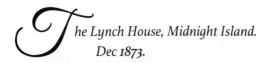he Lynch House, Midnight Island.
Dec 1873.

HE SHOULD'VE BEEN SLEEPING but the screaming had woken him. He'd called for Sarah, but she hadn't answered. The room was freezing. The fire had long since gone out in the grate, nothing but cold ash and cinders. It would not be lit again until morning.

The scream came again, this time followed by a crash and the sound of breaking glass. He climbed from his bed and dropped down on the floor, avoiding the half-filled chamber pot and sliding beneath the heavy wooden frame in nothing but his nightshirt, the freezing floor chilling his small body as he placed his hands over his ears to block the desperate cries.

His father would punish him if he left his room. He could still feel the barely healed strokes of the switch across his backside and the backs of his thighs. The cries came again, filled with pain and fear. His heart clenched, and his eyes filled with tears even as his bottom lip began to quiver.

It sounded like Sarah, screams which had turned to violent sobs, the word no, chanted over and over. He pressed his hands so tightly against his ears his fingers turned white and his ears began to burn from the pressure. The first tears dripped onto the wooden floor and his heart pounded in fear, his father hated it when he cried. Only babies and women cried, his father said.

He wondered if his father had taken the switch to Sarah, wondered what she had done wrong. He liked Sarah; he didn't want her to leave like the others had. Nancy, Olive, Alice, the maids, his nurses, they'd all promised him they would stay, that they wouldn't leave him, but they had. They'd all broken their promises to him, and it was all his father's fault. He'd made them leave; he was sure of it.

The screams quieted and he released his ears, laid there for a moment on his belly, breathing hard, his palms pressed against the floor, leaving tiny little star shaped handprints in the dust. He should just go back to bed and close his eyes, pretend he hadn't heard anything like he had before, only this time it was different.

It was Sarah and she'd been his favorite. She'd sung to him and told him tales of the old country as she'd called it, in her lilting Irish brogue. He liked to listen to her voice, to the funny way she talked. If his father had taken the switch to her, she'd be hurting.

His own pain still fresh in his mind he slowly slid out from under the bed and headed for the dresser. Pulling open the bottom drawer he retrieved a little tin pot of salve she'd hidden in there to soothe his hurts whenever his father punished him. He tucked it into the pocket of his nightshirt and shoved the heavy drawer closed.

He crept across his bedroom to the door and opened it slowly, before slipping out into the hallway. He navigated the darkened corridor easily. He tried Sarah's room first; it adjoined his own in case he woke in the night when he was younger. The room had seen many occupants but for now it was Sarah's. He checked but found her bed empty.

Confused, he slipped back into the hallway. He should've gone back to his room, but he saw a sliver of light spilling from the doorway of his father's room and he was drawn toward it. Silent as a mouse, he crept forward on bare feet, pressing his eye to the slight crack in the doorway.

His mouth went dry and his chest pounded in fear, like the wings of a fragile bird dashing itself in panic against the bars of its cage. His eyes widened at the scene before him, his mind too young to comprehend what he was seeing.

Sarah was pinned to his father's bed by his large commanding frame, her skirts shoved roughly up and bunched around her small waist. His father's clothing was loosened, his pants shoved indecently down his hips revealing his naked buttocks as he rammed himself violently between her pale limp thighs, grunting loudly.

He couldn't look away, his innocent eyes wide with confusion and wet with tears. His father continued to slam himself against the girl who seemed so small and fragile beneath his powerful body. His breathing was ragged and labored with animal like grunts heaving from his throat. His movements increased in speed as he pounded into her and finally with one last violent jab and a vicious growl, he collapsed on top of her, panting heavily.

The boy glanced at her face, his sweet Sarah. She no longer screamed or cried; she made no sound at all. His father's huge meaty fist was still wrapped around her slender throat like a snake constricting its prey. Her head lolled limply to the side, as if she were watching him, as if she could see through the tiny sliver of the crack in the doorway and somehow knew he was there.

But she couldn't; the whites of her eyes appeared red as she stared lifelessly at nothing. His heart jolted when his father moved. He should have run then, back to his room, back to his bed, back to the childhood innocence that would never be innocent again, but he didn't.

Instead he watched as his father climbed off her and moved aside. Sarah didn't move, she laid there across the bed, her legs grotesquely splayed out, revealing the most secret part of a woman he was too young to know. But he could see it now, a patch of fair hair between her legs to match the long locks braided over her *shoulder.* Blood was smeared between her thighs staining the bedclothes.

His father, with no care for the girl, walked over to the dresser and calmly lifted the china jug, pouring a generous amount of water into the wash basin. Reaching for a square of muslin he dipped it in the water, squeezing it out before washing the sweat from his face and neck, exposed by the open collar of his shirt.

The boy's eyes widened as his father turned slightly revealing his penis. It jutted out, swollen and painful looking. It was hard and angry, nothing like his own, but it didn't seem to bother him as he took the cloth and washed himself. Tucking himself into his smalls he pulled his pants back up and fastened them. He tossed the dirty muslin onto the girl carelessly before wrapping her body in the soiled sheets until she was no longer visible. Then he picked up her slight frame and tossed her easily over one shoulder.

The boy scrambled silently out of the way as the door swung wide open. He pressed himself as far back into the shadows as he could, pressing his trembling hand to his mouth to stop himself from whimpering in fear.

His father stood there for a moment, the white shrouded girl draped over his shoulder like a sack of coal. One of her hands hung from the sheet, swinging limply as something dropped from her fingers with a tiny, almost inaudible clatter, and his father turned in the direction of the sound.

For a second of pure terror he thought he had seen him but after several long moments his father turned back and passed by him, so close in the darkness he could smell the sweat and cologne clinging to his skin, underlaid with another primal scent he couldn't place. He listened silently as his father's footfalls echoing against the wooden floor became fainter.

He crawled along the polished floor, groping in the darkness for whatever it was that had fallen from Sarah's grasp.

His tiny fingers closed around a metal object attached to a thin chain. He held it up against the light from the doorway and found *that it was a small, plain gold cross. The one she always wore tucked beneath the collar of her dress.*

Once again something deep inside him told him to go back to his room, to his bed and pretend that he had been asleep this whole time. That the confusing and distressing scene he had witnessed was just a bad dream. That Sarah would come in to comfort him, laugh in her silvery way and tell him a story of her homeland...of skelps and pixies, but that wasn't going to happen.

Sarah was never coming back to him.

Maybe it was that thought which had him climbing to his feet in the darkness. Maybe it was the heartsickness and sorrow that had him creeping slowly down the stairs at a distance behind his father.

Wondering where he was taking her, he followed him to the study, and peered around the door, watching as his father reached for a secret catch on the bookcase.

There was a strange sound, a series of clicks and whirrs as the bookcase slowly swung open, revealing a hidden doorway into which his father disappeared.

The boy crept into the room, one of the places he was not allowed. He barely glanced at the ornate heavy desk nor the glass fronted cabinets containing rows upon rows of books. Instead he headed for the hidden doorway which was still open a fraction. Reaching out he slipped inside, the entire back of the doorway was made up entirely of tiny mechanisms, cogs and wheels, and metal pulleys, reminding him of the delicate watches and clocks his father made.

Turning away from the door he found a plain staircase. Following it down, he came to a long corridor with a deep plush runner down the center. His frozen toes sunk into the springy carpet as he snuck down the corridor like a sneak thief. A few of the candles had been lit in the sconces and had burned down almost halfway, casting dim light and long shadows.

At the end of the corridor was another door. This one stood wide open and spiraling down into the darkness below was a shiny black metal staircase.

He padded down on silent feet, circling endlessly into the black well below, until his feet hit cold solid ground and he found himself face to face with another door. Reaching out toward the handle the door suddenly slammed open and when the boy looked up, the huge imposing figure of his father stared down at him with black eyes. The white tiled room at his back was well lit, making the pure white wings of hair at his temples amidst the black almost glow incandescently, but the boy paid no notice. His wide terrified eyes were locked on his father. He lost control of his bladder, feeling trickles of hot urine rolling down the inside of his legs and staining his nightshirt.

His father did not speak. He reached out and grabbed his upper arm, dragging him roughly back up the stairs. He pulled him along the corridor; the boy couldn't keep up, couldn't move his feet but it didn't matter, his father dragged him along the ground his feet dangling almost a full inch above the floor. His arm was numb, and his bicep pinched painfully where his father's fingers dug into his tender flesh, already leaving dark purple and black bruises.

Once they reached the well-lit study, he didn't stop there but dragged him out into the foyer. Ignoring the stairs, he marched toward the back of the house, through the butler's pantry to the scullery. He stopped in front of the back wall and shoved the rough wooden table out of the way, so violently it skidded across the flagstone floor with a loud grating noise.

He knelt down next to the bare, whitewashed brick wall. There was a mark in the wall, little more than a dent, tiny and innocuous. The boy watched fearfully as his father withdrew his watch from the pocket of his finely embroidered silk waistcoat of deep maroon. He flicked the pocket watch open and turned the face counterclockwise slowly, until with a quiet click a small skeleton key emerged. He placed it into the dent which was deeper than it appeared and suddenly there was a series of clicks and whirring, like the innards of the carriage clock he'd watched his father make.

A small door, barely large enough for a child, certainly not big enough to accommodate a grown man, swung open and the boy saw a small dark space barely three feet by three. There was nothing in that hole but a small metal grate covering an envelope sized air vent.

'NO PAPA!' he tried to pull away, his feet slid and scrambled against the cold stone floor. 'I'M SORRY...I'M SORRY...'

But his father was too big, too strong, he simply tossed him into the darkness and the door slammed shut behind him. The clicks and whirs began again, and as the footfalls of his father's boots faded away, he reached out. His tiny fingers felt the rough cog like edges of a clockwork mechanism, just like the ones his father made, just like the hidden door in the study and he knew, with a heavy sinking heart that he was trapped for however long his father wanted to leave him in that tiny black hole.

He shivered violently against the freezing cold; the wetness of his urine-soaked nightshirt clammy against his skin. Pulling his legs up underneath him he wrapped his arms around his knees, folding himself into a ball and with the small plain gold cross still clutched in his tiny fist, he laid his head on his knees and wept bitterly.

---

*A*va woke with a start, her heart pounding as she sat up and dragged in a shaky breath. Her hands trembled as she shoved her heavy, damp hair back from her face.

'Are you okay?'

She glanced over to the bed next to hers and saw Kelley propped up on a pile of pillows reading a book, wearing nothing but a hospital gown, just as she was. She swung her legs over the side of the bed, her feet dangling inches above the cool sterile floor.

'Yeah,' she swallowed against the dryness in her mouth. 'Bad dream.'

'Wanna talk about it?' he asked.

She shook her head. Even now the dream was quickly fading, and she found she couldn't quite recall the details. It had upset her, she knew that much, but every time she reached for it, the dream tattered and fell apart, slipping through her fingers as fragile as a spider's web.

'How long was I asleep for?' she swung her legs slightly as she straightened her gown.

'About an hour,' he replied as he watched her.

He didn't add that it hadn't been a very restful sleep. She'd tossed and muttered in her sleep, her brow furrowed and her body tense. He'd spent more time watching her in concern than he had reading the book one of the nurses had loaned him.

There was a knock at the door and they both looked up as it swung open and Gus walked in.

'Dad,' Kelley greeted him, 'what's going on?'

'Jesus,' Gus removed his hat and ran his hand through his hair to smooth down the wild tufts. He dragged a chair across the room and sat down, his elbows propped on his knees as he clutched his hat in his hands. 'I don't know what to tell you, it's like a three-ring circus up at the house right now.'

'What do you mean?' Ava frowned.

'The forensic pathologists were called in because we're dealing with human remains. We've opened an investigation but it's obvious the bodies have been down there for some time, decades even. The county coroner's office has called in a forensic anthropologist from the University of Maine. Apparently, no one knows bones like she does, but because of the high concentrations of arsenic found at the scene, amongst other things, we've had to call in the CDC and the New England Poison Center have gotten involved too.'

Kelley nodded, 'I figured as much.'

'The bodies are to be carefully removed for further examination but again, because of the poison, it's a slow painstaking business. All work on the house has been halted until the site is cleared by the CDC.'

'I wouldn't have thought it would take too long,' Kelley mused. 'Once the bodies are out and the place decontaminated it should be safe. It's the bodies themselves that are dangerous.'

'How the hell did you know?' Gus asked his son, 'that they were embalmed with arsenic?'

'Last year I covered one of the senior classes while Rachel Solomon was out on maternity,' Kelley told him, 'and one of the books we covered was Mary Shelley's Frankenstein. As a fun extra credit project, we looked at the Victorian preoccupation with re-animating corpses and briefly we touched on 19th century pseudo-science and anatomy.

One of the things we discovered is that in the 19th century they used to embalm the deceased by flushing out the veins with water and filling them with arsenic. It worked incredibly well. There's nothing, not even modern-day practices, that can preserve a corpse like arsenic, however it was extremely dangerous to anyone handling the body. Many doctors and medical students were accidentally killed by heavy metal poisoning. Eventually they discovered formaldehyde and discarded the use of it.

When we were in the mortuary room, I saw volumes of books about anatomy and on the desk scientific papers and illustrations detailing the embalming process. There were large bottles labeled arsenic on the trolley, next to a porcelain autopsy table and yards of rubber tubing. When I walked into the other room and saw the bodies it just clicked.'

'You always were a smart kid,' Gus murmured as he watched his son thoughtfully.

The three of them looked up at another knock at the door. It swung open and the doctor peeked his head around.

'Mr Ryan, Miss Cortez,' he nodded as he entered the room carrying a clipboard, 'and?'

'Sheriff Ryan,' Gus stood and held out his hand for the doctor to shake.

'Any relation?' the doctor looked to Kelley.

'My dad,' he nodded.

'Ah alright then,' he reached into the pocket of his white coat and retrieved a pen, clicking it before he scribbled something on his notes. 'Well, we've sent your blood work off to the lab for analysis, but it won't be back for a little while longer. You've not displayed any symptoms of arsenic poisoning so far and that's a good sign, although because you inhaled fumes rather than ingesting the poison directly, symptoms can take longer to manifest. However, I believe your exposure was very minimal from what you've told me, so I'm confident the test results should come back negative.

Your clothes have been disposed of as a precaution and you've been decontaminated. We'll keep you under observation for a few more hours then after that I'm happy to release you, but if you feel at all unwell, you're to come straight back. Symptoms to watch out for are changes in your fingernail pigmentation, a metallic taste in the mouth and garlicky breath. Also, excess saliva and/or problems swallowing. Also be aware of blood in the urine, cramping muscles, hair loss, stomach cramps, convulsions, excessive sweating, vomiting and diarrhea.'

'Sounds delightful,' Ava muttered sourly.

Gus's phone rang loudly, and the doctor excused himself as the sheriff stepped back and talked quietly.

'Damn it,' he swore as he hung up.

'What?' Kelley asked.

'We've got a problem,' he scowled angrily. 'I need to get back as soon as possible. Some idiot leaked this whole mess to the press, they're arriving on the island by the boatload. I'm not sure whether or not they know about you two, but just as a precaution I'm going to request the local PD put a couple of guys on the door, just in case they show up here. We have to wait a few more hours for your test results so I'll have someone bring you both some clothes and escort you back to the island when you're ready. Ava, I don't want you staying in the RV on site alone tonight, so we'll have to make other arrangements.'

'But everything I own is there, and what about Bailey? She's there on her own at the moment. I need to get back to her.'

'Bailey's fine,' he assured her. 'She's at Killian's place being spoiled rotten by Hope and the kids.'

'What?'

'My grandkids fell instantly in love with her, they think she's a wolf.'

Ava's eyes softened, 'Killian didn't have to do that.'

'We take care of our own Ava,' he murmured absently as he read a message which had pinged through to his phone. 'I'm sorry you two, I really have to go. I'll see you back on island later. Kelley don't worry about the bar; Miranda is going to cover.'

'Cousin,' he told Ava as she glanced at him curiously. 'One of many.'

Gus bid them a hurried goodbye and slipped from the room as Kelley lay back down on the bed and tucked his hands under his head.

'Guess we're stuck here for a while longer,' he remarked easily.

'You just take everything in your stride, don't you?' Ava watched him.

'I try not to let things bother me,' he replied, 'if that's what you're getting at. Especially if I can't change it.'

The daylight in the room had dimmed and turned gray. Ava turned her head to look as the first patters of rain hit the window. After a few moments the rain came down harder, perfectly mirroring her mood as it streamed down the glass like rivers of tears.

'What is it Ava?' Kelley asked softly.

'I don't know,' she watched as the sky lit up suddenly and there was a loud crack followed by a long roll of thunder. 'Everything, I guess. From the moment Serenity died, I feel like I've been trapped on a rollercoaster.'

'A good one or a bad one?' he asked as she looked over at him. 'I'm just saying; sometimes rollercoasters can be fun.'

'Honestly?' she replied, 'I'm not sure whether I want to laugh, cry or throw up.'

'You tried that earlier.'

'Thanks for reminding me,' she shook her head. It was true though, when he'd carried her out of the house and set her down, she'd heaved and heaved. She wasn't sure if it was the shock or the lack of oxygen underground but thank god, she hadn't actually eaten anything, and her stomach was empty. She'd have been mortified if she'd actually vomited in front of everyone.

'Did you know, Serenity didn't even tell me she was sick,' Ava told him quietly.

'What?' he frowned.

'My mother didn't tell me she was dying, that she was leaving me all on my own. I never got the chance to say good-bye. First I knew about it, was a phone call from one of her friends who was high on something at the time, telling me she was dead. Then I find out she was loaded and that I'd inherited a house on an island I'd never heard of. Now I'm here and the house is full of dead bodies, and your dad is telling me I'm 'one of their own' but I don't feel it. I still feel like a stranger, like I don't know what the hell I'm doing. I'm just floundering.'

He didn't say anything for a moment, he just opened his arms to her. She didn't stop and think, didn't allow herself to second guess. She crawled onto the narrow hospital bed beside him, taking the comfort he was offering as he wrapped his arms around her and pulled her into the warmth of his body.

'I think my ass is hanging out the back of my gown,' she frowned, 'I can feel a breeze.'

She felt his chest jiggle beneath her cheek as he chuckled.

'I'll bet it's a beautiful ass too, but to prove what a gentleman I am, I won't look.' He reached for the thin, pale blue, hospital blanket and draped it over them both, tucking her into him comfortingly.

For a few moments they just lay there in silence.

'You know when I said I wanted to get you naked again,' his

voice rumbled quietly, 'I didn't mean with us wearing hospital gowns, in an isolation room, with suspected heavy metal poisoning.'

This time she laughed.

She tilted her head back and found his piercing green eyes watching her.

'You know, I don't think I've ever met anyone like you,' she murmured.

His mouth slowly curved.

'Back at you.'

He watched slowly as she stretched up and pressed her soft lips to his. This time it was just the two of them, cocooned in the dim room with the patter of rain against the glass as he sank into the feel and taste of her. His fingers tangled in her damp hair and she unconsciously pressed closer to him, her arms wrapping around him.

He took his time Ava noticed, like with everything else he did. He was unhurried as he explored her mouth like he had all the time in the world. It was a devastating kiss, rich and warm, filled with promise and underlaid with heat. It smoldered just below the surface; a need that was so potent she ached from it.

'Kelley...'

She wasn't even aware she'd breathed his name until the word was hanging between them, a promise, an invitation, she wasn't even sure which. His hand trailed down her body and she could feel the heat of his touch through the hospital gown. They rolled slightly, aware they were on a narrow bed and she arched into him, helpless to do anything else when she felt the hot hard length of him pressed against her.

She wanted him, everything else just seemed to fade away until there was nothing but the feel and taste of him. He groaned and pulled away reluctantly, pressing his forehead to hers, his breathing ragged.

'You have no idea how much I hate myself right now,' he panted, 'but we shouldn't do this. Not here, not like this.'

He was right, she hated that he was right. Her whole body was humming with need, but she certainly didn't want any doctors, cops or even worse reporters walking in and finding them in a compromising position.

He rolled back over onto his back taking her with him, so her cheek was pressed to his chest. She could feel his heart pounding beneath her as his breathing began to slow.

'We need a distraction,' he murmured as the lightning slashed across the sky outside, once more followed by a sulky roll of thunder, mirroring his mood perfectly. 'You want to read?' he picked up the book he'd been reading earlier and held it out to her.

She shook her head.

'No, but you can tell me a story,' she idly traced the pattern on his gown with her fingertips. 'I love stories.'

'You love stories, but you don't like to read?' he frowned.

'Yeah.'

'You're a woman of fascinating contradictions Ava.'

'Keeps you from being bored.'

'One thing I haven't been, since meeting you, is bored,' he glanced down at her brushing his lips against hers once more.

'Distraction,' she murmured against his lips, 'or hospital sex. The choice is yours, because if you keep kissing me like that, I'm gonna make the decision for you.'

He huffed out a silent laugh against her mouth as he picked up the book once again. Wrapping his arm around her and pulling her in close he returned to the first page and began to read aloud. His deep rumbling voice was accompanied every now and then by the pitch and roll of the storm rattling against the windows. There, in their perfect cozy little cocoon, she listened to the warm comforting timbre of his voice and the lulling patter of the rain.

. . .

By the time they arrived back on island it was really late. The worst of the storm had blown over and the moon was high in the sky, casting a silvery glow over the damp island. One of the police squad cars met them off the last ferry of the night and drove them both up the steep curving road toward Ava's cliff top. If they'd expected to find the site quiet and shut down for the night, they were in for a huge shock.

They had to make their way through crowds of people with cameras, who banged on the windows of the car, the lights from their cameras blinding through the glass as they yelled random questions. It was disorganized, chaotic and somehow out of place. When Gus had said the media had shown up, she had been prepared for a few news vans and some reporters but nothing like this. It was off the craziness scale.

When they finally made it through the blockade of people, the police barriers were lifted out of the way so they could drive onto the site.

Ava barely recognized it; her quiet sleepy little site was lit up like the fourth of July with huge temporary floodlights. There were dark colored vans everywhere and plastic sheeting hung over square tent-like structures. People milled around wearing protective coveralls and masks, and for one crazy brief second, Ava wouldn't have been surprised to see E.T wheeled out.

'What the hell?' she muttered.

'It looks worse than it actually is Ma'am,' the young deputy told her. 'Most of its just procedure, the rest is for privacy. The Press are notorious for telephoto lenses. They've managed to retrieve one of the bodies so far and until they're ready to release a statement they don't want them getting any photos.'

Slowly the pair of them climbed out of the car, surveying the bustling activity. After a few moments a figure broke away and crossed the distance to them. She was a slim built, middle-aged woman with curly blonde hair, cropped short and tucked behind one ear, and a friendly face.

'Ava Cortez?' she enquired.

'Who wants to know?' Ava asked warily.

'Dr Casey Valentine,' she held out her hand, 'University of Maine, forensic anthropology.'

'Oh,' Ava reached out and shook her hand. 'This is Kelley Ryan.'

'Of course,' she shook his hand also. 'It was my understanding you both discovered the bodies?'

'That's right,' Kelley nodded, 'hell of an experience.'

'I can imagine,' Dr Casey replied sympathetically. 'Usually they're not quite so well preserved when they get to me, however I do have Dr Brightman with me,' she glanced around and frowned. 'Oh well, you'll meet him at some point, he's a forensic pathologist. We'll be partnering up on this case as it's so unusual.'

'How long do you think they've been down there?' Ava asked.

'Can't say for certain yet, we're just in the preliminary stages of the investigation. We've managed to remove one of the bodies so far, but it's slow going as we have to remove them in their caskets without breaching the sealed glass. They'll then be opened in a more controlled environment for a complete analysis. I have however been able to have a look at the two damaged coffins, and the girls inside.'

'Girls?' Ava replied.

'We've been able to roughly estimate that all the victims were between the ages of fifteen and nineteen,' she told them confidently.

'Do you have any idea how they died?' Ava asked quietly.

'Again, I couldn't really say without further examination and even then, after all this time, the cause may be indeterminate. But the one girl I did get a look at appears to have what looks like fractures of the second cervical vertebrae. I need to get X-rays to be sure, but those types of injury can be consistent with death by strangulation.'

'They were murdered then,' Ava murmured as her gaze tracked over to the house, which was a hive of activity.

'Well they certainly didn't end up down there of natural causes.'

'I know,' Ava frowned, 'I just, I've never seen anything like that before.'

'I understand,' Dr Casey patted her arm kindly. 'I also understand from the Sheriff you've been living on site?'

'That's right,' Ava nodded.

'Well, you're going to want to rethink that for a couple of days at least, until the initial excitement dies down a bit. The Press are a bit voracious, not to mention rude and intrusive. They'll make your life hell if you give them the opportunity.'

'We saw them on the way in,' Kelley replied. 'I have to admit I wasn't expecting to see that many.'

'That's because they're not all reporters.'

'They're not?' he replied in confusion.

'No. Given the local urban legends and mystery already surrounding the house, and the fact that bodies have been discovered, it's brought out all the crazies and the paranormal hacks,' she warned them. 'I hate to say it but you two are in for a rough ride.'

'For how long?' Ava frowned.

'Until they get bored or something more interesting comes along,' Dr Casey replied sympathetically. 'Best thing you can do is avoid them.'

'Easier said than done when they're all camping on my doorstep,' Ava replied angrily.

'Like I said, you're going to have to rethink that, at least temporarily,' she turned and nodded to one of her colleagues. 'I have to go, but we'll try to make this as quick and painless as possible. Hopefully once we get all the bodies out it'll thin the herd some.'

'I hope so,' Ava mumbled unhappily.

'I'll be in touch as soon as we have an update,' she patted Ava's shoulder in solidarity before turning and heading back to the house.

'You can stay at my place tonight,' Kelley told her softly. 'I'll take the couch.'

'I guess,' she kicked the ground in annoyance. 'I suppose I should get my stuff.'

She turned and headed toward the RV. She could feel Kelley slowly trailing along behind her as he watched the constant stream of people in and out of the house. She didn't have it in her to stand and watch it all unravel. She was too tired, too annoyed, too... well everything.

She opened the door and frowned; she thought she'd locked it. She climbed the steps and flicked on the light, gasping in shock as her wide eyes took in the carnage in front of her. Kelley, hearing her loud gasp of distress, ran up the steps behind her and stopped dead.

The interior of the RV was almost completely destroyed. The cushioned chairs and sofa had been violently slashed open, the fluff and stuffing yanked out and scattered across the floor like puffs of cotton candy. All of her belongs were strew haphazardly throughout. The flowers that Kelley had given her, with their cute whimsical little cardboard cut-outs of mermaids and frying pans, were tossed across the floor, stamped on repeatedly until they were nothing more than crushed, shredded petals and bent twisted stems.

The several cans of money she'd received from the crew for their lunches for the past couple of days were also tossed, with crumpled bills and coins everywhere, which was weird. The motive obviously wasn't robbery.

Her gaze continued to scan the space. All the doors hung open with plates, cups and silverware dumped amongst the rest of the debris but worst of all, sprayed all over the walls, windows and the cupboards were bright red angry letters.

'GET OUT!'

It was scrawled in furious jagged slashes, and not just that. There were smaller ones, sprayed over every inch of surface telling her to leave, to run, to get out before it was too late, before she got hurt. The writing was so chaotic and disorganized that Ava couldn't even tell if the person responsible was trying to warn her or threaten her.

'Ava,' Kelley whispered, and she felt him wrap his hand around her arm comfortingly. It was only when he slowly turned her to face him and cupped her jaw, wiping her cheek with the pad of his thumb, that she realized she was crying. 'I'm so sorry.'

Her back straightened and her jaw clenched.

'Doesn't matter,' she replied flatly, 'it's just stuff.'

'Of course it matters,' he held her face gently even when she tried to back away. 'It matters,' he repeated firmly, 'and we're going to find the sonofabitch who did this.'

He was right. As much as she didn't want to admit it, it did matter, because like an idiot she'd started to let herself believe. Even though the RV technically didn't belong to her, it had been the first time she'd had something of her own that had even resembled a home and now it was gone. Sure, they could clean up, fix it up, repair it, make it good as new, but that sense of safety, of security was gone. It was no longer her little slice of heaven, her private space and once again she felt like she was being forced to leave.

'I'm going to have to call my dad and the guys in,' Kelley told her quietly. 'They'll need to document everything.'

'Well isn't this the day that just keeps on giving,' she replied coldly. 'It feels like it's never going to end.'

'I know,' he rubbed her arms soothingly. Her skin felt ice cold to the touch and her eyes were flat. It was worrying. 'It shouldn't take too long, and then we'll grab what we can of yours and take it back to my place. What you need is a hot bath and a good night's sleep.'

'It's nearly midnight already,' she replied numbly. 'I don't think there's much of the night left.'

'There's nowhere you need to be first thing so you can sleep in as late as you like.' He wrapped his arms around her and pulled her in close, trying to give her some of his body warmth. 'It'll be okay.'

'It won't Kelley,' she muttered as she pressed her face into his chest, 'it really won't.'

13

*A*va still woke early, despite the lack of sleep, despite the sweet way Kelley had tucked her into his bed and then gone to his brother's in the middle of the night to fetch her dog, because he instinctively knew she needed something familiar to anchor herself too.

Damn that man. If he kept this up, she was in very real danger of falling for him.

Bailey was still snoring on the bed, the familiar and comforting weight of the dog pinning her legs until they were almost numb. She sat up and rubbed her fur as she considered whether or not to just lie back down and see if she could sleep some more, but she knew she wouldn't. Her mind was too full, too active; she needed to burn off some of this restless energy.

Shoving both Bailey and the covers off her legs she padded barefoot out of Kelley's room. His apartment was small but neat for a guy. She stopped in the doorway to the living room and her heart gave a helpless knock against her ribs.

Kelley was laying, sprawled out, face down on a couch that was not built to accommodate a man of six two. His feet hung off the end and one of his arms trailed along the carpet as he snored softly. That didn't look at all comfortable, but he'd made it work. He'd given her exactly what she needed last night, space and the company of her dog. He hadn't made one single move on her, despite the fact they both knew it was only a matter of time before they ended up in bed together. Although, hopefully not with a seventy-pound dog parked between them.

Feeling slightly better than she had the night before she crept quietly into the kitchen to see what he had in the refrigerator. After all the man had given up his bed for her and her huge beast of a dog, the least she could do was feed him.

KELLEY WOKE up to the mouth-watering scent of bacon and a crick in his neck only a chiropractor could fix. He awkwardly climbed off the couch and stretched out the kinks in his spine as he followed that heavenly scent into the kitchen. He stopped in the doorway, leaning against the frame with a small smile playing on his lips as he watched Ava.

She was barefoot and wearing one of his shirts. His green eyes slid down her golden legs as she moved around his kitchen with ease, as if she'd done it a thousand times before.

'Hey,' she looked up and smiled at him as she scooped a stack of warm pancakes onto a plate. She opened a bottle of maple syrup, sniffing it experimentally before liberally applying it to the pancakes. Finally, she set the crispy bacon on the edge of the plate and slid it across the breakfast bar, before turning to pour him a coffee. 'I was just about to wake you. I was debating on whether or not to let you sleep after last night, but I was restless, and cooking calms me.'

He walked silently across the kitchen his gaze locked on hers as he slid his arms around her and pulled her in close, kissing her slowly.

'It's hard to mind,' he broke the kiss and glanced down at her, 'being woken by a beautiful woman cooking me breakfast.'

He smiled softly, 'where'd you get the ingredients? I don't think I've ever cooked pancakes before in my life.'

'Oh,' she smiled as she stepped back out of his embrace, 'it was only a box mix. I found it at the back of the cupboard.'

'Did you?' he frowned in confusion. 'Mom must've bought it. Lately I've been busy juggling teaching and working at the bar, so I haven't had much time. She's taken to doing my grocery shopping; I think she's worried I'm going to starve.'

'That's sweet,' Ava picked up her mug of coffee and sat down on one of the bar stools, watching as Kelley sat down beside her and pulled the plate in front of him.

'Where's yours?' he frowned.

'Oh um,' she placed the mug on the counter. 'I'm not hungry.'

He rolled his eyes and grabbed her stool, pulling her closer as the legs scraped loudly against the floor. Picking up his fork he cut a mouthful of pancake and dipped it in the syrup, holding it up to her mouth.

'You need to eat Ava,' he told her. 'I've watched you; you spend all your time feeding everyone else the most delicious food I've ever tasted but you always forget to feed yourself.'

She smiled softly as she leaned forward and took the mouthful from his fork, licking her lips slowly as he watched her.

'Damn it, Ava,' he muttered. The words were on the edge of his tongue, they both knew it but neither spoke. Neither of them was ready to admit to feelings they didn't know how to handle much less put a label on.

'Eat,' she nudged him as he stared at her, 'it's getting cold.'

In the end they shared it, taking turns with the fork, on alternate bites each, until the plate was clean. It had occurred to them both, that either one of them could have leaned over a fraction and retrieved a spare fork from the drawer but they were both enjoying the intimacy of sharing.

'What are your plans for today?' Kelley asked. 'There's not much point in going back up to the house until they've finished removing the bodies.'

'There's a sentence I never thought I'd hear,' she shook her head, 'but actually, I was thinking something else.' She finished her coffee and moved toward the sink to rinse the cup out.

'Oh?'

'I keep thinking about those girls,' she leaned back against the counter and chewed her lip thoughtfully. 'All the legends and rumors I've heard about the house have centered around the myth of Luella Lynch and the missing children, but those young women were too old. They wouldn't have been students at the school.'

'No,' Kelley agreed, 'they wouldn't have.'

'So, who were they? And how did they end up hidden below the house for god knows how many years. I feel like...'

'Like what?'

'It's going to sound really stupid.'

'I thought we'd already established that I love stupid,' he smiled as he raised his mug to his lips.

'Fine,' she snorted softly, 'I just feel... kinda responsible for them. They were found in the house that's been owned by my family for over a century. I feel like I need to figure out who they are and how they ended up there.'

'Sweetheart,' Kelley replied, 'that's what the police are for.'

'Yeah I know, I get that,' she frowned. 'It's just the other day when all the ladies from the historical society came up to the house...'

'I do recall,' he cringed. 'I accidentally gave them more than an eyeful as they were hiking through the woods and now Ivy won't leave me alone. The woman's downright terrifying. She's like one of those spiders that mate and then rip the male's head off and eat it.'

Ava laughed softly.

'Well, apart from that, when they were telling me the story of the house and the Lynches, I was watching Bunty's face. She was holding something back; she knows way more than she's letting on.'

'You want to go see Bunty?'

Ava nodded.

'I figure it's worth a shot at least,' she shrugged. 'I've got nothing better to do right now.'

'Well okay then,' Kelley rose slowly from his seat, picking up his empty plate and placing it in the sink.

'Do you... do you want to come with me?' she offered, a little unsure.

'Do you want me to?' he turned toward her.

She nodded.

'But don't you have summer classes to teach or something? Plus, you've got the bar.'

'Nope,' his lips popped on the word. 'No classes until tomorrow afternoon and like my dad said, my cousin Miranda is covering the bar for a few days.'

'I just feel like I've taken up so much of your time already, you wouldn't have even been in the house yesterday if it wasn't for me. You certainly wouldn't have ended up falling through the floor and being exposed to a potentially lethal poison.'

'Ava,' he stepped closer, 'don't do that. Don't feel guilty. I'm exactly where I want to be, doing exactly what I want to do and right now, apparently, that means going to visit a bunch of crazy old ladies,' his mouth curved slowly.

'You know, Ivy's probably going to be there, right?' her own mouth twitched in amusement.

'Yeah, and I'd like it noted, the lengths I'm willing to go to for you, including being pursued by a praying mantis.'

'Don't worry,' she smiled, 'I'll protect you.'

'Damn right you will,' he huffed. 'I'll be using you as a human shield.'

. . .

BY THE TIME they'd showered and dressed, and convinced Bailey to remain in Kelley's apartment, most of the morning was gone. They strolled easily down into the town, breathing in the salty air coming in off the tide as the temperature of the mid-day sun approached sweltering.

Kelley's hand slipped around hers as he guided her through the streets that were second nature to him, and she found that she didn't mind. Her mind was gently trying to remind her not to get too attached so it would hurt less when she moved on again, but the more time she spent in Midnight... the more time she spent with Kelley, the less she could picture leaving.

'You're so lucky,' she breathed as she watched the sparkling blue ocean at the end of the sloping street.

'Yeah?' he replied, his brows raised, 'because of my great sense of humor? My awesome intellect? Or is it because I'm so good looking?'

She laughed easily, everything was easy around him and there was a comfort in that, that she'd never experienced before.

'No, I mean growing up here,' she tugged on his hand gently. 'It's such a beautiful place.'

'It is,' he agreed. 'I think sometimes we islanders forget that. It's a great place to live, to grow up, to raise a family and not just because of its natural beauty but because of its sense of community too.'

'Did you ever think about leaving?' she asked curiously. 'I mean my mom did, so did Drew.'

'Well I can't answer for your mom,' he replied, 'but Drew, well he always wanted the bright lights and big city. He lives his life at only two speeds, a hundred miles an hour and unconscious.'

'Having met Drew, I can believe it,' she smiled. 'He has this energy about him, he never stops.'

'Yeah that's Drew. I love the guy but sometimes it's exhausting being his friend.'

'You never thought about leaving the island then?'

'No,' Kelley shook his head comfortably, 'I've got everything I need right here. Don't get me wrong I've traveled a bit, Boston, New York, we even headed over to the West coast for family vacations in California when we were kids. One year I begged my mom and dad to take us to Salem.'

'Salem?'

'Yeah, we'd been studying the witch trials in school and I don't know, it just fired my imagination. I was desperate to see it.'

'And did you?'

'Yeah,' he smiled softly in remembrance, 'they took me and Killian for Halloween. First Danvers, which historically was Salem village and then on to Salem itself which back in the 17th century was known as Salem Town. I tell you, no one does Halloween like Salem; they've got this incredible candy store there too.'

'Sounds like you had a great childhood,' she said a little wistfully.

'We did,' Kelley nodded, 'we were lucky.'

'San Francisco was the longest I ever stayed anywhere,' she told him quietly, 'when my dad was still alive.'

She reached into her back pocket and pulled out her phone, scrolling through until she found the picture of her and her dad sitting on his motorbike. The framed original Baz had given her was still packed away safely in her truck, but she'd taken a picture of it to keep on her phone, so she'd always have it with her.

She held it out to Kelley, who took her phone in his free hand and studied the picture with a smile.

'This is you?'

She nodded.

'Damn you were a cute kid,' he stared at her five-year-old self sitting astride the huge black shiny bike, with curly pigtails, aviator sunglasses that were too big for her face and a huge grin. 'This your dad?' his eyes moved to the bare-chested guy sitting comfortably behind her, barefoot and wearing nothing but cut-off jeans. A small chain of brown beads sat around his neck as he smiled widely. 'He looks a bit like Jim Morrison.'

'Yeah,' she laughed, 'he did. He'd listen to The Doors all the time,' she took the phone as he handed it back and slipped it into her pocket.

'Do you remember him much?' Kelley asked. 'You were quite young when he died, weren't you?'

'He died just a few months after that photo was taken actually.'

'Jesus,' he swore, 'that's rough.'

'It was a long time ago,' Ava shrugged, 'but I can still remember the heat of his skin when he'd been out in the sun on his bike. He was nearly always shirtless during the summer months. He'd scoop me up into his arms and hold me, he always smelled so good.'

'It's a good memory of him to have,' Kelley looked down as he studied her.

'After he died, we moved around a lot. When I got a little older, we even left the country for a while and traveled.'

'Really?' he replied in interest.

'Yeah,' she nodded. 'I think Serenity needed it, needed something completely different that didn't remind her of my dad. We made a pilgrimage to India.'

'Wow seriously?'

'We also spent some time in Thailand, but India was what really stuck in my memory.'

'What was it like?'

'Truthfully?'

'Yeah.'

'Filled with slums,' she breathed quietly. 'Once you get past a lot of the touristy places and into the real India, it's filled with poverty.'

'I've heard that,' he nodded.

'But the thing is,' she shook her head, 'I mean, sure we had to be real careful. It's very dangerous in places for unaccompanied women, but it's also full of history and secrets. Little gems hidden away, palaces and temples that you wouldn't even believe and long since abandoned. We made the Hindu pilgrimage to Galtaji, which is about 10 kilometers from Jaipur in the Indian state of Rajasthan.'

'Galtaji?'

'It's a series of temples built into the hills that surround Jaipur. There's a natural spring high on the hill that flows down into a series of pools in which pilgrims bathe. You can climb to the highest pool, to a hilltop temple and...' she broke off shaking her head. 'You can't even begin to imagine. I stood at the apex as the sun rose; the air was warm and humid, but there was a slight breeze. The small monkeys chattered all around me, running around my feet and as I looked out, the sky was on fire. All I could see for miles were slashes of red and orange, and there down below, was Jaipur nestled in the shadow of those towering hills, spread out across the valley floor.'

'It sounds incredible,' Kelley murmured as he watched her. 'How old were you?'

'Thirteen I guess, maybe a little younger.'

'You weren't scared?'

She shrugged.

'It was an adventure, well for me I suppose,' she replied thoughtfully. 'For Serenity it was something completely different. I don't know why she took us to India. Maybe she was searching for something... something spiritual, a kind of peace, I guess. There was always something so restless about her spirit, a weight she carried with her.'

'I have to admit,' he breathed heavily, 'I'm a little envious. Of places you've been, the things you've seen.'

'But you had a home to come back to,' she replied matter of factly, 'my life was like one never ending road trip.'

'Ava,' he stopped abruptly and turned to face her, 'can I ask you something?'

'I guess,' she replied warily.

'Did you go to school?'

'I'm not stupid if that's what you mean,' she snapped angrily and stalked away.

Knowing he'd hit a nerve he darted after her and caught her arm gently, turning her back toward him.

'I didn't say that,' he said gently. 'You have this real hang up about people thinking you're stupid and you're not. I don't think that for one second, just for the record. It's just little things. The lifestyle you were raised in leaves no opportunity for a consistent school-based education, but it also doesn't lend itself to home schooling either. Especially if your mom was constantly stoned as you've implied.'

'I didn't imply anything,' Ava replied flatly, 'she was stoned all the time.'

'When we were in those hidden rooms below the house, the bottles were all clearly labelled but you didn't know they were poison. You love stories, but you don't like to read,' he continued as he watched her face carefully, as the pieces began to fit together. 'You can't read very well, can you?'

Her spine straightened defensively and for a one long, endless moment the silence stretched out between them.

'I can read well enough to get by,' she finally replied, 'but my education was never real high up on Serenity's priority list.

217

Why do you think I waitress in cheap dives and diners? Because I'm too dumb to do anything else.'

She turned away from him, humiliation burning in her cheeks at having to admit her lack of education to him, to a college graduate and a teacher, for god's sake. It was so obvious that he was way out of her league.

'Ava,' he called out, jogging to catch up with her as he grasped her arm again. 'Ava, just stop. You're not dumb, far from it. I hate that you think that about yourself. It's even worse that you actually believe it. You...' he sighed in frustration, 'I've never met anyone like you Ava. I know you won't believe it, but you're incredible. You're fearless and resourceful and intelligent.'

She scoffed.

'Don't do that,' he scowled, 'there's a big difference between lack of intelligence and lack of education. Shockingly there are over 32 million adults in the US who are considered illiterate. They're not all stupid, their life circumstances simply meant they didn't have the opportunity or access to education. You may not have a high school diploma Ava but that doesn't make you less.'

'Do you have any idea how mortifying it is for someone like you to know?'

'Someone like me?'

'You know what I mean,' she frowned.

'Ava look at me,' he said quietly. 'What do you see?'

'A hot nerd in glasses,' she muttered sulkily.

He tried to hide the grin.

'Try again.'

'Fine,' she sighed. 'I see Kelley... the guy who makes me laugh. The guy who... makes my days brighter. The guy who makes me feel...'

'Makes you feel?' he unconsciously leaned closer.

'Who makes me feel like anything is possible.'

'There,' he smiled genuinely. 'When you look at me, you don't see a bunch of diplomas or certificates and credentials, you see a guy.'

'What do you see when you look at me?'

'Everything,' he murmured as his green eyes deepened.

'Kelley,' she stepped back and took a breath.

Seeing that she was struggling, and deciding to give her some breathing room, he also stepped back and held out his hand for her.

'Come on, let's go see Mrs McCarthy and her merry band of misfits. You know it'll cheer you up to see me getting hit on by senior citizens.'

Her mouth twitched slightly.

'Your face was priceless when Ivy pinched your butt.'

'There you go,' he smiled when she slipped her small hand in his, 'that's the spirit.'

They turned the corner and crossed the street to Bunty's Boutique, stopping when they realized the little shop was closed. Kelley leaned in, cupping his hand over his eyes as he pressed his face to the glass to look in. Stepping back, he glanced up at the building and frowned.

'The shop should be open,' he murmured. 'It's not like Mrs McCarthy to be closed at this time of day. If she's not able to work, she has Amy who covers part time. Come on,' he took her hand once again and towed her away from the sweet little blue shop with the snow-white trims.

'Where are we going?' Ava asked as she jogged to keep up with him.

'Not far, Mrs McCarthy's place is over on Jefferson. We should check in just to make sure she's okay.'

He was such a sweet guy, Ava thought to herself, and frustratingly, she had no defense against him.

They arrived at a catalogue perfect, two-story in biscuit beige with pretty gables. It sat on the corner of Jefferson and

Emery, surrounded by an immaculate picket fence and neatly trimmed lawn.

It suited Bunty, Ava decided. The woman was neat as a pin, with never a hair out of place, she thought as she lifted her hand and rang the dainty little bell.

After a few moments the door opened, and Ava's eyes widened a fraction.

'Uh...'

'Aaaava,' Bunty smiled widely as she elongated the vowels in Ava's name and leaned against the door frame, 'and Kelleeee.'

The normally pristine woman was not looking herself at all. Her usually perfectly groomed hair was sticking up in small tufts, her cheeks which were never without a fine dusting of Estée Lauder were pink and flushed. Her eyes wide and her pupils dilated as she continued to smile like a toothpaste commercial. Her signature string of pearls was pulled up to her throat and hung down her back, almost like she was wearing them backwards, and her dove gray pants suit was wrinkled.

'So nice of you to visit,' she beamed, 'I do lovvvvvvvve visitors.'

'Do you think she's having some sort of stroke?' Ava whispered to Kelley.

'Oh, you must come in,' she clapped her hands together and then paused, and clapped her hands together again as if she just loved the sound it made.

'Oh my god she's having a breakdown,' Ava murmured.

'Come in, come in, come in, come in....' she stepped back and frowned. 'What was I saying?'

'Come in,' Kelley supplied helpfully.

'Yes! what a good idea! The ladies are here; we're having tea and we have the loveliest guest.'

Kelley and Ava gasped as Bunty turned and wandered back into the house leaving them standing on the stoop, staring at each other in bemusement. Given no choice, they stepped in and closed the door, following the sound of voices into the living room.

Bunty was right, the entire group of them were there, plus a few extras Ava noted as she scanned the room.

Norma was parked on a floral couch of pale pink and purple, knitting ferociously. The last time Ava had seen her she was laid back and knitting rather languidly. With no real thought or purpose to what she was creating, it was more like the action of clicking needles and looping yarn soothed her.

Not now, she was a demon on a mission. Her needles clacked together so savagely Ava wouldn't have been surprised to see smoke rising from the melting metal. Norma leaned forward, her tongue poking out slightly in concentration and her gaze fixed on the task, holding the knitting inches from her nose. The monstrosity she'd been knitting last time had grown to almost Jurassic proportions. It coiled and looped in great green woolen entrails over the person who had the misfortune to be sitting next to her clutching a cup of tea. Although who it was Ava couldn't tell, as only the torso covered in a white cardigan, followed by a neat skirt and sensible shoes were visible.

Barbara, the prim and proper club secretary was sitting close by, fanning herself with a magazine, her face beet red and her neat blouse untucked.

'It's so warm in here,' she muttered to herself while the others completely ignored her. 'Why is it so warm?'

Betty sat on the other side of her, her eyes wild and her pupils dilated while she dug ravenously into a giant bag of potato chips. Bunty hovered on the edges of the room, a little jittery and not at all herself.

Sitting sedately on one of the couches, happily planted between Betty and Ivy was the reason why.

'BAZ?' Ava blurted in surprise, 'what the hell are you doing here?'

'Ava,' he smiled up at her, 'I was looking for you.'

'You know this guy?' Kelley asked curiously as he took in the loud, bright red Hawaiian shirt, the pink and blue harem pants and the lime green Birkenstocks.

'This is Baz,' she sighed, 'he's a friend of my mom's, he lives in Arizona, he was also her lawyer.'

'He's a lawyer?' Kelley's brows rose.

'Yeah,' she frowned. 'Baz what are you doing here?'

'Oh well,' he replied, 'I was looking for you. I came off the ferry and met Bunty here,' he winked in her direction which sent her into girlish giggles. 'When she found out I knew your mom and I was looking for you, she introduced me to the ladies here and they invited me in for tea.'

Ava glanced around at the assorted ladies.

'Baz,' her eyes widened in realization, 'please tell me you didn't get the Ladies Historical Society, Book club and literary luncheon, STONED?'

He smiled beatifically up at her and lifted a china plate.

'Brownie?'

'BAZ!' she hissed.

'I didn't want to take my stash across state lines. You know how they can be about that sort of thing and they seem to always want to pull me over.'

'Can't imagine why,' she replied dryly.

'Anyway, I figured I'd bake up a batch of brownies, you know, for the road,' he continued, 'but when the ladies here were kind enough to ask me in for tea, I felt it was only fair I brought something along.'

Ava pinched the bridge of her nose and sighed.

'What did you use Baz?'

'I made them with dragon butter,' he shrugged.

'Dragon butter,' her eyes widened, 'are you mad? They're little old ladies.'

'I'll admit it's a little strong, but it won't hurt them,' he picked a brownie off the plate and bit into it.

'Oooh, don't mind if I do handsome,' Ivy leaned over and batted her eyelashes as she retrieved a brownie and daintily bit into it, giving Baz a coy look.

'Oh, sweet baby Jesus,' Ava rolled her eyes to the ceiling.

'Are they going to be alright?' Kelley asked in amusement as he watched Barbara staring at the ticking hand of a carriage clock as if it were the most riveting thing in the world.

'They'll be fine,' Ava frowned in annoyance. 'Trust me, within an hour they'll be out cold and sleeping it off. You might want to go to the kitchen though and see if Bunty has any cookies or chips. They'll be getting the munchies soon and we need to try and prize the brownies away from them before they eat any more.'

She glanced over at Esther who was already snoring loudly in the corner.

'KELLEY?' a muffled voice came from underneath the green toadstool of knitting next to Norma. 'KELLEY is that you?'

The pile of green wool wriggled a bit and as the layers fell away, it revealed another lady, but one Ava didn't recognize.

'GRANDMA?' Kelley's eyes widened.

She gave him a wide stoner's smile, filled with affection.

'Awww look it's my grandson! Everyone look, my grandson, isn't he a handsome boy!'

'He sure is,' Ivy turned her predatory gaze on him and licked her lips, which wouldn't have been the least bit seductive even if they weren't smeared with brownie crumbs.

Kelley slowly grasped Ava's arm and inched her in front of him.

'Come and kiss Grandma!' his grandmother held out her hands and made grabby motions.

'Maybe later,' he replied as he eyed Ivy warily.

'That's your grandma?' Ava whispered in horror. 'Oh my god Kelley,' she hissed, 'what's your dad gonna say when he finds out my dead mom's lawyer got his mom stoned?'

'Life is never dull with you Ava,' he shook his head.

'Ava!' his grandma grinned widely. 'OH! So, this is Ava! I'm Alma dear, Kelley's grandma. Don't you worry about my Gus, he's too stuffy for his own good anyway.'

'Grandma, he's a cop, he's supposed to be.'

'Pffft,' she waved him away. 'You're so beautiful, isn't she beautiful? Doesn't my Kelley know how to pick 'em? Oh! they're going to make me such pretty great grand babies.'

'Er... no... I...' Ava's eyes widened, 'that's not... we're not...' she flapped her hand, indicating back and forth between her and Kelley with her finger, trying to find the right words.

'Oh no need to be shy dear,' Alma winked conspiratorially. 'I've heard all about you and Kelley naked in the back of a truck, from my Gus.'

'Oh my god,' Ava pressed her fingers tightly into her temples hoping to wake herself from this very weird, very vivid nightmare. 'We weren't naked.'

'We kinda were,' Kelley whispered.

'Not helping,' she glared at him and he stepped back with his hands raised in surrender.

'Look,' Alma reached into her purse which was tucked at her side. She placed her little wire framed glasses on and lifted her phone. 'Now how does this work again.' She poked at the screen experimentally a few times with awkward fingers before beaming and turning the phone around to show everyone the picture of Kelley standing in front of Ava's truck, wearing nothing but a frying pan and a scowl.

'Um hmmmm,' Ivy hummed in pleasure, her eyes narrow and heavy lidded as she puckered a kiss in his direction.

'GRANDMA!' Kelley growled, 'I'm going to kill Killian!'

Alma smiled and leaned over, helping herself to another brownie.

'Alma I really wouldn't...' Ava protested, but Alma ignored her, biting into the brownie with glee and grinning widely, with chunks of brownie stuck to her teeth.

Click.

Ava turned around to stare as Kelley lifted his own phone and snapped a picture.

'Forget the family album,' he told his grandmother with a smirk, 'that one's going on the front of this year's Christmas card!'

Betty crunched her potato chips loudly, shoveling them rapidly into her mouth, as her eyes darted back and forth between them.

'Baz,' Ava sighed in exasperation, 'what are you doing here?'

'I told you, there was tea and a ferry...'

'No, I mean what are you doing on Midnight Island?'

'I came to see you,' he frowned.

'So you said,' she almost rolled her eyes in frustration trying to get a straight answer, 'but WHY?'

'Oh, didn't I say?'

'No,' she shook her head.

'I came to bring you these,' he shuffled forward on the couch and reached into his pants pocket. He emptied out the contents, searching through the fluff, spare change, cherry life-savers and finally picked out two items, handing them over to Ava. 'These were part of your mom's will; you forgot to collect them before you left Bisbee.'

Ava looked down at the items nestled in the palm of her hand. One was a delicate little golden locket the size of a half dollar, on a long chain. It was slightly old and tarnished. She clicked it open but there were no pictures inside it, just the green velvet inserts. All in all, it was a plain, unremarkable piece of jewelry that was not at all her mother's style. More often than not Serenity would be found in moonstones and beads. Ava couldn't understand why her mother would keep the locket, but not only that, why she actually went to the trouble, in her will, of ensuring it came to Ava.

Slipping the chain around her neck so she wouldn't lose it, the locket settled between her breasts, hanging down almost to her rib cage. Looking down at the second object in her hand her heart jolted slightly in recognition. Although she'd swear blind she'd never seen it before, there was something unsettlingly familiar about the old pocket watch attached to a short chain and clip. Something she couldn't quite remember. Pressing the tiny shell shaped button at the edge the lid flipped open to reveal the watch inside. It was no longer working, the hands had long since stopped moving and were frozen at midnight, or midday, depending on the point of view.

She held it up to her ear. Although the hands no longer moved and could not tell the time, she could still hear a quiet ticking sound, almost like the watch had a heartbeat.

Closing the lid, she brushed the worn, slightly dented metal with her thumb. Etched elegantly into the face were the initials *E.L.*

Ava glanced up at the sound of Bunty squeaking slightly in distress. When her dark gaze landed on the older woman, she saw her standing with her hands pressed tightly to her mouth, her eyes wide and locked on the old pocket watch in her hand. Her eyes flitted up catching sight of Ava watching her curiously, she gave another squeak of distress and scurried from the room.

Ava glanced at Kelley who shrugged in confusion and nodded toward the door. Taking him up on his suggestion Ava followed Bunty, finding her in the kitchen sitting at the table pouring herself a brandy.

'Bunty are you alright?' Ava asked.

'Yes, yes dear I'm fine,' she tossed the contents of the small glass back in one un-ladylike slurp.

'I don't think you are,' Ava crossed the room and sat down next to her, 'and it has something to do with this, doesn't it?'

She held out the small battered gold watch.

'Don't,' she shook her head.

'Don't what?' Ava asked in confusion. 'What is this all about Bunty? Do you know who the watch belongs to?'

Bunty nodded slowly.

'Ephraim Lynch,' she whispered.

'Bunty what the hell is going on?' Ava breathed heavily. 'I know you know more than you're letting on. Please tell me.'

'You don't know what you're asking,' Bunty replied desperately. 'Once you know, there's no going back and she made me promise.'

'Who did?'

'Hari,' Bunty answered, her eyes filled with indecision and worry.

'What did she make you promise?'

'Ava, the house,' she took a deep breath, 'it's always been about the house and now they've found the bodies, it's only a matter of time before they find the rest.'

'The rest?' Ava's eyes widened. 'Bunty are you telling me there are more bodies in the house?'

Bunty shook her head.

'So many bad things went on in that house, they left a terrible scar, a wound that never fully healed. Once it has you it will never let you go. Hari was trapped here, Caroline ran to save herself and you,' she reached out and gripped her cheek with frail papery hands, 'sweet girl you should never have come to the island. Now I fear it is too late for you.'

'What do you mean?' Ava swallowed slowly her throat suddenly dry.

Bunty suddenly climbed to her feet, the chair screeching

loudly against the floor. She crossed the room and retrieved something from a drawer and handed it to Ava.

'What's this?' Ava stared down at the old dog-eared envelope.

'Your grandmother left that for you before she died. Take it and read it. Once you do, you'll have a choice. You either get on the ferry, leave the island and never look back.'

'Or?'

'Or you come back and find me, and I will tell you everything, but I warned you once before Ava, truth comes at a terrible cost.'

14

*A*va sat Indian style, crossed legged on the long dry grass, as the breeze rippled and tugged at her hair. One of the things she loved about the island was that despite the summer temperatures, the cool breeze coming in off the Atlantic made the long summer days pleasant rather than stifling. At night the temperature would cool enough to make sleeping easier, unless plagued with strange dreams, which Ava had been most nights. Dreams that were made even worse by the fact she couldn't remember.

It was infuriating. She'd wake in the early hours of the morning, sometimes drenched in an icy cold sweat and feeling such strong emotions.

Sometimes she'd be so sad, filled with loss and sorrow. Other times she'd be filled with anger and fury. Then there were the times she felt completely helpless and afraid, but every single time she couldn't bring to mind the cause of these emotions. She couldn't understand where these feeling came from. It was almost like they weren't her emotions, like she was experiencing someone else's pain.

She reached out and idly stroked Bailey's pointed ears as she lay out on the warm grass and stared up at the brooding, silent house in front of her. She'd been sitting on the letter Bunty had given her for almost two days. She wasn't entirely sure what was stopping her from reading it. Maybe it was the dramatic, over the top, theatrical warnings and predictions about the house. Maybe it was her own growing paranoia over the property, or maybe it was just as simple as she didn't want to risk rejection, even from beyond the grave.

Her grandmother, whom she'd never met, had gone to the trouble of writing a letter to be read posthumously to the daughter, of the daughter who'd abandoned her. Call her crazy, but Ava was certain that was not going to make for happy reading.

It felt like she had so much crap going on in her head that she couldn't seem to sort it into neat little piles. A week ago, she'd been happy. Not just content but actual, honest to God, happy, right down to her bones. The work on her house was well under way, she was making friends and being accepted into the community. She also loved cooking for everyone, nothing else had given her such a sense of satisfaction before.

Then there was Kelley...

The guy who'd gone and snuck right under her radar and set up camp. The guy who made her want to look ahead, to plan a future. She'd had this crazy idea in her head that she was going to ask him to help her get her high school diploma. In the day to day reality it wouldn't make a difference of course, it wasn't like she was going to go to college or suddenly get all career orientated, but it would mean something to her. She wanted to prove to herself she could do it.

She shook her head.

Damn it, the longer she was on island the more she could picture herself staying. That was another reason for not reading the letter. Bunty had implied that the information revealed in the letter would force her into a choice, stay or leave. What if she found out something she really didn't want to know? What if she had no choice but to leave? The thought made her chest ache and her stomach burn.

She didn't want to leave.

There, she'd admitted it. She was madly in love with the island and pretty intensely in 'like' with Kelley, the kind of like which could all too easily trip over into something a hell of a lot scarier if she let it.

She stared back up at the house once again and still felt that tug. It was just a house. Okay, sure, so they'd actually found dead bodies in the basement. Not ideal; worst case scenario one of her ancestors was possibly a deranged would-be serial killer, but all that other crap? There was no such thing as ghosts. The place wasn't haunted. Stuff like that just wasn't real. It couldn't be. She was just letting herself get carried away with everyone else's overactive imaginations.

The truth was, she had come to a crossroads. With or without the letter, she needed to make a choice. The summer was drawing to a close, they were already heading into September. Kelley would return to teaching for the new semester and there was really only a couple of months before the weather turned. She had a small window of opportunity to either continue restoring the house or cut her losses and bull-doze it to the ground, with all of its secrets.

At that moment she couldn't say either was particularly appealing. She flopped back against the grass with a frustrated sigh, staring up at the cloudless blue sky. With the breeze rippling over her skin like a playful lover and the sounds of the ocean crashing at the foot of the cliff, she found her eyes drifting closed.

'Ava...'

She bolted upright, her heart hammering in her chest as she sucked in a deep breath. She thought she'd heard her name, a husky whisper, so close she could've sworn she'd felt a puff of breath against her ear. But now sitting up on the grass, there was no one there but her dog, who was looking at her strangely.

She glanced up at the sky. The bright blue cloudless sky was now overcast, gray clouds drifted above her, casting shadows across the cliff top. She shuddered, wondering how long she'd slept for. The air was ripe with the strong hazy scent of ozone as the first fat drops of summer rain began to fall.

Ava looked toward the house, the only shelter other than her RV which was sealed with crime scene tape and still not repaired. She stood and dusted the grass from her shorts, but as Bailey began to bark loudly, she glanced up and her heart jolted in her chest.

Just for a split second she was sure she'd seen a little boy standing in the doorway of the house. The doorway which, she realized uncomfortably, had been closed when she'd fallen asleep and now stood wide open. She shifted, as if she were going to head toward the house but hesitated at the last moment.

Maybe she was more spooked by Bunty's dire warnings than she'd thought. It was stupid, she shook her head, annoyed with herself. There was no such thing as ghosts and she was going to prove it, to herself and everyone else.

She took one very determined step toward the house when a car suddenly appeared at the top of the road, pulling in and parking next to her. A tall, lanky, familiar body climbed out and approached her.

'Kelley?' she asked, blinking through the rain, 'what are you doing here? I thought you had a class to teach?'

'I did,' he replied, 'hours ago. When you didn't come back, I was worried. My dad still doesn't have any leads on who trashed the RV and it makes me nervous when you're up here all alone. Whoever it was doesn't seem to have good intentions, not to mention the few die hard reporters who are still sniffing around, as well as the obsessed ghost hunters.'

Although there was a police perimeter and a couple of security guards hired to protect the property until the fascination with the recovered bodies died down, he was right, it was stupid to be up there alone.

'I fell asleep,' she shook her head. 'I didn't realize what the time was.'

'Well,' he glanced up at the sky as the rain came down harder, 'we should probably head back.'

Ava glanced at the open door once more.

'There's something I have to do first,' she headed toward the house.

'Ava?' he hurried after her, 'what are you doing?' He climbed up the stone steps and grasped her hand, stopping her just outside the open doorway, partially sheltered from the rain by the second-floor balcony above them.

'I saw,' she frowned, 'I thought I saw a little boy.'

'Where?' Kelley replied, 'in the house?'

'Standing in the doorway,' she looked up at Kelley.

'Jesus Christ,' he shook his head. 'Fearless,' he muttered. 'You're the only person I know who would go charging into a haunted house after admitting to seeing a little boy standing on the doorstep.'

'I have to check, Kelley,' she frowned. 'What if it's some kid up here on a dare; what if he falls through another part of the floor like we did? And gets hurt?'

Kelley blew out a heavy breath. He hated to admit it because the scared little kid part of his brain was screaming GHOST! RUN! at the top of his lungs, whereas the adult part of his brain was saying, go check it's not a real kid. Damn it, he hated being responsible.

'Fine,' he frowned, 'let's go check. But if it is a ghost, please try not to think less of me when I scream like a little girl and pass out.'

'I'm not making any promises,' her mouth curled, and she reached out, taking his hand. 'Bailey,' she whistled for her dog, frowning when she remained resolutely seated next to Kelley's car.

Ava whistled again but she flat out refused to move.

'That can't be a good sign,' Kelley muttered as they took a deep breath and stepped into the house.

'Hello?' Ava called out.

'Don't do that,' Kelley turned to her with wide eyes, 'because if someone answers back, I swear I really am going to pass out.'

Ava chuckled as they began to check the rooms one by one. Although she knew some part of him really was scared, she also knew he'd protect her with his dying breath.

One by one they checked all the rooms on the lower floor, but they found nothing. Finally, they arrived back in the study with the huge hole still in the floor where they'd fallen through. Standing at the top on reinforced planks of wood looking down, it seemed like such a long way down and she couldn't understand how they hadn't seriously injured themselves.

'Seems a bit surreal now doesn't it?' Kelley mused as he too stood staring into the pit.

'Is it safe down there now?'

'Why?' he asked suspiciously.

She looked up at him.

'NO,' he shook his head, 'no way. You want to go back into the creepy ass murder room?'

'Don't you?' her mouth curved slowly.

He hesitated, struggling with the curiosity versus the fear.

'Yeah,' he burst out finally, 'yeah I do.'

She grinned a little wider.

'No flashlights this time,' he told her firmly, 'if we go down, we go down safely. They hooked up temporary lighting down there while they were bringing up the bodies.'

'Okay,' she nodded, waiting while Kelley disappeared back through the doorway. After a few moments the huge hole in the floor was flooded with light.

'Is it on?' his disembodied voice called from the main foyer.

'Yeah,' she called back.

He headed back into the room and stopped beside Ava as they stared down into the hole. There was a ladder propped against the edge, descending down into the corridor below. There were also several sturdy canvas straps which they'd obviously used to haul the coffins up.

'I guess we climb down then,' Kelley muttered, his stomach flipping nervous somersaults.

'Yeah,' Ava frowned.

'What is it?'

'I don't know,' she replied quietly, her forehead furrowed in confusion as she looked up from the hole and glanced around the room. 'There's something familiar.'

'Ava you've been in this room a dozen times.'

'No,' she shook her head, 'it's stronger than that. It feels like Deja vu. There's something about this room, something important. I just can't remember.'

It hovered at the very edge of her consciousness, like a shadow standing just outside her field of vision, a half-remembered dream. It was there, so close she almost had it.

Kelley watched in silence as she stepped away from the hole in the floor, wandering slowly around the room, her fingers brushing along the surfaces of the bookshelves leaving trails of fingerprints in the heavy dust, like fairy footprints.

'He was so scared,' she whispered.

'Who was?' Kelley asked curiously.

'What?'

'You said he was so scared,' Kelley replied.

'Did I?' she frowned, that was weird. She hadn't realized she'd said anything at all.

She turned her attention back to the room. It was speaking so loudly to her now; she couldn't focus on Kelley at all. It was almost as if he'd disappeared from her field of perception altogether. Her skin prickled with awareness. Her vision narrowed and there was a strange buzzing across her scalp making her feel almost dizzy. Without thinking she reached out to the bookcase in front of her and her fingers brushed the aged wood. Feeling a familiar indentation, she hooked the very tips of her fingers under the tiny concealed lever and lifted.

The was a loud clanking and whirring noise, followed by a series of clicks. Stepping back, she watched as the bookcase slowly creaked open.

'Well I'll be damned,' Kelley's eyes widened. 'How the hell did you find that?'

'Watched too many classic horror movies I guess,' she muttered, her brow furrowing, but even as the words left her mouth, she knew they weren't true.

She'd found the hidden lever, because she'd known exactly where to look. Somehow the information was planted deep in her subconscious and she was at a complete loss as to how to explain it.

Kelley whistled low as he moved to stand beside her, studying the concealed side of the doorway in fascination.

'Will you look at that?' his eyes widened, 'it's like a vault at Gringotts.'

'What?' she replied in confusion.

'Harry Potter? Never mind,' he shook his head as he continued to study the door raptly.

The front of the hidden door was a bookcase but the back of it was like the innards of a clock. Hundreds of tiny cogs, spirals, springs and wheels, of brass, silver and gold made up the strange locking mechanism.

'Look at the detail in this,' Kelley breathed, utterly transfixed by the strange sight. 'Can you imagine how long it must have taken to painstakingly create a concealed locking system this complex?'

'It seems a bit like overkill,' Ava managed as she swallowed hard. For some reason her heart was pounding with a kind of nervous trepidation.

Kelley peered into the darkness. The space it opened up into had curved walls, just wide enough to accommodate a metal, spiral staircase, which wound down into the darkness below, like the descent into a deep well. At the bottom was a burst of light spilling into the turret-like room from the corridor below the study.

'This must've been the original entrance to the passageway, until we crashed through the floor and made our own,' Kelley mused. 'You still want to go down?'

She nodded slowly as Kelley slipped her cold trembling hand into his larger warm one.

'You don't have to,' he told her, noticing her pale face. 'We can leave right now.'

'No,' she decided, swallowing hard. 'I want to... I think I need to.'

Stepping out onto the staircase, he tested it. Satisfied it was solid, he led Ava slowly down the stairs, circling and circling until he was beginning to feel slightly nauseous. Finally, they reached the bottom step and were greeted, this time, not with a doorway but an entire section of wall, covered once again in the intricate clockwork mechanism.

The wall had slid to the side revealing the corridor stretched out before them. Stepping through they looked behind them to see that the wall blended in perfectly. Once the entrance was closed, it was undetectable.

'Clever,' Kelley clicked his tongue thoughtfully. 'Unless you know it's there, it's completely invisible. I wonder how many more secret passageways and rooms there are?'

Ava looked up at him silently.

'Well, if you think about it,' Kelley continued, 'the legend of Luella and the missing children could be explained by hidden rooms beneath the house.'

'I don't even want to think about that right now,' she shook her head. 'We've already got enough bodies to worry about.'

Kelley nodded as their hands once again entwined then they turned and began to move down the corridor to the doorway at the far end. The space was now well lit. Dozens of wires ran from the portable generators above ground, down through the hole in the study, and had been temporarily mounted along the walls either side of the corridor. From each of the old candle sconces on the walls, hung at intervals, were bright lights, the power cords looped along the wall, bunched together and strung out like entrails.

The carpet beneath their feet was a faded crimson and covered, almost silver in patches, from thick decades old layers of spiders' webs.

Scattered at their feet were chunks of wood and nasty, spiky looking splinters, the only remnants of the desk which had crashed through the hole in the ceiling above them, nearly crushing them. The desk had been removed and the way was now clear.

They headed to the other end of the corridor without a word. The wires trailed down the second winding staircase, once again accompanied by thick canvas straps.

It must have been a bitch to get those coffins out and winch them up the narrow staircase without breaking them.

At the bottom, they stepped through the doorway, which was open a crack, with the wires from the lights winding around and through into the room beyond.

The mortuary room was bigger than she remembered, but then again, she had been looking at it through the confined beam of a flashlight, Ava thought, as she stepped into the room.

It was circular, something which had also slipped her notice the first time. She glanced around at the well-lit room. The porcelain table was still butted up against a deep rectangular sink fed by an old water pump. Beside it was the metal wheeled trolley which was now empty.

Ignoring the desk and the stacks of books, and medical texts Kelley was pouring over, she turned instead to the shelving containing rows upon rows of apothecary bottles and jars of varying shapes, sizes and contents. Every so often she'd encounter a void, a tell-tale ring imprinted in the dust where bottles considered too dangerous had been removed and scheduled for destruction.

Her gaze glided over the labels, which she struggled to read. The lettering was in faded ink and the penmanship dated, a curly slanted script that made reading the names even more difficult. Eventually she gave up, her gaze straying to another doorway.

Again, the door was ajar from the electric wires, which lit the room beyond. Unable to help herself Ava slowly lifted her hand and pushed the door open fully.

This room was square, but equally as large. Pushed against the far wall and facing out into the room was a huge, heavy wooden framed bed with a canopy. Tattered curtains in a heavy brocade hung from each corner, in the same faded emerald green of the bedding.

As she stood in front of the creepy masculine bed, she

turned slowly and in her direction line of vision were several huge gaping spaces in the wall alcoves, where the coffins had been set.

'Ava?' Kelley spoke from the doorway.

'The sick son of a bitch liked to look at them,' she muttered, a shudder of revulsion sliding slickly down her spine as a greasy roll of nausea churned in her belly. 'Like trophies,' she whispered as she turned back to the bed. For a split second she could see him. A filmy insubstantial image flashed through her mind, of one of the dead girls in his bed.

She blinked, sweat beading on her forehead. Her stomach roiled treacherously as she stumbled back and in that second, she knew, she couldn't say how, but she knew what he'd done. He'd brought the dead girls to his bed so he could play with them before he embalmed them, then he would stare at them for hours, sealed away in their coffins while he pleasured himself.

The vomit was rising in her throat, almost choking her with disgust. She could smell him in the room, sweat and tobacco, could feel his sick, disturbed arousal.

She needed to get out. It was too much, she felt like she was suffocating.

She staggered past Kelley, through the mortuary room and out into the corridor, trying to take in a calming breath, in through her nose and out through her mouth so she didn't throw up.

She didn't stop until she was at the top of the staircase and through the doorway into the corridor. Clammy sweat pinned her rain-soaked t-shirt to her back as she leaned forward, resting her hands on her knees as the wave of dizziness passed.

It was the same as before, when Kelley had to carry her out. The same dizziness and nausea but this time the room hadn't been filled with corpses and poison. It was as if the house itself was trying to tell her its secrets and she wasn't sure if she could handle it.

'Ava?' Kelley called her name, his voice filled with concern, 'are you okay?'

She nodded as she swallowed past the tight dryness in her throat, wishing she had a bottle of water. Despite the lingering shakiness she pushed herself back to standing and looked up.

Kelley had been standing in the doorway watching her worriedly, but suddenly, like an unlocked door, a window opened in her mind and she saw him, the strange man, standing in that same doorway. He had been huge and imposing, the sheer brute strength of him, dressed elegantly in a gentleman's shirt and waistcoat, the chain of his golden pocket watch draped across the expensive silken material. His eyes were as dark as his jet-black hair, which was punctuated by two pure white wings at his temples.

'Ava?' Kelley grasped her arms; her face was so white she looked like she was about to pass out. 'AVA?' he called to her again.

She blinked and her eyes cleared. Locking on Kelley she saw the rich forest green of his eyes, and the warm brown of his sun kissed hair, felt the soft gentle touch of his hands on her and it grounded her in a way nothing else could.

'I'm okay,' she whispered. Her eyes widened in a sudden realization and they locked on him determinedly, 'but there is something I have to do.'

'WHAT?' he called after her as she turned and ran back down the corridor and up the staircase. Kelley was right behind her as they emerged from the hidden entrance into the study. 'What are you doing?' he asked as he followed her out the room, trying to keep up with her as she darted through the main foyer and toward the back of the cavernous house, where she finally ended up in the scullery.

'I have to know,' she breathed heavily as her gaze landed on a heavy wooden table pushed up against the wall.

'Know what?' he asked in confusion.

'If its real,' she looked up at him with wide eyes, 'or if I imagined it.'

Before he could question her further, she purposefully crossed the room and shoved the table a couple of inches. Going with it and curious at her determination, he helped her push the heavy old table out of the way, watching as she dropped to her knees and ran her hands over the rough brick wall.

'What are you looking for?'

Her fingers felt a small groove, and she froze, looking up at Kelley. Reaching into her pocket she retrieved the pocket watch Baz had given her a few days earlier and which, for some unknown reason, she'd taken to carrying around with her.

She pressed the little shell shaped button at the edge and watched as the lid flipped open, revealing the watch beneath. Drawing in a slow breath, her heart pounding in her chest, she turned the face counterclockwise. It moved smoothly as if it were well oiled, and with a small click a skeleton key appeared.

'What the...' Kelley muttered with a frown.

She slipped the key into the groove in the wall with a small click and looked up at Kelley who was watching her silently. She turned the key and once again heard a series of clicks and whirs. The bricks split, a line which up to that point had been almost invisible, appeared and a tiny door opened.

'You're beginning to scare me a bit,' Kelley said quietly.

'I'm beginning to scare myself a bit,' she replied with a heavy breath.

She opened the door which was scarcely bigger than the door of a stove, revealing a tiny, uncomfortable looking space, barely three feet by three feet of cold hard stone. There was a small envelope shaped brass air vent but that was it. The space was empty.

She was about to step back and close the door when she noticed Kelley's eyes fixed on one of the walls inside the confined space.

There were scratches and as she traced her fingers gently over them, she realized it was a named, etched into the stone.

'Edison.'

ew York City.
Mar 1892.

SHE RESTLESSLY PACED THE FLOOR, her heavy skirts brushing the polished wood as she wrung her hands in deep concern. She could hear the ticking of the small clock on the mantle, the only sound in the room other than her frantic pacing. It seemed like an eternity had passed but her mind refused to focus on anything else.

'Don't let him die, please Lord don't let him die...'

She turned her head abruptly and ceased pacing, with the click of the handle turning as the door slowly opened.

The doctor appeared, grim faced beneath his heavy moustache, his black case in one hand and his hat in the other.

'Doctor?' she rushed forward.

He nodded slowly and she released the breath she wasn't aware she'd been holding. She turned to brush past him, heading for the door to the bedroom but his raised hand halted her.

'Madam, a moment if you will.'

'What is it?' she turned her worried gaze upon him.

'A word of caution,' he sighed, his voice a deep rumble, 'to prepare yourself. His convulsions have subsided, but they will return, gaining in frequency and strength. A legacy of the injury to his head. As you already know, his body no longer functions due to the damage to his spine. Other than breathing, there is very little he can do. He will not return to the man you knew, there is no hope for his recovery. It is a mystery that he has survived this long. He cannot feed himself; his speech will deteriorate, and his body will waste away.'

'You're wrong Doctor,' she replied fiercely, 'the Lord spared him for a reason, you will see. He will prove you wrong.'

'He will require more care than you are able to give on your own,' he told her bluntly as he reached into his pocket and presented her with his bill.

Unfolding the piece of paper, she carefully schooled her features not to show any emotion, as she'd been taught. Her back straightened and she purposefully crossed the room, opening the small chest on the bureau and retrieving a few dollars from their measly, dwindling supply.

'Here,' she handed it to him, 'thank you for your time Doctor.'

'Madam,' he nodded, as he placed his hat back on and tipped it politely.

She saw him out, closing and locking the door behind him, once again standing alone in the stillness of the room with only the ticking clock for company. The two rooms they rented were small but expensive. New York was an expensive city and with her husband no longer able to work to support them it would not be long before they would be homeless. She could take a job as a seamstress in one of the big department stores but then that would leave no one to see to his care. She could not afford a nurse and the rent, and food. She closed her eyes and took a deep breath. There was no other choice.

They would have to return to Midnight Island.

It would have to be done soon, before their funds ran out completely and they couldn't afford the transport. It wasn't as simple as getting on a train and then the ferry across to the island. Her husband could no longer walk, and he was not yet strong enough to sit unaided in a wheelchair. He would have to be transferred by stretcher. She would have to hire men to carry him, make special travel arrangements. She wasn't sure they could afford it... but her father in law could.

Her husband had been so adamant that they would not ask him for a single dime. In the six months since their wedding, and their hasty departure from the island, she wasn't even sure he'd spoken with his father. She hated going against his wishes, but she would have to do so now.

She sat down at the bureau and retrieved a fresh sheet of paper, dipping her quill in the ink pot which had almost run dry. She wrote eloquently, imploring her father in law, for the love of his only son, to send for them and to allow them to return to Midnight Island, to her husband's childhood home atop the cliffs, where perhaps the familiarity and bracing sea air might aid in reviving his health.

Once finished she sealed it in an envelope and dug a few coins from the chest. Stuffing the letter and the coins into the pocket of her skirt she grabbed her shawl and wrapped it around her thin shoulders. She would have to be quick; she couldn't leave him for long.

She headed out of their rooms, navigating the huge apartment block down to the ground floor and stepped out into the smog filled street. Pulling the shawl closer around her, she squinted through the heavy air. She could see the lamp lighters from the sooty orange glow appearing at intervals along the street. She kept her head down, hurrying along the sidewalk, the clatter of horses' hooves and the blare of the automobiles clanking along the uneven streets, filling the misty gray air.

It didn't take her long to leave the letter with the postal service. By the time she returned to their apartment the chilly evening air was already seeping into her bones. She was tempted to light the fire in the parlor, but she couldn't waste the coal. She would need it to make sure the small fire in the bedroom kept burning, his frail body couldn't afford to take a chill.

Locking the door behind her, she crossed the room, opening the door to the bedroom softly so as not to disturb him if he was sleeping. She quietly clicked the door closed behind her, stoking the fire and adding more coal before she settled in the chair beside the bed and pulled the blanket over her legs. She'd not slept in their bed since the accident, not wanting to cause him any pain as he recovered.

But he wasn't recovering, not significantly. He'd been struck by one of those awful automobiles. It had been late, and thanks to the smog, visibility had been low. He'd been pulled under the wheels; it was a miracle he'd survived they said.

She reached out with gentle fingers and drew a lock of his jet-black hair away from his forehead, revealing an angry red scar which ran from his hairline to his temple. His face was gaunt and pale, he'd lost such a lot of weight in a very short amount of time, his arms and legs laying useless against the sheets.

He'd been so vibrant, so full of life. He'd held her and swung her around and danced with her. She would have given anything to have him hold her that way again. To just feel the strength in his arms as he wrapped them around her small frame.

She stroked his cheek, feeling the stubble scratching the pads of her fingers. She'd have to shave him in the morning. She didn't want to disturb him while he slept. The fits took so much out of his already weakened body.

She took his lax hand in hers and held on; he couldn't feel it, but she needed the contact. Turning her head, she stared into the flames of the meagre fire and her heart ached.

After a while, she sensed him begin to stir, his head turning toward her, her name a slurred whisper on his dry cracked lips.

'It's okay my love,' she soothed him, 'I'm here.'

She tried not to show her pain, to put on a brave face, for his despair was enough for the both of them and it was etched deeply into his face.

'I'm sorry,' he whispered, 'this was not the life I promised you.'

'Hush now,' she soothed the bedclothes over his torso, touching

the small gold cross at his throat which he had worn ever since he was a child. 'Things will look up soon enough. I've sent word to your father. As soon as arrangements can be made, we'll be returning to the island and to Lynch House.'

'No,' his tired eyes widened in panic, 'no we can't.'

'My love there is no other choice. I cannot work and take care of you, not with the kind of care you require and with what I would earn as a seamstress I cannot afford a nurse.'

'Please,' he begged, his eyes filled with desperation, 'please, you cannot stay in that house. I cannot protect you like this.'

'Protect me?' she frowned, 'protect me from what? Your father is the only one who lives there, and he is very well off. He can afford the care that you need.'

'No!' he whispered harshly, 'listen to me. Do you love me?'

'More than anything,' her eyes filled with tears, 'you know that.'

'Will you do anything for me?'

'Of course,' she promised.

He closed his eyes and dragged in a painful breath.

'Then take the pillow and smother me.'

'WHAT?' she gasped in horror, feeling certain she had somehow misunderstood the request.

'Kill me,' he replied as his eyes burned with seriousness. 'It's the only way you'll be free, and you must run my love. Run as far and as fast as you can. Don't let him find you.'

'Who?' she shook her head as the hot tears began to fall, 'please I don't understand.'

'This is my final gift to you,' a single tear slid down his cheek, 'the only way I can protect you. Kill me my love and run, there is no other way.'

'I can't,' the first sob broke free of her chest. 'How could you ask such a thing of me? Even if I could bear to lose you, it is a sin. I'll burn in Hell.'

'No, you won't,' he breathed heavily, wishing with all his heart he could lift his useless hand and brush away her tears. Her pain, her anguish was destroying him. 'I will find you, I swear I will. God will forgive, for only he and I know the dark secrets held in that house.'

'I can't,' she sobbed, 'you cannot ask this of me.'

She tore her hand away and ran from the room in tears, leaving him to curse God for allowing him to come to harm in the first place, after all he'd suffered. Just when he'd finally escaped, when he'd found her to love and was happy, it was all snatched away from him and it was about to get much worse. If she persisted and they returned to his childhood home, he would not be able to protect her, and the thought terrified him.

16

'This is incredible.' Drew sucked in a sharp breath and leaned in closer to study the intricate clockwork mechanism covering the back of the concealed entrance in the study. 'The detail and precision.'

'Have you ever seen anything like this before?' Ava asked the young architect. 'You said you'd studied, what was his name... Talbot?'

'George Talbot,' Drew nodded.

'The guy who built this house, you said you'd studied his other buildings. Did any of them have anything like this in them?'

'Yes and no,' Drew straightened up from his scrutiny of the strange door. 'Hidden rooms, yes. That particular period of architecture loved concealed staircases, hidden rooms and secret corridors. It's very gothic. In some of Talbot's follies, there have been the odd hidden room, but nothing on this scale, and definitely not with this kind of intricate locking system. I've never seen anything like it before. It's most definitely not Talbot's work.'

'So, did he build the hidden rooms or not?' Ava frowned.

'I imagine he probably did,' Drew scratched his chin thoughtfully. 'They would have had to be built when the house was. I won't know for certain until I can get my hands on the original blueprints.'

'Still no luck?' she asked.

He shook his head.

'No,' he mused as his gaze locked on the door. 'It's possible the hidden rooms were built when the house was and that Talbot commissioned someone else to put in the strange locking mechanisms, or...'

'Or?'

'Or they were added at a later date,' Drew frowned. 'There's really no way of telling.'

'I just don't get it,' Killian's voice drew their attention.

They turned to where Killian was crouched down next to the gaping hole in the study floor.

'What don't you get?' Ava asked.

'Why this happened,' he frowned. 'I've checked a dozen times and the floor, the supports from underneath, it's all solid. There is no reason why this section of the floor should have collapsed underneath you.'

'This whole house is full of weird,' Ava replied. 'File it with the rest and don't stew on it. You'll drive yourself crazy.'

Killian straightened; his brow still fixed in a dissatisfied scowl.

'Are you sure you want to continue with the restoration of the property?' he asked. 'If I can't figure out why this section of floor collapsed, I can't guarantee it won't happen again. You and Kelley got lucky. I don't know how the hell you walked away with just bruises but it could have been a lot worse and if something like this happens again, the next person might not be so lucky.'

Ava glanced around the room and at the two men staring at her expectantly. Did she want to finish the house? Killian warned her right from the beginning that the house was a money pit, but that seemed to be the least of her problems.

The bodies had been safely removed as well as any poisons, the rooms below ground had been cleared and were safe. Although she'd yet to hear from Dr Casey about who the women might be or how they died, there was really nothing stopping her from continuing with her original plan of restoring the house. After all, it would never sell in its current condition but then again, it might not sell at all now they'd literally found skeletons in the closet, only in this case it had been more like preserved bodies in the cellar.

She found herself releasing a slow sigh. The truth was she didn't want to sell it, she couldn't imagine anyone else owning it. In fact, if she were completely honest with herself, she'd already begun to think of the house as hers. Even if she never actually lived in it, she was bound to it in a way she didn't quite understand.

She was in love with the island. There was no point in denying it, especially not to herself. In the short space of time she'd spent there she knew she'd found her place. She could no longer imagine living anywhere else, her days of driving aimlessly back and forth across the country and sleeping in her truck were behind her now. She was still far from having a permanent home, but whatever happened she knew that home would be on Midnight Island.

The letter from her grandmother burned a hole in her back pocket but she ruthlessly squashed the doubt as it reared its ugly head. It had taken a long time for her to find a place she'd fallen in love with and nothing a dead woman had to say to her was going to change her mind.

'Call the crew back in,' Ava decided, 'the build is going ahead.'

'Are you absolutely sure about this Ava?' Killian asked seriously.

'Yes,' she straightened her spine and looked him directly in the eye. 'I finish what I start.'

'Okay then,' he nodded, 'I've got some calls to make.'

She watched as he left the room, his phone already in his hand, leaving her alone with Drew.

'I have a suggestion,' Drew turned to face her, 'and it's a little out there, but it's something for you to consider.'

'I'm listening,' her eyes narrowed thoughtfully.

'I know you've been struggling with what to do with the house. It's obvious you want to keep it but it's a lot of house for just one person. Using it as a private residential home is probably not the best use for it.'

'What do you suggest?'

'Open it to the public.'

'Sorry?' she blinked.

'It's perfect, on several levels,' he replied, the excitement showing in his eyes. 'We restore it as much as we can to its original features. It's an amazing example of gothic architecture at its best. It's hands down the pinnacle of Talbot's career. You've got all these hidden rooms, with complex clockwork mechanisms, the like of which no one's seen before. Then on top of that there's the fact of the bodies you found, the creepy ass secret mortuary. The local legends surrounding the house, the mystery of Luella Lynch and the missing children.

They'll come, and they'll come in droves. Architectural enthusiasts, mystery buffs, paranormal lovers, ghost hunters. Charge them an entry fee. Hell, you could even open the bedrooms and have people stay the night. It'll bring you in an income and recoup some of the ridiculous amounts of money you'll have to pay out fixing the place up, and...'

'And?' she asked curiously.

'And we can take out the Butler's pantry, and the scullery

and build a huge kitchen. The massive glass sunroom can be used for seating. Out back we can put in a sun terrace with more alfresco seating and build a summer kitchen outside with a permanent fire pit, given how much you love to cook on one, and you can open your own unique restaurant.'

'My own restaurant?' she whispered; her eyes wide.

'Think about it. You get to stay on the island, you get to keep the house and earn an income from it. Plus, you get to do what you love more than anything, which is feed people. The islanders will probably get fat considering how much they love your cooking,' he laughed, 'but it'll be worth it. The tourism it will bring in will be a massive boost to the island's economy. It's win, win.'

'Damn it,' she muttered, the more he kept talking, the more she could see it, and now she could see it, she wanted it.

'So, where's my kitchen going?' she asked.

He grinned widely and grabbed her hand, pulling her through the house until they reached the butler's pantry. He talked fast, his words tumbling over themselves, his hands gesticulating wildly every time he came up with a new idea. His excitement and passion for the project was infectious and Ava found her stomach churning with endless possibilities.

He showed her around the sunroom pointing out where the various types of seating would go. The huge double doors opened out into an overgrown garden with spectacular sea views. He described the terrace, the fire pit, where her summer kitchen would be built and how it would function.

There, in that one moment, she fell utterly and hopelessly in love. For the first time in her life, she could picture her home and she knew, she wasn't just going to run it as a business, she was going to live there with her dog, on her cliff top, over-looking the sea.

. . .

THERE WAS SO much to be done. Drew had filled Killian in on their provisional plans for the house and returned to the mainland on the noon ferry to begin drawing up the designs. Killian had begun to call back in the crew to resume work on site. Most of the reporters had lost interest and things largely began to return to normal.

As Ava left the house, she headed to her truck where Bailey had been waiting patiently. Opening the door and waiting for her to jump down next to her, they headed for the RV.

She ripped the police tape from the door and entered. Her stomach once again jolted at the destruction of her sweet little temporary home. Angry red letters still stared mockingly at her, slashed across the walls and windows, dire warnings she chose to ignore. Gus and the rest of the Midnight police department had no leads as to who had been responsible and had concluded, in the midst of all the excitement of the bodies being discovered and the grounds crawling with press, paranormal hacks and amateur ghost hunters, that the incident had been nothing more than a prank.

'Well,' Ava sighed out loud, 'I guess we'd better get started.'

She glanced down at Bailey who was sitting on her haunches chewing a mouthful of the ruined flowers Kelley had bought her, and that up until that moment had been strewn across the floor of the RV.

'That your idea of helping me clean up?' Ava asked her dryly.

Bailey stopped chewing and spat out the ball of congealed leaves and stems dripping with drool, onto the toe of her boot.

'Thanks,' Ava replied flatly.

Bailey thumped her tail against the floor as Ava rolled her eyes.

One by one she threw open all the windows. She scraped up all the trash from the floor, the broken mugs, the scattered silverware and the flowers. Saving what she could she dumped the rest and made a note of all the things that would need to be replaced for the Wilsons, who owned the RV and had been good enough to loan it to her, even though they didn't know her. She felt terrible that their things had been ruined, every bit as much as hers.

Gus had assured her, that they weren't holding her responsible, but she still felt guilty. Scrubbing the RV clean seemed to be the least she could do. So, she did. She rolled up her sleeves and set to work. It took her most of the afternoon, but by the time she was finished there wasn't a hint of red paint anywhere.

With Bailey dozing on the couch Ava headed into the bedroom, which had escaped more or less unscathed. There had been no permanent damage or graffiti, but the bedding had been ripped off and the mattress upended.

Bit by bit she righted the mattress, picked up the bedding and remade the bed. She was just folding one of the sheets under the mattress when she noticed something sticking out from under the edge of the bed. Reaching down she retrieved it carefully and turned it over in her hands. It was the black leather-bound notebook she'd bought the first week she'd been in Midnight.

Opening it on the first page she flicked through pages and pages of her untidy handwriting. Notes of everything that everyone she'd met had told her about the house. Tucked neatly into the pages was the photograph, of the woman, the man and the blond-haired boy. She turned the photo over and there was a sudden jolt in her chest as her belly clenched.

There, in neat block letters, was a message.

'SHE'S COMING FOR YOU AND SHE WON'T LET YOU GO.'

That hadn't been there before. She could only imagine that whoever had been responsible for trashing the RV had left this message too. It didn't make sense though. Why trash the RV, why graffiti it with such angry messages, and then calmly write on the back of the photo and tuck it back in the book, leaving it hidden on the floor, where she may or may not have found it. Ava sank slowly down onto the bed as she stared at the book and the photo.

There was so much more to the house and to the Lynch story, Ava was certain of it. It seemed her grandmother had known, and Ava would have bet money that her mother had known too. Why else had she run and never stopped to look back?

Ava leaned over onto one hip as she retrieved the tatty envelope from her back pocket, clenching it in her hand. If she wanted to stay on the island, if she truly wanted to make it her home, then it was time she knew the truth.

She climbed up on the freshly made bed and tucked her legs under her, propping herself up on the pillows as she set the photo and notebook beside her. Turning the envelope over she found herself involuntarily drawing in a slow breath. Hooking her fingers under the paper she tore along the seam and reached in, but as she withdrew the letter a small photograph dropped in her lap.

It was slightly crushed and a little bit creased from where it had sat in the envelope for the last few years and then where she'd spent the last several days carrying it around in her back pocket. Smoothing out the photo she found herself staring at a woman who looked a lot like her mother, only slightly older and with less love beads. She was holding a tiny baby wrapped in a white blanket and gazing down at her with such love.

Ava flipped the photo over and read the handwriting on the back.

'Hari and Ava... San Francisco...'

Ava read the date below and realized the picture was taken only a few days after she was born. The baby in the picture was her and she was being held by her maternal grandmother

Harriet Wallace. She had obviously come to see her in San Francisco where Ava had spent the first five years of her life.

It was clear from the picture Hari was enchanted with her granddaughter and she had bothered to travel all the way from Midnight to the West Coast to see her. So why hadn't Ava known her grandmother? Had she never visited again? And why hadn't Serenity ever mentioned her mother?

Tucking the photo carefully inside the notebook, Ava unfolded the letter from her dead grandmother and slowly began to read, struggling slightly with the slanted handwriting.

Dearest Ava,

You may never get to read this letter, and to be honest I'm not sure if I'm happy about that or not. If you are reading it then it means you have found your way to Midnight and that you have met my dearest friend Bunty McCarthy. She has promised to keep this letter and the secrets of our family. If you find your way to us, they will pass to you and for that I am so very sorry. If not, then Bunty will take them to the grave with her.

I have so much to tell you, to say to you, sweet girl. My only wish is that I could have been there in person to speak with you, to get to know you, to guide you, but now I fear you must navigate your own path and I'm sorry to say your mother will be of no use to you on that score.

First, I feel I must apologize, for not being there for you while you grew up. For missing the chance to be a part of your life, but your mother asked me to make an impossible choice. I chose, not to do what I wanted, but to do what was right. Your mother never under-stood the grave responsibility that was placed upon our family when the Wallaces first came to Midnight Island and how closely we are tied to the Lynches. Their fate became our curse.

I am giving you a choice Ava; one I should have given your mother, but one she made for herself regardless. Do what I could not, burn the house to the ground it stands on, with all of its secrets, and leave. Never look back and be happy.

If you stay, the burden you will have to carry is great. You will be bound to the house. I imagine even now you can feel it, calling to you, calling to your blood. The very walls are filled with secrets of dark deeds and deeper pain. It left a scar, a darkness in that house and gave birth to a terrible evil.

She walks its deserted corridors, her eyes filled with pain and madness. She was born of violence, the lady in white. I have seen her.

You must think me crazy. I know this sounds like madness, but it is not, I assure you and the longer you stay the more you will come to understand. She won't let them go.

I wish things could have been different. I came to San Francisco when you were just a baby. I held you in my arms and I loved you, the same way I loved your mother, the way I still love her. I've missed her every day since she left. She doesn't understand my choices, she wants me to leave to live with you by the Bay and I was so tempted. I had never wanted anything as much in that moment, but Midnight is my home and the house is my responsibility.

I'm sorry Ava, I'm sorry this curse has passed to you and I am sorry for the secrets you will have to carry, for I know only too well the weight of them.

Be at peace my love, whatever your choice.

Your loving grandmother, Hari x

WHAT THE HELL was this woman smoking? Ava sat back with a frown of confusion. The lady in white? She'd expected the letter to give her some answers but all it did was highlight the rather questionable state of mind of a dying old lady. This was ridiculous, innuendos, half-truths and superstitions, that's all it boiled down to. Grabbing the letter, she stuffed it back into the envelope and placed it in the notebook, before climbing purposefully off the bed.

She was going to pay a visit to Mrs McCarthy and this time she was not leaving until she had tangible answers. No gossip, no mysterious legends, just cold hard facts and proof. She wanted to know just what the hell went on in that house and this time, she was not stopping until she knew the truth.

17

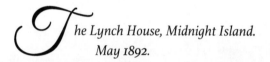he Lynch House, Midnight Island.
May 1892.

IT WAS strange being in the house she thought to herself, as she walked along the corridor the gas lamp in her hand guiding her way through the darkness, her bare feet padding along the cool wooden floor as she pulled her shawl closer around her shoulders.

She'd never spent any real time in the house before. After the wedding they had left the island immediately and headed for New York where her husband had been offered a very prestigious job with Jennings & Co. It was to be their fresh start, a new life filled with exciting possibilities and the fast pace of the city.

All that had ended the moment an automobile had struck her husband and dragged him under its wheels. Now they were back on Midnight Island, where they started, a full circle. Only this time, she was forced to live off the largesse of her wealthy father in law while she watched the slow painful decline of her beloved husband.

There would be no children for them now. The home she'd

dreamt of, filled with family and love and laughter, was fading before her eyes.

Her father in law was a cold, enigmatic man. His black eyes seemed to bore holes in her whenever he looked her way, sending shivers down her spine. Her husband had not said as much but instinctively she knew he was not a man to be crossed.

Since they'd arrived at the house she'd tried to stay out of his way as much as possible, spending her time at her husband's side, reading to him, trying to engage him. But he had fallen into a deep melancholia since their departure from New York and try as she might she could not lift his spirits. Even his boyhood home and the bracing sea air could not revive his mood.

She entered her richly decorated room, closing the door and setting her shawl on the nearby chaise. Crossing the room to climb up into the luxurious bed she sunk into the soft mattress as she set her lamp on the table and pulled the blankets over her.

Her father in law had flatly decreed the night of their arrival that she would not share her husband's room in order to aid his recovery. She wasn't pleased but she'd obeyed just the same. After all, without him they would have nowhere to go.

Each night she'd kissed her husband goodnight and retired to her richly furnished room alone. It was lonely, her only solace was that as she was once again on her home island, she could see her sister. Once a week they met for tea and she had come to look forward to their visits as the only spark of brightness in her dark days.

Feeling the beginning of her own despair tickling the edges of her mind, she turned down the lamp and settled back against the soft down filled pillows and closed her eyes, hoping for the escape of pleasant dreams.

She drifted off; she couldn't have said how long she'd slept for when she suddenly came awake. At first, she wasn't quite sure what had awoken her, until she realized the room was flooded with light. She knew she'd turned the lamp down and as she turned to look, a startled gasp escaped her lips.

Her father in law stood beside her bed, his broad frame towering over her and casting most of her slim willowy frame into shadow. The white wings of his hair seemed to glow incandescently in the lamp light and his eyes burned coal black as he watched her silently.

She pulled the blankets up to her chin, pressing them against her chest. Although, thanks to the modest style of her nightgown with its long sleeves and lace collar buttoned all the way to her neck, she was not showing any more flesh than that of her hands and face, but still it was highly improper for him to be in her room with her wearing only her night attire.

She cleared her throat, hoping to sound firmer than she felt.

'Is something wrong Father?' she tried but her voice shook. 'Is there something wrong with my husband?'

She tried to emphasize the word husband, in an attempt to remind her father in law of the impropriety of his presence in her room but he continued to stare at her with those cold obsidian eyes and just when she thought he wasn't going to respond, his deep voice echoed through the room.

'The only thing wrong with him was that he married you.'

'Excuse me?' she whispered, 'I cannot collect your meaning. You had no objection to our marriage when the banns were read, nor at the service.'

'If he hadn't married you, he wouldn't have left the island,' he continued slowly and deliberately, sensing her unease. 'He wouldn't have been injured and I wouldn't have been forced to the inconvenience and expense of bringing the both of you home. You must understand that a debt is now owed.'

'A debt?' she frowned, 'but he's your son, your only child. Surely you would wish to help him from the goodness of your heart?'

'A debt is a debt, regardless of blood.'

She suppressed a shiver of fear, her mouth dry as she attempted to straighten her spine, forcing a strength into her voice she did not feel.

'Then I shall repay it,' she replied coolly. 'I have a fair hand with

needlepoint, I shall find work as a seamstress. If you would be so kind as to draw up a bill, I shall see that you are reimbursed all expenses for our transport to the island.'

'You think I would allow my daughter in law to work as a common seamstress?' his voice dropped deadly low.

'I do not understand,' this time she did shudder at the darkness in his eyes. 'How am I to repay the debt if you will not allow me to work?'

'Oh, you will repay the debt,' he replied slowly, 'but not with money.'

'I don't...'

Her protest was cut short as he grasped the blankets and ripped them away revealing her modest nightgown.

'No!' she gasped in horror, 'what are you doing?'

He roughly shoved her back onto the bed and climbed on top of her, his legs astride her narrow hips. Reaching up he grabbed the collar of her nightgown and tore it open, the tiny little pearl buttons scattering, as the material gaped down to her ribcage, exposing her pink tipped breasts.

'NO! PLEASE!' She slapped at his hands as they kneaded her flesh, painfully squeezing her breasts viciously, his fingers digging into her soft skin leaving dark painful bruises.

'NO!' She cried out again, struggling to shove him away, to wriggle out from underneath his heavy body.

This time he raised his hand and cracked her across the cheek. Her head snapped to the side sharply, filling the soft palette of her mouth with the metallic tang of blood. Not giving her time to recover he hit her again, harder. This time she felt her eye begin to swell and throb. It was a horrible shock; she'd never been struck before. Even as her mind struggled to comprehend the pain, she felt him moving down her body, grabbing her nightgown and shoving it up her body so roughly it grazed her skin, leaving her body bare to his terrifying black-eyed gaze.

He rose up on his knees, not enough for her to escape but

enough for her to see what was coming. Her eyes widened in terror as he slowly and deliberately opened his trousers, exposing his engorged, angry penis, wet at the tip and eager for her pain and humiliation.

'NO!!' She fought him then, like a wild, feral cat, she scratched and bit and clawed. She wriggled and bucked but it was no use, he was too strong.

He forced her legs apart, then grabbing a handful of her night-gown he shoved it in her mouth to muffle her screams. Nothing could have prepared her, as she felt the hot tip of him between her legs, for the vicious thrust and the white-hot pain as he penetrated her. She cried out, her eyes wet with tears, her sobs muffled as he continued to beat himself between her spread thighs.

He leaned forward; her arms were pinned beneath his chest as he pressed her into the bed. She felt like she was suffocating, she couldn't breathe through the weight of him and the nightgown shoved in her mouth. She felt him grab her hair and twist her head, so his hot breath gusted against her ear.

'Do you like it Daughter?' he taunted, his voice low and breathy as he continued to ram himself inside her. 'Shall I give you what my useless cripple son can't?'

She felt him bite her neck savagely, but it was nothing compared to the pain of the vicious assault she was enduring between her thighs.

'Shall I spill my seed inside you?' he whispered hotly against her ear as his fingers dug into her bruised breast and twisted her nipple sharply. 'Shall I plant a babe in your womb? Would you like that? To feel me growing inside you?'

The horror of the thought was too much to bear. She struggled uselessly, but he didn't even break his rhythm as he pounded sharply inside her.

'You will learn your place Daughter,' he growled. 'Under this roof, you belong to me. Just like every stick of furniture. You're mine to do with as I please. I will come to your bed when the mood takes

me, I will ride between your thighs until you're hurting and then I will leave you wet with my seed.'

She screamed again, but he simply laughed and yanked her hair harder, snapping her neck back into an unbearable position as he forced himself inside her repeatedly, harder and harder for what felt like an eternity, until he hissed loudly with satisfaction and she felt a warmth gush inside her.

The fight left her body as he pulled out of her wetly, breathing hard, his softening penis trailing against her thigh leaving a string of semen.

'There Daughter,' he climbed off the bed, leaving himself exposed and blood stained so she could see what he'd done to her. He leaned forward and removed the wad of nightgown from her lax mouth. 'I gave you a child tonight, a beautiful gift that my son could not...' he whispered coldly. 'Say thank you.'

She stared at him numbly, through eyelashes spiky with tears.

His huge fist wrapped around her throat, squeezing until she thought she was going to pass out.

'Say...' he whispered harshly against her ear, 'thank you...'

'Thank you,' she croaked brokenly.

Satisfied he straightened up and tucked himself back into his trousers before turning and leaving the room as if nothing had happened.

For a moment she just lay there, her body still exposed, her nightgown shoved up to her chest. Her mind couldn't seem to process what had happened. She would have thought it a nightmare if it were not for the agony between her legs. Slowly she pushed herself off the bed, her legs collapsing underneath her as she dropped to the richly embroidered rug.

Sucking in a sharp breath she pushed herself to her feet, using the bed to steady herself. She limped over to the washstand feeling the wetness between her legs, and cringing. She lifted the jug of water, but her hands were trembling so badly it clanged loudly against the bowl as she filled it.

She pulled the soiled nightgown over her head and threw it to the ground in disgust. Her neck and breasts were covered with ugly bruises and vicious teeth marks. She dipped a muslin cloth into the cold water and scrubbed her body until it was raw. Wetting the cloth again she hissed as she washed between her legs, her eyes filled with tears as she choked back a sob. She scrubbed and scrubbed through the pain, trying to rid her body of his semen, praying she didn't conceive and equally terrified that if she didn't, he would return to hurt her again.

Finally, when she could bear no more, she threw the blood and semen stained cloth on the floor next to her nightgown. Pulling her thin shawl from the chair she wrapped it around her body, shaking violently as she collapsed against the wall and slid down it slowly, folding herself into a small ball in the corner where she sobbed quietly until dawn.

*A*s the door swung open Bunty didn't look herself. Not quite as polished and sure of herself as usual as she stared down at Ava, looking slightly uncomfortable.

'You'd better come in,' she said before the young woman could speak.

She stepped back and allowed Ava to enter.

'None of the other ladies here?' she asked.

'No,' Bunty replied flatly, 'just me.'

Ava followed her through to the kitchen and took a seat at the table where Bunty indicated. She watched silently as the older woman set the kettle to boil and retrieved two cups from the cupboard. Ava waited patiently, giving her time to settle.

'I owe you an apology,' Bunty flushed, 'for being so out of sorts the other day.'

'No, you don't Bunty,' Ava shook her head. 'Baz owes you an apology for not warning you about the brownies.'

Bunty flushed again.

'Still,' she shook her head, 'I'd like to apologize for my regrettable behavior.'

'Trust me,' Ava smiled slowly as Bunty set a cup of coffee

down in front of her and took a seat opposite cradling her own cup, 'I've seen worse.'

'I must confess, I expected you to visit me days ago,' she took a small sip.

'I had some things to figure out,' Ava replied.

'Did you read your grandmother's letter?'

'I did,' Ava frowned, 'and I have to say Bunty it didn't make a whole helluva lot of sense.'

'And now you want to know what I know?'

'You promised you would tell me and besides, I think I've earned the right to know. The house is mine now and I'm staying on the island permanently.'

'Does that have something to do with Kelley Ryan?' she asked curiously.

'He's not the sole reason,' Ava replied carefully, 'but he might have factored in, slightly.'

'He's a sweet boy,' Bunty nodded, 'I'm glad.'

'Bunty,' Ava set her cup down. 'Look, I don't mean to be rude but I'm getting real frustrated with all the hints and dramatic warnings. I get that the house comes with a history and given the bodies we found I'd like to know what I've sighed up for.'

'Very well,' she sighed.

Ava grabbed her notebook from her backpack and laid it on the table. Opening it up she slid the old-fashioned photo across to Bunty.

'Do you know who they are?'

Bunty's mouth tightened into a disapproving line.

'Yes, I do,' she nodded. 'The boy is Peter Merrick, the gentleman is Jonathan Sedgewick and the woman... well, the young woman is Luella Lynch.'

'Luella?' Ava's eyes widened as she took the photo back and studied it with renewed interest. 'This is definitely Luella Lynch? The woman who everyone seems convinced is haunting the house?'

'Yes,' Bunty sipped her coffee again, 'it's definitely her.' She stared at Ava for a few moments, tapping her nails against the cup. 'Come with me.'

She stood abruptly and disappeared through the doorway into the living room. Ava scooped up her notebook and the photo before following the other woman. She stepped into the living room and noticed several large file boxes stacked on and around the coffee table.

'I had these brought out of storage the other day, just in case. There are more of course but these are the most important.'

'What are they?' Ava asked as she sat down on the couch beside Bunty.

'They are the history of your family,' she replied.

'You mean the Lynch family?'

'I mean your family,' Bunty shook her head. 'I'm not even sure where to start.' She reached for one of the boxes and opened the lid. Deciding that wasn't the one she wanted she checked a couple of others until she pulled a large heavy photo album from a box. 'It took Hari a long time to track down all these photos from various sources and compile them into one comprehensive album.'

She opened the first page, carefully peeling back the tissue paper separating the pages to reveal a large rectangular photograph in black and white of a tall, powerfully built gentleman with jet black hair and pure white streaks at his temples. He was immaculately dressed, with the chain of a pocket watch hanging across his waistcoat which immediately put Ava in mind of the pocket watch she'd been left by her mother, in which there was also a skeleton key to one of the hidden rooms.

'That's Ephraim Lynch, isn't it?' Ava whispered.

'Yes,' Bunty replied, 'he's always been where this sorry story begins.'

'I don't understand,' she frowned.

'You will,' Bunty replied resignedly. 'The Lynches were one of the wealthiest families on Midnight Island. Ephraim had a younger sister, Eloise, younger by a full decade. There were other siblings but due to infant mortality back then, none of them survived beyond childhood. That's why there was such a big age gap between them. You're descended from Eloise.'

Ava settled back against the couch to listen as Bunty placed the album in her lap and turned the page, to reveal a photo, in sepia, of a sweet young girl of no more than maybe ten or twelve.

'That's her,' Bunty pointed. 'Very few pictures of her survived. This came from the Lynch house itself. Eloise was only fifteen years old when her parents died. She was left in the care of her older brother, but within months of her parents passing, Eloise ran away.'

'Why?'

'That was the big question, nobody seemed to know. By all accounts she was a happy child. Hari spent years searching records across New England before she finally managed to track her down. It seems that within six months of leaving Midnight island Eloise gave birth to an illegitimate daughter.'

'She was pregnant?' Ava's eyes widened, 'at fifteen?'

Bunty nodded.

'She was one of the lucky ones.'

'How the hell was that lucky?' Ava frowned.

'Back in those days, unmarried mothers were a shame upon their families and society. She would've been classed as a fallen woman, even though she was barely more than a child herself. In most cases back then, and you have to remember this was the mid-19th century, the children were either taken from the mothers or the mothers were forced to give them up. A lot of the mothers themselves then ended up in a Poorhouse.'

'What happened to her then? And to the child?'

'Pure luck,' Bunty shrugged, 'or maybe fate stepped in. She went into labor on the streets with nowhere to go; a gentleman happened upon her and took pity. He'd recently lost his wife in childbirth. I don't know, maybe it was this that caused an empathy for the girl who was obviously about to become a mother. He took her in and sent for the midwife. Once the child was born, instead of turning her out, he allowed her to stay and more unusually he allowed her to keep her child with her under his roof. In return she would nurse his youngest infant as well as her own and tend his three older children.'

'She became a servant?'

'In the beginning,' Bunty replied. 'Like I said she was one of the lucky ones. Not only was she able to keep her child but to find employment, you can't imagine how rare that was. After a few years the gentleman moved away, and Eloise went with him. Hari lost track of them for about a dozen years or so. When she finally picked them up in the records again, Eloise was married to her gentleman, who had generously given her daughter his name. They then went on to have two more children of their own, in addition to his four children.'

'So, who am I descended from?' Ava wondered.

'Her oldest child, her daughter whom she named Lottie.'

'Do you have any idea who her father was?' She watched as Bunty's mouth tightened once again into that thin line of disapproval. 'What?'

'There was some unfortunate speculation that the child was fathered by her brother,' she reluctantly admitted.

'What?' Ava's eyes grew round, 'are you telling me that I may ultimately be the product of incest?'

'If you were, I doubt it was intentional on her part,' Bunty muttered.

'Are you saying that he forced her?' Ava whispered in horror.

'Okay let's back up here, we're getting ahead of ourselves.

There was no way for Hari to find out for certain without modern genetic testing. The only way to do that would be to procure samples from Ephraim's remains which are interred at Midnight cemetery. Which would mean exhuming his body, which can't be done without special permission. Now, there has always been a lot of gossip about the Lynches over the years, and some of it is a matter of public record but the research Hari did, that I helped her with, was strictly private. None of the ladies of the historical society know the truth about the family. That was the way Hari wanted it and I respected her need for privacy. I mean, it's hard to find out you may be descended from a woman who was born the product of rape and incest. If it is true, she certainly didn't want it to become public knowledge.'

'I don't know how to feel about this,' Ava sat back stunned and slightly nauseated.

'There's a lot more to the story,' Bunty warned her. 'Are you sure you want to know the truth?'

Ava nodded slowly.

'I guess there's no backing out now.'

Bunty leaned forward and turned the page of the album revealing a picture of Eloise, who was now much older, beside a gentleman. He was sitting, and she was resting her hand on his shoulder, his own hand placed atop hers affectionately. Beside them was a group of children, seven in all.

'That is Sterling Harper, Eloise's husband.'

'He looks kind,' Ava muttered.

'I always thought so,' Bunty nodded. 'I try not to think of who Lottie's true father might be. I prefer to think that Eloise was happy and that her husband was a good kind man, whom she learned to love and who loved her in return. It may not be true, but I like to think it is.'

'Which one is Lottie?'

Bunty pointed to a tall beautiful girl with jet black hair and dark eyes.

'She was a beauty,' Bunty murmured. 'Can't say the Lynches weren't a handsome family, even if they were a bit twisted.'

'What happened to her?' Ava asked quietly her eyes studying the young girl.

'She grew up,' Bunty told her, 'married a man by the name of Victor Wallace. She gave birth to a son they named Thaddeus and so on. In fact, it was Thaddeus' son Louis who inherited the Lynch house some years after Luella and the children disappeared.'

Ava glanced up at Bunty.

'But again, I'm getting ahead of myself. Eloise ran away and married her gentleman, which left Ephraim alone on the island. He left the family home when he bought Talbot's house. The original Lynch home was on the other side of the island, but it's not there anymore. It was demolished sometime back in the fifties. Anyway, he moved into Talbot's house where he lived alone for the next twenty years or so. Now, as I said before, the Lynches were always very wealthy, but Ephraim expanded that wealth exponentially. He was a rather talented watchmaker.'

'A watchmaker?' Ava repeated abruptly.

'Yes dear,' Bunty frowned, 'I'm sure I'd mentioned that before. Anyway, his time pieces were so exquisite he was commissioned several times by European royalty to make bespoke items for them. Not just watches and clocks but he was also known for making dolls.'

'Dolls?' Ava frowned.

'Mechanical dolls, automatons with intricate clockwork actions. He only ever made a few and they are very hard to get hold of, but...'

She reached into another box and carefully lifted out the most breath-taking thing she'd ever seen. It was a young lady in a lavender gown, seated at a miniature harpsichord. Bunty wound it up with a brass key and the doll began to play, the haunting notes of the harpsichord surprisingly clear for its age.

Ava leaned in closer and examined it. It was incredible; its fingers were actually moving in time to the keys and its delicate head moved from side to side as its tiny eyelids blinked.

'He made this?' Ava whispered.

'Yes,' Bunty nodded, 'among other things. It's said he made one of his automaton dolls for Queen Victoria herself.'

Leaning over she turned the page to the next photograph.

'Ah yes,' she nodded when she saw which picture was next. 'This is Clara Cooper, Ephraim's wife. She was only sixteen, poor love and he was, at that point, in his forties.'

Ava looked down at the photo and her stomach tightened. 'She looks younger than sixteen,' Ava swallowed uncomfortably. 'She looks about twelve.'

'Well she definitely was sixteen,' Bunty nodded, 'but very small for her age. You can see now why she didn't survive the birth of her son.'

'He certainly liked them young, didn't he?' Ava frowned. 'Why did he marry her? I mean, he doesn't strike me as the kind of man to care about an unwanted pregnancy. I would have expected him to just cast her aside.'

'I expect he would've done,' Bunty nodded, 'if he could have, but the truth is her father was a local governor. It was only her social status that secured her a marriage, whether she wanted it or not. Although it wasn't illegal, it caused a huge scandal at the time.'

Ava stared down at the wedding photo of Ephraim and young Clara.

'She doesn't look unhappy,' Ava noted, 'she looks scared.'

Bunty nodded.

'Clara gave birth to Ephraim's son, Edison.'

Ava swallowed uncomfortably, thinking of the childish scrawl etched into the tiny, dark, hidden cupboard in the scullery. She was starting to piece together a picture of Ephraim Lynch and it wasn't a pretty one.

'During the time Edison was growing up in the house, he had a constant stream of nannies and wet nurses. Most of them never stayed long. Some of them, the older ones moved on to other employment but some... disappeared.'

'Disappeared?' Ava repeated quietly.

'It's a long story. I'm just giving you the highlights here; the information is all in these boxes. Hari spent most of her adult life researching everything she could about the Lynches and the house. In one of the boxes are copies of the employment ledgers. Ephraim was meticulous about keeping accounts. In one of them there are wages for several young girls, maids and nurses. They break off abruptly and then, later on, there were some fairly large payments to the families of those girls.'

'Pay offs?'

Bunty shrugged.

'Supposition,' she replied, 'but its plausible.'

'Do you think that the girls who went missing are the ones we found beneath the house?' Ava asked a little sickly.

'It does seem to fit doesn't it?' Bunty frowned, 'but I couldn't say for sure. However, moving on, Edison grew up and married a young woman by the name of Eleanor Williams. A sweet young thing of eighteen, a local girl who by all accounts Edison was madly in love with.'

Ava glanced down at the photo album in her lap, skipping a couple more pages before Bunty reached out and stopped her, tapping her nail against a picture of a tall slim dark-haired man and a young woman.

'That's them,' Bunty told her. 'This is their wedding picture, it's the only picture of them together. They married on the island and then left for the city. Edison had been offered what would have been considered a very prestigious, not to mention, well paid job at the time. They'd only been gone a short while when a tragic accident left Edison a cripple. They returned to

Midnight and came to live in Ephraim's house. It's here that the story really begins.'

'This Eleanor, gave birth to Luella, didn't she?' Ava cast her mind back to what she'd been told by the gossiping ladies of the historical society when she'd first arrived on the island. 'Betty seemed to imply Edison wasn't capable of fathering a child and that Luella was Ephraim's, but there was no proof.'

'There is proof,' Bunty replied quietly.

'What?' Ava whispered.

Bunty rummaged in several of the boxes before she managed to retrieve a stack of handwritten letters tied with a piece of rough string.

'Eleanor wrote to her sister,' Bunty handed her the letters, 'they're heart breaking. Ephraim was a sadistic son of a bitch. He didn't just rape her and force her to bear his child, he did it repeatedly. She was horribly abused under the roof of that man and he didn't trouble to hide what he was doing from his son, knowing there was nothing he could do about it. He wanted to hurt Edison as much as he hurt Eleanor.'

'That's sick,' Ava frowned.

'Ephraim Lynch was a sick man,' Bunty shook her head. 'Eleanor gave birth to Luella, and there were several other births, almost one a year but none of those children survived, until Edward. He was born six years after Luella and died at a young age.'

'Why didn't Eleanor's sister do anything? Why didn't she help her?'

'The letters never made it to her,' Bunty replied. 'They were found bound together in amongst Ephraim's papers and ledgers. I suspect he intercepted them before they could leave the house.'

'So much death and tragedy,' Ava breathed quietly, 'no wonder it feels so heavy inside the house.'

'What did you say?' Bunty looked at her sharply.

'It's probably just my imagination but sometimes when you step into the house the air feels heavy, buzzing almost and the hairs on your arms rise. It feels like static electricity.'

'Ava,' Bunty breathed heavily, 'that house is cursed. Please, please give it up for your own sake.'

'Why?' Ava shook her head. 'All of this is very sad and to be honest, really quite disturbing, but all of these people are long dead. It's just a house.'

'It's never been just a house,' Bunty murmured, her eyes worried. 'Eleanor disappeared from all the records. She's not buried in the cemetery with her husband and Hari could find no record of her death.'

'That's weird.'

'Luella left home for a while and moved to the mainland, but eventually returned to Midnight, with a small boy, a foundling she said.'

'A small boy?' Ava glanced at her notebook, to the photo just peeking out from its pages.

'Peter Merrick,' Bunty nodded, 'the boy in your picture. There was some local gossip that he was her illegitimate son but it never came to anything so I couldn't say for sure. She opened the house as a school and after that there was no more mention of her mother. She simply ceased to exist in the official records, but Luella... she was a different matter altogether, cool, aloof, many would say hard. She ran that school until the night of the great storm, the night all those children disappeared.'

'And you have no idea what happened to them?'

'None,' Bunty shook her head, 'neither did Hari. That was the one part of the puzzle she never managed to figure out. Whatever Luella did to those children remains a secret.'

'Bunty,' Ava rubbed her forehead tiredly as she tried to assimilate the mountains of information her dead grand-mother had managed to compile over the decades. 'This is all terrible, I mean it sounds like Ephraim Lynch was every woman's worst nightmare. Edison was dealt a rough hand and it wasn't fair. Eleanor,' Ava shook her head sympathetically, 'I can't imagine what that poor woman must have suffered. As for Luella, coming from the family she did and being raised in that house... in that environment... I can imagine that she would have been a bit unstable, but it's all in the past. It's over. There's nothing we can do about it, except move on.'

'It's not that simple,' Bunty frowned. 'I know you think I'm crazy and that maybe your grandmother was too, but Ava, there is a darkness inside that house. True evil walked its corridors, a darkness born of violence and hate. Those cruel and heinous deeds perpetrated within its walls left a scar, a stain that birthed something evil, something angry, something terrifying.'

'Oh come on Bunty, that might work for the paranormal nut jobs but it's crazy. The house is not haunted, and it's not cursed,' Ava let out a heavy frustrated breath. 'I just want a home... my own home, is that too much to ask?'

'Then pick a house and buy one on the island,' Bunty replied desperately. 'With what Hari left you, you could afford to buy three or four houses and still have change, but not that house, please not that house. I'm begging you, do what your grandmother could not and bulldoze it to the ground.'

Ava rose slowly from the chair and picked up her notebook.

'I'm sorry Bunty, I really am but I just don't believe in all this.'

'Just,' Bunty sighed tiredly, 'just take the boxes, they belong to you anyway. Look through them and see for yourself.'

AVA LAY in Kelley's bed staring up at the ceiling. She didn't need to look at the neon lights of the clock blinking on the nightstand to know how late it was, or rather how early. She'd heard

Kelley come in from the bar in the early hours and collapse on the couch.

It'd been the same since the first night she'd stayed. He'd given up his bed without a second thought. Despite the fact his couch was not built for a guy his height he'd slept on it without complaint. He'd never once pushed her for something more, even though it had always been there, hanging in the air between them.

She'd have to be stupid not to recognize the chemistry between them. In fact, if he'd been anyone else, just some random guy in a bar she'd have scratched that itch the moment she met him and probably broken her own rule of going back for seconds.

The whole time she'd stayed at his apartment they'd had plenty of chances to make something happen, but he seemed content to let her dictate the pace of their relationship and make no mistake, there may not have been any sex as yet but it was definitely a relationship. Something else she'd never experienced before.

She'd been holding back; she knew she had. It all seemed way too good to be true. He seemed too good to be true, ridiculously good looking, smart, funny and just the right amount of nerdy. She was a goner. She wasn't aware she had a type, but if she did it was definitely Kelley Ryan.

If she had any sense, she'd have been cozied up to him naked. Instead she was laying alone in her pajamas pinned to the bed by her heavy half dog, half woolly mammoth, staring at the ceiling, surrounded by stacks of boxes of god only knew what, that Bunty had insisted she took with her.

Her mind was spinning. She felt like she was stuck on some kind of maniacal merry-go-round, unable to slow down or get off. Her brain churned with facts and gossip and rumors, half-truths and supposition. She didn't want to think about the Lynches with their dark, dysfunctional issues, or the house which everyone seemed convinced was haunted. She just wanted her brain to shut up for one damn minute.

She crawled out of bed, careful not to disturb Bailey and slipped silently out of the room. She'd intended to head into the kitchen for a glass of water but instead she'd stopped dead, watching Kelley as he splayed out on his stomach, half hanging off the couch.

'Are you just going to stand there and ogle me? Because I can get naked for your viewing pleasure,' his sleepy voice rumbled in the near darkness.

An unexpected laugh bubbled from her chest.

'I'm sorry I woke you,' she replied.

He grunted and rolled over onto his back, propping his bare feet on the end of the couch.

'Doesn't matter, was thinking about you away,' he murmured.

'Really?' she stepped a little closer.

'Constantly,' he rumbled.

She could feel the warmth spreading through her chest at his sleepy heartfelt admission and before she could give herself a chance to second guess, she crossed the space and crawled on top of him, pressing her body against him until there wasn't an inch of them that wasn't joined.

'Am I dreaming?' his arms wrapped around her, anchoring her to him.

'No,' she replied, her face so close to his, he could feel her smile against his lips.

She yelped in surprise, followed by a giggle, when he somehow managed to roll them, sliding her underneath him without them ending up in a heap on the floor.

'Is it my birthday?' he breathed against her mouth.

'Yes,' she grinned, 'it's your birthday.'

She arched as his hand grazed up her ribcage, sliding underneath her shirt to cup her naked breast, his thumb skimming her nipple and his face pressing into the curve of her neck as he breathed her in.

'Will there be cake?' his voice was slightly muffled against her skin.

She tilted her head back and laughed. Whatever it was that was coiled in her stomach instantly loosened and the tension drained out of her, replaced by genuine happiness and contentment. She didn't know how he did it, but whenever she was with him everything just seemed right.

She slid her fingers into his thick wavy hair and dragged his head up, pressing her lips to his as her hands trailed down his sides and grasped the hem of his t-shirt, pulling it up and over his head.

With a lot of wriggling he managed to draw hers up her body and over her head, tossing it aside carelessly as they pressed together in the darkness, skin to skin, the burning heat of him to her soft lush inviting curves.

He was drowning in the scent and feel of her arching beneath him. Her lips parted on a sigh and he tasted her, her lips soft and yielding.

She felt his fingers burning a hot trail down her skin as they hooked into her pajama pants and drew them over her hips. She wriggled once again and kicked them away, leaving her free and gloriously naked beneath his aching body.

'Kelley,' she lifted her arms, wrapping them over the side of the couch behind her, arching helplessly as his fingers pressed between her legs and stroked her maddeningly.

'Are you sure this is what you want,' he breathed against her lips, his body burning against hers.

'I want you,' she whispered.

His lips crashed down on hers, his kiss devasting as he drove her to an orgasm so loud, her dog started barking in the other room.

He chuckled against her mouth as she caught her breath,

coming down from her high. 'She probably won't let up until she knows you're okay.'

'Tough,' Ava whispered against his mouth, 'I'm not done with you yet.'

He felt her fingers pop the buttons on his jeans and slide them over his hips before her hand closed firmly around him.

'Thank god,' he muttered against her mouth as they sunk down into another kiss.

She shoved the jeans further down his legs until he kicked them to the floor. Then he sank into her slowly. For one brief second it was like the whole world slowed down and stopped. She drew in a deep sharp breath, her heart pounding against his as he watched her, vivid green eyes in the darkness.

Then he rocked against her and the world restarted. She wrapped her legs around him, his arms snaked underneath her, and they held on for dear life. Tangled together and so lost in each other it was tough to tell where one ended and the other began.

Nothing else existed but the two of them, and when she finally arched and shattered, tightening her thighs around his hips, she dragged him down with her, into sated oblivion.

They lay there, breathing ragged, sweat drying on their heated skin, and hearts pounding, like the survivors of some kind of wreck, and this time when they closed their eyes, they both slipped easily into dreams.

19

'*D*id you move in without me realizing?'

Ava glanced up from her cup of coffee.

'The boxes in the bedroom?' Kelley smiled.

'Oh those,' she shook her head as he walked into the kitchen, freshly showered, and poured his own cup. 'I finally went to see Bunty yesterday. She gave them to me, I'm sorry I just dumped them in there. To be honest I didn't know what else to do with them. I couldn't leave them in the truck or the RV.'

'What are they?'

'Part of the whole sorry Lynch family mess,' she blew out a resigned breath as she stared aimlessly down into her cup.

'Hey,' he moved closer, 'what is it? What did she tell you?'

'A whole bunch of stuff,' she looked up at him. 'Apparently Ephraim Lynch was a serial rapist with a liking for teenage girls. He spent years mentally and emotionally abusing his crippled son while he physically and sexually abused his daughter in law, and then ended up fathering his own grand-children, one of which died and the other may or may not have been a pyscho killer.'

'Holy shit.'

'Yeah,' she muttered sourly. 'Those boxes are everything my grandmother managed to track down over the years, ledgers, journals, letters, photos. I had a look at them briefly last night but...' she shrugged, shaking her head.

'You're struggling to read them?' he guessed.

'Most of the time I manage okay, but the style of hand-writing and the dated language makes it harder,' she frowned.

'I could help if you like?'

'Be my guest,' she waved her hand toward the doorway. 'To be honest I'm not even sure what I'm looking at half the time, there's so much stuff there. Just... whatever you find out, keep between us, okay? After discovering those bodies, I'm not ready to stir up the reporters' nest again. Sooner or later they'll find out what a sick bastard Lynch really was, but I'm not ready to deal with it yet. Not when I'm still trying to get my head around it.'

'Ava,' he stroked the length of her arm soothingly, 'you can trust me.'

'I do trust you,' she replied, 'otherwise I wouldn't be here with you, but do you know what I just don't get?'

'What?' he sipped his coffee as he looked down at her.

'I mean I get that the Lynch family was a nightmare and that it would be embarrassing for my grandmother or my mom to be related to them, but what's with all the dire warnings about the house? I don't know why everyone is so obsessed with the idea that it's haunted.'

'I suppose, it's the mystery,' Kelley replied thoughtfully, 'all the unanswered questions. We all grew up with the legend of Luella Lynch and the story of the missing children. It sort of lends itself to a ghost story.'

'Yeah, I get the local gossip, but Bunty was deadly serious. She doesn't want me to have that house, she practically begged me to demolish it.'

'She's an old woman,' Kelley shook his head, 'and from what you've said, both she and Hari were studying the house and the family for years. I guess it's just deeply ingrained now. She's convinced herself its real, or maybe it is real, who knows?'

'Your overactive imagination again?' her mouth twitched in amusement.

'Hey, it's overactive imaginations like mine that are gonna pay the bills from what I hear,' he replied. 'Killian mentioned yesterday that you're going to make the house into some sort of local attraction?'

'Oh,' Ava chuckled, 'that... Drew had this idea that I have the house restored to its factory settings and open it to the public. He thought it would bring in loads of crazy ghost hunters and boost the island's economy.'

'He's probably not wrong,' Kelley mused thoughtfully.

'I don't know,' she frowned. 'At first I was really excited. I thought it was a great idea and in addition to that I could open a little cafe or restaurant space in the house, but now...'

'Now?'

'Knowing what I do I'm not sure if I want to make it public knowledge.'

'Ava,' Kelley told her softly, 'you don't have to air any dirty laundry if you don't want to. You control the spread of information; trust me people would flock to the house regardless. Just the local legends and the fact you found bodies in a hidden room deep beneath the house would ensure visitors flock to the house.'

'But how do I explain the creepy mortuary and the sex bed in front of the coffins... that's just nasty.'

'You don't explain it,' he laughed. 'Trust me, their overactive brains will fill in the blanks. Half the fun is to keep them guessing, but equally, its entirely up to you. You don't have to do anything you don't want to.'

'What if I want to?'

'Then I'd say there's nothing stopping you,' he shrugged.

'Except I don't have the first clue how to run a business.'

'People will be there to help Ava; you don't have to do this alone.'

'It's not just that,' she chewed her lip.

'What then?'

'I just,' she chewed restlessly at one ragged fingernail.

Kelley calmly moved her hand from her mouth as he watched her patiently.

'I just... will you do something for me?' she asked quietly.

'Sure I will,' he moved her hand again when she unconsciously began to chew her nail once more. 'Tell me what you need sweetheart.'

'I um... can you help me get my high school diploma?'

His mouth curved into a wide smile.

'I'd love to,' he replied genuinely. 'There's a couple of night courses we can enrol you in at the school, or if you'd prefer something a bit more private, I can tutor you. I'm a great study buddy. I don't like to brag,' he grinned, 'but all my lab partners in high school aced their final grade.'

'You really think I can do it?' she asked nervously.

'Sure you can,' he set his coffee down, 'plus you have a teacher all to yourself, for one on one learning.'

'And what does this one on one learning entail?' she smiled as he leaned against her, pinning her against the counter and cupping her face with his hands.

'All the things I could get fired for,' he smiled against her mouth as he sunk in and kissed her.

She felt that kiss all the way down to her toes, heating her blood and flushing her skin. She wrapped her arms around his neck pulling him in closer, and as he lifted her easily and set her on the counter, stepping between her legs and sliding his hands under her shirt, she found herself hoping for a replay of the night before, this time hopefully involving a bed and a lot more maneuvering room.

She was dimly aware of a strange buzzing somewhere nearby, and the counter beside her thigh seemed to be vibrating slightly. She ignored it and threw herself back into the kiss until Kelley pulled back slightly.

'Ava,' he murmured between kisses, 'your phone.'

She blinked and glanced down at her phone on the counter next to her. She still hadn't quite gotten used to it. Picking it up she glanced at the screen.

'It's Drew,' she murmured as she hit connect and raised the phone to her ear.

'Tell him to get lost,' Kelley replied as he kissed his way down her neck.

'Tell Kelley I heard that,' Drew responded by way of a greeting.

'Hey Drew,' Ava laughed pushing Kelley away slightly, 'what's up?'

'I've found out some stuff about the house,' his signal kept cutting out. 'I'm on the ferry now, can you meet me at Rosie's diner? It's down on the waterfront.'

'Sure?' she glanced down at her watch. 'When?'

'My ETA's about half an hour.'

'Okay I'll see you then,' she hung up.

'Problem?' Kelley asked.

'No, he's on his way over to the island. He says he's found some information about the house.'

'The missing blueprints?'

'He didn't say,' she hopped down from the counter. 'He wants me to meet him at Rosie's diner.'

'Good choice,' Kelley nodded, 'great pancakes.'

'You wanna come?'

'I wish I could,' he glanced down at his own watch, but I've got a delivery for the bar coming in this morning that I need to sign for, then I have a stock check. Rain check on the pancakes?'

'Sure,' she nodded.

'You going up to the house later?'

'Yeah, the building work has resumed so I've got hungry mouths to feed. Today its smoked chicken samosas and mango chutney.'

He knew it would be something amazing as all her prep work was currently chilling in his refrigerator, and every time he opened the door it smelled mouth-watering.

'Sold,' he grinned and dropped a kiss on her lips. 'If I hustle, I'll be up at the house in time for lunch. Do you need any help getting everything in the truck?'

'I'm good,' she shoved him playfully, 'get going.'

He gave her one more glance before heading out. Smiling to herself she whistled for Bailey who had made herself at home on Kelley's couch, wincing when she saw the sheer amount of dog hair stuck to the fabric.

'We're definitely going to have to brush you later,' Ava announced.

Bailey howled and rolled over onto her back.

'Drama queen,' Ava rolled her eyes. 'He won't love you if you keep shedding everywhere you know.'

Still, she thought to herself as she grabbed her keys and headed out of the apartment, he certainly wouldn't be sleeping on the couch tonight.

Kelley's apartment was more or less right on the edge of town, so she left the truck and took a pleasant walk down to the waterfront. Although she'd not been before, Rosie's wasn't hard to find. She opened the door to the merry tinkle of bells and found Drew already sitting in one of the aqua colored booths.

'Hey,' she greeted as she slid in opposite him.

'Hey,' he returned as a well-rounded, middle aged woman headed toward them with a pot of coffee and two mugs.

'Drew,' she smiled widely, 'nice to see you back on the island. You back for long? Your mama was in the other day with Kelsey.'

'My sister,' he told Ava. 'Ava this is the famous Rosie, best pancakes on the island.'

'Oh, go on with you,' Rosie flushed.

'Rosie this is Ava,' he grinned. 'She's the one who's inherited the scary ghost house.'

'So I hear,' she smiled warmly and offered her hand to Ava. 'You're braver than I am, but welcome to the island sweetheart. I heard you're giving me a run for my money, "cooks like a dream" is the word.'

'I don't know about that,' Ava shook the offered hand. 'I'm looking forward to trying your pancakes though, Kelley says the blueberry's the best.'

'Oh, that boy,' she shook her head fondly, 'the blueberry was his favorite. He ate his way through stacks of them all the way through high school, I have no idea how that boy stayed so skinny. I had the three of them in here constantly. Drew, Killian and Kelley, the three musketeers.'

'I'll try the blueberry then,' Ava decided.

'Me too,' Drew grinned.

Rosie grabbed a rolled-up order pad from the front pocket of her apron, and a stubby pencil from behind her ear, and made a quick note. Then with a smile in their direction she headed behind the counter.

Ava took a slow sip of her coffee and turned to study Drew.

'You said you found out something about the house?'

'That's right,' Drew replied with an excited smile, reaching for his briefcase.

'The blueprints?'

'Still in the wind,' he shook his head, a little of his frustration bleeding through the excitement, 'but I managed to get my hands on these instead.'

He lay out a folder on the table and flipped it open; the pages appeared to be copies of something.

'The originals are all part of an exhibit about Talbot's life and work, housed in Boston, but I managed to get the curator to send me copies. These are all the original notes and ledgers.'

'Okay,' she stared down at them, not really sure what she was looking at. 'Why don't you explain it to me.' She eyed what appeared to be a hand drawn sketch of some sort of honeycomb.

'These here are all the ledgers he kept while building the house on Midnight Island. It details all the materials and laborers etc. It's mostly boring stuff, but it's the notebooks that are the real find. He talks about finding naturally occurring caves in the cliff.'

'My cliff?' Ava replied.

'Yeah,' Drew nodded. 'These sketches are of the caves he found, though it's drawn by hand and not entirely accurate. After all it's not like they had access to ground penetrating radar or anything, but it gives you a rough idea of the size and scale of the tunnels and caves that ran through the cliff. It was like honeycomb.'

'Isn't that dangerous?' Ava frowned. 'I mean, if there's caves beneath the house won't it collapse? Is that why the floor gave way?'

'No,' Drew shook his head. 'We still don't know why the floor gave way, but the caves, their natural formation gave them stability, just like the honeycomb. Talbot loved the caves so much he strengthened them and then made them into hidden rooms and corridors for his children to play in.'

'So, they were part of the original building?'

'Definitely,' he replied, 'and it looks like there are more of them down there.'

'More hidden rooms?'

'Yeah,' he nodded. 'I don't exactly have a map to work with

here, but this is what I've been able to find out from the notes. There's the one in the study, there's the one in the scullery, there's one hidden somewhere in the butler's pantry, and another in the billiards room.'

'They all have concealed entrances?' Ava asked.

'They do. Some of them are small, little more than hiding spaces, like the one in the scullery. Talbot originally designed those ones as hiding spots for when the children were playing hide and seek. He created a few more of these tiny spaces on the second and third floors, and in the attic space, but it's the ones on the ground level that are really interesting. These lead down to lower levels inside the cliff itself. Many of these were made from the naturally occurring caves.'

'They didn't look like caves.'

'That comes from his need to make everything look neat and tidy. He clad the walls in plaster and paneling to hide the fact that they were pure stone. I only noticed myself when I saw the part of the wall that had collapsed in the room you and Kelley found the bodies in. Although, on closer examination it wasn't the wall that had collapsed just the plaster and wood paneling.'

'So, there's a load more hidden rooms, but we don't really know where.'

'We have a rough idea, with the exception of one.'

'What do you mean?' Ava asked.

'Talbot talked of a tunnel, the biggest of all of them. He implied it ran all the way down from the top of the cliff to the private beach at the bottom, but he didn't say where the entrance to it was in the house and I've been down to the beach. I've never seen any caves or entrances down there.'

'Could it be underwater now?' Ava wondered. 'I mean, it's been over a century and a half.'

'It's possible I suppose,' Drew scratched his freshly shaved jaw. 'I'll look into any documented cases of costal erosion on the island. Tom, who mans the lighthouse at the other end of the island, would probably know the most about that.'

'Well if there are more hidden rooms,' Ava grimaced, 'I just hope there are no more bodies.'

'Could you imagine it though,' Drew grinned, 'if after all this time, we managed to solve the mystery of what happened to Luella Lynch and all those missing kids.'

'I guess,' she frowned,

'I wonder if she did kill them.'

'I'd rather not think about that,' Ava frowned. 'There's enough sadness and misery connected to that house without adding in the corpses of little children.'

'I know,' he replied softly in sympathy. 'Sometimes I get carried away and I forget you weren't raised with the legend. I guess after all this time, you kinda stop thinking of them as real people.'

'Well they were real people,' Ava muttered.

'Do you think all the other rooms and passageways are hidden by those same clockwork mechanisms?' Drew changed the subject slightly, leaning back and smiling as Rosie delivery two plates stacked with delicious looking pancakes dripping with butter and syrup.

'Enjoy,' she smiled before disappearing again.

'I don't know,' Ava picked up her fork and cut away a mouthful, 'maybe... oh my god.' Ava almost purred as her eyes rolled back in her head, 'this is so... I wonder if I can convince her to give me the recipe.'

'Good luck with that,' Drew laughed, 'many have tried and failed. Family secret and all that.'

'Damn,' Ava muttered as she went back to devouring her stack with gusto. 'Anyway, I think that I know who designed the clockwork locks,' she mumbled around a mouthful of pancakes.

'Ephraim Lynch?'

She swallowed hard.

'How did you know?' she reached for her coffee.

'I didn't,' he took a mouthful of his own breakfast. 'I just put two and two together and came up with a master horologist. There's no proof as of yet, but it seems like too much of a coincidence. Those locking mechanisms didn't come off an assembly line, they took time and an insane amount of skill. I have had trouble coming up with anyone of note during that time period, who would have been capable of producing work not only on that scale but of that quality, but it was widely acknowledged that Ephraim's work was commissioned by royalty. We need to get a look at the other hidden rooms to see if they also have the same mechanisms. How did you find the one in the study?'

She stared at him as she slowly chewed and swallowed.

'Luck,' she finally answered carefully, 'just stumbled across it.'

She wasn't ready to tell him the truth, not when she didn't fully understand it herself. Somehow, she'd just known where it was, just as she had with the one in the scullery. The same way she'd known how to reveal the skeleton key concealed inside the pocket watch.

Drew leaned back in his seat, patting his completely flat belly beneath his expensive suit.

'Damn I've missed Rosie's pancakes.'

Ava smiled softly.

'You grew up here then?'

'Yeah, with the two Ryan assholes,' he grinned.

'Do you come back often?'

'Not as often as I'd like,' he shook his head, 'not as often as I should. I started my own architectural firm about two years ago and it keeps me pretty busy.'

'I don't know, you seem to be here quite a lot.'

'At the moment I am, I cheated,' he smiled. 'I passed some

of my workload off to some of my staff. I'm not known to do that usually. I'm pretty picky but I couldn't pass up this project. It's a once in a lifetime opportunity, to not only work on a Talbot but to help unravel one of the greatest mysteries of the town I grew up in. There's still enough of the boy in me that I can't resist.'

Ava nodded in understanding.

'It's too easy to get caught up,' Ava stared out of the window. 'There's something about that house, that just...'

'Pulls at you?'

'Yeah,' she turned back to look at him, finding him staring at her with a small smile playing at his lips.

'Kelley's a lucky guy,' he chuckled. 'If he wasn't one of my best friends, I'd steal you away.'

Ava laughed. She liked Drew, there was something very honest and open about him. She'd never liked pretenses and inherently distrusted anyone in a thousand-dollar suit, but Drew just had this way about him. Just like Killian and Kelley, maybe because they'd grown up together. Killian was quiet and sturdy; the practical one you could always count on. Kelley was smart and funny, the one who'd always make you smile when you were down and who was so easy to be around. Drew was all fire and manic energy, driven and ambitious but not in a bad way. He was the kind of guy who could make you believe anything is possible if you just set your mind to it and work hard enough.

'Well,' Drew drained his coffee and nipped the bill off the table before Ava could protest. 'I'll take care of this and visit the restroom. I've got to stop by and see my mom quickly or she won't forgive me. Then I can meet you guys up at the site later?'

'Sure,' Ava nodded, watching as he headed to the cash register.

She glanced at the guy sitting in the booth behind them as Drew moved. For a second they made eye contact but then he quickly looked away, turning his attention back to his phone. Picking up her coffee she turned to gaze once more out the window, watching the gulls circling the bay and the ferry heading back out for another run.

Suddenly she felt a tight grip on her wrist and turned sharply to look. It was a woman in her thirties, with dirty blonde hair and brown eyes. She was leaning in close, her eyes wide and her skin pale.

'GET OUT!' she hissed.

'Excuse me?' Ava frowned, pulling on her wrist, trying to get the woman to let go.

'You need to get out, it isn't safe. She's watching you.'

'Who?' Ava tugged her arm again but for such a slight woman she had a fearsome grip. 'Who's watching me?'

'She's watching you and she won't let you go,' the blonde woman's fingers tightened causing Ava to wince in pain. 'There's so many of them, she won't let them go.'

'That's enough!' Rosie's voice cracked firmly. 'Let her go Julia.'

'You have to listen to me,' the woman called Julia yanked on Ava's arm, causing a sharp pain to shoot through her wrist. 'Why won't you listen to me?'

There was a jangle of bells and the diner door swung open with a clatter. Another blonde woman, this one older, hustled into the room and headed for Julia.

'I'm sorry,' she apologized, 'I'm so sorry, she got away from me for a moment. I was at island market and I turned around and she was gone.' She grasped onto the younger woman and pulled her away, 'Julia let go of her.'

'BUT SHE HAS TO LISTEN, SHE HAS TO RUN! SHE'S WATCHING HER!' Julia yelled desperately.

'It was you,' Ava frowned with a sudden startling realization as Julia finally released her wrist and was pulled away from her. 'You were the one who trashed my RV?'

'I'm sorry,' the older woman shook her head, 'my daughter is unwell as you can see. Please, we'll pay for any damages or inconvenience but please don't involve the sheriff. I'll keep her away from you I promise.'

'NO!' Julia began to struggle, 'NO YOU HAVE TO LISTEN, SHE'S COMING FOR YOU! SHE'S GONNA HURT YOU!'

'Come on Julia,' Rosie took her other arm gently. 'Joyce, I'll help you get her to your car, you should probably get her home.'

Joyce nodded miserably.

She turned back to Ava. 'Once again, I'm so sorry for my daughter's behavior. She doesn't mean anything by it.'

Ava watched in shock as they pulled her from the diner, still yelling.

'Are you okay?' Drew asked softly as he reached for her wrist.

She flinched slightly as he examined it carefully.

'You're gonna have a nasty bruise, but I don't think it's damaged.'

'She had a really tight grip,' Ava frowned. 'Who was she?'

'Julia Mays,' Drew blew out a slow sympathetic breath. 'She's something of a local legend around here herself.'

'Oh?'

'As a teenager, Julia, her boyfriend Todd and their best friend Declan all thought it would be a great idea to break into the Lynch House and spend the night. No one knows exactly what happened that night, but she was the only one who walked out alive and she's never been the same since.'

'Poor thing,' Ava murmured as she glanced at the door the woman had been dragged through. 'I think I remember Killian or Hope mentioning them when I first came to the island. Didn't one of the boys fall off the cliff?'

'One of them took a dive from the second-floor balcony and

the other ran screaming from the house and ran straight off the edge of the cliff.'

'I wonder what made him do that?' she frowned. 'Was he depressed?'

'No,' Drew shook his head, 'honors student with a full ride to college. Loving home, great friends, just like the other two. There have been a lot of rumors over the years, but like I said, no one really knows what happened that night except Julia and no one's ever been able to get a straight answer out of her.'

Ava wrapped her arms around herself, suddenly feeling cold and uneasy.

'She's watching you...'

'Come on,' Drew wrapped his arm around her, 'why don't I make sure you get up to the site safely? I can visit my mom afterwards.'

She should have declined but she didn't. At that moment something churned uncomfortably in her gut. She couldn't put a name to it, but if she had it may have been something like dread. She found herself wishing she had Bailey with her. It didn't feel right without the solid comforting presence of her furry best friend, instead she took the comfort Drew was offering and was grateful for it.

But as he held the door for her and shuffled her out into the warm sunlight, neither of them noticed the guy who'd been sitting behind them lower his phone, having filmed the entire strange exchange.

20

*B*y the time she was firmly settled at her makeshift, street food shack on the cliff top her nerves had settled, but then again cooking had always soothed her. She stirred the jasmine rice and checked on the samosas while Bailey settled happily at her feet. It felt good to have her at her side again, and although Killian had asked her to make sure she wasn't roaming free about the building site, she had to admit she was missing spending time with her dog, so she was keeping her very close. She also realized that the altercation with Julia Mays had shaken her up more than she thought.

'Hey,' a familiar voice called as Bailey leapt up, not just her tail but her whole-body wagging in excitement.

'Hey,' Ava moved the pan off the heat, as Kelley strode toward her. 'I didn't think you'd be done for another hour or so.'

'Miranda is covering for me,' he reached down and scrubbed Bailey's fur, until she collapsed to the ground in paroxysms of delight. 'Drew called me,' his serious green eyes fixed on her. 'Are you okay?'

'Is that why you came?' she tilted her head, her heart thudding in her chest, 'to check on me?'

'Why wouldn't I?' he straightened and crossed the distance between them. 'You're not just the woman I'm sleeping with Ava, I care about you.'

In fact, what he felt for her went a helluva lot deeper than just care, but he didn't think either of them were ready to deal with that yet.

'Kelley,' she replied softly, 'I'm fine.'

He lifted her wrist carefully and saw the dark purple bruises already blooming along her skin.

'It's just bruises,' she told him, 'it looks worse than it actually is.'

'It's not just bruises,' he murmured as he searched her face, 'something spooked you.'

'It's stupid,' she shook her head.

'You know...'

'Yeah, yeah, you love stupid,' she huffed out a laugh and her belly began to uncoil slightly, as it always did when he was near her. Damn it, she didn't want to be charmed by him, but she was.

'Tell me what's wrong sweetheart.'

'I don't know,' she blew out a breath, 'it was just something she said. I don't even know why it's bothering me.'

'What did she say to you?' he frowned.

'She said,' Ava drew in a deep breath, 'she's watching you.'

'She who?'

'That's just it I don't know but given the circumstances I'm willing to bet she meant Luella Lynch, which is just dumb.'

'You think she's the one who trashed the RV?' he asked.

Ava nodded.

'Have you spoken to my dad yet?'

'No,' she frowned. 'She's just a very disturbed woman

Kelley. Whatever happened to drive her to this, calling the law on her isn't going to help her.'

'You have a very sweet and forgiving heart Ava,' he replied softly, as he wrapped his arms around her and pulled her in close. 'But whether you want to press charges or not, it's an open investigation and you need to report it.'

'I guess,' she sighed.

Kelley held her, rocking slightly as she laid her head on his shoulder and drank in the comfort and strength he was offering, like a woman dying of thirst. It was too easy, way too easy to rely on him and she didn't trust easy.

'Don't do this Kelley,' she whispered as she pulled back.

'Do what?' he looked down at her.

'Don't make me need you.'

'Is that such a bad thing?' he tucked an errant strand of inky black hair behind her ear.

'I don't know,' she admitted, 'I have no experience with this. I don't know what I'm doing.'

'Neither do I,' he cupped her face and stroked her jaw slowly with the pad of his thumb. 'Why don't we just figure it out together?'

She leaned in and pressed her lips to his. She didn't want to talk she just wanted to feel, to quieten her unsettled mind and soothe her nervous belly, and for some reason Kelley was the only one who could do that.

'GET A ROOM!' a loud voice broke through their tangle of lips and tongues, followed by several loud whistles.

Ava chuckled, 'I guess it's time to feed the kids.'

She looked over as Bo, Luke and Aiden came striding over.

'Sorry Ava,' Luke grinned, 'can't wait any longer. My stomach has been growling for the last hour with the smells coming from over here.'

'Take a seat, boys,' she laughed stepping away from Kelley and reaching for a stack of plates.

'You want some?' she glanced at Kelley as she began to load up a plate.

'Always,' he dropped a kiss on her lips, 'but I just need to speak to my brother and then I need to make a phone call.'

She nodded, knowing that he was probably going to call his dad about the incident in the diner that morning. Although she didn't want to cause trouble for Julia Mays, after all the woman was troubled enough, she could see Kelley's point. They did need to know, and she found that she rather liked that she had someone to look out for her.

'Miz Cortez?'

Ava glanced up and saw a stranger approaching her. No not a stranger she realized, she recognized him. He was the man who'd been sitting behind her and Drew in the diner.

'Derek Carpenter,' he offered his hand.

Ava's eyes narrowed warily, her grip tightening on the plate she was holding in one hand and the spatula in the other. After a moment, he realized she wasn't going to shake his hand and he dropped it, giving her a harmless easy going smile that she instantly mistrusted.

'It's quite a little business you've got going here,' he inhaled deeply. 'It smells real good, I'd love to try some.'

'I would have thought you'd be full, from all those pancakes at Rosie's,' she replied flatly.

'Ah.'

'What are you doing here Mr Carpenter?' she asked bluntly.

She watched wordlessly as he handed her a small business card. Her gaze flickered down to the card and then back to the man in front of her, with his mousey brown hair and glasses.

'You're a reporter,' she stated flatly.

'That's right,' he smiled with what he probably thought was a friendly, approachable smile but all it did was raise all of her hackles.

'I have nothing to say except that this is private property and you are not welcome here.'

'I'm not here to cause trouble,' he lifted his hands innocently, 'but I did witness that unfortunate altercation in the diner this morning. Miss Mays seemed quite upset and warned you that someone wished you ill. One might assume she means the ghost of Luella Lynch. Do you believe in the legend Miz Cortez? Do you believe in ghosts?'

'I'm too old for fairy tales Mr Carpenter,' she replied coolly, 'now please leave my property.'

'Miz Cortez,' he ignored her request, 'if I may...'

'Is there a problem?' a deep voice growled from behind the short stocky reporter.

He looked up to find two huge, burly guys flanking him, one with a beard and tattoos and the other shaved bald and built like a pro wrestler.

'Luke, Aiden,' she smiled warmly, 'would you please see that Mr Carpenter finds his car.'

'But Miz Cortez, if I could just have a moment of your time,' he said quickly, 'I'd be willing to pay.'

'She said this is private property,' a familiar voice appeared beside her.

'And she asked you to leave,' another voice materialized the other side.

She glanced over to find Killian and Kelley standing beside her protectively.

'Luke,' Killian nodded.

Luke dropped a heavy hand on the guy's shoulder and leaned in.

'You wanna go under your own steam or you want us to haul your ass out of here?' he asked.

'I'm going,' he brushed Luke's hand off as if it were a minor annoyance and Ava guessed that being a reporter he was used to getting tossed out of places on his ass. 'You have my card, if you change your mind.'

Ava tossed the card into the fire pit, watching as it blackened and curled.

'No thank you,' she replied politely, 'you have a pleasant trip back home. I believe the next ferry leaves at three.'

Kelley chuckled beside her as Luke and Aiden escorted the disgruntled man back to his car and watched as he turned and drove back down the road toward town.

'I can't leave you alone for five minutes without you getting into trouble, can I?' Kelley's mouth curved.

'Thanks guys,' she blew out a breath.

'Like I said,' Killian patted her shoulder, 'we take care of our own.'

She watched him head over to his foreman Bo, who'd already finished eating, and the two of them headed back to the house.

'My heroes,' Ava smiled as Luke and Aiden wandered back her way.

Aiden stood a good couple of feet taller than her, built like the Rock and with just as little hair. He was also one of the biggest sweethearts Ava had ever met and she'd met a lot of people on her travels.

She handed him a loaded plate which he took with a grin, patting her on the head, the way he would a kid sister or a kitten.

'Thanks Ava,' Luke also smiled through his bushy beard as he took his plate from her.

She was just fixing a plate for Kelley when Bailey suddenly started barking. She glanced down and noticed her dog's gaze was fixed in the direction of the house.

'What is it?' she muttered as she reached down to calm her.

There was an alarmed shout and a sudden clanging. Ava

looked up in time to see part of the scaffolding on the second-floor collapse underneath Bo.

They all dropped everything and ran toward the house. Killian and Luke clambered over the piles of broken wooden planks and metal poles calling for Bo, as Hank, who'd been standing almost under it, was helped further away from the house.

'Have you got him?' Hank wheezed, having inhaled some of the dry dust thrown up from the collapse.

Killian heard Bo moan and slid down between the metal rods.

'I've got him,' Killian called, 'he needs an ambulance.'

Ava turned to look but Kelley was already on his phone calling for help, while Aiden and Judd were quickly checking the rest of the scaffolding to make sure it was stable and not about to collapse on top of Killian and their injured foreman.

'Paramedics are on their way,' Kelley called to his brother. 'How is he?'

'Looks like a broken leg and a head injury,' came the reply. 'I don't want to move him in case of a spinal injury. Somebody find me a blanket before he goes into shock.'

Ava didn't need to be told twice. She ran for the RV, grabbing the blankets off the bed and running back to the collapsed scaffolding. In almost no time at all the ambulances arrived on scene. She backed up and watched for a few minutes while they clambered into the gap to assess Bo's injuries, before she turned and headed over to check on Hank.

'Hey,' she sat down on the back of the ambulance next to Hank, handing him a bottle of water.

'Hey Ava,' his voice was a low growl.

'You okay?'

'Just a bit banged up,' he indicated his elbow, where he held a pad to the scratched and torn flesh. 'How's Bo doing?'

'Don't know yet,' she shook her head, releasing a worried breath.

Hank swore profusely.

'He's gonna be okay Hank,' she soothed him. 'I know it's not much consolation but at least it was only a drop from the second floor not the roof.'

'Hey Hank,' Killian marched over, 'you okay?'

'Yeah,' he nodded, 'just a few scrapes and bruises. How's Bo?'

'He's okay,' Killian nodded, 'he's awake and talking. They're stabilizing him for transport but it's just a precautionary measure. They seem to think it's probably just a concussion and a broken leg.'

'I should have been watching more carefully,' Hank scowled, 'but I was distracted by the kid.'

'What kid?' Killian replied in confusion.

'The kid in the window on the second floor, blonde kid.'

'Blonde?' Ava replied sharply.

'Yeah,' Hank scratched his chin, 'he was pointing to the ground beneath the scaffold. I was looking at what he was pointing at when it dropped, barely dived out of the way in time. You know it's one thing to have reporters and ghost hunting nut jobs creeping around, but they shouldn't be bringing kids up here. It's not safe.'

'I'd better go take a look,' Killian frowned, 'just in case.'

Ava watched as he took off across the site shaking his head and muttering.

'What did he look like?' Ava asked quietly.

'Jesus, I don't know, like a kid. Short...' he murmured thoughtfully, 'maybe 'bout seven? I dunno I'm no good at guessing kids' ages, young though.'

'And he was pointing to the ground?'

'That's what it looked like,' Hank nodded, 'directly beneath Bo.'

'Did you see anything?'

'Nope,' Hank blew out a breath. 'I don't know, it all happened so fast but for a second...'

'What?' she leaned in closer.

'I probably imagined it, it was probably just a shadow or a trick of the light.'

'What was?'

'It looked like the ground had split open, like a wound that's busted its stitching,' he shook his head. 'Probably just imagined it.'

Ava turned back to where they were hauling Bo out, strapped to a bright orange back board.

'Be right back,' she muttered, 'take it easy Hank.'

She crossed the distance snagging a hard hat as she went. She waited until everyone was watching Bo loaded into an ambulance, before climbing over the metal rods and split boards.

'Ava!' Kelley called, 'what the hell are you doing? It might not be safe.'

'I just need to check something,' she called back as she climbed down inside the collapsed scaffold.

Carefully she moved a few pieces of loose boarding out of the way until she could see the ground and sure enough, just like Hank had said, the dry ground had split open like an abscess.

Kelley swore mildly and grabbed a hard hat for himself before climbing in behind her.

Ava kneeled down and stared into the gaping earth. A loud gasp caught in her throat when she found herself staring into the wide vacant eye sockets and grinning teeth of a human skull.

'What is it?' Kelley climbed down behind her.

'You're gonna need to call your dad,' she looked up at him. 'We've got another body.'

'Miss Cortez you seem to be sending a lot of business my way,' Dr Casey strolled toward her, peeling off a blue latex glove and holding out her hand.

'Dr Casey,' Ava shook her hand, 'can I get you a coffee?'

'That would be great,' she nodded, looking back toward the house, which was once again a hive of activity.

The part of the scaffolding that had collapsed had been cleared away and the rest of it checked and braced. Now that it was safe, the strange split in the earth was being very carefully excavated around the human remains.

Kelley's dad was standing not far from the burial site, drinking his own coffee as he spoke quietly with one of his own deputies. After the media circus when they'd recovered the other bodies, this time they were trying desperately to control the flow of information in order to avoid another frenzy. Although, once Dr Casey Valentine had been called in once again from the University of Maine, it was only a matter of time before the news broke that another body had been unearthed at the Lynch property.

Ava filled a paper cup from the urn she'd set up and handed it over.

'Thanks,' she smiled, taking a sip. 'You seem to be keeping me in business at the moment, although I have to say this one's more up my alley. The others were fascinating but a little too well preserved for me. I'm used to bare bones, makes things easier.'

'Have you come to any conclusions about the women we found?' Kelley asked curiously.

'Not so much,' Dr Casey pursed her lips, 'it's a slow process. We've dated them to roughly the late 1870's or maybe just after, definitely just before the turn of the century. They're all in their early to late teens and judging by their bones and teeth, I would say lower class.'

'Like maids and nannies maybe?' Ava asked quietly.

'It's possible,' Dr Casey nodded. 'A lot of lower-class women their age would have entered into service with richer, more affluent families.'

'What about the newest addition?' Kelley nodded toward the freshly dug pit.

'We're bagging and tagging her for transport now.'

'Her?' Ava replied.

'Definitely,' Dr Casey nodded. 'We thoroughly documented her in situ, and after my preliminary examination I can confirm the remains to be female, most likely late forties.'

'Not Luella then,' Ava muttered.

'How do you know?' Kelley asked.

'Luella was in her twenties when she disappeared,' Ava replied.

'Ah yes,' Dr Casey nodded, 'the infamous Luella Lynch. Since the bodies were recovered, I've been reading up on the local lore regarding the house and the disappearances. I can tell you it's very unlikely this woman was Luella. Not only was she about twenty years too old but from the separation in her pelvis I can tell you this woman gave birth several times. In all my research so far, I cannot find any evidence to suggest Luella had any children of her own, but anyway we'll transfer her to my lab where I'll be able to run a full analysis.'

'I don't suppose you know how she died?' Kelley asked.

'Well she has a lot of broken bones, but under these conditions I can't tell you if they occurred peri or postmortem. However, she had a large wound to the back of her skull. I'd say that was probably what killed her.'

'Not natural causes then?'

'She was buried in the back yard without even the most rudimentary coffin. I'd say that's a giant red flag,' Dr Casey nodded. 'Anyway, I'll get back to you as soon as I have anything concrete.'

Ava nodded and stepped back. She'd wait for Dr Casey's report of course, but she had a pretty good idea who the bones pushing up daisies belonged to, and if she was right, that meant they'd just discovered the fate of Eleanor Lynch, Luella's mother. But instead of answering questions it had only created more.

21

*A*va woke with a start, breathing hard, but once again the dream was fading quickly. She could only remember a sense of fear and of falling, then nothing. She glanced over at Kelley who was sprawled naked over the other side of the bed, the sheets tangled around his narrow hips. The thought of waking him was extremely tempting, but after everything that had happened the day before he'd still gone and worked a full shift at his uncle's bar and she found she didn't have it in her heart to disturb him, considering he still had a summer class to teach later that day followed by another shift at the bar.

Glancing at the clock she realized it was still really early, the sun was barely even up. Creeping from the bed, with Bailey scampering along behind her, Ava headed into the kitchen to make some coffee. Even as she stood there pressed against the counter, slowly sipping her second cup, she found it wasn't helping. She felt as if she hadn't slept at all. Her brain felt heavy and sluggish and she couldn't stop yawning.

She briefly considered crawling back into bed and wrapping herself around Kelley's warm naked body, until she either fell asleep or he woke up and kept her awake in a much more entertaining way. Neither were really fair to Kelley though.

What she needed, she decided, was some fresh air and the ocean. A swim, down in her small private cove at the bottom of the cliff would be perfect. It was still too early for Killian and the rest of the crew to be there, so she'd have some privacy. She'd already bought herself a bathing suit, anyway, so wouldn't be naked this time... just in case.

The more she thought about it the more the idea appealed. Just thinking about her private little beach at the foot of the cliff reminded her of the conversation she'd had with Drew the day before and she found herself wondering if there were any hidden caves down there. She felt a pulse of excitement in her veins and without stopping to second guess herself she gathered up her things, leaving a note and a pot of fresh coffee brewing for Kelley, before slipping out the door with her dog.

It was a pleasant drive, through the winding streets, through the town and past the docks, watching as the sun began to rise. The small fishing fleet were just heading out of the bay and slowly the little island was beginning to stir. They travelled up the coast road, the window cranked down as Bailey hung her head out, her long pink tongue flapping in the breeze as it hung out the side of her mouth.

They drove under the lush green canopy of trees, the bright light of dawn dappling through the leaves and casting patterns across the road ahead. They passed through the woods, and out of the corner of her eye Ava caught sight of a small blue car parked off road amongst the trees. She slowed down to a crawl. It seemed somehow familiar, but she couldn't place where she'd seen it before.

She glanced around but she couldn't see anyone who needed help. If it was a breakdown, she assumed the owner of the car probably hiked back down into town for assistance. Mentally shrugging she sped up, heading through the woods that were now so familiar to her and up to the cliff top. Beyond the tree line she could see the house looming up, from this angle and distance it looked like it was surrounded by metal toothpicks.

The work on the house was coming along nicely, despite the constant interruptions. They'd managed to finish replacing the roof; all that was left to do was replace the tiles. Killian's wife Hope had managed to track down roof tiles almost identical to the originals from an old reclamation yard and have them shipped to the island to replace all the damaged and missing ones.

Although there was still more to do, a lot of the loose brickwork on the exterior of the house had been cemented firmly back into place. Likewise, the balconies had been strengthened and the black metal decorative balustrades repaired. One of the biggest surprises was discovering that the house wasn't a dull depressing gray stone but in fact a sunny warm sandstone, the exterior was just dirty. A little investigation by Drew had revealed that for about seventy-five years after the house was constructed a tannery had operated across the bay on the mainland and the smoke and fumes had been carried across on the sea air. As soon as all the exterior work was completed, Killian had promised her they were going to clean the staining to reveal the original sandstone colored brickwork and she couldn't wait to see it.

The bottom row of windows was now back in on the ground floor. Although there was still a lot more to do, it felt like they were beginning to make progress. She hadn't picked out a new front door yet, they'd just put in a temporary one to keep the voracious ghost hunters and reporters out, but she knew she wanted something that let in the light with some kind of stained glass.

Sooner or later she'd have to see about a landscape designer too, but she could already see it. For the first time in her life she could picture it and despite all the dark past that had been linked to the house she found she still wanted to save it, like the house deserved a second chance.

She pulled up to the top of the road and waved to the deputy sitting in his squad car as she bypassed him and parked by the RV. They now had a permanent police presence since the bodies had been found, on account of the house being even more tempting for thrill seekers to break into.

Climbing out of the truck with Bailey jumping down beside her, she glanced over to the house and frowned. The front door was wide open. She crossed the yard and headed up the stone steps and as Bailey bounded ahead, she caught a scent and started barking loudly. Suddenly Ava realized where she'd seen the small blue car concealed in the woods. It belonged to the reporter who'd been bothering her the day before, Derek Carpenter.

Her expression darkened and her jaw clenched in irritation as she marched up the remaining steps and through the wide-open doorway. She stopped in the foyer with Bailey pressing heavily against her legs.

'MR CARPENTER?' she called out into the house, her voice echoing in the stillness. 'I KNOW YOU'RE HERE SO YOU MAY AS WELL COME OUT.'

She waited a few more moments.

'YOU'RE TRESPASSING ON PRIVATE PROPERTY. IF YOU DON'T LEAVE, I WILL HAVE TO CALL IN THE DEPUTY.'

Still nothing.

'MR CARPENTER?'

Bailey suddenly gave a ruff and wagged her tail. Heading toward the steps, she ran up the first few before stopping and running back down.

'Gotcha,' Ava whispered as she grasped the bannister and placed her foot on the bottom step.

She climbed the stairs slowly with Bailey running back and forth on the steps in front of her, her tail wagging playfully. When Ava finally reached the top, she stopped, glancing around for the rude reporter.

'Hello?' she called out.

Bailey gave another short ruff next to her.

Ava's blood ran cold as a small leather baseball rolled slowly across the floor towards them, a ball Ava knew without a shadow of a doubt she'd left in her RV.

Bailey picked up the ball in her mouth, tail wagging. Ava slowly turned to look in the direction her dog's gaze was fixed on and her heart slammed against her ribcage, thumping erratically in her chest and pounding in her ears.

There in front of her, peering shyly around the corner, was a tiny boy. His blonde hair was messily parted on one side, and he was wearing much the same as in the photo which was tucked away carefully in her notebook. He watched her carefully through pale eyes, his skin chalky white. He pointed to the ground at her feet. When she looked down, she found a small bunch of wildflowers tied with a long strand of grass. She reached down slowly and picked them up, looking back at the boy who smiled shyly.

Ava tried to swallow past the dryness in her mouth, blinking rapidly like she couldn't quite believe what she was seeing.

'Are you... are you Peter?' she whispered into the stillness.

Suddenly the boy looked up, his pale eyes alarmed. He shimmered and disappeared like a mirage.

Ava turned abruptly and sucked in a loud breath. A scream caught in her throat, but no sound came out. Her entire body froze. She was staring into the pale, colorless eyes of a face that, although she'd only seen it in an old photograph, was burned into her mind.

It was the face of Luella Lynch.

Her skin was sickly white, the shadows under her eyes were deep purple bruises highlighting those cold eyes. Her hair was scooped off her face in a huge loose bun on top of her head, wild, with serpent like tendrils escaping, but before Ava could register what was happening, she'd raised her white claw-like hands to Ava's face and gripped either side of her head.

It was like being blasted with white hot electricity. Pain lanced through her skull, until she thought it was going to explode with the pressure. She screamed and stumbled back, and felt her foot miss the top step. Her arms windmilled wildly and for a split, terrifying second everything froze, then she was falling, and everything went black.

SHE COULD HEAR SCREAMING; the children were screaming. They were terrified. A woman was crying, the sound of lightning slashing across the sky and the violent crash and roll of thunder too close. The rain hammered down loudly, violent jagged spears that pierced anything they touched.

Ava moaned quietly and turned, her eyes fluttering open, blurry and unfocused. The rain was still hammering loudly only now it was against glass. Her eyes rolled as she tried to focus. There was a window, she could see streams of rain running down its surface. Somewhere in the background there was a low hushed beeping.

'Ava.'

She knew that voice. She turned and opened her mouth to speak but her voice sounded strange; dry and croaky, and not at all like her.

'Kelley,' she whispered.

'Thank God,' he breathed heavily, the relief clearly etched into his exhausted face as he unfolded himself from the chair beside her bed and leaned in, taking her hand and pressing it to his mouth.

'Where am I?' she glanced around to find a sea of brightly colored flowers and balloons.

'You're in the hospital Ava,' he replied quietly. 'Jesus, you scared the shit out of me.'

'Sorry,' she apologized, 'I know you have classes to teach this afternoon.'

'Classes? Ava,' he blinked slowly, 'that was days ago.'

'What?' she frowned in confusion.

'You've been unconscious for nearly four days.'

She blinked as her slow sluggish mind tried to assimilate what he was telling her.

'Where's Bailey?'

He smiled then, huffing out an unintentional laugh. It was so like her, for her first thought to be about her dog.

'She's with my brother, getting hopelessly spoiled by my niece and nephews. She's probably going to be the size of a walrus by the time they hand her back to you.'

There was a quiet knock at the door and as they looked over, it opened and a woman with honey blonde hair and warm brown eyes looked in.

'How is she?' she asked in a hushed hospital tone.

'She's awake,' Kelley replied.

'Oh,' the woman smiled widely as her eyes landed on Ava and held her gaze.

She stepped into the room and closed the door behind her. As she approached, she was carrying a large potted plant.

'Another one?' Kelley asked.

'Rosie from the diner,' she replied with a shrug as she set the plant on the table at the end of the bed.

'Ava,' Kelley turned to look at her, 'this is my mom. Cecelia.'

Ava swallowed once more, her mouth feeling like Velcro.

'Mrs Ryan,' she croaked, uncomfortably aware she probably

wasn't looking her best, having apparently not showered for four days and wearing a rather attractive standard issue hospital gown.

Although, it wasn't any worse than when she'd met Kelley's father. That time she'd only been wearing a towel and had smelled faintly like fish guts.

'Call me CC honey,' she smiled as she rounded the bed and stood beside her son. Her hand automatically lifted and stroked across his tense shoulders, as she looked down at Kelley. 'Why don't you go fetch the doctor, I'll sit with her.'

Kelley nodded, casting a worried glance at Ava before leaving the room.

'Well,' CC sat down in the chair he'd just vacated, 'you gave everyone quite a scare.'

'I guess,' she struggled to sit up.

'Here let me help you,' CC stood up and helped her adjust the bed, puffing up her pillows and making sure she was settled against them comfortably. It was such a mom thing to do that for a moment Ava had to blink back the tears. She might not have always seen eye to eye with Serenity, but it was times like this she missed her mom.

Taking a moment to compose herself Ava glanced around the room. Almost every surface was covered with flowers, teddies and balloons.

'What is all this?' she frowned.

'From a whole bunch of very distressed well-wishers,' CC smiled. 'It's seems in the short time you've been on the island you've made quite the impression.'

Ava turned to CC and blinked in astonishment.

'These are all for me?'

CC nodded.

'While you've been out, you've had more or less the entire Midnight police department in here, as well as Bunty

McCarthy and all her cronies, and a rather colorful gentleman named Baz I believe.'

'Baz is back?'

'He never left,' CC winked. 'I've heard all about what happened at Bunty's with the brownies, from my mother in law Alma.' She chuckled, absolutely tickled with amusement. 'Don't worry I didn't say anything to Gus, what with him being the Sheriff and all, but I would bet money that he already knows. Not much escapes my husband's notice on the island. Anyway, apparently Baz has been holed up at Barbara's house. Barbara, who has been very vocal over the years about sexual promiscuity and sex outside of marriage and now she has a gentleman staying with her in her one-bedroom cottage, if you know what I mean,' she wiggled her eyebrows.

Ava couldn't help the laugh that escaped at the thought of the strait-laced Barbara shacked up with the colorful hippy stoner.

'It's been quite the scandal,' CC laughed.

Ava's gaze landed on a strangely folded blob, which consisted of coils and coils of green knitting tied into a parcel shape with a lopsided bow. Clearly a gift for her, from Norma who loved to knit but couldn't seem to actually knit anything specific.

'Still it was sweet of them to stop by,' Ava murmured, ridiculously touched.

'Oh, they weren't the only ones. Killian has been by with all of his crew. It was kind of sweet actually, to see all of these huge tough looking guys tiptoeing around you carrying teddy bears and flowers. Even Bo, was wheeled down from his room on the 3rd floor.'

'How is Bo?' Ava asked.

'He's doing just fine,' CC nodded. 'Had a bit of a concussion, but the break in his leg was worse than they first thought. He had to have surgery, a few pins and screws and he's right as rain. They released him yesterday.'

'God,' Ava frowned, 'all these people coming in and out to see me, I hope I wasn't snoring or drooling.'

CC laughed in amusement as she stared at the beautiful woman with jet black hair. While she'd been unconscious, she'd looked as pretty and as unreachable as Snow White. She'd watched her son, as he'd watched over Ava. She didn't think she'd ever forget the look on his face, or the moment she realized he was completely in love with her.

'Kelley never left your side,' CC murmured.

Ava turned to stare at her.

CC opened her mouth to say something else, but the door opened suddenly, and Kelley strolled back in, followed by the doctor.

'Miz Cortez,' the doctor looked up from his chart. 'Back again so soon.'

She recognized him as the doctor who'd treated them before for suspected heavy metal poisoning.

'What can I say Doc,' she replied, 'I like the Jell-O cups.'

'Well you'd be the first then,' he smiled.

CC rose from the chair and smoothed her skirt. 'Why don't I go grab some coffee and give you some privacy,' she excused herself and slipped out the door.

'How are you feeling?' he dropped the chart on the bed and reached into the breast pocket of his white coat, retrieving a flashlight pen and shining it in her eyes as he spoke.

'I'm okay,' she frowned, 'a little confused, my head hurts and I'm a little dizzy.'

'Any pain anywhere?'

'No,' she shook her head.

'Well we seem to have a bit of a mystery,' he frowned. 'There's nothing wrong with you.'

'Why am I here then?' she asked in confusion.

'According to your fiancé...,' he nodded toward Kelley.

Ava slowly turned to Kelley who had the grace to look slightly embarrassed.

'...you were found at the bottom of a rather large staircase. The general consensus is that you fell.'

'What do you remember Ava?' Kelley asked.

'I remember going into the house,' she frowned thoughtfully. 'I remember climbing the stairs. I was standing at the top when...'

'When?' he prompted.

'I don't know,' she blew out a breath, 'it's all a bit blurry, then I woke up here.'

'The thing is Miz Cortez, you haven't sustained any injuries, not one single bruise, scrape or broken bone. That simply wouldn't have happened if you'd fallen down the stairs, there'd be some evidence of trauma.'

'So why was I out cold for four days then?'

'We don't know,' he shook his head, 'there's the mystery. We've run every conceivable test we could think of, CT, MRI, bloods, we can find no head injury or illness. It's like, your brain, for whatever reason just went offline for four days and then rebooted. I'm at a complete loss as to how to explain it.'

'Oh,' Ava frowned.

There was another knock at the door and this time a nurse looked in.

'Doctor you're needed down in the ER for a consult.'

He nodded.

'Get some rest,' he told Ava, 'we'll check in on you later.'

She waited until both the doctor and nurse left, closing the door behind them before she turned to Kelley.

'Fiancé?'

'You don't have a next of kin listed,' Kelley explained. 'When we arrived, they wouldn't tell me what was going on, so I had to tell them I was your fiancé. Apparently, fiancé trumps boyfriend.'

'Is that what we are?' she tilted her head as she watched him.

'Aren't we? I mean you're practically living in my apartment and having sex with me.'

'Oops sorry,' CC blinked in the doorway.

'Mom!' Kelley rolled his eyes in exasperation.

'Sorry, sorry,' she tiptoed into the room, 'I just thought Ava could use some caffeine after four days.' She placed a disposable cup down on the table over the bed. 'I'm just going to...' she indicated to the door, 'but it's not like I didn't know you two were pounding the bed springs...'

'Mom!' Kelley's eyes widened.

'Sorry sorry...' she backed toward the door, 'I'll just...' she pointed toward the door, before smiling impishly and disappearing.

Kelley turned back toward Ava who was trying not to smile.

'She does that on purpose,' he sighed.

'What?'

'Mom and Dad have had this contest going since Killian and I were kids, over who can embarrass us the most. They think we don't know about it.'

'Really?'

'It's really quite elaborate,' he nodded, 'it resets every year on their anniversary. Each year they up their game.'

'What's the prize?'

'Winner gets to choose where they go for their anniversary date.'

'That's nice.'

'Uh uh,' he shook his head, 'that in itself is another game. Each year they both choose somewhere they know the other one would hate.'

'Seriously?' she replied in fascination.

'Yeah. One year, Dad made Mom get all dressed up real fancy and I mean dinner at the Ritz fancy, took her over to the mainland in a private water taxi, had a limo waiting and then took her to Chucky Cheese for their anniversary meal.'

'Oh no,' Ava laughed.

'Yeah and the following year, Mom won so she made Dad take burlesque lessons with her. He had the long satin gloves and the feather boa and everything. He thinks we don't know about that,' he leaned in closer and whispered, 'but there's photographic evidence. We're having it blown up and printed on his birthday cake when he turns sixty.'

'No!' she laughed in horrified fascination, 'how do you know about all this?'

'One year, Killian and I found their score sheet.'

'They actually have a score sheet?' she dissolved into helpless laughter as he watched her with a smile.

'Anyway, enough about my parents,' Kelley shook his head. 'Where were we?'

'Defining the level of our relationship,' she replied, her eyes glittering with amusement.

'Right, so,' he began to tick items off his fingers, 'practically living together, having sex... hmmm I should probably take you on a date,' he mused. 'Anyway, it's a bit 7th grade but do you need me to like, ask you formally?'

She watched as he plucked a flower from a nearby arrangement, smoothed down his hair nervously like he was about to ask her to prom and dropped on one knee, blowing out a mock breath, 'so here goes. Ava... wait, do you have a middle name?'

'Uh uh,' she shook her head, 'not telling.'

'Oh, come on.'

'Nope,' she smiled.

'How bad can it be?'

'I'm the daughter of a hippy,' she reminded him.

'Come on,' he coaxed, 'I mean you are my fake fiancée; don't you think that's the type of information a fake fiancé would have?'

She shook her head.

'Okay I'll make a deal, you tell me yours I'll tell you mine and as a bonus, for blackmail purposes, I'll even throw in Killian's. Trust me, they're pretty embarrassing. I think it was another one of my parents' competitions to see who could come up with the worst middle names in the universe.'

'I've got to hear this,' she laughed.

'You first,' he dared.

'Okay fine,' she rolled her eyes, 'Summer Rain.'

'What?' he smiled.

'Ava Summer Rain Cortez.'

'That's not so bad, seriously mine is way worse,' he told her confidently.

'What is it?' she asked eagerly.

'Oreo.'

'No way.'

He nodded, 'and Killian is Snickerdoodle.'

'Now I know you're making this up,' she laughed.

'Am I?' he grinned, 'anyway, we're getting off topic.' He cleared his throat and comically smoothed down his hair once again, as he lifted the flower for her. 'Ava Summer Rain Cortez, wanna be my girlfriend?'

'You're such an idiot,' she grinned.

'Is that a yes?'

She rolled her eyes, 'yes.'

He laughed and leaned in to kiss her just as her stomach growled loudly.

'Hungry?'

'Wow that was loud,' her cheeks flushed.

'Want me to get you a Jell-O cup?'

'I haven't eaten anything solid in four days. I think it's gonna take more than Jell-O.'

'Your wish is my command,' he replied. 'Can't have my girl-friend slash fake fiancée going hungry. I'll go find a nurse to remove the IV bag and find you some proper food. I'll be right back.'

He dropped a kiss on the top of her head as he stood and headed for the door.

She looked down at the flower in her hand and found herself smiling foolishly.

After a while a nurse appeared and unhooked her from everything, clearing away the monitors and leaving her alone once again. While Kelley was off finding her food, she decided it would probably be a good idea to freshen up.

Pushing the bedding off her legs she swung them over the side and gingerly slid to the cool floor. Her head spun slightly but she was upright. Taking a few hesitant steps, she lurched, a bit like a drunk, but managed to make it to the opposite wall and open the door into the bathroom. She flipped on the light, listening to the hard patter of rain against the window in the room behind her as she leaned against the sink and turned the faucet on. Scooping up a handful of water she splashed her face and glanced up at her reflection in the mirror.

A sudden flash of images had her swaying and gripping the edge of the sink with white knuckles. A face in front of her at the top of the stairs and a tight grip on her skull. Ava closed her eyes and shook her head, taking a deep breath and waiting for the flood of images to stop.

She had been at the top of the stairs and she had fallen, so why had she not sustained any injuries? It didn't make any sense. In the moments before she'd fallen, she'd seen a face. The face of a dead woman.

Rubbing her face in confusion she ran her hands through her hair, stopping suddenly when her fingers felt small rough patches on her scalp. Turning her head and leaning in closer to the mirror she parted her hair and saw what looked like small oval marks on her skin, in fact they looked like electrical burns.

Slowly she ran her fingers through her hair once more. This time she stopped every time she encountered a rough mark and placed one of her fingers on top of it. By the time she'd finished, her fingers of each hand were splayed out across her skull, five marks each side of her head and she realized they weren't burns, they were finger marks.

___

22

*A*va stared out across the choppy gray water, as the ferry rocked more than usual under her feet, although the hard driving rain had eased up to a fine mist. It had taken a while to convince them to release her from hospital but considering there was no actual medical reason to keep her there, she'd signed herself out.

She couldn't explain it, there was a strange uneasiness in her belly. She needed to be back on the island. It was more than just a desire to go home, it was almost a driving compulsion. There was something she needed to do but she wasn't sure what.

'Hey,' Kelley's warm voice rumbled in her ear as he wrapped his arms around her waist and leaned his chin on her shoulder, while they both stared out across the water. 'You just got out of the hospital; you probably shouldn't be standing out in the rain.'

'It's not raining that hard,' she wrapped her arms over his at her waist and leaned her head against him.

'You've been really quiet since yesterday,' he said quietly. 'What's wrong?'

'Just thinking,' she replied. 'Kelley…'

'Yeah.'

'Do you know where Julia Mays lives?' she asked.

'Are you kidding? She's the town crazy lady, everyone knows where she lives. Kids dare each other to go knock on her door at Halloween… why?' he asked suspiciously.

Ava sighed and turned in his arms so her back was pressed against the railing and she was looking up at him.

'Because I want to go see her.'

'Ava she's crazy,' he frowned, 'and I don't mean that in a cute, she has too many cats and yells at the neighborhood kids, kinda way. She's legit crazy. No one can understand half of what she babbles.'

'Kelley,' she shook her head, 'I don't know how to explain it.'

'Try.'

'The night Julia broke into the house with her friends I think she saw something and…' she broke off and took a deep breath. 'I think I saw it too.'

'What?' he whispered in confusion.

'When I was at the house, I'd climbed the stairs to the second balcony and as I was standing there, I saw a little boy.'

'A little boy?' Kelley repeated slowly. 'Where did he come from?'

'I think he's been there all along,' she replied.

'You mean he's….' he almost couldn't bring himself to say it.

'He's a spirit. I think he's the one Hank saw; I think he was trying to warn him. He's been giving his baseball to Bailey to play with and he's been leaving me bunches of wildflowers and seashells. At first, I didn't understand but I think they were gifts. He's not trying to hurt us, it's almost like he wanted to be friends.'

Kelley stared down at her, his expression unreadable as his eyes narrowed.

'So, you're telling me that the ghost of Lynch House is in fact not a homicidal school mistress, but Casper the friendly ghost?'

'No,' her mouth curved slightly. 'I'm saying there's more than one spirit in that house.'

'But you don't believe in ghosts.'

'I didn't,' she shook her head, 'then I saw him, and he smiled at me. Then in the next second he looked... I don't know... scared. He disappeared and when I turned, I saw her.'

'Who?' Kelley asked suspiciously.

'Luella Lynch,' she replied reluctantly. It sounded so crazy when she said it out loud, but she didn't have anyone else to talk to about this and if she couldn't trust Kelley, she couldn't trust anyone. 'Look, I know it sounds crazy and you probably think I hallucinated the whole thing, but...'

'Hey, hey,' he wrapped his arms around her and pulled her close, cupping her jaw with his hand. 'I don't think you're crazy. It's kinda hard to explain, but I've always been terrified of that house. It was a ghost story from my childhood that I carried through to adulthood. But I exist in that weird space most people do, where I'm not quite sure it's real, but I'm scared of the thought of it being real. Does that make sense?'

'Weirdly, yes,' she admitted.

'I don't know if I believe it or if I'm just scared of the idea of ghosts in general, but I do know that if you need to speak with Julia then that's what we'll do. We'll figure this out.'

They both looked up at the cliff as the boom of the waves hitting the base reached their ears. The house stood tall and gloomy in the stinging rain as it picked up pace once more.

'Something is going on in that house Kelley,' she muttered, 'and I need to find out what it is.'

HE WAS as good as his word as they drove off the ferry and

through the town. Heading toward the other end of the island where Ava had not yet been, they passed the orchards and saw the lighthouse in the distance as they turned toward a small single-story property with a neatly manicured garden and a white picket fence, that stood apart, isolated. The rain was coming down harder as they climbed out of the car, pulled up their hoods and jogged toward the porch.

As Ava lifted a hand to knock Kelley slipped his hand into the other and squeezed reassuringly. After a moment the door opened a crack and the older woman, she'd seen rush into the diner the other day, appeared. Her eyes wide and suspicious.

'Mrs Mays?' Ava said softly.

'I told you we don't want no trouble,' she went to close the door abruptly, but Ava reached out to stop her.

'Please Mrs Mays, we're not here to cause trouble,' Ava told her as the woman continued to stare at her. 'Please?' The woman relaxed her white-knuckle grip on the door, and it slid open a little wider.

'What do you want?'

'I'd like to speak with Julia,' Ava replied honestly.

'She's sick,' the woman moved to shut the door again.

'Mrs Mays please,' Ava held onto the door, 'please,' she whispered. 'There's something in that house, and I think you know that. I've seen it too. I need to speak with Julia, I need her help.'

'I'm sorry for you, I am,' the older woman replied tiredly, 'but Julia can't help you. She can't even help herself. My daughter went into that house fifteen years ago, but what came out wasn't my Julia. I lost my daughter that night.'

She stood there for several long moments just staring at Ava before sighing slowly and opening the door.

'I suppose you'd better come in.'

'Thank you,' Ava heaved out the breath she wasn't aware she'd been holding.

They stepped through the doorway and stood dripping in the hall.

'Julia's in her room,' she nodded, 'second on the left.'

'Maybe I should speak with her alone,' Ava turned to Kelley. 'She's already familiar with me and it might be less stressful for her.'

'Are you sure?' he replied worriedly.

'She won't hurt her,' Mrs Mays told him flatly. 'My daughter's crazy but she's not violent.'

'Tell that to Ava, when she nearly broke her wrist,' he frowned.

'Sometimes she holds on too tight,' her voice was sad and tired. 'She only does it when she's scared.'

'Are you saying she was scared of me the other day in the diner?' Ava asked,

'She wasn't scared of you,' she shook her head, 'she was scared for you.'

'Why?'

'Only she can tell you that,' she shrugged, 'but don't go expecting a straight answer from her. You can wait in the living room,' she turned to Kelley, 'I'll make some coffee.'

Casting one last look at Kelley, Ava turned and headed toward the door Mrs Mays had indicated. She knocked quietly so as not to startle the disturbed woman on the other side. When there was no answer she slowly and carefully reached out and turned the handle.

Julia was sitting on the floor with a box filled with plastic 2d shapes. She was arranging them on the floor in front of her until it resembled a geometric pattern. For a moment it looked familiar, but Ava couldn't quite place where she'd seen it.

'Hello Julia,' Ava said softly.

The woman paused, she didn't make eye contact, but her gaze flickered in her direction, so Ava knew she was aware of her presence. She inched slowly into the room and sat down on the bed nearby.

'That's pretty,' she told her softly, 'what are you making?'

'It's a door,' Julia whispered as she reached into the box and pulled out another piece, 'it's a door, it's a door, it's a door, it's a door....'

Ava watched as Julia chanted to herself in a hushed tone, while adding more shapes to the repeating pattern.

'Julia,' Ava said quietly, 'I need your help. I'm sorry I wasn't listening to what you were trying to tell me before but I'm listening now.'

'The door is weak,' Julia whispered, 'it's weak.'

'Julia,' Ava slid down from the bed to sit on the floor next to her. 'I've been inside the house, I've seen things.'

Julia placed a black shiny diamond shape down and slowly her eyes rose to Ava. They stared unnervingly at her as if they were reaching right down into her soul.

'You've seen her,' she whispered to Ava.

'Yes.'

'She won't let them go,' she muttered, 'they're screaming.'

'The children,' Ava nodded. 'I can hear them, they're scared.'

'She won't let them go,' Julia repeated agitatedly. 'Born of a violent act, you have to send her back.'

'I don't know how,' Ava replied.

'Have to send her back, they can't get out, can't get out, the door is weak, they can't get out.'

'I don't understand,' Ava shook her head.

Julia pushed herself up from the ground roughly and grabbed onto Ava, dragging her across the room as she stumbled to try and keep up.

'Julia?' Ava called to her.

'You'll see, I'll show you and you'll see,' she muttered as she dragged Ava into the bathroom and rummaged through the cabinet.

Ava watched in horror as Julia grabbed a set of buzz cutters and before she could stop her, she grabbed a handful of hair at her temple and sheared it off at the roots.

'Julia stop!' she tried to reach for them as huge clumps of hair fell into the sink and to the floor, but Julia shoved her back and shaved several more strips before turning back to Ava.

'You have to send her back.'

Ava gasped, a loud sharp intake of breath as she stared at the woman in front of her, clutching the buzz cutters tightly. Half of Julia's hair was missing from the side of her head, save for a few uneven clumps and random patches, but what really demanded Ava's attention was the five small oval shaped burns in her scalp, exactly the same size and shape as fingerprints.

Ava's own hand involuntarily lifted to her own hair.

'I'm so sorry Julia,' she whispered, 'you didn't deserve any of this.'

Julia's knees folded and she collapsed to the floor rocking and muttering.

'They can't get out, she won't let them go, can't get out...'

Ava's eyes filled with pity as she slowly dropped to her knees. Reaching out and placing her arms around the rocking woman, she stroked what was left of her hair, and soothed her.

'It's okay,' she murmured quietly in her ear, 'we'll figure this out. I'm going to do whatever it takes to help you. It's going to be okay I promise.'

As she soothed her, Julia's murmurs and rocking gradually slowed and her eyes drifted closed. Ava looked up and saw her mother standing in the doorway watching her wordlessly.

Ava gazed at the clumps of hair strewn over the floor and sink, and the half bald woman in her arms, at a loss as to what to say. In the end she didn't need to say anything.

'Help me get her to the bed,' Mrs Mays told her quietly. 'She'll sleep for a while.'

She stepped into the bathroom. Taking the buzz cutters from her drowsy daughter's hand she calmly switched them off, as if she dealt with this kind of thing every day. Between them they walked the woman back into her bedroom and lay her down on the bed. Ava stepped back and watched as the older woman tucked her under a pale pink blanket and stroked her sleeping face tenderly.

'Thank you,' she looked up at Ava.

'For what?'

'For treating her like a real person,' she sighed. 'I know what they say about her. They pity her, gossip about her, make fun of her... the kids are afraid of her... she used to love kids...' she muttered as she watched her daughter sleep. 'She's my only child, I'll never have grandchildren and when my time comes, I worry who'll care for her.'

She turned to Ava.

'I hope she was able to help you.'

'Thank you for allowing me to speak with her,' Ava nodded before turning and walking out of the room and straight into Kelley's chest.

'Are you done?'

She nodded, 'let's get out of here.'

'Where are we going?' he asked.

'To see your dad,' was her cryptic reply.

HE FOLLOWED her out into the rain and drove her straight to the sheriff's office. By the time they'd been bustled into the small office and Ava had been fussed over by all the deputies, most of which she'd met while they'd taken turns watching her property, he was afire with curiosity.

'AVA!' Gus's voice boomed through the small office as he

crossed the distance briskly and enfolded her in a huge bear hug.

'Hi Gus,' she whooshed out a breath as he wrapped his arms around her and squeezed, adding a little sway just like Kelley did when he held her.

It was such a dad hug, she could feel the warmth and affection as he held on and patted her back, and she found herself blinking back the tears.

'You worried us,' he pulled back and looked her over as if checking that she was indeed alright and fit to be released from hospital.

'I'm okay,' she reassured him.

'What happened?' Killian seemed to think you'd fallen down the stairs, but the doc said you didn't have any injuries consistent with a fall.'

'It's still a little unclear,' she murmured, not wanting to admit that the ghost of Luella Lynch was not only real, but had knocked her out cold by trying to fry her brain. 'But I'm here about something else, I need to ask you something.'

'What's that?' his eyes flicked to his son who shrugged.

'It's about...' she looked around and dropped her voice, 'the two boys who died at the house, Declan and Todd.'

'What about them?' he asked carefully.

'This is going to sound a bit weird but when you recovered their bodies, did they have any strange marks on their heads, five each side. They would've looked like small oval shapes but when you look closer, they'd have been more like electrical burns.'

Gus stared at her for several long seconds.

'Come with me,' he said finally.

Ava and Kelley followed along obediently as Gus led them back into his office. They both took a seat and waited as he rifled through an old battered file cabinet. Taking a handful of files, he moved behind his desk and sat, dropping the files in front of him and folding his hands over the top of them.

'First,' Gus said seriously, 'tell me how you know about the marks.'

'Then I'm right?' Ava replied quietly, 'they did have them?'

Gus picked up one of the files and flipped it open to an autopsy photo which he tossed in front of Ava.

'Jesus,' Kelley swore next to her as he glanced at the picture of an eighteen-year-old kid laid out on an autopsy table.

'I won't show you the other one. He went over the cliff and he wasn't too pretty by the time we scraped him off the rocks.'

Ava picked up the photo with trembling fingers and stared at the side of his exposed skull. The burns didn't just mark his scalp, they went all the way down to the bone. She swallowed hard and looked up at Gus.

'Julia Mays has them too,' she whispered.

'What?' Gus frowned, 'how do you know?'

'We've just come from her house,' Kelley told him. 'Ava wanted to speak with her.'

'What? Why?' Gus looked at Ava.

'I wanted to know what she knows,' Ava shook her head. 'I've seen things, in that house, things I can't explain, and I just wanted to talk to her, but she got really upset and before I could stop her, she grabbed the buzz cutters and shaved part of her hair. She was trying to show me the marks on her scalp.'

'It didn't occur to us that she might have them too,' Gus shook his head. 'Both of the boys had them, but it was more than that. During their autopsies it was discovered that the prefrontal cortex of the brain in both cases, was swollen to twice the size it should have been. At the time of death both boys would have been in agony with the swelling in their brains being constricted by their skulls. It was suggested that possibly they were exposed to some kind of mold or fungus in the house that may have caused an allergic reaction and that their deaths were a tragic accident, but it was never proven.'

'So much death,' Ava looked down at the file in front of her.

'Are you okay Ava?' Gus asked quietly.

She shook her head.

'I'm actually more tired than I thought I was. I think I need to go lie down.'

'Kelley,' Gus glanced at his son, 'why don't you get Ava home. We'll talk more when she's feeling better.'

Kelley rose from his seat and held his hand out to Ava. With a final goodbye to Gus and a promise to check in with him, they walked out of the building, hand in hand, and into a torrential downpour.

'What is it with all this rain?' Kelley remarked as they climbed into the car. As soon as the doors were closed, he turned to Ava. 'Okay, what's going on?' he asked directly. 'What was it you didn't want to say in front of my dad? How did you really know about those marks?'

Ava stared at him for a moment, sighing quietly as she leaned over and lifted her hair so he could see the marks on her scalp.

'Because I have them too.'

'Jesus Christ Ava, what the hell?' he gasped in shock.

'Luella touched me, she put her hands either side of my head and it felt like I was being electrocuted.'

'Are you telling me that's what happened to Julia and those guys?'

'It must be,' she frowned thoughtfully. 'It's the only explanation because it sure as hell wasn't mold or fungus that did this.'

'Ava, we need to get you back to the hospital now,' Kelley started the car. 'You heard my dad; those kids' brains were swollen.'

'Kelley wait,' she grasped his wrist before he could put the car into gear and reverse out of the parking lot. 'There's nothing wrong with me. You heard the doctor, they performed a CT and an MRI, they would've immediately picked up any swelling or discrepancies with my brain.'

'I don't get it,' he sighed and switched the engine off again. He turned back to look at her as the rain hammered against the windscreen.

'I don't either,' Ava shook her head in confusion, 'as far as I know four of us bear the same marks. Two died almost instantly, their brains swelled, one took a dive off a second-story balcony and the other swan-dived off the cliff. Julia survived but anyone can see she's not able to function normally, but me... it knocked me out cold for four days straight but other than that I don't seem to be affected.'

'That we know of,' Kelley frowned, but looking over and seeing the distress in her eyes, he pushed back his own frustration. 'Come here,' he pulled her into his arms, pressing his face against her damp hair and breathing in the smell of shampoo and rain.

'I'm scared Kelley,' she whispered.

'I know,' he murmured over her head, his own eyes filled with worry, 'but I won't let anything happen to you Ava, I promise.'

'$\mathcal{A}$*nd the weather front is moving east across Maine from Canada, causing a string of unseasonable summer storms. They appear to be gaining in strength as they approach the coastlines. The advice to the residents of the costal islands is to stay inside. Don't travel unless it's necessary and wait until it's blown past and out to sea.'*

AVA PICKED up the remote and switched off the TV. She reached down and stroked Bailey's fur as the huge dog lay sprawled across her lap, taking up most of the couch. The rain continued to hammer relentlessly against the window like tiny little fists demanding entry.

Her head dropped tiredly back against the couch as she stared out the window, the clatter of the rain and the howl of the wind lulling. Bailey let out a contented whine and snuggled closer, and with the heavy reassuring weight of her dog pressing her into the couch, Ava's eyes drifted closed.

It was an assault of painful images which left her raw and

bleeding. She could hear the children screaming, the worst kind of screaming, children screaming for their lives. She could feel their terror and it slammed into her chest, her heart pounding so fast she couldn't breathe. Somewhere close by a woman cried out in despair, her sobs soul wrenching.

Ava shot upright on the couch, breathing heavily, her t-shirt sticking to her back, heavy with sweat. Pushing Bailey off her she dropped her legs down to the floor and cradled her head in her hands as the last of the images faded from her mind. She felt sick, her stomach churned, but as the dizziness receded the feeling in her belly was replaced with a sense of urgency. She needed to get out of the apartment, she was suffocating.

Leaving Bailey behind her, barking in protest, Ava grasped her keys from the table by the door and ran out of the apartment, slamming the door behind her. She couldn't focus, her mind was churning, driven by pure instinct.

The second she stepped out into the storm she was soaked through, her long black hair dragged down her back, heavy and cumbersome, as she headed toward her truck. The sky lit up with streaks of jagged light and the thunder rolled, growling ominously. The air felt hot and heavy, the reek of ozone lay over everything, so strong it almost made her dizzy as she climbed into the truck and gunned the engine. She wasn't even sure where she was going, she just drove.

MIRANDA SLAMMED the cash register shut and turned to her cousin.

'Hey, you actually working tonight?' she propped one hand on her hip, her red hair blazing in the neon light of the bar.

'Sorry,' Kelley frowned as he lifted his phone and shifted his position. 'No reception. I guess the storm knocked out the signal.'

'Kel,' she smiled as she placed a couple of glasses in the dishwasher and wiped down the bar, 'if you're that worried about her, why don't you just head home for the night?'

'I can't leave you on your own again,' he frowned. 'You've covered for me plenty over the last few weeks.'

'Seriously?' she shook her head. 'It's dead in here.'

Kelley looked around; she was right. They'd already closed up the kitchen early so their cook could get home safely and there were only a few diehards left nursing their drinks.

'I'll give them another hour then kick them out,' she told him, 'and I'll stay in the apartment upstairs tonight. There's no point in trying to drive across the island in this crappy weather.'

'Are you sure?'

'Go,' she laughed, 'before I change my mind.'

'Thanks Mira,' he dropped a kiss on her cheek. 'I owe you one.'

'Yeah, yeah,' she shoved him playfully, 'I'm keeping score.'

He threw her a disarming grin and grabbed his jacket.

THE MOMENT he pulled up outside his apartment he knew something was wrong; Ava's truck was gone. He glanced up to the floor above and saw Bailey barking behind the window. He launched himself out of the car, sliding on the wet sidewalk as he ran through the driving rain and into the building. He repeatedly pumped the button for the elevators, but nothing happened. The power must have been knocked out by the storm.

He took the stairs two at a time, sweaty, panting and rain soaked by the time he reached his apartment. She wasn't there. Bailey was barking madly, but he shut her back inside the apartment for her own safety and headed back to his car, pulling out his phone and checking it for bars.

He tried calling her, but her phone went straight to voice mail. He tried his dad and it managed to connect on the third ring.

'DAD!' Kelley shouted into the phone above the howl of the rain. 'DAD! AVA'S MISSING... DAD!'

He heard a faint answer but after that it just kept cutting out. He couldn't even be sure his dad had heard what he'd said.

Shoving the phone roughly into his pocket he got into his car and tore out. He wasn't sure where she was heading but his gut told him there was only one place that could be. He sped through the almost deserted streets of the town and turned onto the coast road which led straight to the cliff top and to the Lynch House.

AVA CLIMBED out of the truck and stood, staring at the house. The rain was beating against her, her t-shirt and her jeans were plastered to her body and the rain was stinging her skin. She stared up at the house. A single lone candle burned and flickered in one of the topmost windows.

The double front door should have been closed and locked but instead stood wide open, blazing with light. She took an involuntary step forward, she could hear it, pounding in her blood. The house was talking to her, drowning out every other thought. The logical part of her brain was screaming at her to stop, to not go in, but she brushed it aside, as harmless and irritating as a fly.

She took another step and another, climbing the steps slowly as the storm raged around her until she stepped through the door and into the brightly lit foyer. All of the floodlights Killian had installed were switched on, powered by the portable generator. She glanced up to the second-floor balcony above her, which stretched between the two curving staircases.

A small face and an unruly mop of blonde hair appeared, peering through the spindles of the banister, his pale eyes wide with fear. He looked across and was joined by a little girl slightly older but not by much, her sweet round face framed by ringlets bound at her temple by a lopsided bow and wearing a white apron over her dress.

Ava turned to the entrance to the parlor which had served as the school room. Two more angelic faces peered around the doorway watching her. Directly ahead of her, beneath the balcony, the foyer led into another huge room from which she could see another three children peering around the corner.

'She won't let them leave,' Ava muttered.

Her gaze slowly tracked down to the floor beneath her feet. Killian had laid down some protective plastic but some of it was scuffed and torn away, revealing the tiles beneath. Ava tilted her head as her brain slowly began to process what she was seeing.

She leaned down and grabbed some of the loose covering and pulled it back, watching as the plastic split and tore away revealing the original foyer floor. She sucked in a sharp breath; the geometric pattern of the tiled floor was the exact pattern Julia Mays had been recreating with her childish 2d shapes.

Ava stepped back and stared at the floor, to the huge stain which looked like rust, and which spread across the foyer, stretching between the two staircases.

She heard a door slam violently somewhere upstairs but as she looked up all the children had once again disappeared.

KELLEY SPED up the road as the trees weaved and swayed alarmingly in the storm. Lightning struck the tree in front of him in a shower of sparks and a thick branch collapsed into the road. He swerved violently to avoid it, the car fishtailing on the slick road. Suddenly a figure appeared in the bright glare of his headlights. He slammed on the brakes and swerved, the car skidded, hit a downed branch and flipped, rolling over and over in a screech of crunching metal and smashing glass. The car skidded to a halt on its roof, bumping up against a thick tree trunk, the wheels spinning, the wipers still moving and the headlights cutting through the dark woods.

For a few seconds Kelley didn't move, just hung suspended upside down in his seat. Then he sucked in a deep shuddering breath. Dazed, he reached for his seat belt and unclipped it, falling forward heavily with a pained grunt.

He crawled over the broken glass and painfully hauled his battered body through the shattered side window. He rolled over onto his back and lay for a moment, breathing heavily as the rain slanted towards his face.

His head throbbed painfully. Reaching up he felt a gash at his temple and when he pulled his fingers away, they were covered in blood. He rolled over once again and pushed himself painfully to his feet. His body was badly bruised and aching but thankfully he didn't seem to have more serious injuries.

An urgent feeling slammed into his gut. It felt like something was trying to stop him from reaching the house, from reaching Ava. He pushed himself away from the wreck of the car and staggered through the woods. The heady scent of wet loam and wood filled the air. The rain beat down on his head and neck obscuring his vision. Praying he was heading in the right direction he continued to climb steadily uphill.

The lightning strikes would randomly light his path until finally he saw a light through the trees. Hurrying toward it, the trees parted, and the house loomed out of the darkness. A single light burned in the topmost window and bright light spilled from the open doorway.

He hurried up the stone steps and almost fell through the doorway.

'Ava!' he gasped in relief as he saw her standing in the foyer, her back to him.

Hearing her name Ava turned and saw Kelley, bloodied and covered in mud, lurch through the doorway.

'KELLEY!' She rushed forward wrapping her arms around his shivering body. 'What the hell happened to you?'

'The car,' his teeth chattered as he swallowed, 'flipped in the rain, I crashed it in the woods. I thought I saw someone in the road, I swerved to miss them.'

'Who?'

'I don't know,' he pulled her in close, 'they disappeared.'

'Jesus Kelley,' she cupped his face, pushing his hair out of the way to examine the cut, 'you could've killed yourself.'

'I came for you,' he grasped her face urgently, 'you shouldn't be here. It's not safe.'

'Well isn't this sweet?' a familiar voice intruded.

They both turned to look and saw the reporter Derek Carpenter standing in front of the open doorway, watching them with a smirk. He wore a yellow raincoat with the hood pulled up, his glasses were steamed up and his bangs clung to his wet forehead, but as he watched them, he held up his phone as if he were filming them.

'What are you doing here Carpenter?' Kelley glared dangerously at him.

'Same thing you are,' he smirked, 'came to see a ghost. I saw Ava here take off like a bat outta hell, then not long after you followed. How could I resist?'

'You're crazy being out in this storm,' Ava scowled at him.

'Just following your lead princess.'

'You saw me wreck my car and you didn't stop to see if I was okay?' Kelley growled.

'Hate to burst your self-righteous bubble there Mr Ryan but by the time I got to your car you were already gone.'

Suddenly there was a loud clunk, the generator stopped

whirring, and the lights went out plunging the three of them into darkness. The phone Derek had been holding in his hand flew across the room and smashed hard against the opposite wall, shattering.

'What the hell?' his eyes widened.

Suddenly a shrill scream echoed through the house. It was chilling, filled not with fear but rage and malice. They could feel the sheer fury vibrating through the walls.

Kelley turned to look at Ava.

'I don't think so.'

He grabbed her hand and started toward the door, with Derek already moving in that direction but before any of them could reach it, the doors slammed violently shut. Kelley grabbed the doors and rattled them, but they were locked tight. There was no getting out that way.

'The windows,' Ava tugged on his arm and they ran toward the schoolroom where the original windows had just been rein-stalled.

Kelley grabbed the sash window yanking on it hard, while Ava tried the one next to it and Derek grabbed the third which made up the curve of the window alcove, but none of them would open.

'Stand back,' Kelley grabbed the old rusted iron poker from the fireplace and lifted it to swing at the glass.

Ava watched in horror as Kelley was thrown violently across the room by an invisible force.

Both Ava and Derek stumbled back as the wooden desks suddenly parted down the center of the room and shot across the floor in a loud ugly screech of wood, piling up against the walls. The lightening lit up the entire bay window and standing in front of it was Luella Lynch.

Her pale bruised eyes stared at them from a stark white face, her hair wild and bushy, escaping the bun at the top of her head, her lips peeled back into a snarl.

Ava felt Kelley grab her and they ran through into the smaller parlor and out the doorway which opened into a hallway.

'I know another way out,' Ava yelled breathlessly, 'follow me.'

She took them through the butler's pantry, and across to the other side of the house, past the music room and into the billiards room, slamming the door behind them.

'What the fuck?' Derek was breathing so rapidly he was almost hyperventilating.

'I need a light, I can't see anything in here,' Ava cried out in panic.

'Hang on,' Kelley fumbled in his pocket, one hand still clutched around the poker and the other dragging his phone out of his pocket and turning on the flashlight setting.

She ran her hands underneath the edges of the old billiard table.

'Where is it... where is it...come on...'

Suddenly there was a click and as Kelley lifted his phone, he saw a panel in the wall open up. It was another hidden room.

'How did you know that was there?' he asked as they rushed toward it.

'I don't know,' she panted, 'I just did.'

Derek crammed in after them and she slammed and locked the door with a deadbolt.

'What is this place?' Kelley asked as he lifted the light and saw roughhewn stone walls, not paneled like the other hidden corridor, and instead of carpeting and wooden parquet flooring there were just stone steps leading down.

'It's an escape route,' she breathed heavily, her heart pounding in her chest from the fear and adrenalin. 'It leads down in stages to the foot of the cliff.'

'I don't remember there being any caves or openings on the

beach at the foot of the cliff,' Kelley frowned. 'If we follow it, how do we know we can get out the other end? What if its collapsed?'

'We'll have to risk it.'

'Oh, hell no,' Derek shook his head. 'I'm not getting trapped in a secret tunnel in the cliff and suffocating to death.'

'It's that or face the ghost.'

'Come to think of it, if we just breath shallowly...'

'I thought so,' she nodded, 'come on.'

They started to climb, but it didn't just descend straight down, every now and then it would flatten out into landings then turn and descend again. They'd passed two of these strange little plateaus when they suddenly came to a dead end.

'I thought you said this went all the way to the bottom of the cliff?' Derek frowned.

'It does,' Ava murmured as she stared at the pile of rocks in front of her.

'There's no way we're at the bottom already,' Derek replied.

'We're not,' Ava shook her head, 'we're not even halfway.'

'Ava, this isn't part of the passageway. The roof has collapsed in over the original tunnel,' Kelley whispered as he examined the rocks. 'Do you remember me telling you that the night of the storm in 1919 the cliff was struck by lightning? I think it might have brought the ceiling down in this section.'

Ava turned to look at Kelley. As he moved the phone, the light fell on something poking out from under a rock. Kelley kneeled and shifted it out of the way, revealing the cracked face of a doll.

'Oh no,' Ava's breath left her in a rush.

She stepped back and looked up toward the top of the pile near the ceiling. Grabbing the poker from Kelley she scrambled up the rockslide.

'Ava be careful,' Kelley warned, 'you don't know how stable it is.'

'It's okay,' she reassured him.

She lifted the poker and stabbed it into a gap between two small boulders. She repeated it a couple of times then wiggled it back and forth. When it was loose enough, she dropped the poker back down to Kelley and yanked out a couple of the rocks. Shingle and pebbles rained down, skidding down to the floor in a shower of smaller rocks. She used her hands to dig a hole big enough to climb through.

'Kelley give me your phone,' she scrambled halfway back down the rock pile.

Once she had it in her hand she climbed back up and looked through the gap she'd made. There was a huge void beyond.

'It doesn't look as if the whole thing has collapsed, just sections,' she called back to him. 'I'm going to take a look.'

'Be careful,' his voice echoed in the darkness.

She wriggled her body through the gap and climbed down the rocks on the other side. When she hit the ground and turned, her heart shattered.

The beam of light carried through the corridor to where another section of rock had fallen in at the far end, sealing a void in between, and lined against the walls huddled together in the darkness were the skeletons of the children.

She heard the skittering rocks behind her and turned to see Kelley climbing down with Derek behind him.

'Damn it,' Kelley cursed softly, 'they must have suffocated in here.'

'Yeah,' Ava whispered.

She moved the beam of light and watched as it fell on the skeleton of a fully grown adult. It was a woman, judging by the severe corset, high necked shirt and full-length skirt holding the bones together. Her dark hair hung either side of her vacant eyed skull. In her lap, undisturbed for a century were the remains of a child, her arms wrapped around him holding him close. A small tuft of blonde hair was still visible against his bleached white skull.

There was a sudden rush of sound, like an indrawn breath. Ava felt the hairs on her arms rise and her skin prickle. She turned her head slowly to find herself staring into the eyes of Luella Lynch.

Kelley jolted and raised the poker like a club.

'KELLEY NO!' Ava stopped him.

They froze, breathing heavily as the spirit in front of them watched with frightening pale eyes.

Ava's gaze landed on a small gold locket hanging against Luella's blouse, just below her breasts and her gaze narrowed. Her hand fumbled for the locket she wore beneath her t-shirt; the one Baz had given her. It was the same one. Luella's eyes landed on the locket in Ava's palm.

Ava flipped it open. This time she peeled back the green lining paper and realized there was a small photograph concealed behind it. A small fair-haired boy.

'Peter.'

Ava turned to glance at the bones of the woman cradling the child and the pieces slowly began to fall into place.

'That's Peter, isn't it?' Ava whispered as Luella's eyes locked on her. 'He's yours.... he's your son, isn't he?'

Luella continued to stare at her but didn't move.

'You couldn't claim him because he was illegitimate,' she guessed, 'so you brought him here and opened the school. It was the only way you could keep him close to you, wasn't it?'

Ava looked back at the bones of Peter, then across to the other children.

'You tried to save him,' she murmured, 'you tried to save all of them. You were trying to get them to safety when the passageway collapsed.'

She turned her attention back to the spirit who watched her carefully.

'You weren't trying to hurt Julia and those boys,' Ava realized, 'you weren't trying to hurt me. You were trying to warn us.'

'Warn you against what?' Kelley asked.

'Whatever it is that's trapped in the house.' Ava stepped
closer to Luella, her mouth dry and her heart pounding. 'Show
me, like you did before.'

'Are you crazy?' Kelley hissed as he grabbed her arm. 'Last
time she knocked you out for nearly a week, this time she could
kill you.'

'She won't,' Ava shook her head, keeping her gaze on
Luella. 'She's not trying to hurt me; she's trying to tell me
something.'

'Ava, you don't know what will happen. What if you end up
like Declan? Like Todd?'

'I won't.'

'You don't know that,' he argued.

'Yes, I do,' she replied firmly. 'Last time it was a shock, I was
unprepared. This time I'm not, this time I'm giving her my
permission.'

'And if you're wrong?' Kelley whispered. 'I don't want to lose
you Ava.'

'You won't,' she replied softly, 'but if we don't figure this out,
whatever it is up there will kill us and we'll be trapped here
forever just like they are.' She nodded toward the children's
bones. 'They've waited long enough,' she told him, 'we have to
help them.'

He reluctantly let go of her arm as she stepped closer to
Luella.

'Try to be a little gentler this time,' she murmured and for a
second she could've sworn she saw her thin lips curve a
fraction.

'Okay,' Ava blew out a nervous breath, 'show me... show me
what really happened that night.'

Luella lifted her hands slowly and deliberately, her fingertips crackling with blue energy. Ava felt her grip her head, felt the shock and then there was blackness.

he Night of the Storm.
31ˢᵗ Oct 1919.

'MOTHER PLEASE, *you have to eat something,' Luella held the spoon to her shriveled lips, but they remained tightly closed.*

The left side of her face permanently drooped, and she'd lost the ability to speak, but there was still intelligence behind those eyes and a coldness Luella had learned to fear as a child.

'Mother come now,' she tried again, lifting the spoon, but Eleanor turned her head sharply and the mashed stew slid off and landed with a plop on Luella's skirt.

'Oh, for goodness sake mother,' Luella sighed in frustration, 'I'm trying to help you.'

Eleanor resolutely kept her head turned.

Luella took the napkin and wiped up the mess, then picking up the tray, she headed across the room. Eleanor still refused to look at her, barely acknowledged her. It had always been the same even as a child. It had been different for Edward, as a boy her mother had seemed to hate him even more.

The sudden random thought of her younger brother still made her heart ache. When she'd woken on that morning and found he'd died in her arms during the night she'd wept bitterly, and she'd vowed never to forgive her mother for what she'd done to him.

She'd left the house and the island as soon as she was old enough. Her intention was to gain employment in one of the big houses over on the mainland. It had worked for a while, she'd been free. Then she'd met a handsome young servant who'd worked in the same household as her. He'd won her heart, seduced her, and then ultimately abandoned her the moment he'd discovered he'd planted a babe in her belly.

Peter had been born soon after and it had been the happiest moment of her life. The second she'd held her son in her arms she knew she'd do anything to protect him.

Still exhausted from the hard labor, and bleeding heavily from his birth, she'd run, stolen away into the night with him tightly wrapped in her arms before they could take him from her. She'd moved from place to place, stealing if she had to, finding work where she could.

When word finally reached her that her mother had taken ill, paralyzed down one side of her body, Luella had hesitated, but the truth was they were slowly starving. It was getting harder and harder to find work. Peter, who was barely a year old, was sickly and getting thinner by the day. They were staring at a long hard winter with nowhere to live.

She'd vowed she'd never return to the island, to that house, but she had no choice. Her son would die if she couldn't provide better for him. So, she'd returned with a small blonde boy in her arms. She could've lied, told them that she'd been married and that her son was legitimate, but she couldn't, not on Midnight Island. She didn't want him tarnished by the Lynch name. No one could know he was her son.

She knew what the islanders whispered, about the crippled father she'd barely known, about the young brother she'd lost far too soon, and about the frightening grandfather she'd avoided at all costs while he'd been alive.

Ephraim Lynch had terrified her. She'd heard the whispers about him, heard what kind of man he was. She'd witnessed herself on more than one occasion what he'd done to her mother, the perversions he'd inflicted on her, things she'd been far too young to see.

No, she didn't want Peter to be compared to any of the Lynch men. So, she'd lied, she'd told them he was an orphan in her care. She'd returned to the house to find it in a shocking state of disrepair.

She'd found her mother had suffered a stroke and in her condition was no longer a threat to her or her child, but she required constant care.

Luella had stayed.

She moved her mother to the topmost room in the house, the room she'd once sentenced her and her brother to. It was petty, but at least she'd given her mother a constant warm fire and had all her bedroom furniture moved into the smaller room. It was more than her mother had given her and Edward.

She'd cared for her mother from a sense of duty to the woman who'd given birth to her. She'd always harbored a seed of hatred for what she'd done to her brother, but it battled with the barest hint of sympathy, knowing what she'd suffered at the hands of her cruel grandfather. It was a messy knot of emotions that, no matter what she did, she couldn't untangle.

And so, they continued on, Eleanor in her small room which Luella kept locked, just in case. Not that Eleanor could've moved on her own but there was still that little kernel of fear in her belly, that she would harm her son the way she'd harmed Edward.

Luella had turned her attention to the house. The repairs had been costly, and it was then she'd realized that the family fortune was all but gone. She would need an income if they were to survive. The solution was so simple, she would open the grand house as a school. It would bring in a good income, especially if she boarded children from the mainland. Peter would have children his age to befriend and the house would be filled with laughter, chasing away the dark memories of the past.

They'd come, a few at first, then more. After a while she'd been forced to hire another teacher to help her manage so many beautiful rambunctious children.

Jonathan Sedgewick had come to them from Boston that spring. He was a good man, sweet and he loved the children as much as she did. He was not handsome as such, not like the rakish boy who'd stolen her heart and given her a child. No, Jonathan was quiet and self-effacing, slightly rounder, soft rather than fat. He had a comely face and the sweetest temperament and as the years passed, she came to love him fondly.

They married in the January and were content in their house filled with children.

THERE WAS a knock on the door startling Luella from her thoughts. She looked up and saw her husband peek around the corner, pushing his thin spectacles back up his nose.

'It's time to settle the children for bed Ella,' he told her softly, 'but Edith and Hugo are both running fevers. I've isolated them for the sake of the other children but I'm going to need your help.'

'I'll be right there, love,' she smiled warmly.

He nodded and closed the door with a quiet click. Luella stood and smoothed down her skirt, before lifting the tray of barely touched food.

'I'll be back in a while to settle you in bed mother,' she told her but was once again resolutely ignored.

Luella sighed and headed out the door.

Once on the other side Luella found her husband waiting for her.

'How is she?' he took the tray from her.

Luella glanced back at the closed door.

'The same,' she sighed, 'she won't eat.'

'MISS LUELLA!' *a small girl with fiery red pigtails ran up to her.* 'Agatha was sick all over the floor!'

'Oh lord,' *Luella sighed, taking the girl's hand.* 'Come on Effie I'm going to need your help.'

Luella hurried away with the small child, Jonathan following close behind with the tray, neither of them realizing that they hadn't locked the door.

ELEANOR'S EYES *jerked toward the door; she hadn't heard the click of the lock. She waited a few more moments, the candle on the window ledge flickering as rain pounded against the window. The wind howled, rattling the glass but she couldn't hear anything else. The voices outside the door had gone quiet.*

She grunted, unable to speak as she flexed her hand against the arm of the chair. Slowly she pushed herself up until she was standing, the strength flowing back into her body.

Her daughter thought she was weak. Her body may still be damaged, but she had found strength. Every time she was alone, she'd practiced, pushed herself, with sheer will and determination. She knew she'd be able to walk again and now finally she could.

She'd bided her time, watched her daughter flaunt her fat stupid husband and her bastard child, filled her house with other bastard children, and yet she'd waited... waited for her moment.

She shuffled forward as the lightning lit up the sky in the window behind her. Slowly reaching out she grasped the handle and turned it. With a small click the door creaked open. She blinked and shuffled forward into the hallway, her eyes glittering dangerously.

She moved toward the stairs, her left foot dragging slightly behind her. Her long white nightdress fluttered around her legs as she slowly descended the second staircase down to the foyer. The tiles were cold against her bare feet as she moved with a lopsided, purposeful gait toward the kitchen and when she returned moments later, her fist was wrapped around a large knife.

Her long, prematurely white hair spilled down her back in matted locks as she climbed the stairs, her feet sinking into the carpet.

As she reached the top of the stairs at the second-floor balcony she stopped, peeling her lips back in a snarl. The small blonde-haired boy stood frozen in fear, staring at the wild-eyed woman with matted hair wearing nothing but her nightgown and clutching a carving knife.

The boy turned to run but her hand shot out and grasped him by the collar. He cried out, struggled and kicked, but she was surprisingly strong.

'MOTHER!' Luella's voice cried out in alarm as she rounded the corner. She dropped the bucket of water she'd been carrying, sloshing it everywhere, her sleeves still rolled to her elbows where she'd just scrubbed the floor clean.

Eleanor glanced up at her daughter and growled, an almost inhumane sound.

'Let him go, please,' Luella begged as she slowly stepped closer. 'He's just a child.'

Eleanor ignored her pleas as she stared down at the child, her daughter's bastard. It didn't matter what she told people, she knew, she'd known the truth the moment she'd seen the boy. She could see Ephraim in his face, just like her own son. She could see the darkness in them, the stain of evil. She'd tried to purge Edward of it. She'd tried to wash away the stench of his father from him, she'd held him down in the scalding water though her own hands had bubbled and burned.

Now her daughter had borne a child and still Ephraim stared back at her mockingly through those eyes. It didn't matter that his hair was a different color or that his eyes were paler, the same blood flowed through his veins, the same evil.

She should have killed her daughter when she'd had the chance, like she had the others. The other bastard babes she'd birthed because of that monster, she'd torn them from between her thighs, wet and bloodied, and smothered them with the soiled sheets before he could stop her. He hadn't stopped her; it had almost amused him to witness her descent into madness.

He'd simply smiled and just planted another one in her, no matter what she did she couldn't escape him. It was only when she finally gave birth to a son, he'd left her alone. At least, he'd stopped trying to impregnate her. Instead, the few more times he'd visited her bed he'd sodomized her instead, just another punishment. Another way to control her. The few times she'd tried to kill herself he'd simply tied her to the bed and left her there, starving, covered in her own feces, until she'd capitulated.

She'd celebrated the day he died. She'd stolen away into the room where his body had been placed on show, with a knife. She'd gleefully cut his penis off.

'Say thank you...' she'd whispered as she threw it on the fire and watched it blacken and burn. Then she'd urinated on his corpse and laughed, while he burned in hell.

Now she had to end it, she had to end his blood line. She grabbed the boy's blonde curls as he squealed in pain and raised the knife.

'NO!' Luella launched herself forward, but it was too late. Eleanor sank the knife into his small body and tossed him aside like a rag doll.

Luella screamed in rage and anguish, but Eleanor lunged forward slashing furiously, and the blade sliced through Luella's bicep, blood blooming against her white shirt. The two women grappled desperately. Eleanor grabbed the golden locket at her daughter's throat and yanked it hard. It fell over the balcony to bounce once and skitter across the tiled floor of the foyer.

Eleanor shoved Luella hard, throwing her to the floor and knocking the air from her lungs. She looked up and saw her mother towering above her, her eyes filled with hate and madness as she raised the knife to strike.

'NOOOOO!!!' Jonathan shouted as he ran at the old woman, pushing her away from Luella. She stumbled back unable to stop her

momentum as she went backwards over the balcony and plunged to the foyer floor.

Jonathan leaned over the edge and stared at her body laying broken on the tiles, her eyes wide, her limbs splayed grotesquely, a lake of crimson creeping out from underneath her and spreading across the foyer.

Luella crawled over to her son and rolled him over, pulling him into her arms and pressing her hand to his wound to stem the bleeding.

'It's alright love,' she whispered to him, her eyes blinded by tears. 'It's going to be alright.'

'Mama,' he whispered quietly.

She blinked as she stroked his hair, he'd never called her mother before. They'd never spoken of it.

'Yes Peter,' she told him quietly, 'I'm your mama and I promise I'll never leave you.'

'Ella,' Jonathan called to her urgently.

'Is she dead?' Luella asked coldly.

He nodded.

'Take her out back and bury her,' Luella told him bluntly.

'Ella we can't,' he protested, 'we have to report her death.'

'Do you want to hang for it?'

Jonathan turned back to glance at the corpse and slowly shook his head.

'Get rid of the body,' she turned her attention back to the boy in her arms, 'no one will ever have to know.'

'What about Peter?' he asked in concern as he eyed the boy, whose skin was now chalky white as he bled profusely from his stomach.

'I will get him to Doctor Grayson,' she lifted him into her arms. 'You stay here with the other children.'

Jonathan stared down at Peter, worried that it was already too late to save the boy. Not giving his mind time to process what he was about to do he ran down the stairs and into the study. Tearing down one of the drapes he returned to the foyer and wrapped Eleanor's body in it.

Picking up her slight weight he opened the front door into the dark night and stepped out into the rain. He moved around the side of the house quickly and purposefully, dumping her in the wet grass while he retrieved a shovel from the shed.

The sky churned and boiled above him as he buried the mad woman in a shallow grave.

When he re-entered the house, drenched to the skin, covered in earth and blood, he expected Luella to be gone, but she wasn't. She sat on the bottom step of the foyer with Peter cradled in her arms as she slowly rocked him back and forth. The children, all disturbed by the commotion had appeared and were sitting on the stairs, surrounding Luella, as they watched sadly.

In that moment Jonathan knew Peter was gone.

'Ella my love,' he whispered as he knelt in front of her, 'I'm so sorry.'

She didn't speak, tears streamed down her wet face as she rocked him in her arms, pressing her lips to his blonde curls.

SUDDENLY THE FRONT door banged open loudly, the shriek and violence of the storm beyond suddenly building. The sky churned and boiled, and lighting streaked across the black clouds. The thunder crashed and roared so loudly the children jumped and a few cried out in alarm. The gas lights suddenly cut out, plunging them into near darkness.

Unable to explain what had extinguished the lamps, Jonathan stood slowly. The hairs on his neck began to rise and his skin prickled. His gaze was drawn to the huge pool of blood on the tiled floor beneath the balcony.

For a moment it almost seemed as if his eyes were playing tricks on him. The blood on the floor began to bubble, and he watched in horror as a pale spectral light began to appear, hovering above it.

'ELLA!' he shouted in alarm, 'get the children out of the house!'

He sprinted for the stairs, heading for one of the isolation rooms. He burst through the door and scooped up the two fevered children into his arms, feeling the heat of their skin burning through his wet, soiled shirtsleeves. He held their limp bodies against him as he looked out to see Effie, the little red-haired girl wiping Agatha's brow with a damp cloth.

'Effie!' he called to her urgently, 'bring Agatha. No matter what you see, no matter what you hear, you stay close to me, do you understand?'

Effie stared at him with large frightened eyes, nodding quickly, having never witnessed such panic and intensity from the mild mannered, softly spoken man. Effie helped Agatha out of bed, and they headed out into the hallway and down the stairs.

Luella quickly stood, still clutching onto Peter.

'COME CHILDREN QUICKLY!' she ordered them. She didn't know what was happening, nor did she know what the strange light was, all she knew was they had to get the children out of the house. She rushed towards the door with the children clustered around her, but the doors slammed shut and wouldn't budge.

Jonathan hurried down the stairs cradling the two sick children, one in each arm, with Effie dragging the pale faced Agatha behind her.

They couldn't get out, the doors held fast.

Luella turned and watched in horror as the light hovering above the pool of blood began to coalesce into a form. Strange tentacle-like threads of light undulated in the air and gradually a face appeared.

Eleanor.

She hovered above the ground stained with her blood, floating, her white nightgown rippling around her and her long white hair splayed out as if she were floating underwater. Her eyes were black and wild against her white face. Her lips peeled back in a scream of rage as her sharp claw-like fingers flexed.

The children screamed, faced with such a terrifying sight.

'COME!' Luella turned and ran, the children following her and her husband last to make sure no one was left behind.

They navigated their way through the maze of the house in the near darkness, from memory and instinct alone, fumbling and tripping until they finally reached the billiards room. There Luella flicked the catch to open the hidden door in the paneled wall. As it swung open Jonathan entered first to guide the children down the dark steps and through the passageways. Luella came through last as an ear-piercing shriek of utter madness and rage rang through the house.

Luella slammed the door and hurried after the children. The ground heaved and shook beneath their feet as they stumbled along in the darkness.

Suddenly there was a loud cracking, grinding sound and the ground lurched again, this time so violently they were all thrown to the ground. The ceiling gave way and smashed down to the floor. For a few horrifying moments it didn't stop; it felt like the whole cliff face was going to break away and fall into the sea.

When it finally subsided Luella turned to look but she couldn't see anything. They'd been plunged into total darkness. She reached out but found nothing but rock. The passageway behind her was blocked.

'Jonathan the passageway is blocked,' she called out.

'This end is too,' came the muffled reply in the darkness.

Luella slid down the wall helplessly, cradling Peter's limp body in her arms. She could hear the children crying softly in the dark, but it was no use, there was no way out.

'NOW YOU'RE TRAPPED HERE FOREVER...' she heard her mother's voice whisper loudly in the darkness, harsh and filled with venom. 'I will never leave this house and now, neither will you...'

*A*va stumbled back and doubled over, gasping in a desperate lungful of air. She couldn't breathe through the excruciating wave of grief pressing down on her chest and the feeling of absolute hopelessness. Her emotions were too deeply tangled with that of Luella and for a moment she couldn't break free.

'Ava?'

She felt Kelley's hand on her back soothingly.

'Ava, talk to me.'

'She killed him,' Ava whispered, her face wet with tears. 'She killed Peter.'

'Who, Luella?' Kelley frowned.

Ava pushed her hands against her knees and straightened, sucking in a calming breath as the intense emotions of the dead woman began to fade. She glanced around and realized Luella had disappeared again and that she was standing alone with Kelley and Derek, who was looking a little wild eyed at the events he'd just borne witness to.

'No,' Ava shook her head, 'not Luella. It was her mother.'

'Her mother?'

'Eleanor,' Ava explained quickly, 'she killed Peter and tried to kill Luella. Her husband Jonathan saved her.'

She turned to look at the end of the corridor and sure enough, there was the remains of an adult male, his arms wrapped around two young children.

'He pushed Eleanor away from Luella as she tried to stab her and she went over the balcony, she died right there on the floor of the foyer. Her spirit came back violent and angry, she trapped Luella, Jonathan and the children down here and they suffocated. She's the one who's keeping their spirits trapped in the house.'

'Jesus,' Kelley raked his hand through his hair, 'what the hell do we do? Now she's awake she's plenty pissed, and I don't think she's going to let us leave.'

'We have to try and find a way to send her back. She's not supposed to be here.'

'Just how are we supposed to do that?' Kelley frowned.

Ava turned to Derek.

'Because we have him,' she replied confidently.

'ME?' his eyes widened.

'You're a ghost hunter, aren't you? You must've heard all the lore, the rumors, the myths, you're basically a walking almanac of the weird and occult,' she replied.

'I'm not a ghost hunter,' he protested.

'But you said earlier,' Kelley interrupted, 'you said you were looking for a ghost.'

'Yeah,' he replied sarcastically, 'to disprove it. I investigate claims of paranormal disturbances, not because I believe but because I don't. I spend my time proving that these people who claim to have encounters with the paranormal are nothing more than con artists and frauds. I debunk more hauntings than any other reporter I know.'

'Good luck debunking this,' Kelley murmured.

'That's just semantics,' Ava waved her hand dismissively. 'It doesn't matter if you believe it or not, what matters is the knowledge you've accumulated over the years. Just think back to anything anyone has ever told you about getting rid of a violent spirit.'

'Well we don't have an old priest and a young priest,' he replied.

'It's not a demon possession,' she replied dryly, 'this is an angry ghost we're dealing with.'

'Okay,' he blew out a breath shaking his head thoughtfully, 'salt and burn the bones.'

'This is also not a TV show,' she scowled.

'Hey, aren't you supposed to get their bones to consecrated ground?' Kelly interrupted.

'That would be great,' Ava nodded, 'if we had consecrated ground and her bones weren't fifty miles away in a lab.'

'Wait!' Derek shouted, 'her bones aren't here on site?'

'They're not even on the island,' Ava replied.

'Then what's tying her to the house?'

'You mean apart from her bad decisions and sucky attitude,' Kelley muttered.

'Hang on,' Ava frowned, 'he's got a point. Let's think this through logically. She died in the house, she went over the balcony of the second floor and died there. When I went to see Julia, she was recreating a pattern with these 2d shapes she had. At first, I couldn't place where I'd seen it. She kept telling me that it was a doorway and that it was weak. That's what that stain is, Eleanor's blood. It's the doorway she used to come back.'

'I suppose it makes sense,' Derek agreed. 'A lot of people believe that angry spirits are born of a violent act.'

'Born of a violent act,' Ava closed her eyes in realization, 'that's what Julia, Bunty and my grandmother all said. They kept telling me whatever was in the house was born of a violent act. I thought they meant Luella because she was the product of rape, but it wasn't. It was her mother all along. Her murder was the violent act, it's what brought her back.'

'If that was the case, we'd have violent spirits cropping up all over the place,' Derek protested.

'Who says we don't?' Ava shrugged, 'but I don't know, maybe it was the perfect storm of events. It was Halloween, which is meant to be the one day of the year when the veil between life and death is at its thinnest. It was during a violent storm, all that electricity and energy in the air. Eleanor's madness, Luella's grief, the children's fear, all strong emotions, somehow she was able to come back and she used the exact location of her death as a doorway.'

'So how does this help us?' Kelley shook his head.

'Julia said that we have to send her back,' Ava replied. 'If she used the blood stain as a door to come through, maybe it's still open, maybe that's how we send her back.'

'You really think that'll work?' Kelley asked

'You got any better ideas?'

'Okay,' he breathed heavily, 'so how do we draw her to the blood stain?'

'I'll get her there,' Ava replied confidently.

'How?'

'Just trust me,' she nodded, 'right now, we need to get back up into the house.'

'Well, we just have to....' Kelley cut off and turned around sharply as the ground began to shake under their feet. The rocks stacked up behind them began to vibrate and shimmy fiercely.

Suddenly they exploded outwards into the corridor they'd crawled in from. They seemed to hang motionless in the air for a second before clattering to the ground and there, hovering in front of them in all her terrifying glory, was Eleanor Lynch.

All three of them stumbled back from that awful sight. Her hair was wild, streaming ribbons of white, snapping in all directions, as was her nightgown. Her eyes were soulless dark pits, filled with rage and torment. Her thin lips peeled back into a snarl and as she opened her mouth a bone chilling, birdlike screech filled the air.

Luella suddenly reappeared between them and the nightmarish woman in white, blocking her way. Eleanor bared her teeth in a snarl, her cruel needle pointed fingers curling into claws as she launched herself at her bastard daughter. Luella lunged forward to meet her and as they clashed the whole tunnel shook viciously and the two of them disappeared.

'Why did they vanish?' Derek demanded in a shrill panicked voice.

'She's buying us some time,' Ava took off through the rubble which had been blasted back along the tunnel and up the stairs. 'We need to get to the doorway.'

Kelley rushed after her with Derek close behind, they ran up the stairs and didn't stop until they reached the doorway. Ava unbolted the door and they burst into the billiards room. A chair flew across the room and smashed into the opposite wall, the paintings on the wall began to rattle and shake as they ducked and weaved their way out of the room to avoid flying debris.

They tripped and fell out into the hallway, Kelley reached down and hauled Ava to her feet and they ran, past the study toward the foyer. Ava felt herself shoved forward roughly, sending her colliding into the wall, her head cracked sharply causing a wave of dizziness.

Kelley lunged toward her but found himself launched through the air and pinned up against the solid opposite wall a foot off the ground. The air in front of him shimmered and Eleanor appeared, her eyes crazy and her hand wrapped around Kelley's throat as he kicked, and he struggled and fought for breath.

'HEY! ELEANOR!'

Eleanor turned her head slowly her black eyes fixing on Ava as her nostrils flared slightly, like a predator scenting its prey. Ava stood over the blood-stained circle on the floor, one hand curled around a bloodied broken tile and the other she held out in a fist as a trickle of bright red blood spilled from her clenched palm.

'That's right,' Ava replied, 'you can sense, it can't you? Ephraim's blood, I'm the last of his bloodline. You want to end it? You're gonna have to kill me.'

Eleanor dropped Kelley and screeched in rage, plunging across the foyer toward her. Ava felt Eleanor's icy fingers wrap around her throat but before she could get a grip, Ava's breath was knocked out of her as Kelley launched himself across the circle, tackling her midsection and throwing them both clear. They hit the hard floor with a painful thud and skidded a few meters.

Eleanor howled in rage again and pitched toward them only to find she couldn't move. She glanced down in confusion to find the blood stain beneath her was writhing and bubbling, the dark pitch-like liquid slithering up her white nightgown like poisonous vines, wrapping thin tentacles around her legs and torso.

Eleanor shrieked again, only this time it wasn't a murderous rage, it was more like panic when she realized she couldn't get free.

The tentacles began to split until they resembled blackened hands grabbing at her arms, her hair, her face. She screamed again. The dozens of arms and hands dragged her down, pulling her through the floor as if it were a tar pit. She scratched and screamed and clawed at the edges of the circle, but it was no good, she was being pulled inexorably down. In desperation her flailing arm lashed out and managed to catch hold of Ava's ankle.

Ava screamed as she slid across the floor. Kelley reached out and grabbed her wrist, as he gripped onto the staircase to stop them both from sliding into the hell pit or whatever it was, but the woman had a hell of a grip. Ava screamed again, partly in panic, partly in pain. She slipped further across the floor, Kelley desperately trying to hold onto her.

A hand reached down and grasped Eleanor's wrist, forcing her to release her grip on Ava's ankle. Kelley yanked Ava back out of the way and wrapped his arms around her protectively. Luella held onto her mother's wrist tightly, their eyes met and for one brief second something passed between them.

Then Luella let go and Eleanor sank down, disappearing into the thick black goo. Luella stood and stepped back as it frothed and bubbled viciously, folding in on itself again and again, reducing in size until it finally disappeared, leaving the tiles as they once were. Nothing more than a simple Victorian geometric pattern with a century's worth of dirt on it.

Ava crept forward and reached out warily, running her hand across the tile. The blood stain was completely gone and so was Eleanor. Ava looked up at Luella, then following her gaze she turned and looked around her as all the children began to appear one by one, until the foyer was filled with them.

The front doors suddenly unlocked and slowly creaked open, allowing the fresh air to rush in, but Ava couldn't see anything, outside was filled with a blinding white light.

She climbed slowly to her feet, feeling Kelley rise next to her. Side by side they approached the door, flanked by the trembling and traumatized reporter.

Ava stepped out onto the porch. The storm had passed, blown out to sea. The sky was filled with pale gray clouds, there was no more rain or thunder, instead there was a heavy fog. It covered the entire cliff top obscuring everything including her truck, the RV and all the heavy machinery.

Ava stared at the strange undulating mist, until she realized it was moving toward the house. More than that, as it got closer, she could see individual shapes, gliding along the ground. Her mouth opened, and she gasped as her eyes filled with tears.

'Kelley look,' she whispered, 'they've come for their children.'

Derek's eyes rolled back in his head and they heard him drop to the ground with a thud.

They were spirits, dozens of them, men and women in pairs, creeping closer to the house. Ava turned to see all of the children crowded into the doorway behind them, looking up at her expectantly. Ava turned to Kelley and they smiled to each other and stepped aside.

A little girl with red pig tails stepped out. She turned to Ava and Kelley, giving them a wide grin before skipping down the steps. She ran across the yard and launched herself into the arms of a man, the woman standing beside him smiled and wrapped her arms around them both until the three of them coalesced into a bright beam of light which shot up into the sky like a shooting star, igniting the clouds above.

The children surged out of the doors, running down the stairs and across the yard, leaping into their parents' waiting embraces. One by one the beams of light shot up into the sky, the clouds glowing with microbursts of light. Gradually as the last one disappeared, the yard cleared, the mist gone, everything was damp with rainwater, fresh and somehow cleaner.

'Ava,' Kelley rumbled beside her and pointed.

When she turned to look, she saw two teenage boys smiling at them.

'Todd and Declan,' she realized, 'she trapped them here too.'

One nodded and the other threw a cheeky little mock salute, then the pair of them looked up into the sky and as they disappeared two beams of light shot up into the sky.

Ava turned when she felt someone else standing next to

her, a sweet looking, slightly round-faced man. He adjusted his glasses and smiled at her, nodding in acknowledgement, before lifting his face to the sky and another beam of light shot into the sky punctuating the clouds.

Ava and Kelley turned around to look back into the house and saw Luella standing in the foyer and in her arms, wearing a wide smile, was Peter. He waved to Ava and she lifted her hand in a small wave as he blew her a kiss. Her gaze moved to Luella and the two women stared at each other. Finally, Luella nodded, and smiled as her arms tightened around her son. The two of them began to glow, brightening until it was almost impossible to keep looking at them. Ava and Kelley both raised their hands to shield their eyes and when the light subsided, they were gone.

Derek Carpenter climbed to his feet his eyes a little wild and headed resolutely down the steps toward his car.

'Derek,' Ava called in amusement, 'where are you going?'

'Down to the dock to wait for the next ferry off the island,' he replied without a trace of humor.

'Hey,' she called out to the traumatized paranormal reporter, watching as he paused and looked back at her. 'You going to write about this?'

'Who would believe me?' he replied and opened his car door, he rummaged around the back seat and then headed back to the bottom of the steps, tossing up a bottle for Kelley to catch.

Kelley turned it over in his hands, it was a full bottle of Johnnie Walker.

'Thanks,' he replied.

'I think you two have earned it,' he nodded.

They watched as he climbed back in his car and disappeared into the trees. Slowly and tiredly Ava and Kelley collapsed down on the front stoop, feeling every cut, scratch and bruise. Kelley unscrewed the top and handed the bottle to Ava who took a long gulp and passed it back.

'Hell of a night,' Kelley remarked as he tilted the bottle back and took a deep swig himself.

'Yeah,' she chuckled, 'hell of a night.'

'What are you going to do now?' he asked looking up at the house. 'You still keeping it, the house I mean?'

Ava took the bottle back and drank again thoughtfully.

'Yeah,' she concluded, 'yeah, I am. I feel like I have an obligation. I need to get those kids out; they deserve a proper burial. I need to search the official records and see if I can find their names then I need to get licenses to have them buried.'

'Sounds like a lot of work,' he drank slowly.

'It does, doesn't it,' she replied with a slow smile.

'Sounds like the kind of thing you could use a hand with,' Kelley continued.

'You offering?'

'Looks like,' he nodded, 'and I was thinking, you know, in between getting thrown around by a psychotic ghost that maybe you might like to upgrade the fake fiancée to just fiancée.'

She paused for a second to absorb what he was saying.

'You asking?' she took another swig.

'I'm in love with you Ava,' he turned to look at her.

Her mouth twitched slightly, 'well I suppose you did run into a haunted house for me and save me from said psychotic ghost... twice.'

'Is that a yes?' he smiled slowly.

'Hmm,' she stared at him, 'does this mean I'm gonna end up with twins?'

'I'm not gonna lie...' he grinned, 'probably.'

'Then yes.'

'Yes?' his brows rose.

'Yes,' she nodded, 'because I love you too.'

He grinned and leaned in, cupping the back of her head as he kissed her deeply. She wrapped her arms around his neck and pulled him in closer, the bottle of black label crushed between them as the first pale rays of dawn broke over the cliff top.

They broke apart breathing heavily and slightly disorientated as a car tore into the yard, lights and sirens blazing.

Gus leapt out of one side and Killian out of the other.

'Fashionably late as always,' Kelley grinned at his father and brother.

'What the actual fuck Kelley?' Killian growled.

'Killian do you mind?' Gus admonished.

'Sorry,' Killian muttered clearly annoyed.

'What the actual fuck Kelley?' Gus growled, 'we've been going out of our minds with worry. We got some garbled message from you about Ava being missing, and you both disappear in the middle of a storm you're not supposed to be out in. Your car was wrecked, abandoned in the woods and covered in what I can only assume is your blood given the state of you and now I find you both with a bottle, sitting on the stoop making out like horny teenagers?'

Killian's eyes narrowed as he took in the state of them, both were covered in layers of mud and dirt, and blood. They were both severely bruised and cut, and Kelley was sporting a rather nasty cut at his temple surrounded by an egg-shaped lump which was beginning to turn an interesting shade of purple.

'What happened?' Killian demanded. 'It looks like you've gone ten rounds with the ghost of Luella Lynch.'

Ava and Kelley looked at each other and burst out laughing.

'What?' Killian frowned, 'what did I say?'

But the more that Kelley and Ava looked at each other the harder they laughed.

CLICK.

'That's one for the family album,' Gus looked down at the

photo of Kelley and Ava, bloodied and bruised, looking like the survivors of some intense battle, holding onto each other with a bottle of booze planted between them while they threw their heads back and laughed.

'I think they're having some sort of breakdown,' Killian muttered as the sound of the laughter echoed through the empty house.

EPILOGUE

hree years later.

KELLEY CLIMBED the stone steps and stepped through the wide double doors into the brightly sunlit foyer.

'Do you know where Ava is?' he asked his sister in law.

'I'm not sure,' Hope leaned down to strap her daughter into the stroller beside her twin sister.

'Hey Bean, hey Button,' he leaned down to their level. 'Got a kiss for Uncle Kelley?'

They both giggled as he dropped a sound kiss on each of their chubby cheeks.

'You know one of these days, you guys will have to start using their actual names,' Hope sighed.

'Can't,' Kelley replied, 'it's stuck now. You can blame Killian.'

'Oh, trust me,' she smiled, 'I blame him for plenty.'

'Okay, if you see Ava before I do, tell her I'm looking for her.'

Hope waved him off.

He passed by the welcome desk set up at the front of the foyer, stacked with glossy flyers. In front of it stood a small sign stating that the next tour would begin at 1.40pm.

He veered off to the left, poking his head into the study. It still gave him a little thrill to see it fully restored with its glossy wood and glass fronted cabinets, completely restocked with the literary classics, including Harry Potter and Captain Underpants, especially for him, Ava had told him with an impish smile, the hint of a dimple in her cheek.

The large hole in the floor, where he and Ava had fallen through and discovered the first of what turned out to be many hidden passageways, remained. They'd decided to keep it, instead choosing to cover it over with toughened reinforced glass so the tunnel could be seen from above. The hidden door also remained permanently open, revealing its intricate clockwork locking mechanism, and sectioned off with velvet ropes. Tours ran three times a day so people could explore the underground mortuary and the room of the sleeping angels, as the press had dubbed it, although it was not in any way accurate and tended to romanticize what essentially had been the sealed tomb of several murder victims. Still, it brought the visitors into the island in droves.

Heading back out of the room he crossed the foyer to the front parlor which once again was a school room, complete with the original desks, which they'd been able to save, some of them still with the children's names etched into the wood.

Ignoring the visitors milling around, he headed through the back parlor and into the restaurant, which bustled not only with tourists but many regulars from the island. Waving to a few familiar faces he headed through into the glorious glass sunroom and then out onto the terrace, with the warm summer breeze blowing in from the incredible sea views.

His gaze scanned the headland, across the manicured

gardens and immaculate landscaping, and he knew exactly where to find her. He trotted down the steps and headed out into the gardens, past ornamental shrubs and flower beds, until he reached a small garden divided off by ornate metal railings, along which were dozens of bouquets of flowers and wreaths propped up against them. He skirted around the edge of the large plot to the entrance and headed under the archway which was entwined with pale pink roses.

He found her standing there, the sunlight catching the wedding band on her finger as she held a rainbow of different colored roses in her hand. Bailey leapt up wagging her tail and headed toward him. He reached down and stroked her thick fur, as Ava turned and smiled.

'I was wondering where you were,' she said softly.

'Looking for you,' he stopped beside her, rubbing his hand over her hugely swollen belly and dropping a kiss on her lips.

'We were just visiting,' she laid her head on his shoulder as he wrapped his arms around her.

His eyes dropped down to the headstone in front of her, where she'd just laid two of the roses.

'Edison Lynch, devoted husband 28.11.1867 - 24.12.1898 & Eleanor Lynch, beloved wife 13.08.1874 - 31.10.1919'

'It was kind of you to have her buried here, even kinder to have Edison buried with her,' Kelley murmured.

It had taken a great deal of time, money and persuasion to get permission to exhume Edison's body and have him reinterred at the house with his wife, but she was glad she had. Out of everyone in this sorry tale he was the one who didn't deserve to spend eternity buried next to his evil father.

Ava stared at the stone, *'beloved wife...'* she hadn't added the obligatory *'& mother.'* Ava felt that really was going a step too far, considering she'd pretty much either murdered or attempted to murder all of her children.

'She was a terrible person,' Ava frowned, she still hadn't

quite reconciled how she felt about Eleanor. 'She truly loved Edison, she didn't start out to be the person she became, that was Ephraim's doing with his cruelty and abuse. I can't excuse what she did, but she was treated horrendously by that sick bastard. He may be buried on consecrated ground, but wherever Ephraim Lynch is, I really hope he's burning in hell.'

'Amen,' Kelley muttered.

Ava glanced to the left where seven angels stood with heads bowed and wings raised. Each one bore just one name.

'Nancy, Olive, Ruby, Alice, Anne, Catherine and Sarah.'

She handed Kelley seven roses one by one and watched as he propped them up against the foot of each statue, before turning to a large memorial stone. On it, were twenty-six names. It had taken them a long time, but they'd tracked down each of the names of the missing children and had buried them together.

Ava leaned over awkwardly and retrieved a wreath which had been sat at her feet and set it in front of the stone.

Next to them was one lone headstone.

'Jonathan Sedgewick 1887 -1919 loving protector.'

Ava laid a single white rose for him and turned to the final one. It read simply,

'Luella and Peter, beloved mother & son.'

Ava stroked their headstone fondly. Having shared Luella's memories so intensely she found she'd retained a profound and deep connection to the two of them. She kissed her fingers lightly and brushed them against the stone, before laying the final two roses.

Kelley took her hand and together they walked back through the archway. Ava stopped and locked the metal gate firmly.

She'd made the decision not to open the small graveyard to the public because it seemed wrong somehow to put them on display. She didn't want people trampling all over their bones every day, so instead she'd compromised and left the fencing around it only four feet high so visitors could look in, as long as they were quiet and respectful.

Wrapping his arm around her waist Kelley whistled for Bailey who happily trotted along behind them, with the old-fashioned leather baseball in her mouth. It was the one thing she refused to give up and no matter how many times they hid it, weirdly enough she always seemed to find it.

They walked around the house, breathing in the fresh salty air and smiling as they passed by visitors and locals. They reached the front of the house and stood for a moment admiring the beautiful warm sandstone building.

Kelley nudged Ava and nodded toward a familiar face standing across the gravel parking lot, staring up at the building.

'Go on,' Kelley told her, 'I'll wait here.'

Ava smiled at her husband and crossed the distance to the small blonde-haired woman.

'Hello Julia,' she smiled.

'Hello Ava,' Julia replied, as she gazed up at the house. 'I never thought I'd come back here.'

'Would you like to come inside?' Ava asked. 'I would be happy to show you around.'

' No,' she shook her head. 'It's taken me a long time to get to this point, I don't think I'm ready to go inside.'

'How are you doing?'

Julia looked at Ava and smiled slowly.

'I don't hear them screaming anymore,' she whispered. 'I can finally dream.'

'I'm glad,' Ava replied softly.

'I'll never be completely okay,' Julia told her honestly, 'but thanks to you, I'm as okay as I can be.'

Ava reached out and took her hand squeezing gently. 'I'm here for you whenever you need me.'

Julia nodded, turning at the honk of a car horn.

'I gotta go,' she smiled, 'my mom's taking me out to the mainland today, we're going shopping.'

'You have a great time,' Ava told her sincerely.

Julia turned and headed toward the car, stopping impulsively and turning to look at Ava.

'You're going to make a great mom Ava,' she smiled as she climbed into the car.

Ava waved them off.

Walking back to Kelley she took his hand as they headed toward the entrance.

'Well, I'd say it's been a big success,' he stared up at the building. 'I can't say I was too thrilled when you convinced me to move into the house with you, but at least there are no more ghosts.'

'Yeah, no more ghosts,' Ava murmured as she gazed up and saw Luella looking down from one of the upstairs windows, with a smile on her face and Peter grinning and waving by her side.... 'more or less...' Ava's mouth curved.

They climbed up the steps and headed inside the house, past the shiny golden plaque mounted beside the door, which read simply.

'THE CLOCKWORK HOUSE.'

Also by Wendy Saunders
The Guardians Series 1
Book 1 Mercy

The Town of Mercy is hiding a centuries old secret...

Olivia West had no intention of ever returning to her home-town of Mercy, Massachusetts, but when an ancient presence begins to stir beneath the sleepy little town, she feels it echoing in her soul... calling to her witches' blood, a call she is helpless to obey.

Theodore Beckett has a dark past and secrets of his own, born in 17th Century Salem he finds himself dragged through time to the present day and left with nothing but a cryptic instruction to find and help Olivia.

When the town is rocked by a series of supernatural murders Olivia unwittingly finds herself the prime suspect, but the murders are only the beginning.

Thrown into a world of murder and magic and trying to fight their growing feelings for each other, Olivia and Theo must stop a murderer and uncover her family's oldest and darkest secret, but as the killer draws closer and a dark presence begins to awaken... time is running out.

REVIEWS

"What an amazing read this book is. From the moment I started reading I was hooked and could not put the book down and ordinarily that would be fine but I've been a walking zombie at work this week due to lack of sleep but IT WAS WORTH IT." (*Amazon Reviewer*)

"Couldn't put it down. It draws you in and keeps up the pace to the explosive finale. It also makes you care about the characters who are believable and human. This is a book you will want to read and recommend to your friends." (*Amazon Reviewer*)

"Fantastic read!! Starts with a cracker and keeps it rolling perfectly all the way through, you know you need to put down the book to sleep but you have to know what happens next!!" (*Amazon Reviewer*)

FREE TO DOWNLOAD!!!

Available from all Amazon Marketplaces!

MERCY SAMPLE CHAPTER

Welcome to Mercy, Massachusetts
  Pop. 13,623

The blurred letters stared mockingly back at Olivia through the intermittent swipe of her wiper blades. The persistent rain misted her windshield as her whiskey colored eyes narrowed, locking on the offending sign. Her lips unconsciously tightened as her fingers tapped out a restless staccato on the wheel.

'What the hell are you doing Olivia?'

She shook her head as if to rid herself of the relentless question, which continuously pounded through her skull with all the subtlety of a pneumatic drill.

'What are you doing?'

Her gaze flicked to the mirror, demanding, as if her frustrated reflection could somehow give her an answer. Sucking in a breath she shifted the gear into reverse, intent on putting the town into her rear-view mirror and never looking back.

But she didn't.

Instead she paused, dropping the gear once again into

neutral. That small nagging doubt at the back of her mind nipped at her like a vicious and annoying insect. The sudden and renewed tug tightened around her ribcage, dark and earthy, a primitive drumbeat matching her heartbeat.

Something was calling to her, she could feel it even now, pulsing through her blood.

With a slow sigh her head dropped down to rest against the back of her knuckles as she gripped the wheel tighter. Closing her tired eyes, she listened to the idling of the engine and the rhythmic tapping of the rain, allowing it to soothe her turbulent thoughts.

Fighting with herself was so exhausting; maybe being back in Mercy wouldn't be as bad as she expected. She let loose a sudden, unintentional snort of amusement even as the thought occurred to her, loosening the uncomfortable knot in her chest.

Despite the twenty years she'd been absent from her hometown there were some things she was sure would never change and Mercy's small-town mentality was one of them. She knew, without a shadow of a doubt, that the second she set foot on Mercy soil the town gossips would start spreading the word that 'the West girl' had returned.

Before long, her past would be dredged up and picked over, like vultures over carrion. Then all anyone would be talking about was how her father had brutally murdered her mother and grandmother.

Olivia let her head fall back against the seat as her hands dropped from the wheel to rest in her lap.

They didn't know the truth about what happened that night... none of them did.

She'd spent years trying not to think about that night. She'd painstakingly crammed every single blood-soaked memory into the deepest recesses of her mind, where they would never again see the light of day.

And it had worked... for a while.

The closer she got to town the more the memories had tried to force their way back to the surface. With every mile marker her heart began to pound harder, her palms slippery with sweat as she white-knuckled the wheel.

She should never have come. She sure as hell didn't need the inheritance. A rickety old house on the edge of a lake in the middle of nowhere. The stupid thing was probably falling to pieces anyway. She should just put the car in reverse and leave.

Her hand hovered over the gears, trembling for a second before she finally fisted her palm and straightened her spine.

She couldn't leave and she damn well knew it. It was the same reason she'd made the journey in the first place, the same reason she'd ignored the nagging, perverse little voice inside her that hadn't shut up the whole drive from Providence. She'd felt the raw tug of power; whatever had lured her back to Mercy, it was old and very powerful, of that much she was sure.

Olivia glanced up at the sky; the rain had slowed, and the sky was darkening. She couldn't continue to sit at the side of the road and argue with herself all night. She was here now; she may as well deal with it, whether she wanted to or not.

A sudden banging on her window had her sucking in a sharp, startled breath. Her gaze once again flicked to the rear-view mirror and she caught a glimpse of flashing lights. Taking a deep breath to still her jumping heart she lowered the window, blinking as the cold raindrops bathed her face.

'Ma'am,' the officer nodded in greeting, 'is everything alright?'

'Yeah,' Olivia muttered sourly, 'everything's fine.'

Her gaze dipped to the badge pinned to his jacket and she noted the name, 'Deputy Walker.'

'I'm afraid you can't stop here,' he offered with an easy smile, as the rain dripped from the wide brim of his hat.

'I know,' she murmured.

'Ma'am?' his brow furrowed questioningly as he studied her. 'Do you require any assistance?'

'No,' Olivia's mouth curved slowly, 'just a backbone.'

He grinned suddenly, making him seem even younger.

'You be sure and drive safe,' he nodded, 'road ahead can get slippery.'

'You have no idea,' she muttered under her breath as she watched him return to his vehicle.

Given no other choice she pulled out onto the road and headed into town. About a mile down the road she started hitting the outskirts and it was like she'd never left. The place had barely changed in the last two decades. Walker's Auto was still there, as was the Sidecar Diner.

She slowed as she made the turn onto Main St, passing by the Bailey's convenience store on one side of the street and the Irish pub, The Salted Bone, on the other.

The old ice cream parlor was still there, bringing an unconscious smile to her lips. Miz Willow's Scoop'n'Shake. She wondered idly if the sweet old hippy still ran the place. Olivia felt a small, unexpected pang of nostalgia and was forced to admit that maybe her memories of Mercy were not all bad. She still remembered running down to Miz Willow's on a hot day for a sundae with her best friends, Jake and Louisa. She shook her head lightly as the small smile continued to play on her lips.

No, the memories weren't all bad.

Olivia passed by the library, followed by the museum, once one of her most favorite of places in Mercy. Making a mental note to visit as soon as she had the chance, she headed east onto Walnut Drive and then north onto Maple. Her smile slowly faded as she drove further into the heart of town. There was one place in particular she needed to visit, before she headed up to the lake house, and the longer she put it off the harder it would be.

With a heavy heart she pulled up and parked at the side of the street. Her heartbeat picked up and a low-pitched buzz began humming in her ears. Climbing out of the car she pulled her jacket around her tightly, against the wind, noting that the rain had picked up once again.

The moment her foot hit the sidewalk she felt a strange throb of power. It was weird; she didn't remember feeling anything like it as a child, but she could feel it now. It wasn't exactly the same presence which had been calling her back home. No, this was the town itself.

It was as if Mercy was somehow alive. The low thrum of power which ran beneath the ground pulsed and throbbed with magic, almost like a central nervous system with thousands of tiny synapses connecting everything.

She lifted her face to the dying light and, allowing the cold rain to bathe her skin, she breathed in deeply. The air crackled with power.

What the hell was going on? Was it just that she'd been unable to detect it as a child? Had the town always had this undercurrent of power, or was it something more recent and more sinister?

Shaking the worrying thought from her mind she took a tentative step forward. The ground almost seemed to ripple beneath her feet, but she resolutely ignored it and forced herself to focus on the empty plot of land in front of her.

Sandwiched between a pair of cute little, two storey houses was an empty lot where her childhood home had once stood.

She'd ridden her shiny red Schwinn along that very sidewalk, rolled wildly across the lawn with her sweet little golden cocker spaniel, Truman. She'd sat out on the back stoop on clear nights and watched, fascinated, as her father pointed out the constellations.

She closed her eyes and sucked in a sharp painful breath at the sudden memory of her father. Shaking her head, she took another step forward, her chest aching as the memories washed over her in waves.

The house was long gone. It had burned to the ground the night her mother had died, and it seemed no one had bothered to rebuild it. But... she noted curiously, someone had gone to a great deal of trouble to clear the site and plant a beautiful garden. Even this late in the year it still burst with colors, so vivid it felt like she'd stepped inside an oil painting.

The obstinate buzzing in her ears had now become a low murmur, incoherent but insistent. It tugged at her, pulling her forward, urging her closer, almost as if the ground itself was trying to speak to her. Before she even realized what she was doing she lifted her foot and stepped onto the grass.

Everything disappeared.

The air was filled with the acrid stench of burning. The daylight was gone, along with the stinging rain. Instead the dark air was heavy with thick, black, oily smoke. It scalded her mouth and throat as she coughed violently, her lungs burning as they filled. The house burned hotter than any fire she'd ever known. The wall of heat in front of her was so intense it felt like her skin was peeling. The roar of the flames filled her ears, as if the inferno was somehow singing to her, as the windows melted and dripped down the front of the building like great dirty tears.

The roof collapsed inward with a shockingly loud splintering, throwing burning dust and ash into the choking air. The wall of heat was too much, her skin felt too tight and her eyes stung, causing her to stumble back a step.

The second her foot hit the sidewalk the flames disappeared. Once again she felt the fat, clean drops of rain dripping down the neck of her jacket, settling cold and uncomfortable, someplace between her shoulder blades.

The dim daylight returned, hidden beneath heavy storm laden skies and once again the colorful little garden stared innocently back at her. Kneeling down Olivia pressed her hand into the wet soil. This time she felt, rather than witnessed, the violent echo of fire and flame.

Drawing in a shaky breath her fingertips curled involuntarily, digging into the mud.

The garden was an illusion.

Beneath its pretty mask the stench of blood and death lingered. The ground was scarred from that night.

Straightening up, Olivia took another step back. Her heartbeat slowed and resumed its regular pace and the whispering in her ears subsided until once again all she could hear was the clatter of rain against the sidewalk.

'Olivia?'

Her name was little more than a startled breath on the wind, whispered in disbelief.

Olivia turned slowly. Her penetrating gaze fell on a small, familiar looking woman of about her own age. Her vivid blue eyes were wide with shock and the errant locks of blonde hair, which had escaped the hood of her bright yellow windbreaker, were plastered wetly to her pale, heart shaped face.

A small, slow smile curved across Olivia's lips. The face, although older, was one she knew very well.

'Hello Louisa,' she said softly.

The breath whooshed from her lungs and she found herself caught up in a tight, desperate hug.

'I can't believe it's really you,' Louisa whispered past the hot, hard ball of emotion burning at the back of her throat.

Olivia stepped back awkwardly at the sudden embrace.

'I'm surprised you recognized me,' Olivia tilted her head thoughtfully. 'It's been twenty years.'

Louisa blinked back the tears and shook her head.

'What?' Olivia smiled, 'do I look that bad?'

'You look beautiful,' Louisa blinked again and wiped away a tear which had escaped. 'I'd recognize you anywhere.'

She didn't want to add that Olivia also happened to be the image of her dead mother. That had given Louisa as much a jolt as seeing her childhood best friend, something she was sure Olivia probably wouldn't want to hear so she wisely chose to keep her mouth shut.

'You look good Louisa,' Olivia nodded to fill the awkward silence.

'We thought you were dead,' Louisa frowned.

'What?'

'We thought you were dead,' she repeated, 'after what happened...you know, with your mom. Jake and I didn't know what had happened to you. We kept asking mom and dad where you were, but they just kept telling us that you were gone. Even the people in town didn't seem to know what had happened to you.'

'This'll certainly give the gossips something to talk about then,' Olivia muttered in resignation.

'I mourned you,' Louisa swallowed quietly, 'Jake and I both did, every damn day.'

'I'm sorry,' Olivia stared at her friend.

She could feel the hurt and confusion pouring off her in waves, so she did the only thing she could think of. She reached out and wrapped her arms around her.

'Olive,' Louisa breathed as she returned the hug.

There, in that one moment, that one childhood nickname, she understood why she'd come back. Because no matter how much it hurt her, this was the one place that had always been home.

'Where have you been?' Louisa asked in confusion.

'Everywhere,' Olivia pulled back with a sigh and shook her head. 'Nowhere...' she added with small self-deprecating smile, 'and every place in between.... it's complicated,' she finally shrugged.

'Why don't you come in for a coffee?' Louisa nodded toward the tidy little house opposite.

Olivia stared at the little blue house, with its cheerful doll-house shutters.

'You still living with your parents?'

'God no,' she laughed, releasing some of the tension. 'I've got my own place in town. Mom and dad are on vacation; I just stopped by to pick up the mail and water the plants.'

'I can't,' Olivia muttered, her eyes still locked on the house she'd spent a good deal of her childhood running tame in, along with Louisa and her brother Jake.

'Please,' Louisa asked quietly, 'I'd really like to talk to you.'

Olivia shook her head.

'I can't,' she answered again, 'it's getting late and I need to get up to the lake house. I don't even know if the electric is still on.'

'The lake house?' Louisa's eyes widened a fraction, 'that's where you're staying?'

'Yeah,' Olivia admitted, 'Evie left it to me in her Will.'

'I heard about Evelyn,' Louisa nodded, 'I'm so sorry.'

'Don't be,' she shrugged. 'I'm not even sure why she left me the house.'

'Why wouldn't she?' Louisa frowned in confusion, 'she adored you.'

There was nothing Olivia could say to that. Even as close as she'd been to Louisa as a child, she wasn't about to admit the sad pathetic truth to her. Her great aunt hadn't wanted her. After the death of her mother and grandmother, and the subsequent arrest of her father, the authorities had contacted Evelyn as her only living relative, but she hadn't wanted her. In fact, she'd flat out refused to take custody of her. The hurt had stung hot and bright at the time, after all she'd only been eight years old, but over the years she'd learned to live with the rejection.

Shaking off her bleak mood she turned back to Louisa.

'I should get going, it was good to see you though.'

'Olivia wait!'

She turned back to her friend and stared thoughtfully for a moment before pulling in a slow inhale.

'Look,' Olivia offered, 'why don't you give me a couple of days and then come up to the house and we'll talk.'

'Do you really mean it?'

'Sure,' Olivia nodded.

'Give me your phone,' Louisa held out her hand.

Olivia watched as she took her cell and programmed her number into it before sending herself a text, so she'd have her number too.

'Call me if you need anything,' Louisa offered genuinely.

Olivia nodded in acknowledgement before turning and heading back to her car. While they'd been talking the rain had let up to a fine mist, but it was already too late. She was pretty much soaked to the skin and shivering.

Sliding back into the driver's seat she blew out a long breath. She was going back to the lake house. As a child it had been her favorite place in the whole world, but after the last twenty years of pain and resentment she had no idea how she was going to feel when she actually walked through the door.

She started the car, pulling away while a hot, uncomfortable ball of awareness churned once again in her stomach. Part of her still couldn't quite believe she was back in Mercy. She'd spent the last two decades bouncing around from place to place. From Lawrence to Georgetown, Philadelphia to Boston, New Hampshire to Rhode Island, until she'd ended up in Providence where she'd stayed the longest.

She'd spent most of her childhood bounced from group home to foster family and back again. After all no one wanted to adopt the kid of a murderer, not even her great aunt it seemed, but she supposed she couldn't blame her.

When she'd gotten word that Evelyn had passed away she'd grieved. Despite everything that had been left unsaid between them she hurt regardless. When her great aunt's lawyer had tracked her down in Providence and informed her that she was the sole beneficiary of Evelyn's estate, to say she'd been surprised would have been an understatement.

In fact, she'd opened her mouth with every intention of telling the lawyer to just sell the house but somehow that wasn't what came out. She'd signed the papers, taken the keys, then she'd packed up her beloved, banged up old Camaro and hit the road.

She headed across town to the outskirts until she reached the edge of the woods, then turned onto a dirt road which wound between the trees. Despite the number of years that had passed she knew exactly where she was heading. Everything was so heartbreakingly familiar her heart clenched painfully. The last time she'd been down this road, she'd been with her mother.

Swallowing hard against the deep ache in her throat she blinked back the hot tears stinging her eyes and focused on the road. The light was failing and although the rain had almost completely stopped, the wind had picked up. Even with the windows rolled up she could hear the roar of it through the trees, vast and ponderous like a freight train. With every gust, a myriad of colored leaves broke over the windshield like a wave, catching in the wipers.

Suddenly the canopy of trees parted, and the house came into view. Cradled lovingly by the surrounding trees, the house tugged at her. She stopped the car and gazed up at the familiar steep gabled roof and overhanging eaves.

It was a stick style Queen Anne built on the site of its prede-cessor, a wooden framed house built by her ancestor Hester

West and her sister Bridget when they co-founded the town back in 1704.

The original West house had been little more than a cabin and had nestled amidst the woods overlooking the lake, until it was damaged by a fire in the late 1800s. Unable to be salvaged, they'd pulled down the ruins and built the Queen Anne in its place.

Local legend said that a West had lived on this land for the last three hundred years. Maybe that was why she found it so hard to let go or move on. She felt the bonds of blood, love and hate, wrapped around her like vines, binding her to the end, and to the house itself.

Olivia stepped out of the car and gazed up at the house. The wind tugged and pulled at her, teasing her clothes and dancing up her spine with sly spindly fingers. The hiss of churned up leaves filled the quiet air, making it sound as if the house itself was sighing, like it had been waiting for her.

She slowly climbed the steps to the wraparound porch and pressed her palm to the door, drawing in a breath.

'This is my house now...'

The old porch swing to her left suddenly moved in the wind, creaking loudly on rusted chains. A wave of leaves rustled, rolling over her feet in a mad tumble of yellow, red and gold. Feeling a strange prickle of awareness at the back of her neck, and a heaviness settle somewhere between her shoulder blades, she turned around, her narrowed gaze scanning the tree line, but nothing seemed out of place.

Her brow creased at the sudden sense of unease that washed over her. It was strange, she'd never been afraid of the woods or the seclusion before. The house, the woods, the lake... they'd always been a place of wonder and magic to her, but now, standing on the porch gazing out into the dying light... it almost felt like she was being watched.

Rolling her shoulders to shake off her uneasiness, she

fumbled in her bag for the keys the lawyer had given her and quickly unlocked the door.

The air inside the house was silent as she stepped into the hallway. She could hear the shriek and call of the wind and the rustle of leaves behind her, but the house was still, like it was holding its breath.

The dust sheets hung like great shrouds across the furniture, twitching slightly in the errant breeze that had followed in her wake.

She dropped her bag to the floor just inside the threshold, as the door clicked quietly closed behind her, leaving her standing in the oppressive stillness.

Slowly she stepped forward, wandering down the hall. Her heels clicked against the parquet flooring as her fingertips lightly pulled the dust sheets from mirrors and framed pictures, letting them drift ghost-like to the floor, setting the dust motes spinning madly in the dying light, like tiny fairies.

Reaching out, she flicked the light switch, but nothing happened. She tried a couple more times, nothing. She'd obviously have to call the electric company, first thing in the morning she realized, looking down at her watch. It was later than she thought.

Making her way through to the kitchen she stared at the dark cherrywood cabinets and worn rose-colored walls. Some things never changed, no matter how many decades passed. Rummaging through the drawers she finally managed to locate a flashlight, but when she flicked it on, it sputtered once, then twice, before it died.

Muttering under her breath Olivia headed back through the rapidly darkening house to the library. Opening the door, she felt a rush of recognition. Despite the failing light, the feel and smell of the room was so familiar her stomach jolted.

Her gaze scanned the room, noting the candles scattered

throughout. She headed toward the fireplace, to the two tall pillar candlesticks book-ending the mantle.

Her fingertips grazed the cool metal of the candlestick and traced upward along the smooth scented wax. Taking in a quiet breath she blew slowly and deliberately against the wick. It burst cheerfully into flame, hiccuping and dancing merrily, bathing her face with a soft warmth.

Olivia's gaze slid to the opposite end of the mantle where the candlestick's twin waited patiently. Once again, she drew in a breath, feeling the warmth and heat gather in her throat as she blew gently against the wick. This time the heat radiated outward, rippling through the room, like a small pebble breaching the surface of a still pond. Each candle placed carefully around the library simultaneously burst into flame, illuminating the room with a soft warm glow.

Holding her hand close to the flame, as if she were coaxing a small skittish animal, she watched as the flame bobbed on the wick a couple of times before tipping onto her fingertips. It danced along her skin until the flame sat in her palm.

It didn't burn; it was nothing more than a warm tingle. She studied the flame, her gaze tracing the fine threads of gold, red and orange which made up its substance as the memory of her grandmother's voice whispered at the edge of her mind.

'Fire, little one, is the first skill learned and the last lost...'

The flame burst into life in her palm and Olivia smiled. Fortunately for her it was also her strongest skill. The power pulsed along her skin, the fiery threads wound down deep into her flesh like the roots of an ancient tree, separate, but also very much a part of her. Dropping to her haunches, she blew against the flame in her hand, watching as it separated and scattered across the fireplace in a rush of heat, igniting the dry logs and roaring to life.

Satisfied the fire had caught, she stood and stretched. As she did her gaze caught on a silver-framed photograph of a familiar face. Sucking in a sharp and painful breath, feeling her heart pounding loudly in her ears, Olivia reached out with trembling fingers to grasp the frame.

The night her mother had died, she'd been dragged away from Mercy with nothing but the clothes on her back. She didn't own one single photograph of her mother. For the last twenty years her mother had existed only in her memory.

Tracing her shaky fingers across the dusty glass, Olivia found herself gazing upon the face of her mother for the first time in two decades and found her memory to be nothing more than a pale specter.

Seeing her mom smiling back through the lens of a camera, frozen, immortalized in that one moment of time, caused a deep, painful ache in her chest. She'd been so young, so vibrant, and completely unaware of the violent fate which awaited her.

Olivia tried to swallow past the hot, hard lump burning at the back of her throat, but as she tore her gaze away, her eye caught her own reflection in the mirror mounted above the fireplace and she realized, for the first time, how much she looked like her mother. It wasn't just her long, dark wavy hair, or her whiskey colored eyes, but her face, the shape of her nose, the curve of her jaw. She was the image of her mother. No wonder, she thought with a heavy heart. No wonder her aunt hadn't wanted her, she probably couldn't bear to look at her.

The sudden wrench of grief drove Olivia to her knees. Her legs simply collapsed beneath her as she clutched the photograph to her chest and rocked. The tears came hot and fast and she allowed herself to finally do the one thing she'd held back since she drove into town.

She curled into a tight ball of misery and wept bitterly.

She couldn't say when she fell into an exhausted sleep, but her dreams were filled with flame and ash and dust. The house burned around her. She could hear the groan of the timbers as they splintered and gave way. Her father's face towered above her, cold and malicious as he clutched a knife in his hand, dripping with her mother's blood.

Turning away from that terrible image she saw her grandmother in a crumpled heap in the corner of the room, lying in a pool of her own blood, her dress alight as she was consumed by the inferno.

The flames licked against Olivia's skin and she shivered. Her brow folded into a confused frown; the flames should have burned but instead they were cold. She shivered again and this time her breath was expelled from her mouth as a fine mist. Suddenly, her body was wracked by a deep shudder and her eyes opened on a gasp.

It took her a moment to realize where she was. Unfolding her stiff limbs, she pulled herself up from the shabby, threadbare rug. The fire had now burned down to embers and the candles in the room had gone out. Looking up into the dim light, she realized the window was wide open, the curtain billowing ghostly white in the freezing night air.

Frowning to herself, Olivia walked stiffly over to the window and leaned out. The cloud cover from the earlier storm had burned away, leaving the night air crisp, clear and freezing. The moon split the sky like a great silver disc, reflecting upon the surface of the lake and bathing the surrounding woods in its ethereal light.

Shivering, she closed the window and locked it. Strange, she thought to herself, she didn't remember opening the window.

Turning her back, she once again felt the uncomfortable prickle which started at the back of her neck and rolled slowly down her spine. She couldn't seem to shake the feeling of being watched.

Convinced it was just the stress of being back in town, she

shook her head, dismissing the vague feeling but as she turned to move back into the room, she froze mid-step.

The photograph, which had caused her so much grief, no longer lay upon the rug in front of the fireplace where she'd left it, but instead rested once more on the mantle, looking for all the world as if it had never been moved.

FREE TO DOWNLOAD!!!

Available from all Amazon Marketplaces!

ABOUT THE AUTHOR

Want to know more about me and my books? Come find me on my official website!

www.wendysaundersauthor.com

Don't forget to subscribe to my mailing list via my website to receive a free copy of my e-book Boothe's Hollow, a companion/prequel short story to Mercy. You can find them here!

http://promo.wendysaundersauthor.com

<u>On Facebook</u>

www.facebook.com/wendysaundersauthor

<u>On Twitter</u>

www.twitter.com/wsaundersauthor

<u>On Instagram</u>

www.instagram.com/wendysaundersauthor

If you would like to rate this book and leave a review at Amazon or Goodreads.com I would be very grateful. Thank You.

Manufactured by Amazon.ca
Bolton, ON